हर HER DIL KA DOCTOR

AANZOOMAAN KHALEQUE

REDGRAB books
redgrabbooks.com

RG
books

Published By

Redgrab Books Pvt. Ltd.

942, Mutthiganj, Prayagraj, 211003

www.redgrabbooks.com

contact@redgrabbooks.com

First published by Redgrab Books in 2025

Printed and bound in India

Cover Design & Typesetting by Redgrab Books team

ISBN : 978-93-95697-48-4

ACKNOWLEDGEMENTS

Writing can be a lonely affair. Spending hours in front of a laptop and letting words weave tales and dreams on a blank canvas is not always easy. Several individuals deserve special mention for making this journey easier and more beautiful.

To begin with, my heartfelt thanks to my husband and daughter for understanding my constant need to drum my fingers on the keyboard and patiently waiting for the magic to happen.

To my parents and brother, for always believing in me and never questioning my decisions.

To my friends, Jayashree, Sujata, Prasanti, Moonmoon, Angita, Abishmita, Bishmita, Sangeeta, Jyoti, Shaheen, Sagarika, Anaxee, and Upanita, for being my ardent cheerleaders. Your love and blind faith give me the strength and motivation to keep going. A special mention goes to Zubishmita and Bandana for their unwavering support and affection.

I owe my gratitude to Monalisha Ma'am, Jonali Ma'am, and Mehbooba Ma'am for their warmth and encouraging words. Your belief in me helped me overcome self-doubt and persevere despite the odds.

To my friend, Bandita, for not only liking what I wrote but for being a true champion of my work and urging me to keep writing.

To my youngest reader, Isha, whose sweet feedback after reading my first book warmed my heart.

To dear Kyan, my youngest cheerleader, thank you for understanding the nuances of writing and the effort it takes to turn thoughts into words.

My heartfelt gratitude to Antara for helping me explore various avenues and opportunities as an author.

To my dear school friend, Sangeeta, thank you for reaching out after so many years. Your kind gesture brought me immense joy.

Thank you to the incredible team at Redgrab Books for believing in this book and sharing it with the world.

And lastly, to my readers, you are the reason I write. Thank you for your continued support and for taking the time to read.

Happy Reading!

CONTENTS

PROLOGUE

Mumbai,

Sunday, 6 A.M.

Looking sinfully tempting, he approached her. Dressed in a white coat, he looked nothing less than a knight in shining white armor. Oh, wait! In fact, he was hotter than any man she had seen so far. Her cheeks heated in anticipation, and butterflies had started running errands in her stomach. He stopped just at arm's length. His hair ruffled in the wind, and he came close to her—very close! He wrapped his arms around her waist, and she was entrapped in his warm embrace. The surrounding air buzzed with electrifying intensity. Her heartbeat increased and raced with excitement at his proximity. He bent down, and his hazel-brown eyes bore into hers. His lips twisted into a wicked, possessive smile. He gripped her chin in a warm grasp and said, "Well, Ms. Patel, I know you intend to fight me, but I wasn't lying when I said I have the habit of winning, and tonight you will have no escape. I will kiss you and wipe that smirk off your pretty face. You will have no defenses left except to surrender and be mine completely."

As he bent down to claim her, her lips began to tingle. His mouth was about to crash into hers when a sudden darkness enveloped them.

Hell! What just happened? Did I pass out from a single spell of a kiss? She wondered.

And then someone spelled her name in a sing-song voice, "N Y S H A D I D I."

Slowly, she brushed the hair away from her eyes and rubbed them before opening them completely. Confused, she found herself staring at the round, plump face of her house help, Sushi. Sushanti, aka Sushi, smiled at Nysha with her arms stretched out, displaying her uneven dentures. Her wide smile spread across her face, almost touching the back of her head. It took a moment to realize that Sushi was holding her phone in her outstretched hand.

"Didi, Pia didi call kari thi," she said.

("Sister, Pia sister had called," she said.)

Nysha took the phone from her and said, "Thanks, Sushi. Tu coffee bana de jaa ke, behen."

("Thanks, Sushi. Please make some coffee for me, sister.")

But Sushi, it seemed, was reluctant to make a move, as she kept staring at Nysha with an amused look on her face, barely able to suppress a laugh.

"What?" Nysha asked.

"Aap phir se wahi sapna dekhi na, Didi?" she asked.

("You had the same recurring dream again today, didn't you, sister?" she asked.)

Nysha took a deep breath and replied calmly, "Tu jaa, coffee bana, behen."

("Go ahead and make some coffee, sister.")

Nysha's New Proposition

It was only 6 A.M. on a Sunday morning, and Nysha Patel was wide awake, completely in her senses. There was a dull throb in her head, in all probability a hangover from her weekend club outing with her gang of girls, minus her best friend, Pia.

The very thought of her best friend brought a smile to her lips. They had many shared memories together, and she had been so dependent on her that life without Pia Shergill had been very difficult initially. For those wondering where she was at present, well, there was nothing to worry about. She was happily married and settled with her superstar husband, Zain Zaidi. The duo had recently been promoted to the status of "would-be-parents" in the making, and were off to the Bahamas for a week-long vacation for their "Babymoon." Here, her best friend was soon going to have her baby, and Nysha, at 29, was still single, with no boyfriend or prospective husband in sight. She was done giving reasons and excuses to herself.

"Single and successful" "Single and rich" "Single and independent" "Single but a splendid entrepreneur"

Actually, it wasn't any of the above. The fact was that she was single, and her life sucked, to say the least! For the umpteenth time in days, she was having a rerun of the same morning dream, and her recurring dreams were her only source of "guilty pleasure," which, thanks to Pia and Sushi, was doomed today. They had doused the fire and left her "high and dry." A part of her longed to drift back to sleep and finish the kiss she had shared with the handsome hunk of her dreams. The dream had felt so real – from his touch, to the way his lips lingered against hers, or the heat of his breath. But now, all that remained was the faint morning glow seeping in through the curtains and the distant buzz of the city slowly waking up.

God! Her life was insanely fucked up and one huge ball of curled-up mess. Her damn hormones were totally worked up while jumping to and fro.

She rubbed her eyes and throbbing temples to ease the tingling tension. Slowly, she crawled out of bed, only to immediately collapse onto her bedside couch again. Perhaps nimbu paani would have been a better option to combat her awful hangover. She thought about calling Sushi to get her nimbu paani, but then decided against it and shifted her attention to her phone instead. There were three missed calls from Pia. It was 6:30 in the morning, and a quick check of the "Time Zone Converter" on her phone indicated that it would be around 9 P.M. Saturday in The Bahamas. *Should she call Pia at this hour? What if the lovebirds were busy "coochie-cooing" with each other?* Her thoughts were already off on a wild rampage, but she hushed them all in her mind.

Hell! Who cared? After all, Pia was her best friend, and she didn't need to think twice before calling her bestie. Quickly, she video-called Pia and was surprised when her call was answered on the first ring.

"Hello, sweetie! At last! I tried calling you so many times. Where have you been?"

"Damn you, Pia Shergill! It's barely 6:30 in the morning, and I am awake. All thanks to you."

Pia let out a muffled giggle as if someone had just tickled her funny bone. Nysha didn't have to wait long, because the cat soon leaped out of its bag and revealed its... handsome face.

"Whoa! Hold your horses, Zaidi, I have seen wolves with better control than you do," Nysha cried out.

Zain smiled sheepishly from behind his wife and flashed his dazzling, perfect smile at Nysha.

"Hey, Nysh! What's up?" he asked impishly.

"Clear off before I lose my mind, Zaidi," Nysha shrieked, which in turn seemed to amuse him all the more.

Zain's eyes widened and a smile spread across his face, making him look like a teenager playing pranks on his teacher and drawing contentment from it. His boyish charms were truly infectious. No wonder this man was considered the heartthrob of the nation. But today, however, he seemed hell-bent on irritating her, or perhaps she was already irritated. Her continuously throbbing temples and pounding head were driving her crazy, and as usual, Sushi was nowhere to be seen. For God's sake, it was just a simple, readymade, instant cup of black coffee. Going by Sushi's time lag, it felt like she was off to the Southern coffee plantations to pick up the choicest coffee beans, roasting them using the finest methods to unleash their distinctive aroma before brewing that perfect cup with its delectable flavors for the ultimate coffee indulgence, much like the visually appealing coffee ads. However, the hardworking farmers in the ads had been replaced by the not-so-hardworking Sushanti at home.

As if sensing her thoughts, Sushi walked in with her precious cup of coffee. But to her surprise, she let out an audible gasp, loud enough for Nysha to almost jump to her feet. Sushi had managed to spot Zain's face on her mobile screen, and like everyone else, she was awestruck by him. She handed Nysha her cup and positioned herself right in front of the screen.

"Hi, Zain bhaiya," she shrieked. ("Hi, Brother Zain," she shrieked.)

"Sushi, kaisi ho?" he asked. ("How are you, Sushi?" he asked.)

"Main thik," she replied. ("I am good," she replied.)

Then shifting her attention to Pia, she asked her, "Didi, thik ho?" ("Sister, are you okay?")

To which Pia sweetly replied, "Main bilkul thik hoon, Sushi. Tu kaisi hai?" ("I am perfectly fine, Sushi. How are you?")

Irked by the absurdity of the surroundings, Nysha let out a snort. It was loud enough to make Sushi turn her head. She then glared at her, and taking the hint, Sushi smiled nervously at Pia and said, "Main chalti didi, bahut kaam hai." ("I should go, sister. There is a lot of work to be done.")

"Indeed," Nysha growled.

Zain looked at Pia, and then again at Nysha. His mouth fell open, and he gawked like a wide-mouthed dolphin. Pia muffled her hand over her mouth to control her soft chortles. But one disgusted look from Nysha, and both her friends burst into a whirlwind of laughter.

Nysha looked apologetically at her still-sniggering friends and said, "Come on, guys! Stop being so mean..."

Both Pia and Zain tried to control their laughter. They even attempted a serious face, but failed miserably and began to laugh again, louder than the previous time.

"Alright, cool! Laugh your hearts out, morons, I am leaving," she stated.

Her threat worked. Pia almost immediately stopped laughing, though her body was still shaking, and while tears of mirth rolled down her eyes, she gasped for breath. After all, putting a sudden brake in her flow of laughter was a bad idea. Nysha cursed herself and became worried about her friend. How could she forget that her best friend was pregnant?

God damn! Shit! She thought.

She shouted at Zain, “What are you looking at, idiot? Give her some water to drink.”

He immediately rose to his feet and almost jumped to grab the bottle on the bedside table. After drinking water, Pia’s heartbeat normalized and she regained her composure. Then looking at the serious faces of both her husband and her best friend, she sneered at them and said, “Come on, guys, I am just pregnant and absolutely fine. One look at your grave faces makes me feel like I am barely surviving.”

Hardly had the words escaped her mouth when Zain pulled her into a warm embrace. He hushed her with a soft kiss on her lips and mumbled, “Shut up, will you? Don’t you ever say that again. Never ever! Do you understand?” he asked.

“Fine... then stop acting like a dick-head,” she chastised.

“Hey!” Nysha chimed in.

“Have fun, you fanatical grown-up kids,” she said.

Pia shifted her attention to Nysha and said, “Nysha... wait.”

Then turning towards Zain she added, “Zain... please!”

He raised an eyebrow and gave her an “Are you seriously out of your mind?” expression before saying, “What?” he asked.

"Seriously, I need some privacy with my friend," Pia replied.

"I am her friend too... what is it that you can't discuss with me?" he challenged.

To prove his point, he poked the phone screen with his index finger, and that was it. It was enough to ignite a fire at the other end.

"Zain Zaidi, you are the most annoying and obnoxiously awful creature that I have ever come across," Nysha yelled.

"Oh! Come on," he huffed.

Before things could get from bad to worse, Pia practically shoved a reluctant and resisting Zain out of the room, and closed the door behind her.

Her head was throbbing loudly now. Her husband and best friend sharing the same frame was clearly bad news. She collapsed on the sofa and let out a deep breath before adjusting her phone camera to face her friend anew.

"Finally, sweetie, we are alone now. Come on, spell it out. I am all ears," she announced.

"Well, at last!" Pia exclaimed, her eyes shining brightly. "Now, Nysha Patel, can you share the deets, please? I am waiting, darling."

"Oh my God! I hate it when you do this, Pia," Nysha accused.

"Do what, exactly?"

"What you are doing right now. You are eyeing me with suspicion, trying to decode what's going on in my mind. It drives me crazy! Seriously!" Nysha charged yet again.

"Oh, come on, Nysha. You said you wanted to discuss something important. So come on, babes, tell me."

"You know I have a meeting with Papa Patel and the board members, right?" Nysha asked.

"With Uncle? Today? Yeah, you did tell me. But why exactly, and what's cooking in that brilliant mind of yours? Still clueless and counting..." Pia replied earnestly.

"Pia, I fucked up... Big time..."

Nysha was now perpetually pacing up and down the balcony outside her bedroom, pacing every inch of it in a futile attempt to soothe her tense nerves.

"I think you need to calm down," Pia suggested.

"What? You heard what I said, right?" Nysha replied.

"Sure, I did. But seriously, what were you even thinking when you said yes to this dicey proposal... and now you are clueless about your next move. Great!"

Pia raised her hands in exasperation and slapped her palms on her forehead. Nysha, on the other hand, cupped her face between her hands and squinted her eyes before replying, "Weigh my options, honey, both are equally fucked up. This one, though, is a degree less. And to remind you, beggars can hardly be choosers. Trust me, I had none. This happened to be my best move."

Pia looked at Nysha with furrowed brows, still largely unconvinced.

Nysha shook her head and took a deep breath before adding, "Alright then, put yourself into my shoes. What would you have done?" she asked with a slight, vulnerable pout.

Pia pursed her lips tightly into a thin line while contemplating what Nysha had said. Though she hated to admit it, her friend was indeed right. There was hardly any choice between going on a mindless husband search spree and a pathetic hospital restoration project. Nevertheless, saving a hospital could at least benefit society.

Pia arched an eyebrow and let out a huff before replying, "Though I hate to admit it, perhaps you are right here..."

"And...?" Nysha asked while a small surge of hope filled her chest.

Pia winked at her as she bit into her favourite chocolate-coated strawberry. Then, in a soft, sultry voice, she added, "Well, it's time to up your game, Nysha darling. Let's chalk out a smart plan for your new baby."

"Precisely what I have been trying to do for the past three days, only to fail miserably. I realized I know nothing about hospitals and their operations. I am doomed."

"Stop whining, you knew nothing about running a café, too, remember?" Pia pointed out.

"That was different," Nysha shrugged.

"No, it was not. Honey, your job is to provide solutions to your clients. Akshat Ratna Hospital is just another client, and you need to treat it as one," Pia suggested.

Nysha scrunched her eyes and replied, "You know it's not. It's complicated."

"Then work it out. Make it simple," Pia advised.

"I only wish it were that easy... I really do," Nysha sighed.

Akshat Ratna Hospital

After almost half a decade, Nysha entered the hospital, and a familiar stench of disinfectant, mixed with mosquito repellent, antiseptic, and medicines, greeted her nostrils. The place was nostalgia at its best; the emotions, though, were mixed, ranging from love to loss, and grief to relief. A sudden bout of nausea gutted her insides, and she had to fight the strong urge to withdraw and retreat from the place.

She could fathom the various sensations that the place had to offer. From the cries of newborn babies and children to the sense of solace in seeing a loved one recover, or the heart-wrenching sobs and pain experienced upon losing a dear one—a feeling she was hugely familiar with. With every passing moment and with each step she took, her heartbeat increased and her eyes were blinded by the surrounding white color. They glowed as the veil of tears moistened them and now threatened to escape their threshold and wet her face. With great difficulty, she pushed back the unpleasant memories and thoughts. It was not the time to falter. On the contrary, it was time for some real action.

Nysha had always been very confident in her dealings with clients. But today wasn't one of those days. She still couldn't believe that she had said 'yes' to a proposal she wasn't too sure about. Had it only been her dad seeking her help, she would have politely declined, and she was sure he would have understood too. But she didn't have the nerve to say 'no' to Harsha Aunty.

Dr. Harsha Sanghavi was one of the most graceful and enigmatic women she had ever come across. A mother figure, she had been a pillar of strength and unfathomable support during one of the darkest and worst phases of her life. So when Harsha Aunty called and mentioned that 'Akshat Ratna' was in danger, Nysha immediately jumped in to help. She knew quite well what the hospital meant to her and her late husband, Dr. Vasant Sanghavi, both of whom were recipients of the prestigious 'Rashtra Samman Awards'. They could have easily opted for private practice, or joined any big corporate hospital that would have loved to have them on board. Instead, with their limited funds and the help and support of close friends and acquaintances, they chose to start their own hospital. Back then—precisely two decades ago—those individuals had categorically formed the board of members. But the scenario was different today, and things had changed drastically. A few of the eminent members were no longer alive, and with their spouses or children settled abroad, the shared vision and cause with which 'Akshat Ratna' had commenced were slowly beginning to diminish. The next-gen family members were hardly interested in pumping cash to run the hospital. It didn't matter to them as much as it mattered to Harsha Aunty. All they were interested in was selling their shares to big corporate wolves, who were ruthless in their dealings and had no interest whatsoever in disrupting the status quo. If it were to materialize, the legacy of 'Akshat Ratna' would be lost forever, and Nysha could not allow that to happen. She was ready to fight tooth and nail to save the hospital. Her mind was engulfed in confused thoughts when a phone call interrupted them. It was her dad calling. Dropping the formalities of a courtesy greeting, she answered it straight away:

"Already reached, Papa."

"Good morning to you too, beta," the voice at the other end boomed in response. "It's good that you are here early; I would like to introduce you to the board members. Though I must warn you, dear, these are a bunch of grumpy old men and pea-brained youngsters with the least interest in reviving the hospital. I would like to believe that you do have a solid plan up your sleeve," he concluded.

Nysha suppressed a grin and said, "Grumpy old man! Like seriously, Dad? Mr. Davesh Patel, you must be in your jolly forties then," she teased.

"Age is just a number, darling... and by any means, are you suggesting I am old?" he asked.

"Of course not, Davesh bhai, you are as young and sexy as sixteen. Now tell me, where are you?"

"Conference Hall No. 1, on the third floor. While a few members are already here, the rest are about to reach. Come soon," he said.

As she disconnected the call, her streaks of thoughts were back again. She was only hopeful that, in all probability, her dad was exaggerating. After all, how difficult could it be to convince a group of men and women to see things the way she saw them?

Her internal query was immediately met with a spontaneous gut response in her mind. Who was she kidding anyway? It would indeed be difficult to persuade people whose only interest seemed to be minting money. Moreover, she wasn't even sure about her so-called plan. She had hastily agreed to Pia's cringe-worthy proposal since she had none of her own and was only hopeful that presenting the same would buy her some time to pull up her socks.

Nysha took the elevator to the third floor. Upon reaching her destination, she walked past the administrator's office, down the lobby, and straight to the Hall. Stopping in front of the large, artistically designed teak wooden door, she took a moment to admire the proudly displayed 'Akshat Ratna' logo. The hospital, which started twenty years ago with 'service to mankind' as its core motto, was slowly upgraded to a Multi-specialty Hospital and Research Centre. At one point, a team of renowned doctors and healthcare specialists was part of its fraternity. However, with the influx of big corporate hospitals, the growth of 'Akshat Ratna' had somewhat stalled, and its operations had taken a backseat. Today, the hospital was on the brink of closure and in serious need of a facelift; failing which, it was sure to succumb to the competition and follow the footsteps of the preceding smaller hospitals which were forced to shut down entirely without any scope of resurrection whatsoever.

Nysha was about to enter the room when a whiteboard placed neatly against the wall, adjacent to the door, caught her attention. It listed the names of the board members expected to participate in the meeting which was about to begin shortly. Staring at their names didn't help much. There wasn't even a single name that rang a bell, or seemed even remotely familiar. She understood that she would certainly face one hell of a time coaxing and cajoling a group of uninterested and unknown men and women. Without wasting another minute, she muttered a quick prayer, took a deep breath, and stepped inside the hall with a pretentious aura of confidence and a fake smile plastered on her lips.

A silent pep talk in her mind helped to calm her weary nerves.

Bring it on everyone, I'm here to win.

When Nysha entered the hall, she was in for a surprise. The chairs in the front row were nearly empty, and almost everyone was standing at the end of the room. Moving forward and taking a closer look, she saw that two tables were neatly lined up at the rear of the hall, where breakfast and beverages were evidently being served.

Duh! And so much for lack of funds, she thought. She was about to take another step when she felt a light tap on her shoulder. Even without looking, she could tell who it was. She smiled and turned around to greet her favourite person. Nysha gave Harsha Aunty a warm hug. Though they were regularly in touch via phone calls, she hadn't seen her in a long time, and Nysha was dismayed to see that Aunty had changed. No, not her persona, of course; she was still the same warm, loving, and affectionate being, but her appearance had changed a lot, making her look like a different person altogether. Fine, wrinkled lines had developed around her eyes, and the wrinkles near her mouth appeared to rest deeper, making her look older than she was. Most importantly, her dark grey eyes looked tired, while her slightly drooping shoulders gave the impression that she was fragile, which wasn't quite the case. At least that's what Nysha still liked to believe.

Her reverie of sorts was broken when Harsha Aunty spoke in her lively voice:

"And who do we have here, at last? I was actually starting to get worried that you had changed your mind, beta," she teased.

"And why on Earth would you think that I would ditch my favorite Aunty...," Nysha replied with a smile while hugging her back.

Harsha Aunty rolled her eyes in a comical fashion as if to suggest, 'you would soon get to know, my love.'

"Would you like some tea or coffee?" Aunty asked.

"No Aunty, I am good. By the way, have you seen Papa Patel?" Nysha replied.

"Mota bhai? Oh yes, he was here just a minute ago." Dr. Harsha scanned the length of the entire room, almost straining her eyes in an attempt to inspect the far end of the hall. After a moment, she spotted Mr. Patel and a young gentleman, engrossed in deep conversation, and a smile crossed her lips.

"Ah, there they are," she said. "Come; let me introduce you to someone."

Without questioning, Nysha followed Aunty. They stopped at the far right corner of the room, where she spotted her father seated comfortably, sipping his favourite cup of masala chai. She couldn't help but notice a plate beside him, where a tempting, unfinished cinnamon sugar bun was neatly placed in the center.

Sheesh! Mr. Gujju Bhai Patel and his sweet cravings, this man is just way too much! He is unfazed by what sugar can do to his body, Nysha thought, flinching internally. Nevertheless, she managed to keep a straight face. Papa Patel still hadn't noticed their arrival, which made her curious about the other person's identity in their two-way communication model. After all, keeping Davesh Bhai Patel engrossed in conversation for this long couldn't be considered a small feat. She tried looking over Harsha Aunty's shoulder, but the man was seated with his broad back to them, leaving her still clueless about his tentative identity.

"Mota Bhai," Aunty called from behind, and both men got up to greet her. One was her dad, but the other person caught her attention. He was tall with broad shoulders, not very dark but undeniably handsome. Most importantly, he looked familiar—very familiar—but she couldn't place him immediately, not yet. That was until Harsha Aunty shifted her attention to him in an attempt to introduce them.

"Ah! Nysha beta, meet the youngest member of the board, Dr. Samarjeet Attwal," she said.

Dr. Attwal! Why, of course, the name now not only rang a bell but also evoked her sleepy senses. She could remember him bang on, without a streak of doubt or an ounce of confusion. He was the same person to whom her best friend had almost been betrothed before she changed her mind just in the nick of time. Though things eventually fell into place and ended on a high note for Pia, she couldn't say the same for Dr. Attwal. After all, a breakup was a breakup, and it was bound to leave a bad taste in the mouth of the one forsaken.

Holy hell! Shit! Shit! Shit! What was Dr. Samarjeet Attwal doing here? Of all the doctors in the world, it had to be him? Seriously now! This turned out to be a real difficult deal, she thought. To Nysha, it felt like being stranded on a remote island, alone, without a soul for help.

God! What had she gotten herself into? Did he recognize her? In all probability, he did, because she thought she had seen the unmistakable look of shock and evident recognition cross his face.

By now, her head had begun spinning like someone high on drugs and enjoying a double o' ride on the largest Ferris wheel available. Getting a grip on herself, she let out a thin smile before saying, "Hello Mr. Samar, I mean, Dr. Samarjeet... Dr. Attwal, hi...," she finished.

Suddenly, Harsha Aunty eyed her with a visibly interested look. Papa Patel, too, seemed to have forgotten all about the unfinished cinnamon bun on his plate and was looking at her as if she owed an explanation. Seriously! Did she owe one? She was still figuring out a response to wade out of the weird situation she was caught in when Harsha Aunty fired the first query at her,

"Wait! Do both of you know each other?" she asked.

"No, I mean...," Nysha responded.

"Yes," Dr. Attwal said at the same time.

"No, I mean yes, sort of," Nysha replied again.

"Yeah, sort of, I guess," Dr. Attwal agreed, his voice drawling. She couldn't help but notice that it had a slight musical edge and a largely drowsy effect to it.

She gathered her thoughts and saw two pairs of eyes contemplating her with suspicion, still unconvinced by her rather clumsy attempt at offering an equally awkward response. She was saved from further embarrassment when a young lady approached Harsha Aunty and asked her politely, "Dr. Sanghavi, we are done with the refreshments. The members are beginning to get a bit restless now. Should we start the meeting?"

"Ah! Of course, we should," she said. Then, turning towards Nysha she asked, "Beta, are you good to go?"

Am I? (Internal muted, but true response.)

"Yes, absolutely." (Loud and vocal, but fake response.)

Well, cheers to new beginnings, Nysha muttered internally.

Game: Nysha's Hell Squad
Players: Nysha, Harsha Aunty, Papa Patel
Player expertise: Novice
Task Difficulty Level: Outright nightmarish
Score: 0
Comments: Try and try until you dry.

Nysha, Samar, Meetings, and More...

With each step she took, her heart skipped several beats. With a host of thoughts circling her mind, it almost felt like the world was spinning right in front of her eyes. Her breath came in small gasps, and until then, she hadn't even realized that she had been holding it the whole time. Fearing the risk of passing out, she opened her mouth and took a gulp of fresh air.

Upon reaching the middle of the room, she carefully placed her bag on the table and looked at the blank, uninterested, and largely impassive faces around her. Letting out a nervous smile, she started with a greeting,

"Good morning, ladies and gentlemen."

Her voice sounded partly hoarse and largely shrill, even to her ears. There was a chorus of counter-greetings from around the room.

Taking a deep breath, she began, "Well, let me begin by introducing myself. I am Nysha Patel, and I run a business consulting firm, Aura Cosmos. From what I have learned, Akshat Ratna is facing a real cash crunch and desperately needs a fresh infusion of funds. I am here not only to help control this unwarranted crisis but also to chalk out a plan to reengineer its entire process so that we can save it from the predicament of a permanent shutdown."

A loud, disdainful snort reverberated from the corner of the room. Nysha turned to look at the source of the ungracious hoot with glaring eyes. She saw an old man with a permanent sneer imprinted on his face staring at her. He eyed her with visible disinterest and repulsion. His lips were pursed together in a thin line, and he spoke with an evident air of superiority and an equally condescending tone.

"As much as I appreciate your concern, Miss, I believe your technical jargon won't help. No pun intended, but my friends here would also agree that the only way to recover our already invested and drained funds is to seize the earliest opportunity and sell the hospital to any corporation willing to offer the best possible deal."

There were rumbling murmurs and nods of agreement around the room, and Nysha could see that he was right and that most of his loyal friends indeed shared his opinion. Her cheeks heated, and her face became flushed with anger and contempt. She took a deep breath and replied in the most respectful and dignified manner possible.

"Sir, I understand your concern. But I am sure most of us here would agree that Akshat Ratna is more than just a hospital. It's an emotion for us. We have our share of memories here. By handing it over to any corporation, we would compromise its legacy. All we need is a well-planned event to raise funds, and that is precisely why I am here."

However, Nysha soon realized that the old moron was not the least bit interested in listening. He was busy fidgeting with his mobile, and she had a wild inner urge to kick the legs of his chair, simply for the fun and sadistic pleasure of seeing him lose his balance and fall smack-dab on the floor. Her insides seethed with fury and disgust. She took a deep breath to calm her jumpy nerves.

As if sensing her turmoil, Harsh Aunty stepped in to help, "Dr. Pawar, we need to listen to what Nysha has to say. She is an expert in the field, one we need in this current hour of crisis. It's only fair that we give her a chance to explain and share her plan."

Dr. Pawar gave her a nonchalant and dismissive glance before shifting his attention to Dr. Harsha and speaking, "Dr. Sanghavi, try and understand that most of us here have some real work to do. You can't expect us to spend the entire day weaving dreams of saving an almost-dead entity. I have more pressing matters to attend to. Now, if you would kindly excuse me, I would like to take my leave."

Listening to him speak to Harsha Aunty in such a demeaning tone rattled Nysha's nerves. She realized exactly what the old moron was trying to do. He was trying to mess with them and play games with their minds. She had dealt with many ruthless rascals in her line of work, but never once did she think that a senior doctor of his repute could be such an uncouth and mean old fellow. She had to start counting prime numbers in her mind to divert her attention and control her anger.

Like heck! She thought.

She was not allowing misogynistic narcissists like him to belittle their cause or dethrone them in their own game.

Once she was sure that her nerves were settled, she turned towards Dr. Pawar and said in a subtle, unapologetic, and sarcasm-laced voice, "Absolutely, Dr. Pawar, I understand that you are a very busy man. Of course, you can continue with whatever you deem more important than saving the heritage of Akshat Ratna. However, we shall proceed with the meeting, and I am sure we can find a way to save our beloved hospital. Meanwhile, you could have someone trustworthy on the board update you about the proceedings of this meeting later."

Nysha knew she had crossed a line, but she didn't give a damn. For all she knew, the old jackass deserved every bit of contempt thrown his way. Exhaling deeply, she looked around and found the entire room eerily silent. She could see Aunt Harsh and Papa Patel's pale faces staring at her with part surprise and sheer disbelief. She was also somewhat relieved that she couldn't read minds, since she was sure their current thoughts were bound to be direly confusing and massively convoluted, to say the least.

But it was Dr. Pawar's changed expression which caught her attention. Perhaps the mean old fellow had never tasted his own medicine before. His changed demeanour could definitely be considered worthy of a 'Filmfare Laurel' or the 'Golden Globe,' though the Oscars would need to wait their turn. Chiding away her unruly thoughts, she focused on Dr. Pawar with renewed interest.

A sheepish smile played on his lips instead of his deep-rooted sneer, and he eyed her with a challenging look. Finally, he spoke, his eyes never leaving hers, "Impressive! Two weeks…that's all you have, young lady, before you present your ultimate and final proposal to the board."

Turning towards Dr. Attwal, he said in an assertive, but a slight domineering tone, "Samar, you will help the young lady. She seems to be a novice, without the slightest hint of the real-time operations of a hospital. Both of you will report to Dr. Sanghavi. I believe I have made myself clear."

"Yes, Doctor," Samar nodded.

The uncanny silence stretched throughout the room with supreme intensity. There was a dead calm, and for a moment Nysha thought she could even hear the rattled heartbeats of the people around her. Only after Dr. Pawar exited, and the conference door closed behind him, the surrounding air eased, and the environment regained its normalcy. However, the faces of the onlookers remained pale, and their ghoulish eyes were fixed on her, including that of Dr. Attwal's.

Holy Lord, what have I got myself into? Nysha thought with a sigh.

"What the hell just happened?" he repeated in his mind for the umpteenth time.

Dr. Samarjeet Attwal was pacing up and down the length of his cabin inside Akshat Ratna Hospital. He was also trying to decipher the events of the morning board meeting. It had happened so quickly that he was still attempting to get a hang of it. Nysha Patel! The girl was spitfire and completely crazy. Otherwise, who would, in their right mind, mess with the senior-most member of the Board of Akshat Ratna and also the soon-to-be National President of the Indian Medical Association (IMA).

A knock at the door disturbed his line of thought, and his reverie was broken when Dr. Sanghavi entered his cabin. But it was the person walking behind her who caught his attention—the one who had occupied his mind since morning...Nysha!

They had met only once before, precisely three years ago, and interestingly, it was her birthday party. The situation, though, had been entirely different then. He had agreed to the invite only because of Pia, whom he had genuinely liked and started to consider as his prospective bride, only to realize later that her heart was already occupied.

"Dr. Samar, I hope we aren't disturbing you," Dr. Harsha asked.

"Of course not, Dr. Sanghavi, please take a seat," he replied.

Nysha followed suit and took a seat next to Dr. Harsha. Dressed in a coral pantsuit and with her hair tied in a ponytail, she looked extremely professional. But it was her eyes and fragrance that captured his interest. The room was filled with a mix of aromas: mocha, sandalwood, and lavender, and her kohl rimmed doe-shaped eyes behind the gold-framed specs did little to hide her anger and irritation. Her lips remained pursed in a thin line as if she was barely hanging by a thread, and one slight 'peck' or 'prick' could bring out the worst in her. He wondered if she was into swearing. Given her current demeanour, her uttering profanities didn't seem unlikely.

God! The girl sure had temper tantrums, and they were as huge as they could get, he thought.

"Samar!"

Dr. Sanghavi began, "From what I have seen and understood about you, this hospital means something and is important to you."

"Of course, Doctor, it does," he replied earnestly.

"And I hope you will help Nysha and give her a fair chance to explain herself and propose her plan."

Samar visibly didn't seem quite at ease with her request. In fact, he looked as if he was taken aback. Nysha found his behaviour somewhat strange. She tried to open her mouth to say something, but one look at Dr. Harsha made her restrain herself.

"Please, Samar," Doctor Harsha repeated.

"Alright, Doctor, I will," he assured.

"Thank you so much, Samar. Alright then, I will leave you both to discuss, and once you come up with something concrete, call me in," she said.

Nysha turned towards Dr. Harsha, and cupping her hands in her own, she spoke in a soft tone, "Aunty, I hope you understand that this will not be easy. I don't want to give false hope, but I assure you I will do my best."

"Of course, I trust you, beta."

Dr. Sanghavi then turned towards Dr. Samar and said, "I am counting on you too, Doctor."

He gave her a wry smile, but no oral affirmation as such.

Once Dr. Harsha exited, an uneasy silence descended upon the terrain. Nysha eyed Samar expectantly, but without any clear idea or inkling about the entire matter, he couldn't bring himself to say anything, lest he should end up looking like a fool instead. However, when the silence between them stretched for a bit too long, Nysha sighed in exasperation, and losing her cool, finally blurted out in an almost abrupt manner, "Dr. Attwal, are you sure you want to do this today? Or do we have enough time in the whole wide world?" she asked.

Whole Wide World! Seriously! Is she even for real? he thought. Samar still couldn't comprehend whether what he had heard was exactly what Nysha had just said. And damn! Who even uses words like these? Well, he had heard it from his five-year-old niece, who had picked it up from her favourite cartoon series. And who was Nysha Patel, some 5-year-old cartoon-loving kid?

Samar's thoughts went haywire on their own wild rampage. Nevertheless, Nysha's sudden hurled accusation had the desired outcome. He immediately raised his head from the file that he had buried himself in and arched an eyebrow at her before saying, "Excuse me!"

"You heard me," she accused.

He held her gaze for some time, and so did she. There was an unmistakable and unapologetic challenge in those amber eyes. He shifted his gaze downward and noticed her impressive angular jawline and her pouty, luscious, kissable lips.

Luscious, kissable lips! Damn! What was he thinking? He muttered internally. With great difficulty, he looked away and restrained himself from gaping at her. What the hell! His hormones had never really acted this weird and worked up for a girl before. Sure thing, Nysha Patel was bad… bad news!

"What do you want?" he asked.

"Your attention, Doctor, what else?" she replied calmly.

"Why, of course. Well, now you have it." He closed the file he had been pretending to read and placed it on top of the other similar looking files before shifting his attention to her.

"So…you have any idea…any proposal…plan…Anything?" she asked, continuously tapping her foot on the floor, giving away her edgy nerves.

"As far as I can remember, Dr. Sanghavi's exact words were that you are the expert here, the one capable of pulling us out of this distressing situation, or the utter mess, so to speak," he replied sarcastically.

"Whoa! You sound much like old Doc Pawar, full of resent, contempt, and evident bitterness. Life is not so bad, Dr. Attwal, so chill!" she stated. "And sometimes, all we need to do is take a chance, right?" she chastised.

Samar was impressed by Nysha's confidence, or perhaps by her visible, unapologetic overconfidence. He leaned back in his chair and spoke slowly. His voice almost drawled, and Nysha realized it held the subtle undertones of a seductive flair, with a slight nasal tinge and a deep, drowsy resonance—a deadly concoction.

She immediately chided herself for letting her thoughts mess with her mind.

Seductive! Nasal! Drowsy! Seriously! What have you been thinking?

She questioned internally.

Meanwhile, Samar eyed her with interest. In her internal mind brawl, she hadn't managed to pick up his query. She scrunched her nose and asked again, "What? Sorry, I mean, what exactly were you saying?"

"Ah, ha!" Samar gave her an amused look.

"Dr. Attwallllllllll…"

She said in a slight, warbling voice, and as his name lingered on her lips for some time, it did something unexplainable to the pit of his stomach. He felt a sudden tug at his chest while his eyes remained fixed on her face a bit longer than could be considered courteous. Upon realizing his folly, he looked away and answered, "I asked, how much do you know about Akshat Ratna, Dr. Pawar, or the Board members, for that matter?"

"Is this some knowledge test? Do we need to do this right now?" she responded skeptically.

"Oh, no! Of course not. You decide, Ms. Patel; to begin with, should we look for an auspicious date or time? Or, for that matter, do you have any particular venue in mind to do the honors?" he asked in a straight, razor-sharp voice, sans mincing his words.

She glared daggers at him, before replying in an icy tone, "Alright, if you insist… Well, I know as much about Akshat Ratna as necessary. But regarding the board members…"

She puffed out her cheek and exhaled loudly before continuing, "I regret that I don't have much of an idea."

Samar noticed that she looked extremely adorable with her nervous pout. Chiding away his thoughts, he deadpanned instead, "I figured," he stated.

"Hey, don't jump to conclusions, and stop acting like an obnoxious moron. Even your name was not on the list of directors," she charged.

"Okay, now you are deflecting the obvious," he said. "Besides, my name was pretty much on the list, you must have missed it," he added with a nonchalant shrug.

"You bet...," she challenged.

Before he could comprehend her next move, she was already by his side. Clutching his hand, she led him outside his cabin. Slowly, they walked in silence through the long corridor towards the Conference Hall, which was on the same floor. On the way, they crossed several onlookers, and sets of curious eyes greeted them—some smiling, the rest bemused, but none indifferent whatsoever. Finally, standing outside the hall, Nysha proudly pointed out towards the whiteboard where the names of the participating board members were displayed. Not surprisingly, his name was indeed missing. However, he was already aware of it. His name was a last-minute addition at the behest of Dr. Pawar, and so, quite conveniently, the attendant had forgotten to put it up while Samar hadn't even bothered about it. Of course, not until one Ms. Patel had stepped in and well...he thought for some time, and a small smile crossed his lips.

Chaos! Ms. Nysha Patel was living, walking, and talking chaos...

Meanwhile, oblivious to everything around her and with her hand still entangled in his, she gave him a slight nudge that broke his musing. With eyes glistening, she looked at him and pointed towards the board again before speaking (or rather, squeaking excitedly with an endearing streak).

"See, I told you."

"Yeah, that you did," he replied.

Their eyes met for a few seconds, and Samar felt a slight tug at his heartstrings as a subtle ache engulfed his chest. Nysha looked stunning. It was obvious that winning did that for her. It had been quite a while since a girl had managed to have that kind of an effect on him. Or perhaps Nysha Patel was not just any girl; she was strikingly different.

Hard reality and realization began to seep into Dr. Attwal's hardwired brain. The intermingling of emotions and uncontrolled stimuli could be the beginning of a dreaded new ailment: one he could not afford to catch. He prioritized getting his vitals checked, including his cardiovascular system. And, of course, his myocardium needed to be protected at any cost while maintaining a safe distance from the source of his dread: Ms. Patel.

The Beginning of Mayhem (Mr. Cool vs. Ms. Chaos)

Samar was trying to concentrate on a critical case file, but no matter how hard he tried, he could not. It seemed his concentration was amiss. He had agreed with Dr. Harsha, but the prospect of working alongside Ms. Patel posed far too many risks, and the consequences were difficult to ignore. He closed the file, and that's when his eyes suddenly fell on a shiny, oval-shaped object across the table. Clearly, it was a misfit on his well-organized desk. Slowly getting up from his chair, he went near to inspect and look at it. On approaching it, he picked it up and sighed, Ms. Patel had forgotten her shiny, silver-colored clutch.

Well, life had thrown in another surprise in less than 24 hours. His lips curved into a small semblance of a smile. He could even inhale the subtle hint of her fragrance: mocha, sandalwood, and lavender. He shook his head and flinched internally at his splendid eidetic memory. The huracan named Ms. Patel was robbing him of his attention and control, and by no means could it be deemed a good thing. He pondered about his next move for some time. Since they had already exchanged numbers, he could simply call her to inform about her forgotten purse. But that would have been applicable under normal circumstances only, and his gut feeling suggested, standard procedures wouldn't apply too well with Ms. Patel. So he settled for his next best move instead: call Dr. Harsha, inform her about Nysha's misplaced purse, and in turn request her to pass on the information. Sure, it might seem a bit weird, and a tad too much of an effort, merely because of his irrational reluctance to call her. But he didn't want to risk another confrontation with Ms. Patel on the same day itself. However, contrary to his restrained thoughts, a sick part of him also wanted to grasp the opportunity of seeing her again. As the very thought crossed his mind, he clenched his fist at his damn idiotic notion.

He picked up his phone to call Dr. Harsha and inquire about her whereabouts; however, an incoming call from the doctor herself surprised him. He immediately answered the same.

"Hello, Dr. Sanghavi, in fact I was coming to you…" he began.

"Yes, Samar…Actually, I called to ask, did Nysha forget her purse in your room?"

"Why… I mean…Yeah, she did," he replied instantly.

"Oh, thank God!" Dr. Harsha heaved a sigh of relief.

"Yeah, thank the Holiness for her Highness's purse," Samar thought, and immediately chided himself for his internal rude remark.

"Dr. Harsha…," he began, but before he could complete, Dr. Harsha spoke instead, "Samar, I needed your help with something."

"Oh, no! No! No!" Even before Dr. Harsha had completed, Samar knew exactly where she was heading, and hence he was preparing himself internally for a negative response to her request.

"Samar…you there…Are you listening?" she verified at his muted response.

"Ah well, yes…yeah, listening, Dr. Harsha," he replied.

"Oh great, could you please drop Nysha's purse home? The poor girl had freaked out when she realized that her purse was missing."

Samar gave the purse a severe disdainful look and thought, Aha! Poor crazy missy! And what could this rather small, single-compartmental piece possibly hold? Not a lot of money, of course.

"Dr. Samar, I believe that's okay with you," she repeated.

Dr. Harsha's voice managed to pull him out of his thoughts, but he was still undecided of his response. He tried to rack his brain for some plausible answer, without sounding vague or rude, but all he could come up with were certain lame indistinct sounds instead.

"Aah…actually!!…"

"Samar, please…"

And that was it. Dr. Harsha had already uttered the magical word. When someone said a 'please,' Samar could hardly refuse, and saying 'no' to Dr. Harsha had now become an utmost impossible feat. So much to her relief, he mumbled an unwilling and inconvenient 'yes' instead.

Dr. Harsha was truly gratified at his response and thanked him for his help. Before hanging up she added, "Thanks, Samar, I will text you her address immediately. It shouldn't be much of a problem, since I guess it falls on your way home."

If only Dr. Sanghavi knew, and if only Samar could explain, that the address and the distance were never the problem, but Ms. Patel was. She was a huge distraction, and a messy lunatic bite-sized dynamite which came with its own potential danger sign attached, along with a severe warning which stated, "Highly combustible…Mess at your own risk."

Feelings and emotions have an extraordinary way of messing with the human mind. Until morning, Samar had been a strong-willed individual who was capable enough of taking the right decisions for himself. But enter Ms. Patel, and his prefrontal cortex and myocardium had entered into loggerheads, refusing to work in tandem.

Strongly fighting his inner urge to back out and make an escape, he found himself standing and staring at her door instead. It had the quirkiest nameplate attached to it, which showcased three clay elephant figurines with intricate pop-out details. Adjacent to each elephant, the following words were inscribed:

The biggest elephant – Papa Patel (Mr. Davesh Patel)

The medium one – Mamma Patel (Mrs. Riddhima Patel)

The smallest one – Baby Patel (Ms. Nysha Patel)

Samar tried hard to stifle a loud laugh. He was still contemplating on the idea of making a run. Though he could now pretty well understand the source of mayhem for her craziness, he had some serious doubts if he was well equipped to handle the same. Sidelining his line of thought, he inhaled deeply and finally took the giant leap.

He rang the bell.

When Nysha opened the door, she was in for a surprise. Dr. Samarjeet Attwal was the last person whom she had been expecting. At first she looked shocked, and then her expression turned grim. Irritated, her eyes took in his handsome features. He was dressed in a simple lime-colored shirt, minus the white medical coat. His hair as usual was neatly combed back and his day-old stubble gave him a raw appeal, making him look extremely sexy. As the very thought crossed her mind, she became angry at herself. Tearing away her eyes from his face and controlling her lustful thoughts, she finally asked him, "Dr. Attwal…What…are you doing here?"

Meanwhile, Samar's eyes took in the breathtaking beauty that stood in front of him. Dressed in a sleeveless floral yellow midi dress, her hair tied in a messy bun, with a few strands set loose on her face, while kissing her cheeks, she looked extremely adorable. She batted her eyelashes quite a few times, and Samar thought that it was the cutest thing he had seen in a long time. It almost made her look like a doll. Her face, scrubbed clean and devoid of any makeup, radiated an angelic aura.

Doll! Angelic!

Something was seriously wrong with the air. Had someone spiked it with drugs? An affirmation of the same would have been a relief; coz there was no other way to explain the weirdest possible thoughts encircling his mind at the moment.

"What brings you here, Doctor?" Nysha repeated.

Her icy taunt broke his trance. She was looking at him with a devilish sneer. Well, Nysha Patel was no angel, she was actually a nymph from "hell" with a resolve to mess with his mind and jeopardize his sanity and existence. She didn't even have the courtesy to invite him in. Damn! He was not her courier delivery boy. He had a strong urge to push her aside and barge inside. However, controlling his violent streak, he replied with the calm of an ocean instead, "Your purse…," he said.

She looked at her silver-colored, non-essential, shiny little box in his hand as if he were Mandrake, the Magician who had just pulled out a giant king cobra from his hat. But her expression softened, and she replied in a hushed tone, "Oh that!"

In an almost reluctant manner, she reached out for it and took it from his hand. Then under her breath she muttered, "Thanks, but I could have collected it tomorrow."

"Then you should have said that to Dr. Harsha, instead of feigning a panic attack," he snapped back.

His boorish mannerism repelled her. Gritting her teeth, she replied back, "Mind your words, Dr. Attwal…I…y-o-u…"

Samar noticed that she stuttered, in all probably when she was mad, and currently she was straightway mad at him. Though he was absolutely clueless about the reason, he noticed that in her anger directed at him, her cheeks had turned flush red, making her look extremely endearing. A part of him wanted to pull her towards him, hold her against his chest, and comfort her.

Holy hell! Something was seriously wrong with him, he speculated.

He made a mental note to run a few tests on himself the very next day. He couldn't risk his mental imbalance, fuck-up with his decision-making capacity, and wreck up his organized life.

Before further accusations could be hurled at him, a sweet voice came from inside the house and echoed behind her, "Nysha puttar, kaun hai darvaze pe? Aur inna der kyon lag raha hai?"

("Nysha dear, who is at the door? And what's taking you so long?")

Samar noticed a middle-aged woman in her early sixties looking intently at them. She was of medium build, had a radiant complexion, and looked very pretty in her peach-colored salwar suit. He needed no explanation as to who she was because her eyes said it all. She had those same eyes which her daughter had categorically inherited. And she spoke such good Punjabi. Oh, wait! Nysha's mom was Punjabi. Alright! His lips twisted into a playful smile as if he had made the most important discovery on the Planet.

Oh my, this is beginning to get interesting…Aha! Very, very… interesting indeed, he thought.

As Auntyji eyed him with interest, in reflex he folded his hands together and muttered, "Uh, Namaste, Auntyji."

She scanned him from top to toe, and then looked at Nysha with a bewildered expression, and then back to him before replying, "Ah, namaste, puttarji…Enu pehchana nahin, Nysha puttar."

("Ah, namaste, son…I didn't recognize him, Nysha dear.")

Before Nysha could answer, Samar replied instantaneously, "I am her partner…"

The absolute wrong choice of 'word' had the most hilarious and precarious effect on the mother and daughter duo. Mrs. Patel's eyes wobbled in disbelief, while Nysha's mutinous expression suggested that, given a chance, she could slit his throat in one clean stroke. He had absolutely zero doubts regarding her wild ability to do the same. So, without pushing any further, he reframed his response, "Ah! What I mean is, work partner," he added.

Mrs. Patel let out an audible gasp of relief, and Nysha rolled her eyes in a comical fashion, muttering something under her breath, and Samar was sure that she was hurling cuss words at him. But it seemed Mamma Patel was far from being convinced by his response. She wasn't done with her questioning, at least not yet.

"Work partner?" she asked.

Samar's guess was right. A typical Punjabi mom's investigative hormones kick in the moment she finds a handsome but unknown gentleman knocking at their door in the late hours of the night. And that too for a highly silly endeavor like returning a petty clutch.

Darn!! Life had taken a 360-degree flip with the influx of Ms. Patel.

This time however, Mrs. Patel was eyeing Nysha for a proper explanation. The poor girl was pleading with her eyes, straightaway declaring, 'you will get all your answers once he leaves.' Meanwhile, she did try her best to put in place some sort of nonchalant reply, which, of course, was a far cry from sounding convincing.

"I have told you about the Hospital Project, haven't I? Well, about Harsha Aunty…" she tried explaining.

But Mamma Patel simply stood there, while her face showed her unconvinced retort.

When she failed miserably at convincing and eliciting a proper response, Nysha sighed audibly and added, "Papa must have told you… Dr. Samar and I, we just met today…"

However, in a surprising turn of events, Mrs. Patel delivered a master stroke. A move neither of them had expected nor even contemplated. She raised her hand and, turning towards Nysha, declared, "Bas!" (Enough!)

For a moment, the room went silent. Nysha hated it when her mom used that word. In typical Indian families, children are conditioned in such a way that one feels obligated to behave as per certain standard societal norms. And when her mom used that word, it always meant that she was supposed to keep her mouth shut…for good, of course…

Mrs. Patel then turned her attention towards Samar and continued, "It's already late; we were going to have dinner. Do join us, Dr. Samar."

Her tone sounded more like a command than a request. Samar noticed that Mrs. Patel could be quite assertive in her dealings, a trait quintessentially passed down to her daughter too.

If Samar was taken aback by this sudden unexpected proposal, Nysha's deep furrowed eyes clearly conveyed her intense disapproval of the same. Don't you dare consider this, she gestured with her eyes.

Truth be told, she was absolutely right. Samar should have said an outright no. He had no business being there, and he had to be clearly out of his wits, if even for a miniscule second the option of saying a yes had crossed his mind. But that would have been the case, had the situation been normal, and he was being his logical self. With Nysha around, the logical doctor made an early exit, and the one left behind enjoyed the liberty of bending and mending rules for fun. There was a strange charismatic aura about her that unleashed his carefree boyish charm, and for some strange reason he was beginning to enjoy the same. Though good or bad, only time could tell.

As he stared at Nysha's cajoling face, a sudden enthralling idea crossed his mind, which was sure to piss 'her craziness' off. And a sick part of him wanted to do exactly that, piss her off and make her mad...

With a plastered grin on his face, while avoiding Nysha completely and acknowledging Mrs. Patel upfront, he said, "Thank you so much for the offer, Auntyji. It would be my pleasure to join you all for dinner."

A Hint of Sugar, a Dash of Spice, and Lots of Ice

Pain in the ass! That was the first thing that came to her mind when she saw him comfily occupying a chair in their intimate dining area. Reluctantly, she pulled another one next to him and settled her bottoms into the seat. The fact that he chose to ignore her while being glued to his mobile screen didn't quite sit well with her. In fact, it irked her to bits. In an attempt to attract his attention, she cleared her throat, a bit louder than she had intended to, but it had the desired effect. He looked up and asked, "Yes, Ms. Patel? You wanted to say something?"

When Samar had entered the abode of her craziness, Ms. Patel, he took in the tastefully decorated modern interiors. The living area had bright neon-colored walls, with a section of it displaying a few selected paintings from around the globe. Another wall was splashed with bright hues of crimson and copper, and it proudly showcased beautifully framed photographs of friends and family. There were pictures with her parents, cousins, friends, and staff members, but the one that stood out was that of the awesome four: Nysha with her besties, Pia, Zain, and Rajiv. There was another one, a comparatively recent one, which seemed to have been clicked at Pia's baby shower, where the soon-to-be mom was radiating an ethereal glow. She was a lovely human being, and she deserved the best in life. Though he was happy for her, a part of him felt a sudden tug of emptiness, as he wondered if love would ever happen to him in an almost dramatic flair, as it had happened to Pia and Zain.

He had settled himself in one of the comfortable dining area chairs, and was checking his work emails while replying to a few urgent ones, when he felt Nysha's eyes on him. The brat that she was, he was sure she had a lot of questions up her sleeve. So finally when he asked her the same, she gave him a scornful look before replying, "Aren't you getting a bit too cozy, Dr. Attwal?"

"And what makes Her Highness say so?" he asked playfully.

She was astounded by him, addressing her as Highness, and making it sound like she was some spoiled entitled brat. She straightaway wanted to wipe away that smirk from his face. But gathering her thoughts and maintaining her calm, she replied instead, "You could have always said no, Dr. Attwal. Dinner invitation by Mamma was just a courtesy call. I fear now you will have to settle for poor man's roti pizza," she attempted to dishearten him.

Unperturbed by her feeble attempt at deterring him, he replied in his trademark cool demeanor instead, "Why tire yourself, Nysha dear?"

Dear! She couldn't believe he had just called her that. The nerve of the person!

"You are really...like...are you seriously out of your mind?" she fumbled.

Flabbergasted, she stared at him with her mouth wide open.

"Such a liar you are. The aroma coming from the kitchen speaks otherwise. And stop gaping with your mouth wide open; it makes you resemble a hideous fish," Samar stated as a matter of fact, while trying hard not to grin from ear to ear.

"Alright, first you call me a liar, then a fish, and hideous at that…And what are you? No saint, I suppose," she snapped.

"Who, me?" He pointed a finger at himself and then continued, "Go on…What about me? I am no saint; I never claimed to be one," he clarified.

"Of course, you are not," she agreed. "By the way, when were you planning to tell me that vile-mouthed Dr. Pawar is your uncle?" she asked.

"Ah! Now we are talking…So this is all about Dr. Pawar then," Samar replied.

"He is your maternal uncle, your own uncle…for God's sake!" she accused.

"He is, so what? You are still not making sense," he said.

"You don't understand…you never would," she sighed in exasperation.

She looked small and dejected, as if singlehandedly fighting a losing battle, and overwhelmed by the sense of its responsibility. He hated to see her like that. With her spitfire personality, vicious viper suited her better than a tamed submissive cat.

"Nysha…listen to me…," he began softly.

She looked at him, her eyes glistening with unfathomable emotion. He held her gaze, while his warm eyes gently scanned her face. Whatever he saw must have really convinced him, for he leaned closer and whispered lightly, "You need to relax, Nysha…Calm down."

"Samar, this project…It is very important for me…The stakes are very high, and I can't afford to falter. I owe this to Harsha Aunty…I can't let her down," she finished, but her voice quivered and sounded hoarse.

"Don't worry. You will do fine," Samar assured.

"I will?" she asked, as if seeking a reaffirmation.

"Yes…you will," he confirmed again.

"You don't even know me properly, Samar. How can you be so sure?" she asked. A sense of bewilderment crossed her face at his confidence.

"I don't need to. I have seen enough to know that you mean well. Nysha…listen, you need to trust me. Dr. Pawar being my uncle is by no means going to hamper our relationship…"

She immediately raised an eyebrow at him skeptically, and that in turn made him laugh. A rich and warm throaty chuckle escaped his lips. He was happy that she was back to being her normal self, a nasty viper.

"I was talking about work relationship, dirty mind," he guffawed. "And for once please stop glaring at me like a brutal monster," he added.

She squinted her eyes in annoyance and replied, "If you are done talking about my feral instincts, can we please talk business?"

"That's exactly what I have been trying to do, Princess."

"And what's with the use of these adjectives? Dear…Princess…and of all things, Highness …Seriously, are you fucking out of your mind?" she accused.

"Why? Why does it bother you?" he asked.

She looked at him with her eyes wide open and then said, "It does… Aargh! It's irritating…" she replied.

"Of course, it is. Trust me, Nysha, if you find this vexing, then presenting your very proposal before the Board is going to be a Herculean task. I know my uncle very well. To tackle him and the Board, you would need a shitload of patience."

She gave him a meaningful look before replying, “By any chance were you equipping me with patience then?”

He shrugged his shoulders and replied, “Perhaps it’s more like testing it.”

“Hey! That’s so very mean,” she smacked him playfully on his arm.

Their eyes locked for a few seconds, and Samar could feel a pleasant jolt of electrifying sensation pass through him. Her eyes were mesmerizing and deep, capable of penetrating one’s soul. She broke the gaze and looked away before saying, “Mamma is calling. I guess dinner is ready. I should go and help.”

This time Samar simply nodded in response.

Dinner turned out to be a lavish affair with Auntyji’s wholesome four-course spread, consisting of spinach and roasted sweet potato salad, acchari paneer tikka, roti and stuffed kulche, pindi chole, mix veg, and a mouth-watering shahi tukda cooked to perfection to conclude the meal on a high.

“That was the best shahi tukda I have had in a long time,” Samar said as he scooped the last bit of dessert from his bowl.

“Have some more,” Mrs. Patel offered.

“As much as I would love to, but I don’t think I can have any more, Aunty,” he said earnestly.

But despite his protests, a generous portion of dessert was served into his bowl and Nysha couldn’t control her laughter. She chuckled softly and added, “Don’t look at me like that. Mamma loves to feed as much as she loves to cook. Don’t worry, fix an extra hour at the gym and you would be sorted,” she teased.

“Of course, I will take a mental note of it,” he agreed.

Nysha noticed the ease with which Samar was conversing with her mother. Even when she had probed him with certain personal questions, like his marriage plans and family, he had maintained his calm and answered most of them, while skillfully dodging a few without sounding rude and upsetting the opposite person. As if sensing her gaze and reading her thoughts, he turned to look at her with his smile still intact on his face. Her stomach did a flip and a low rumble escaped her gut, the reason for the same she wasn't quite sure of, since it definitely couldn't have been due to an empty stomach. She took a deep breath and cleared her thoughts, Good Lord! I can handle a grumpy, snooty doctor, but a smiling, sexy doc with an irresistible charm is already a lost game.

"Nysha!"

Her mother's voice broke her trance.

"Oh ho! Nysha puttar, you forgot the drinks."

Samar raised an eyebrow at the mention of drinks.

Typical men! She thought.

She whispered, "Don't get ideas; she is talking about homemade coolers."

"Oh, I see…"

The three of them remained so deep rooted in their conversations that they had failed to realize that it was already half past midnight. A self-taught early riser and hardly a fan of late nights, Samar was quite surprised at how easily he had not only made adjustment to his midweek schedule, but also had ended up quite enjoying the same. Perhaps good company mattered, and not the rules, he thought.

"I will take my leave now. I must say you are an amazing cook, and I thoroughly enjoyed, Auntyji," Samar complimented.

"Oh, the pleasure was all mine, beta. Isn't it, Nysha?" Mrs. Patel replied while eyeing her daughter for approval.

Beta! Seriously! Now, when did this happen? As far as her memory served, it had been just a few hours since their cheery introductions. The very thought made her dizzy, and she thought she was about to faint.

Samar eyed her with veiled amusement, waiting for her affirmation.

"Yeah…why not? You can come here anytime you feel like, Dr. Attwal."

Her words were laced with sarcasm, but poor Mamma Patel missed it, and satisfied with her daughter's generosity she added instead, "See, even Nysha agrees."

"Oh, thank you so much Nysha…hun…"

Nysha almost froze on the spot as she thought he would use the forbidden word in front of her skeptical mom. But to her relief, he stopped midway and instead said, "Really? That's quite an honor, I must say."

Nysha glared at him angrily.

Later, as she accompanied Samar outside towards the main gate, they were mostly silent, but there was a sense of heightened awareness, and an unmistakable spark in between them. Suddenly losing her balance, she tripped on a pebble and was about to have a nasty fall on her rear, when strong hands caught her just in time and prevented the same. His hands had gripped her waist, effectively keeping her in place, and she felt a heavy jolt travel up her chest, while jitters ran down her spine at his soothing touch. Her cheeks felt hot, and she must have blushed the deepest shade of crimson. She was thankful that they were outside the house, and was only hopeful that the dimmed street lights didn't give away much of her flushed face.

He whispered in her ears, "You…Okay?"

She nodded and wriggled herself out of his arms.

He looked at her for a few seconds and then suddenly in a drastic mood shift spoke in a baritone voice, "We meet tomorrow, sharp at 9 o'clock."

She scrunched her nose in annoyance and utter disbelief.

"You! How dare you, I don't take orders!" She exclaimed.

Unfazed about what she had to say, he continued, "And yes, don't be late. I hate unprofessionalism and unprofessionals."

Saying that, he proudly strolled towards the main gate, without even bothering to say a proper goodnight or goodbye.

She watched him glued to the spot as he expertly maneuvered the car and drove off, thereby disappearing into the silence of the night. An insane part of her wanted him to turn around just once, but he never did.

"Bossy Jerk!" She muttered.

Then turning around, she huffed her way inside the house…

Game: Mission Save ARH (Akshat Ratna Hospital)
Players: Naive Nysha vs. Smart-ass Samar
Player Expertise: Novice vs. Expert
Task Difficulty Level: Dreadful
Score: Nysha: 0; Samar: 1
Comments: Ah! Better luck next time (i.e., if only next time exists)

To New Beginnings (A New Dawn at Akshat Ratna)

Samar checked his watch and saw that it was already 9:15, and still there was no sign of Her Highness making an appearance. Well, along with all other things, Ms. Patel surely didn't have a penchant for punctuality. He chided himself internally for doing it all over again. She somehow managed to bring out the best motivator and also the worst critic in him. He was afraid that it could do him more harm than good, or perhaps to her as well. He remembered the previous night, when looking at her, scrunching her nose; he had so wanted to nibble at the tip of it.

Surprisingly enough, it had barely been just a few hours since they had last met, and he already missed her and craved her presence. He shook his head in disbelief at the very thought of behaving like a pubescent-stricken horny teenager.

God damn! He was a grown-ass man and needed to behave like one. He could not allow one Ms. Patel to meddle with his brain with her meddling middle finger.

He picked up his file and got up from his chair. Well, he might as well complete his round instead of waiting for Her Slothfulness, he thought snarkily.

Meanwhile, behind the wheel of her hatchback, Nysha muttered a curse and swore to herself under her breath.

"Oh no! No! No! Holy shit! No! What a mess!"

The only vacant parking space she had set her eyes on was now occupied by a pretentious SUV, twice the size of her humble car. The driver of the vehicle, who was responsible for the major screw-up, also happened to be twice her size in both gut and grit. With a bandana tied around his head, broad, muscular chest, and tattooed bulldozer arms with a skull-face imprint, he looked hell scary, to say the least.

Darn him! Such a show-off! A giant machine for a deadly ogre, she huffed.

The muscled giant stepped out of his car and, almost as if he could sense her awful thoughts about him, shot her a death stare.

For a moment, the thought of hurling accusations registered in her mid-sized brain, but the very next second it changed to calling quits and making peace with the fact that a midget-sized mouse such as herself didn't quite stand a chance with a bulk-sized hulk. So keeping in mind the best interest of safeguarding her anatomy, she decided to make a fast retreat. Driving at top speed, Nysha exited the parking area of the hospital. After some struggle, she finally managed to park her car in the only available slot in a scanty bye-lane next to the fish market, about 200 meters from the hospital building, right under the open blue sky and merrily chirping birds.

#Parking struggles are real in Mumbai! She thought, observing the crawling traffic before her.

She rushed her way to the hospital, part walking and part running through the swarming streets, her sling bag dangling by her side. By the time she reached her destination, she was full-on sweating and panting for breath. She made her way towards the elevator and pressed the button. To her surprise, the door opened immediately. She barged in, almost bumping into an elderly lady who was already inside. Nysha muttered a clumsy sorry and thankfully the nice lady didn't seem to take offense. On the contrary she assured her, "It's okay, beta. Relax, it happens sometimes."

The cutie choco-pie that she was, Nysha wanted to hug her tight and place a kiss on her cheeks as a mark of gratitude. But she restrained herself for the fear of baffling the old lady, and settled for a polite thank you instead.

In the meantime, the creaking old lift took ages to reach the destination, but finally when it did, she ran out of the confines of the same, straight into the third-floor hallway. She heard her phone beep, and out of curiosity opened her bag and retrieved her mobile to check the message. It was from an intern in office. She began typing her reply, while still continuing to walk, and had just turned around the corner, when she banged straight into a wall—the wall being a human. A strong scent of musk greeted her nostrils. It was different and refreshing. However, the sudden unexpected blow startled her, and the phone slipped off from her hand. She staggered forward in an abrupt manner to get it, when she heard his irritated voice, "Hey, watch out! And what the hell do you think you are doing?"

She was about to have a hard fall, but he caught her arm just in time. She looked up, and found him scowling at her. Ignoring his angry bull sneer, her eyes fell on her phone instead, which thankfully had gotten rescued by the swift reflexes of 'His Haughtiness in White Coat'. Breathing a sigh of relief, she relaxed and gave him a nervous smile before saying, "Phew! Thanks a lot."

Slowly she pulled her hand out of his vice-like grip, and extended it to get her phone back. But was surprised when without a single word, he calmly withdrew his hand along with her phone. She watched him neatly shove and secure her phone in his coat pocket, making her expression transform immediately from amicable to an impatient and annoyed glare.

"What the f...?"

Giving leverage to the surroundings, she controlled her language and hissed at him, "Dr. Samar, give back my damn phone!"

"I think you know better than that, Ms. Patel, don't you? And...you really...like, really, do have a knack for coming on time..." he scoffed.

Nysha checked her watch. It was already 9:45. Sure thing; 'Mr. Punctuality Personified' had every right to be mad at her. But she could explain, i.e. if only he allowed her to. And how dare he hijack her phone?

"Alright, look...you are mad, I can understand. But I can explain."

Samar gave her a level stare and replied, "Sure, you can."

"God damn it, Samar! I was stuck in super bad traffic..." she tried explaining.

"Go on...that's quite original," he retorted sharply.

Samar had his hands crossed over his chest, which made him look like a sculptured "Greek God Statue," flawlessly crafted and perfectly chiseled. Despite the chaotic and fucked-up situation that she was in, she couldn't help but notice his perfect ten features, and she despised herself for the same.

"Ok, there's more...the parking was full, I had to park my car straight 200 meters away and run all the way here."

She put her hands on her hips and continued, "See, I am huffing and panting...Does that help?" she asked.

As she innocently pouted her lips in order to acquaint him about her faced ordeal, she had absolutely zero idea what it did to his insides. He shuddered as a wild thought crossed his mind. He wanted to pull her against his chest and kiss her pouty lips, a wild and passionate kiss to drive her crazy, and then leave her craving more, as a punishment for her foolish exploits. The most logical thing would have been to back out and walk away from the project, and in turn from the ball of utter chaos that stood right in front of him. But Samar never backed out from a challenge, and Ms. Patel was his biggest challenge till date. She brought out flaws in his anatomy which he had never been aware of, or even knew that they existed in his system. He sighed as he realized that the lines of demarcation between logic and illogic were slowly overlapping and blurring from his being, and it most definitely couldn't be considered a healthy sign after all.

Upon failing to get any response from him, she gave one final try, "Now…now, you won't really believe it, or would you, if I say that I encountered a massive giant downstairs in the parking area."

"Wow! That's epic! Congratulations, you fought a monster," he said with a raised eyebrow.

"Trust me, Sammy! I encountered one. He was one giant muscular monster with a tattooed bulldozer arm."

He stared down at her for some time with narrowed eyes and then gritted through his teeth, "Don't you ever call me by that pet name again," he warned.

Startled, she looked at him with amusement and then spontaneously a smile crossed her lips. God! He was so irritated, and damn! He looked too cute when irritated…

"Aww! You don't like that, Sammy baby?" she teased.

"I am warning you, Nysha."

"You wouldn't dare!" he hissed.

"Oh! Watch me, Doctor," she challenged.

He was about to say something when a voice called out his name from behind.

Both Samar and Nysha turned around. "Hey Sam!"

Samar fisted his hands for control, while Nysha froze on the spot.

It was the tattooed monster, who was now walking towards them. The closer he came, the more gigantic he appeared.

Nysha thought she was about to faint, and in an attempt to get some support, she caught hold of Samar's arm and whispered to him, "Are you effing kidding me? You have hired him to kill me, right?" she asked.

Samar shook his head in disgust and replied, "Get a grip on your wild imagination, hunnie…," his nasal voice drawled.

She glared daggers at him before replying, "Alright, then who the hell is he, and what is he doing here?"

"Meet Dhananjay Pawar, Uncle Pawar's son and the newly elected board member. I guess you have already met him. He is your tattooed monster, isn't he?" Samar asked.

For the first time in years, Nysha ran out of words. She simply blinked at the approaching calamity, and realized that her chances of winning were awkwardly reduced to ashes. With each step that he took, his enormous form became more visible to the naked eye. This bulldozer monster could surely rip her to pieces without a shred of remorse. Compared to his son, Pawar now seemed like a kind "oaf." Too bad, the realization chimed in late. The damage had already been done, and “His Ghastly Beast” now stood right in front of them, smiling from ear to ear with a monstrous grin plastered on his face.

Game: Save Akshat Ratna Hospital (@Part 2)
Players: Nysha, Samar, Bulldoze Monster
Player Expertise: Novice(s) vs. Yet to Decode
Task Difficulty Level: Harrowing
Score: Nysha & Samar: 1+1; Bulldoze Monster: ?
Comments: A Wicked-Licious Monstrous Ploy

A Plan to Please the Giant Beast

Nysha tried to take a deep breath to calm down and soothe her jumpy nerves, but it felt like time had come to a halt. She could hear Samar telling her something, but nothing much registered since she was no longer paying attention and had stopped listening. The only senses that were working actively now were her eyes. Her eyes remained fixated on the object of disaster standing right in front of them. He was smiling like a Cheshire cat (or a spotted leopard), and as he stepped forward and closed the distance between him and Samar, Nysha opened her mouth, gasping for breath. Mr. Beast smacked Samar's arm lightly and wrapped his hands around him to engulf him in a big, tight, monstrous hug.

"Hey, Sammy, such a long time…Look at you, Dr. Attwal, a grown-ass man…No wonder Papa is always so proud of you," he beamed.

"Language! Jay bhaiya, it's a hospital corridor. And Mama Ji is super proud of you, too. Why wouldn't he be? After all, an investment banker in LA is no small feat," Samar replied earnestly.

Nysha scanned Mr. Beast from top to bottom and thought to herself, Whoa! Investment Banker! Modern-Age Popeye had an impressive profile indeed, spinach and all…

As if sensing her thoughts, Mr. Beast's gaze shifted to her. He gave her a savage look, and Nysha thought her heart would stop beating completely.

Sensing trouble, Samar stepped in to introduce them both formally to each other, "Nysha, meet Dhananjay Pawar, the newly elected Board member and Dr. Pawar's son, and Bhaiya, she is…"

The Beast didn't let Samar complete, instead he completed for him.

"She is Ms. Nysha Patel, a business consultant, our specialist of the hour, and the one apparently responsible for reorganizing and restructuring Akshat Ratna, or rather pulling it out of the sheer mess, so to speak."

Nysha noticed that his words were dripping with sarcasm. Well, not that she cared, but it was Samar's veiled grin which caused her annoyance.

Bloody infuriating brothers, she thought.

Making a sorry attempt at masking his grin, Samar replied, "Wow! I must say, that was quite a neat homework," he sounded mightily impressed.

Mr. Beast, however, nonchalantly waved his hand in the air and said, "Actually that wasn't necessary. Papa had already warn, I mean, informed about her in advance."

Gruesome beast! Like father, like son…, Nysha thought.

Holding her gaze, the Beast continued, "We have met before, haven't we, Ms. Patel? Downstairs in the parking lot…"

Nysha wanted to let loose the original beast, His Beastly Wildness, "Mr. Anaconda" on the human "Beast form" just for the fun of watching his bones getting crushed and his savage tongue being ripped off. Her mind almost achieved an internal orgasm simply at the mere thought of it.

Getting a grip on her wild emotions, she replied with a coy and polite smile instead, "That Mr. B, ah! What I mean to say, Mr. Pawar, can hardly be considered a meeting, you see…"

"Call me, Dhananjay…," he said.

"I prefer Mr. Pawar…," she replied.

His ghoulish eyes scanned her face in a challenging manner before replying, "So be it…So, Ms. Patel, tell me what you have got?"

One Hour Later: Dr. Samar's Cabin

When Nysha had first encountered Mr. Dhananjay Pawar, she had thought of him to be a proud, entitled beast just like his father, who had secured his place on the board, simply because of his bloodline and not quite because he actually deserved it. However, what she hadn't realized at that point in time was that she would be in for a surprise for having judged him too soon. They say, 'looks could be deceptive' but in his case, they were charmingly so. For the past half an hour now, the man had surprised her with his knowledge and wit. As he sat next to her in a relaxed mood, minus his bandana, she noticed that he looked more human and less of a beast. He had thick, curly hair which bounced when he talked, and his dimpled smile made him look much younger than his actual age.

Both Jay and Samar looked at her intently as she explained the proposed plan to them. Finally when she was done, Jay asked her in a somewhat serious tone, "All of this, Ms. Patel, seems way too perfect. In fact, honestly, it's too good to be true. I am just worried about how sure you are about the implementation bit though…"

"If I weren't sure, I would have never suggested the same, Mr. Pawar," she replied.

"A fundraising event for a hospital…that too involving celebrities… would it work?" he asked concerned.

"It definitely would. Besides, when it comes to fundraising, I have an ample amount of experience," she stated confidently.

Samar shot an eyebrow at her and asked, "Just for the record, Nysha, how many such fundraisers have you organized till date?"

Nysha glared at him in disbelief and thought to herself, Damn Samar! Moron! You were supposed to be on my side.

Though she was upset with him, she still replied in a balanced and calm tone, "Around ten to twelve, and I assure, all of them were highly successful, Doc."

Jay let out a soft chuckle at her visible over-confidence, and she blushed a light shade of pink. She hadn't even realized that she was speaking way too fast, giving away her irritation and pissed-off persona. Coolly, she reminded herself that she was dealing with two highly intelligent men, one a smart-ass monster, and the other, she looked at Samar and concluded, well, he was a handsome devil in disguise who could accelerate her heartbeat and make her swoon. In any case, she knew that she had stepped into a high risk zone, and the risk of either winning or losing it all made her stomach flutter.

"But, Ms. Patel, how much can we rely on these celebs? You know what I mean, last minute cancellations, handling their tantrums, fussy behavior… and what not," Jay asked skeptically.

"Aren't we being too judgmental here? Fussy behavior and wild tantrums are not just part of celeb personalities, but could rather be associated with anyone in general. Besides, since Mr. Zaidi is family, I am confident that we won't face any undue hassle."

Calling Zain as family had somewhat managed to impress Mr. Beast. He gave a crooked grin and asked, "Are we talking about the famous Bollywood superstar, Zain Zaidi?"

"Of course, we are," she replied.

"And if I may ask, how is he family?"

"Well, for starters, we studied in the same college, and now that he is married to my best friend cum sister, per se, he is more of a family member."

Mr. Beast ran a hand across his slight stubble and replied with a raised eyebrow, "Oh, I see…that's quite impressive."

"Well, Mr. Pawar, from what I can see, you are not averse to the entire 'celeb drama' yourself. You seem pretty close to the famous British Indian Pop Singer JS the RS, aka Jaspreet Singh, also known as The Royal Singh."

And that was checkmate… Jay had an enthralled expression plastered all over his face. To say that he was impressed would be an understatement. He ran his fingers through his hair and asked in an amused tone, "Now, this can't be a wild guess, Ms. Patel…How did you know?"

"By simply being a bit observant…The moment you took off the bandana, I noticed that it wasn't an ordinary one. It had "JS the RS" inscribed with golden zardozi handwork. And that precisely is reserved only for a handful of special people, very close ones of JS. People are crazy to get that stuff. You wouldn't get it even if you are ready to pay a hefty amount for it."

"That's just wow, Ms. Patel! I think I am done for the day."

Jay turned towards Samar and said, "Sam, she is an awesome find, bro…"

Before Samar could reply, Nysha intervened, "I ain't anyone's find, Mr. Pawar. I am just doing my job and, well, thanks for appreciating."

"I didn't mean any offense, Nysha."

"Ah! Very well…I am sure about that."

It was for the first time since their meeting, that he had addressed her by her first name. The equation between them had undergone a drastic change. Instead of animosity then, she could see a genuine liking in his eyes now.

While discussing the plan, both Jay and Nysha hadn't realized that in their excitement of sharing the deets about it, their chairs had been drawn quite close. At such proximity, there came a point when Nysha could almost smell his woodsy male scent which made her a bit uncomfortable. Trying to distance herself from his personal space, she tried pulling away her chair slightly, when her eyes fell on Samar, who was seated at the other end of the table. She thought she saw him clench his jaws, while something flickered in his eyes. Though his expression was mostly passive and unreadable, yet she found his behavior quite bizarre.

God! Sexy Samar and his mood swings! This person definitely had more temper tantrums than sultry celestial nymphs, Nysha thought.

Meanwhile Jay was grinning at her, flashing his sparkling white teeth. He got up from his chair and Nysha followed suit. As he extended his hand to her and she took it, his eyes lit up as he said, "Let's start all over again. Hey, I am Dhananjay. My close friends and acquaintances call me Jay. It was an absolute pleasure meeting you, Nysha, and yes, I would really appreciate it if you call me Jay. Since I already have your number, I will call you for an update and let's set up a meeting next week to discuss the subsequent phase of our plan."

"Cool!" Nysha agreed.

She paused for a moment before adding, "The pleasure was all mine, Jay…Well, this was just the initial idea, and once the board, including Dr. Pawar, approves of it, I will have the final proposal readied."

"Sure thing, I suggest you start working on the proposal. Papa shouldn't have any issue."

Yeah! Your Pha Pha…nearly had me thrown out the last time we met. Nysha thought internally without voicing it aloud for him to hear.

"Hmm…" she whispered silently instead.

Jay added, "And next time we're gonna have to conduct this meeting in a comparatively interesting location, instead of Sam's boring cabin… what say?" he guffawed.

Nysha let out a half hearted smile, but she could feel a prick on her back as if someone's gaze bore straight into her skin, making her skin break into goose bumps. Turning around, she found Samar giving her a disdainful, non-approving look, and she sneered back at him.

Maddening man, what was his problem? She groaned internally.

Meanwhile, apart from the pricking skin sensation, she was beginning to feel a different sensation and subtle itchiness in her eyes, nose, and skin. She had the urge to pull up her sleeves and check, but taking a deep breath, she somehow managed to restrain herself. With two men watching her, it didn't seem like a good or too comfortable an idea.

Nysha watched Samar as he got up from his chair and slowly walked towards her. He stopped right in front of her, and with furrowed eyebrows looked straight into her eyes, before asking her softly, "Are you okay?"

By this time, her eyes had started getting a bit watery. But looking at the obvious concern in his eyes and sensing the same in his voice, her heart skipped a beat and her insides went all mushy. Her senses were in awe of his sensitive persona, but she controlled her thoughts and replied with a straight face, "Yeah, I am okay. I guess some dust particles got into my eyes. I will wash my face, and it should be fine."

Samar took a sweeping glance at her face before adding, "I am going to the parking downstairs to see Bhai off. I will be back…Stay."

Though his tone sounded like part order, but this time Nysha didn't argue. She simply nodded.

Once the duo left, Nysha wasted no time in rolling her sleeves up to her elbow, only to receive a big jolt…She saw small red bumps had erupted all across her skin, and the itchiness in her eyes and nose had also intensified. In reflex, she rubbed her eyes only to make matters worse. She started to feel dizzy and even experienced shortness of breath. Then she sneezed. "Achoo!"

And the sneezing continued…

"Achoo! Achoo! Achoo!"

"God damn! How is it back?"

She understood that something had triggered off her allergy, and it was getting worse than ever before.

Her panic mode got activated when she realized she had neither medications nor her asthma pump with her.

Good Lord! That was it…She was going to die before turning 30… And there couldn't have been a more pathetic way to be dead…!

Samarjeet Attwal! Where are you? She thought.

NYSHA'S ANTICS VS. SAMAR'S HEROICS

The first thing Samar heard upon entering his cabin was the sound of incessant sneezing. It was enough to ring "warning bells" and alert the doctor within him. Next, he noticed Nysha slouched on the chair with her head pressed between her hands. Even her breathing seemed a bit uneven. Her eyes were completely shut, and she was continuously muttering to herself, "Oh shit! Shit! Shit!"

He immediately rushed to her side and took the chair next to her, before turning her around to face him. "Nysha, what happened? Look at me, come on…come on, dammit!"

Still sneezing continuously, she lifted her head to look into his eyes. Her skin tone had acutely changed its color, and there were rashes on her face and hands. Even her eyes were all watery.

"God damn, Nysha! This is severe allergy…What are you allergic to?"

"I…I…Achoo! Achoo! I don't think that's possible…," she replied in between sneezes.

"Forget what's possible or not. Just say it," he ordered.

"I am allergic to cats…"

"Darn Nysha!" he hissed. "Open your mouth."

"What?"

"Stop acting up and open your damn mouth," he snapped.

By that time, Samar had already gotten up from his chair and was now almost towering over her. He held the back of her head in his palms, and flashed his penlight inside her mouth in order to check her throat.

"Any other allergy, anything else we need to know?" he asked.

"Achoo!! I have…I mean, used to have mild intermittent asthma, but the last episode happened almost a decade ago," she replied.

"Doesn't matter…could have been triggered by the cat allergen. We can't take any risks," he asserted.

"But there isn't any cat here," she asked, confused.

"Shut up, Nysha. Where is your pump?" he asked.

"I don't have it on me," she replied honestly.

"That's freaking careless…You suffer from asthma and you roam around without your pump."

"For your information, I wasn't roaming around. If you care to remember, some time back, we were together in a meeting…" she hissed. "Achoo! God! I feel so itchy…Huff!" she started gasping for breath.

Samar held her face between his palms and said softly, "Shhh! Don't panic! I got you."

Next, she saw him dial quite a few numbers and alert the emergency department. Within a few minutes, a nurse came in with an inhaler pump and as Samar helped her with it, the device somewhat managed to relieve her of her breathlessness.

Once the emergency ward was ready, he asked her, "Will you be able to walk?"

"Yeah," she nodded.

"Good, come on."

He helped her to her feet and led her across the corridor to the elevator. The emergency ward was on the 1st floor, and allergist Dr. Devika Gill was already there. Nysha was led to the hospital bed, and before she knew or could resist, she was given the first shot. She wasn't sure if it was a panic attack, an induced dose of sleep drug, or steroid, but she felt dizzy, her vision blurred, and she was knocked out for a couple of hours.

After about two hours, she woke up and heard voices talking among themselves behind the closed curtain.

"You need not worry, Doctor Samar, it's not a case of anaphylactic attack…But she was definitely lucky that you were here for her, just in time," the soft female voice assured.

"Or perhaps lucky enough to be at Akshat Ratna and find you," he said.

"Ah huh! Absolutely humbled, Doctor…," the mild voice replied.

Nysha could hear the sound of soft laughter. Earlier, because of the haste and the gravity of the situation, she wasn't able to see her allergist's face clearly. But now when she heard her voice, she found it to be mushy and captivating. The ease with which both she and Samar were conversing, implied that they were quite comfortable and friendly with each other, which was otherwise normal considering they were colleagues and well acquainted with each other, but somehow it managed to piss her off instead. She felt her heart sink a bit, and a shot of subdued and subtle jealousy flared her insides, which was highly unlikely of her.

Dare he laugh at her expense...and damn! They still owed an explanation for the deadly cat allergen making its way to her nostrils, she thought irritably.

So with the pure intention to disrupt their cozy talks, she called out his name with a soft slur, "Samar!"

The very next moment, just like magic, he manifested from behind the curtain. She noticed that he was wearing his blue hospital scrubs, and, honest to God! He had the impudence to look gorgeous even in those plain scrubs. In fact, the fabric clung to his body just like his second skin, much like a pert lover. Nysha could well imagine the absolutely toned and zero-fat stunning body beneath, a stark contrast to her own with visible 'love handles' which were beginning to show up in all the wrong places. Her wondering thoughts were back on track when she saw the female doctor walk behind him.

"Hey, you are awake? How are you feeling now?" Samar asked.

"Quite better actually, thanks," she replied.

"You should thank Dr. Devika instead. She is the best we have."

Nysha turned to her and said, "Thanks for everything, Doctor."

"Happy to help, Nysha."

Dr. Devika moved forward to examine her.

"Okay, let's get you checked," she said with a smile. "Tell me frankly, any other complaints right now...like dizziness, throat itching, breathlessness...," she asked.

Nysha furrowed her eyebrows and scratched her nose, as if running a mental check before responding, "No, I don't think so...all good. In fact, I think it stopped within minutes after the shot."

"Okay...that's good."

"Was it sleep-induced, doctor? I think I passed out for a couple of hours."

"Yeah, that happens sometimes...It might make you a bit drowsy...But that's hardly a bad thing. The sleep, in fact, helped you," Dr. Gill replied.

"Yeah, sure, it did. Thanks again."

"Alright then, I will prescribe a few more medications, two more shots of steroids..."

"Shots?"

The word had barely escaped Dr. Devika's mouth, when a panic stricken Nysha gasped, "Do you mean pushing needles again...? No...No way, doctor...Thanks, but I have had enough for the day..."

She then turned towards Samar and repeated innocently, almost begging him, "Pleasseee...Samar, no more shots...no needles, please," she whimpered.

Nysha knew she must have looked like an annoyingly petrified kid, but hell with it! She didn't care at all. The mere thought and feel of a nasty injection piercing through her sensitive skin yet again, was more than enough to drive her nuts.

Samar's eyes widened in disbelief, for he had never imagined that a feisty thing like Nysha could actually be terrified of a tiny needle. For a brief moment, the thought of 'laughing out loud' crossed his mind. He almost had to fight the inner 'laughter bubbles' floating inside his mouth, which were threatening to make an escape and spread across his lips like a 'blooming wildflower.' The strong determination and grit with which he controlled them, in turn, brought a tear to his eye.

Letting out a soft chuckle, he turned to Dr. Devika and asked, "Doctor, is it okay if we go without injections?"

Doctor Devika, who was herself grinning now, nodded in response. "Sure, I will replace the injections with tablets. But, Doctor Samar, I would still suggest a complete physical examination and allergy test, just to be on the safe side. Well, I leave that to you," she said with a twinkle in her eyes.

Nysha looked ruefully towards Samar and then said, "Samar, you and I, seriously, it isn't working…From the time that we met, my life has gone kaput…Us, we are pathetic together. Do you even realize that?"

Before Samar could respond, Dr. Devika shot up an eyebrow and blurted out, "Wait a minute…us? Are you guys like, really, us?" she inquired.

"What? No!"

Samar denied vehemently. He turned towards Nysha expecting some help, but she looked at him in a state of daze, confusion written all over her face. On seeing the frustrated look on his face, she raised her hands questioningly at him and muttered under her breath, "What?"

Samar shook his head in exasperation and pursed his lips tight. Then, turning towards Dr. Devika, he said in a deadpan voice, "Medication side effects…Ms. Patel must be hallucinating. Dr. Devika, we are not us. Well, she is she, I am me…and we definitely are not us…," he clarified.

Upon getting a hang of their conversation, Nysha jumped to defend her previous statement, "Oh boy! Are you upset about the…us thing?"

She then turned towards Dr. Devika and defended, "You got it all wrong, Doctor. Eeww! I did not mean a romantic us…Oh, no! No! Not in that way! Not at all!"

Samar looked at Nysha with furrowed eyebrows, glaring at her intensely while Dr. Devika simply laughed away…

"Oh my God! You guys are hilarious…," her voice was still shaking with inward laughter…

"Well, I am off to pick up my kids from school. I will leave you both to figure out the…us, me, him, or we…thing," she said, still smiling.

"Kids! Really! You are married?" Nysha blurted.

"Of course, I am. In fact, a mother to two pesky five-year-old twin brats," Dr. Devika proudly declared.

"Oh!"

"What?" Dr. Devika asked.

"No, you actually look quite young, that's it…," Nysha replied frankly.

"In that case, I am thankful I inherited my mother's genes. Okay, I will take my leave now. I will see you around, Dr. Samar, and Nysha, take care. Do call in case you face any discomfort," Dr. Gill added.

Saying those words she walked away, leaving Samar and Nysha alone in the room, along with an uncomfortable silence, and heightened awareness thumping between them.

SINFUL, SAMAR.....STRAWBERRIES AND MORE

Nysha was sitting upright on the hospital bed, with her back pressed against the headrest. Her hair was no longer tied in a ponytail; it was left open and fell on her shoulders like a mass of curly waves. Her face and hands still had some red, blotchy spots, and she looked annoyed to bits. With raised eyebrows, she looked at Samar and asked,

"Did you inform anyone about the allergy thing?"

"Just Dr. Harsha…," he replied.

She relaxed and said,

"Cool!"

Then suddenly, as if remembering something very urgent, she exclaimed,

"Did she inform anyone?"

"Are you serious? I have no idea..."

"You clearly have no fucking idea what's gonna happen if my parents get involved…all hell would break loose," she assured.

She glared at him, before stretching out her hand and adding,

"Give me my phone."

It took him a while to realize that her phone was still in his custody.

"Oh that! It's in my cabin," he said.

She shrugged her shoulders and replied,

"Wow! Great! Then, give me your phone."

Samar was appalled at her sassy and bossy attitude. No one had ever dared to talk to him in a tone which she was currently using, and interestingly, instead of being miffed with her, he was actually finding it quite amusing.

Smiling inwardly, he handed over his phone to her.

"Password…," she asked.

'Give me...,' he said.

"It's ok, just tell me…," she coaxed.

"Are you kidding?" he replied.

"Stop being so fussy, Sammy," she chastised. "Change it later if you must," she winked.

"Call me that again, and I'm taking back my phone," he retorted.

"Which one? Sammy or fussy?" she giggled.

The audacity of this girl to call him names and drive him crazy, he thought.

He gave her a menacing look, but what irked him more was that even in her dishevelled state, she looked breathtakingly beautiful, just like a wild cat ready to claw its prey. A smile tugged at the corner of his lips as a wild thought crossed his mind. He wanted to tame the feral cat; it seemed rather funny now that the wild cat herself had fallen for the feline blow.

"Why are you grinning like an idiot? Come on, give me the password," she probed further.

Samar shook his head and raised his hands in exasperation before replying,

"Aadhya321#$"

"Spell it."

"A-a-d-h-y-a…"

"Alright, got it."

As she began punching the password on the touch screen keyboard, she chirped casually,

"Hmmm…Aadhya is a nice name. Who's she by the way?"

"Hello, Agent Katty Bell, why don't you mind your own business instead of poking your nose into matters off-limits?"

She shrugged and replied,

"Whoa! No need to get mad, I was just asking…I mean, just like that… you know what I mean…," she blabbered.

"Get done with your call so that I can drop you home…," Samar almost ordered.

"That won't be required. I have my car," Nysha replied.

"Stop acting funny. No way, you aren't driving in this state."

"What state? I ain't drunk," she snapped back.

"You're drowsy. And for God's sake, Nysha, can you for once stop arguing? I'm tired. You've made it a point to disagree with whatever I say," he retorted.

His words had the desired effect. Nysha raised both her hands as a mark of defeat and ran her fingers along her lips, symbolizing zipping it tightly. She then went ahead and completed her call with Harsha Aunty. Despite the flash of animosity in her eyes, Samar found her expression somewhat cute. Ignoring her antics and letting out a low, throaty chuckle, he headed off to his cabin to change out of his hospital garb and into regular clothes. On returning, he found her seated on the raised hospital bed, scrolling through his phone, while jiggling her legs to and fro. He almost snatched the phone from her hand before inspecting the screen and saying,

"It's bad manners to check someone else's phone. Here is yours," he said, handing it back to her.'

"Hell yeah, and it's pretty much ok to hijack another person's phone. Such a snob you are, aren't you? Anyway, I was just checking the news," she defended.

"I might be anything, but not a snob. Anyway, forget it! Come, let's get going..."

She immediately jumped off from the bed and landed on the floor with a thud. As they made their way outside the hospital premises, she updated him about the call to Dr. Harsha.

"So, she didn't inform your parents, right? Which means everything's good," he said.

"Yeah, I guess so, at least for now. I called them, and they said they were at an anniversary party, which works fine for me, since they wouldn't be back till 11. This gives me ample time to sneak into the house without showing my blotchy, splotchy face," she stated.

"Hey, it's not that bad," he said softly. For a brief moment, their eyes met, and Samar felt as if those eyes had the ability to scan right through his soul. Dragging his eyes away from her face, he said in a casually amused tone,

"Well, it does make you look a bit funny though…"

She crossed her arms over her chest and scowled at him before saying,

"Go on…laugh out loud. I'm waiting for you to finish. Until then, I ain't dumping my ass atop that car seat of yours," she huffed.

"Aha!" He shook his head as he chortled. "Come on, I meant no offense, and trust me, it's not that bad," he pacified.

As Samar slowly began to manoeuvre his car out of the parking area, Nysha turned around in her seat and asked him,

"Did you have your lunch today?"

"I…did," he replied.

"Hmmm!"

"Why do you ask?"

"Because all I ate today…ah, sorry, correction! Actually drank today was the awful hospital coffee, which tasted more or less like dishwater mixed in a muddy puddle."

He chuckled at her vivid description and said,

"Aren't you old enough to be a fan of all this kiddie stuff and purple prose?" he asked, before adding, "So, you are hungry?"

"Oh no! That's an understatement, I am famished!" she replied.

"Sorry, I should have asked. Tell me, how can I make it up to you?"

He looked at her, and saw that her face had lit up like a 1000 watt electric bulb. Knowing her, it could mean only one thing; she had undoubtedly been struck by an idea with the speed of a rocket launcher.

Samar felt a distinctive tug at his heartstrings. Her contagious smile and wave of happiness sent a jolt down to his core and rattled his nerves. Even deep down South, 'Mr. Willy Wong' became steady and way too ready for a happy dance. He immediately looked away, fearing misbehaviour from Mr. Wong. Concentrating on the road ahead instead, he asked her casually,

"What's on your mind? Out with it."

She rubbed her hands in anticipation and added gleefully.

"Well, I think I know the perfect place to satiate my hunger pangs!"

"And why don't I have a very good feeling about this?" he asked sceptically.

"That's probably because you think way too much, Dr. Heartless. Just follow my lead, and you'll be fine," she placated.

"Bragger!" he scoffed.

Half an hour later, Samar found himself occupying a chair alone at Nysha's favorite joint, 'Sinful Temptations.' Alone, because the lady in question was way too popular and sought after by the people at the cafe. From the moment they had set foot, she had been surrounded by excited faces, colleagues and acquaintances, all wanting to know about her well-being, and, of course, they were all concerned about the horrid red splotches on her skin. Well, for once, he wasn't complaining. This was her cafe, the brainchild of her and her best friend, Pia. Later, the third partner cum friend, Rajiv, joined in as one of the investors, and together they had managed to reposition it as one one of the most sought-after cafes in Mumbai. He could well imagine the special place it occupied in her heart and their shared memories together. From a distance too, he could sense her vibrant energy and dramatic flair for storytelling while also listening to others. Clearly, she enjoyed being the 'centre of attraction,' and was a favourite among people. As if sensing his gaze, she looked at him and waved. Then, excusing herself from the crowd, she made her way towards their table, occupied the chair opposite him, and joined him.

"I was made to believe that you were dead hungry," he teased.

"Hey…so sorry, visited after a long time…and…," she sighed before adding,

"Well, this place just feels like…home."

"I know…I can see that. It shows in the way people look at you," he said with a knowing smile. "You miss Pia, don't you?" he asked.

"I do…everyday," she confirmed. "She's my soul sister, and though I'm happy for her, things would have been way easier and different with her around," she added.

"Different perhaps…But you are doing a good job, don't ever doubt that," he said.

"You think so?" she beamed.

"Yeah...even Jay was convinced..."

"Well, he was a darling... quite a contrast in comparison to his dad, Dr.

Pawar," she said.

She saw Samar's pupils dilate. For a moment, she thought he wanted to say something, but then he restrained himself, his expressions going back to being seamlessly inscrutable.

She rolled her eyes and asked,

"What was that, Doctor?"

"What?" he said.

"Well…you clearly wanted to say something."

"I did. But I just thought…it's better for you to figure out yourself."

"Oh! Cut the crap, Samar! You can't hint at something and then leave me hanging in the middle. Spill it out, now…," she commanded bossily.

"Well, you're drawing conclusions too quickly again. As much as I like Jay bhaiya, he's a bit of a playboy. I mean…forget it, it doesn't really matter…," he shrugged dismissively.

"How much is that bit?" she probed.

"Quite so..."

"Cliché, isn't it? He's being labeled as a playboy just because he's LA-returned, whereas we have many of our very own desi fuck boys..."

"And do you really think I would have fallen for something cliché? Like I said, you're smart enough to figure it out yourself," Samar asserted.

Nysha shrugged her shoulders and said,

"Ah! I guess so. Thanks for the warning anyway. I'll keep that in mind."

Soon after, the server arrived carrying two large plates of delicious-looking 'paneer shashlik tikka with makhani sauce.'

"Wow! This is as huge as it gets," Samar chortled.

"Trust me, doctor, this is heaven, and this is veg," Nysha assured, almost drooling over the delicious fare.

"Yeah, anything works…as long as it's veg," Samar agreed.

"Oh no! This isn't anything but…"

"Heaven!" he completed for her. "Quite the foodie, aren't you? Girl! You're drooling," he teased.

"I'm a big…big…foodie," she agreed without deliberation. "In fact, I live to eat," she said, as she began serving herself.

"And you?" she asked him through a mouthful of food.

He was about to respond when she interrupted,

"Oh! Don't bother answering that, I already know. You definitely belong to the second category, one who eats to survive only. Pity!" she concluded.

"Now, that was quite a judgmental junk," he accused, while attempting to mask his subtle grin.

"Of course, it's not. Look at you! A perfect chiseled body, athletic physique, lean, muscled arms like that of a fighter, you're totally into the health and fitness thing…a freak, in fact. You don't get into that perfect shape unless, of course, you spend a considerable amount of time dedicatedly at the gym or exercising, which I'm most certain you do. And the zero-fat, hardened pectoral muscles! You could end up featured on the cover of Men's Lifestyle Magazine. And aha! It would be such a welcome change to finally see a healthy mixture of brawn and brains, instead of only brawn, which is, anyway, so totally overrated."

She let out a deep breath. Then, cupping her face between her hands, with an added glint in her eyes, she added,

"Think about it, Sammy baby. You could give the influencers a real tough time. Ever thought about a parallel career alongside surgeon duties? Oh, I bet you could be minting a hell lot of money, you handsome hunk!" she winked.

Once finished, she studied his expressions as if anticipating a response to her just-completed wild rant. Meanwhile, Samar simply stared at her, still trying to process the entire conversation. Seeing the look of astonishment on his face, realization dawned, that probably in her unhinged excitement she had gone a bit overboard with her description. Letting out a nervous laughter she asked,

"Hey! Why are you giving me that nasty look?"

He shook his head and replied,

"Lady, you've been describing my anatomy by using exaggerated adjectives…and you want me to stay calm? What in the name of God have you been thinking…and pretty how much?"

She blushed at his blatant accusation, and God! He was so damn correct. What had she been thinking? And what was her reason to feel so unperturbed with him, when in the first place it had hardly been just a day or two of actually meeting him.

"Oh! You're overreacting now," she replied, avoiding the accusation in his eyes.

"Not at all! The drinks seem to have been spiked."

"This is just plain water. The mocktails are yet to arrive," Nysha muttered.

"We aren't having any tail whatsoever. We'll finish dinner and leave immediately, before you become delusional and uncontrollable...," he stated with finality.

"Stop being so bossy and mean all the time. No way in hell are we leaving before checking out the new live chaat and dessert counter," she said, brimming with unconcealed excitement.

"After finishing all of this, you still hope to eat more...you seriously have an appetite of a lorry driver," he looked baffled.

"Don't you dare cast your evil eye on me," she exclaimed. "Besides, it's just pani puri. You can't refute a fluffy, golden-brown pani puri and walk away from it. It's almost considered a bad omen...," she quipped.

"Wow! What about dessert then?" Samar questioned.

"Desserts, my friend, are auspicious. We are Indians, and Indians are crazy about their desserts. Be it puja, festivals, birthdays, anniversaries... oh, you name it, boy! It would be a real shame if we walk away from the dessert counter without tasting any...," she clarified.

Samar continued to stare at her with awe or annoyance; she wasn't sure. She bet more towards the latter, since by no means could he be in awe of her antics. He probably thought of her as a nuisance and a brat with brain cells loosened at the ends, and in dire need of repair. Before another massive short circuit jolted her insides and in turn created a ruckus to the people and the surroundings, he spoke calmly,

"Finish your food, Nysha. It's getting cold, and we're getting late."

Nysha nodded in agreement. They finished the rest of the food in silence. Before leaving, she stopped by to try the melt-in-mouth pani puris (her version), with two of her favorite flavored waters. And, of course, there was no walking away from the dessert counter without tasting the scrumptious pumpkin pie with whipped vanilla cream. Upon coaxing, when Samar tried a bite of the same, he had to agree that it did taste like a slice of heaven, if not heaven in entirety. After finishing her share of goodbyes, as they began to leave, they saw a young lady approaching them. She was wearing a white apron with her initials inscribed. She wiped her hands on the apron and walked towards Nysha with a big smile on her face. Before she could reach them, Nysha hollered her name with unmasked excitement,

"Oye...Mihika!"

She reached them and gave Nysha a tight hug. Then with a glint in her eyes she spoke,

"How have you been, ma'am? Haven't seen you in a while..."

"Yeah, guilty as charged. Been a bit busy," Nysha replied.

"Can't totally blame you...things here aren't as much fun as they used to be," Mihika replied.

"Yeah, with Pia and Rajiv, right? Does Rajiv visit?" Nysha asked.

"He does, on alternate days...and Pia ma'am video calls regularly to check. She'll be a regular again once she is back."

"Of course, the girl loves her damn job...way too much. Right now, she's busy vacationing, taking that well-deserved break," Nysha added with a smile.

"Right," Mihika agreed, before asking, "Ma'am, what's with the spots on your face?"

"Ah, these!" Nysha said, as she touched her face. "That's a long story, dear…I'll narrate it some other time, I guess."

"Ok…hope it's nothing serious," Mihika replied, concern laced her voice.

"Nah! It's taken care of; it's going to be fine…an old ailment came back to say hello. I'm sure it's just a guest and would be off soon," Nysha joked.

Shifting her attention to Samar, Nysha continued,

"Samar, this is Mihika, our Executive Chef, an expert in international desserts, and Pia's best mentee till date. Mihika, meet Dr. Samarjeet Attwal, a renowned cardiologist."

As they shook hands, Samar said,

"Nice to meet you, Mihika. Well, the pie was an absolute delight."

"Thank you. Glad you liked it, Doctor."

"We should leave, Mihika…we'll catch up later," Nysha intervened, before adding,

"And thanks to your delectable dishes, they provided an absolute pleasant ending to a not so pleasant day," she winked.

"Ah! My pleasure, ma'am," then suddenly, as if remembering something, she added,

"Just a minute, ma'am, stay…," she excused herself and went inside in haste.

Samar looked at Nysha and said,

"I'm waiting outside..."

"In a minute," she replied.

"Come soon."

"Copy that," she smiled.

When Nysha finally reached the car, she found Samar busy talking to someone on the phone. She knocked on the window pane; and he looked up and opened the door. As she slid into the seat beside him, he finished the call and started the vehicle. After driving for sometime in silence, he eyed the exquisite looking box in her hand and asked,

"What is that?"

"Hey, this is for you," she said, as she placed it on the dashboard.

"For me?" he asked surprised.

"Yeah, it's a kind of tradition at Sinful—a new guest gets a welcome gift."

"Ah! A gift! Sounds nice…but I have been to Sinful before."

"Yeah, yeah…I know, three years back…for my birthday party."

"Yes...."

"Well, let's say that was just a party…this is more like being a formal guest, a prospective customer…to new beginnings!" she cheered.

"Impressive! By the way, what's in there?" he asked curiously.

"Homemade chocolates, an assortment of flavours to die for," she replied.

As she elaborated on the delicate flavors, Samar noticed that her eyes had shut on their own accord, as if she had been transported to the 'Land of Chocolates' from the classic tale of 'Hansel and Gretel.' Her words became a soft whisper, almost like a moan, and despite the AC running at full capacity, he thought he could do with a gush of wind blowing straight over his flushed face, which seemed to be getting hotter with every passing second. He looked away, and in an attempt to maintain a straight face, ended up with a scowling one instead.

When Nysha opened her eyes and looked at Samar, she found him with furrowed eyebrows, while a brooding look masked his face. Confused at his sudden, changed demeanor, she asked him,

"Oh my God! What's with you?"

"What?" he asked.

"Look at your sullen face! Whoever blamed girls for being fussy and throwing tantrums would take a step back and most definitely would swallow their words," she grumbled.

"No need to get so dramatic. I ain't fussy, and no, nothing is wrong with my face. It's just my resting face. Not a big fan of chocolates, that's it," he bit back.

"Of course, you're not. Even the selfish giant was not a fan of chocolates. Mean people are never a fan of chocolates," she snapped.

"What are you so mad about? And who the hell is this giant, anyway?" he retorted, part amused and part confused.

"You know what, Samar? Shut the fuck up…or I might not be able to control my urge to shove this entire pack into your damn mouth," she threatened.

"And why in the name of God would you do that?" he asked, exasperated.

"Just a wild, wild urge!" she said in a singsong voice, while smiling viciously at him.

For the next couple of minutes, an uncanny silence floated amidst them. In his mind, Samar knew that he was in the wrong and probably even misunderstood by her. But he couldn't bring himself to apologize. His ego at present was acting way too big to bow down to 'Her Highness.' At least that's how she was behaving currently—a haughty princess of a small princely state. She had accused him of having mood swings, as if she had any less, he thought.

They stopped at the crossing near the traffic signal, where excited young boys and girls wearing tattered clothes were running to and fro while attempting to sell a variety of miscellaneous stuff. One such girl saw Samar staring out of the window, and thinking that he might be interested in her strawberries, came running to them and knocked on the window pane. He rolled down the glass, and she asked him if he needed any. Seeing her smile and sensing her anticipation, he didn't have the heart to say no. Although not a big fan of strawberries, he still bought two small boxes. While making the payment, he offered her some extra cash, which she gracefully declined.

"Aai boli, muft ke paise nahin lene chahiye."

("Mother said we shouldn't accept free money.")

Samar and Nysha were surprised by her words of wisdom at such a young age. Her mother had taught her well, Nysha thought.

"Paise hi toh lene ke liye mana kiya hai, chocolates toh le sakti ho?" Samar asked.

("She has asked you not to take money, but you can accept chocolates, right?" Samar asked.)

For a moment, she looked confused, but then slowly nodded tentatively as if in agreement.

Samar picked up the box of chocolates and looked at Nysha before asking,

"You wouldn't mind if...."

She smiled and replied,

"Absolutely not. You have found the best use for it and the chocolates, their rightful place," she encouraged.

The pretty girl thanked and took the chocolates from him, then singing merrily to herself, she ran away. Samar and Nysha watched her until she disappeared from their line of sight.

"Thank you, Samar," Nysha said softly, taking him by surprise.

He turned around to ask her the reason for the same, when he saw a million-dollar glint in her eyes, while a magical smile played on her lips. Before he could say something, she threw her arms around his neck and pulled him into a hug. With all the restrictions of distance and space blurring and vanishing into thin air, and practically no demarcation between chest and breast, Samar felt a different sort of pressure build up in his thorax, all the way to his heart. His heartbeat had intensified and he had to practically gasp for breath. He could also feel her excited heartbeats beneath his own. When she reached for his ears, her warm breath caressed the sensitive part of his auricle, making him almost lose control. Oblivious to the slow torture being inflicted on him, Nysha whispered in his ear,

"Dr. Attwal, I think I just discovered the perfect pitch and idea for the hospital project—one the board would never be able to reject."

As she raised her head, their eyes locked and Samar murmured,

"Nysha, you will be the death of us."

By this time down south, Mr. Willy Wong had turned shamelessly and uncontrollably alive and was now throwing a fit in his pants, kicking hard to be let out and allowed to breathe into the open air.

The vehicles behind them started honking impatiently, and that's when they realized that the lights had already turned green, thereby giving them a go ahead. A few rowdy drivers had even begun to hurl abuses.

"Get the hell out of the way!" shouted the first.

"Move the damn car," barked the other.

Nysha burst out into a fit of loud laughter, as if those were the funniest and sweetest words she had ever heard.

And God! Did she know how spellbound her laughter was, and how utterly hypnotic she looked! Samar thought.

Giggling, she arched her back to look into the rear-view mirror and muttered a clumsy sorry, before turning back to Samar and declaring,

"Drive on O' Chauffeur, before we become strangulation victims by an unruly street mob."

After a series of maddening events, they finally reached her home. She got down from the car and Samar followed suit.

To their surprise, they found a giant Porsche Turbo parked right in front of the gates.

Without even looking at Samar, Nysha asked him straightaway,

"Does this pretentious, monstrous, hulk-like machine belong to the person I think it does? And if that's true, what in the name of God is he doing in my home at this hour?" she asked, raising an eyebrow in mock disbelief.

She then turned towards Samar. With hands on her hips, slightly furrowed eyebrows and lips pursed into a thin line, she was clearly expecting an answer. Upon realizing there wasn't any room for escape, Samar let out a deep breath. Then, reaching for the top button of his shirt, he opened it in an attempt to breathe in more air and allow a fresh gush of oxygen into his lungs.

Finally, looking directly into her eyes he asked,

"Ah, well, hunnie! Did I tell you how it is that your cuteness-overload, round, splotchy, itchy allergy is back after almost a decade of long and peaceful slumber?"

And there was silence.

The howling of the stray dogs was the only sound that penetrated the stretched deadly silence of the night, and Nysha could swear they were laughing at her precarious position.

Caught between a sexy doctor vs. a bulldozer monster, life had taken a full-on 360-degree non-reversible flip, and truth be told, she wasn't loving it…at all.

Game: Princess Nysha Needs Rescue: Who's the Warrior Knight?
Players: Nysha, Sammy, Jay
Player Expertise: Novice(s) vs. not-so-Novice
Task Difficulty Level: Hell! No Idea
Score: Tabula Rasa
Comments: Aargh!!!!!

WHO WILL BELL THE CAT? (SOLVING THE FELINE MYSTERY)

Nysha eyed Samar as if he had just told her that vampires walking the Earth were for real and that "The Count Dracula" himself, disguised as Dhananjay Pawar, was sitting right across her, occupying a sofa in the aesthetic living room of her abode.

"I am so very sorry... all of this happened because of me. By the way, I had no idea that you were allergic to cats... or rather, that someone could be allergic to cats," he defended.

Nysha smiled wryly and replied, "Yeah... sure, you did not. Well, now you know."

That was precisely the 65th time that Jay had muttered a clumsy sorry. He had also drunk three cups of coffee in an attempt to drown his sorrows completely as a mark of penance for his unintended misdeed, and Nysha wasn't sure how she was supposed to pacify a giant monster with an innocent puppy face. Meanwhile, as Sushi placed the fourth mug of coffee in front of Jay and replenished the tray with what seemed to be the last of the gourmet hazelnut and marzipan bites, along with dark chocolate cigar rolls, Nysha's heart tore to bits as he nibbled on the final pieces of her favorites, the ones she had coerced Zain to bring back during his previous outdoor shoot in Australia. In all probability, the moron had cursed her for bullying him into getting them. What else could explain the pathetic end the cookies had met? She watched in despair as Jay savagely bit into a cookie and chewed for some time before his face turned bright with pure delight as he declared, "These are really good... pretty awesome, in fact."

Those were melt-in-mouth cookies which he had just gorged on, and Nysha wanted to smack him... or better still, suffocate him with her bare hands. But she managed a straight face instead and maintained a polite smile on her face, all for the sake of being dignified and civil.

Sushi eyed them, pretty convinced that they were all overly qualified, educated nutty people, and she threw a murderous glare towards Nysha, just to remind her that it was way past her working hours, and she couldn't miss her late-night chats and calls with her lover, not for an un-emergency, and definitely not for some buffoon for sure. Nysha shrugged her shoulders helplessly and, letting out a nervous laughter, said to her, "Tu sone jaa, Sushi. Mein dekh loongi." ("You go and sleep, Sushi. I will manage.")

Then she turned towards Samar, expecting some help, but to her dismay found him sitting put instead, as if he had vouched not to meddle with crazy people and equally crazy surroundings. Sure, she could give him two extra credits for not devouring her cookies and benevolently declining a second round of coffee. But what could explain his call to not bail her out of the pathetic situation, part of which she held him responsible for, because Mr. Bulldoze Monster was his brother and hissy Pawar, his uncle. And though it might not seem fair at all to be held accountable for someone else's doings, but hello! Whoever said life is fair and square was blatantly lying, so deal with it! Nysha let out an audible huff and then muttered beneath her breath, "Coward!" not very loud, but clear enough for Samar to hear and awake his sleepy, drippy senses. As if taking the cue, he looked up and gave her a menacing look. Then, immediately rising to his feet, he strode towards Jay. "I think we should leave, Jay bhaiya. It's already late... and Nysha needs her rest. Besides, you can't take all the blame for Jahaan's doing," he stated.

"Wait! Who's Jahaan?" Nysha blurted.

Jay let out an uneasy laughter before adding, "Aah! Actually, he is the Persian Cat...."

"You named your cat, Jahaan? It sounds more like the name of your twin brother than a pint-sized monster," Nysha exclaimed, only to regret immediately.

The moment the words escaped her mouth, she could have bitten off her tongue to take them back. But the damage had already been done. Jay was back to being his lost puppy self. He looked so sad, as if someone had just tried to defame him by questioning his manhood and declaring him to be 'impotent'. To save the situation, she turned towards Samar and found him glaring at her as if she were mad and hallucinating. And for once at least, she couldn't blame him.

Still smiling nervously and in a puny attempt to convince her, Jay began, "He...he! It's not like it sounds... I mean, he is actually the most obedient... feline..."

Obedient and a tom cat, it didn't quite sit well with her. Nysha felt dizzy and would have almost passed out had Samar not intervened. Turning towards Jay, he said, "Nysha didn't mean any offence. She just needs some rest, Bhai.... Let's give her that," he asserted.

"Oh yeah... I was just leaving...," Jay replied.

As Jay went forward to hug her goodbye, she flinched internally but maintained a stoic expression upfront. Sensing her reluctance, he gave her an awkward one-armed hug instead and walked away. Both Nysha and Samar went to see him off at the gate outside, when Jay gave Samar a quizzical look and asked, "Aren't you leaving too?"

"In some time, I got to check her night time dose of medications."

"Oh! Ok, I shall take my leave then."

They waved Jay goodbye and once he disappeared down the path, Nysha turned towards Samar and asked him, "Samar, how exactly did I get the allergy from Jay?"

"Trust me sweetheart, you wouldn't want to know..," Samar replied.

"But I insist...," she coaxed.

"Alright, if you must, it could have been anything....from cat fur, dead skin cells, saliva or urine...."

She literally had to push away the thought of throwing up at the mention of the last two allergens... "Samar, kill me now," she said softly as she pretended to faint and Samar caught her in his arms. Tapping her cheeks lightly he said, "Enough... O' Drama Queen! Let's get your temperature checked."

Once they were inside the house, Nysha sat coiled up in a corner of the sofa. Samar could see her eyelids drooping and knew that she was sleepy. She muffled a yawn and looked at him with her drowsy eyes. Her parted lips made him skip his heartbeat. Pushing away his unwarranted thoughts, he walked up to her and said, "Ok Kitten, open your mouth."

For once, without arguing she did exactly as told, and he liked it when she followed his orders without questioning. He put the thermometer inside her mouth and as it beeped, he took it out and happily declared, "Great! No fever... that's really good." "Now, can you stick your tongue out for me, sweetie?" he asked.

She furrowed her eyebrows questioningly and pouted her lips, before opening her mouth. She was about to stick out her pink tongue at him, when he laughed loudly and said, "Hey! I was just joking... You look cute when you listen without complaining."

"Had it been some other time, Dr. Heartless, I would have kicked hard those perfect twin globes of yours. But now is not the time... Hell, I am tired!" she said.

"You need to rinse that dirty mouth of yours," he guffawed. "Anyway.... now, off you go to sleep, Ms. Pretty Dirty Mouth.... I am leaving...," he added.

Samar headed for the door, and Nysha followed behind. "Your parents aren't back yet?" he asked.

"Well, Mr. and Mrs. Patel have a more happening social life than their un-social daughter. They have the keys... so no worries. Just hope, these marks lighten up or magically disappear by morning. Or else, would have to face the music by Mataji, and there is no... Let's just say... Loving it moment about it .....," she replied.

Samar tenderly tapped her cheeks before saying, "Don't worry; they should considerably lighten up by morning. Take you meds and sleep."

At his feather-light touch, a mix of shudder and warmth spread across her body. Their eyes met, and the very next moment he pulled her in for a hug. What was meant to be a casual hug, almost ended up igniting a fire within. The attraction she felt for him was unexplainable. It should have ended, and she should have pulled herself out of his embrace, but she didn't have the heart to do so, and break the bizarre connection between them which seemed too real to be jeopardized. The way she fit into his arms, and the comfort of it made her feel as if she always belonged there, and the safe cocoon of his warm cuddle was her forever safe haven. She felt her heartbeat intensify, and slowly as her hand slid down to his chest, she could also feel his erratic heartbeat under her palm. She looked up at Samar and saw him looking at her with a passionate and desirous look. Her lips parted of their own accord, and as the pad of his thumb stroked her lower lip, a soft moan escaped her lips at his slow and evident torture. He bent his head down and was just a second away from capturing her lips when Nysha's phone rang, breaking their trance. She immediately wriggled away from him, putting a safe distance between them. Lifting her head as she met his intense gaze, she saw that an equally shocked expression masked his face, and mirrored in his eyes as well, as if none could believe that whatever had transpired in the spur of the moment had actually happened for real. The weight of their unspoken words, shared vulnerabilities, and heartfelt emotions hung mid-air in silence.

"It's late Samar, you should leave," Nysha stuttered after sometime.

He nodded and ran his fingers through his hair. Then, without a word, he walked out of the door, and Nysha almost slammed it shut behind him. A shiver ran down her spine, and her legs began to tremble as she thought about the incident that had taken place just a moment ago. Samar was almost going to kiss her, and she in all probability would have responded to it as well. Her heart throbbed and her chest ached, not with pain but with deep desire. "Oh my God! What just happened.... and this is wrong! So damn wrong!" she muttered aloud. "He is just a client... a work partner... I hardly know him!" But deep within, she knew her heart had set foot in a complicated realm, and she had to back away while there were still chances of averting the risk of getting hurt.

Game: Princess Nysha in Danger
Players: Nysha, Samar
Player expertise: Not so sure
Task Difficulty Level: Really! Really! Difficult
Score: Tabula Rasa still
Comments: Seriously! Who's counting?

Of Love, Lust, or...Exactly what?

Nysha

Nysha straightaway ran to her room, then, stepping inside the bathroom, splashed her face with cold water to shake away the incident from her mind, but it didn't help much. Droplets of water slowly traced paths down her face, but that did nothing to calm the raging storm inside her. As she pulled off the hair tie from her ponytail and looked into the mirror, she remembered the heated look on his face, and the tingling of her lips at his touch was a thing to reckon. She could feel her insides shaking still.

Get it together! She muttered to herself. But deep within, she knew, washing away a moment wasn't as easy as washing one's face.

Washing her face for a second time, she stepped out into her room. By this time, she had started to feel a bit giddy. Too many events in a day were surely robbing her of her sanity. Taking the prescribed night-time medicine from her purse, she swallowed the pill in one go, washing it down with a sip of water. As she settled onto the bedside couch and took a deep breath, only one thought consumed her mind: How had she almost ended up kissing Doctor Hot Pants, and would she have ever regretted it?

In an attempt to clear her mind, she checked her phone and saw several missed calls... most of which she ignored... She then stopped at the last one, the one which had pulled them out of their stupor and averted the kiss. It was from her best friend, Pia. "Oh Pia, you saved me, honey....," she whispered to herself.

Nysha dialed Pia's number and she picked up her call almost immediately. The excited voice at the other end chirped, "Hey sweetie... I am back. I called you so many times, where have you been?"

"Ah, Pia! Welcome home, darling. Missed you so much," Nysha replied.

"Missed you much....much, love. And it feels so good to be back...You know what........."

As Pia began to share her travel stories in her over-energized tone, Nysha found her thoughts drifting away. She tried to command her mind to stay, but her weary thoughts were out of control and strayed. Now and then, she mumbled a half-hearted affirmation in response simply for the sake of staying in the conversation. Though a part of her felt guilty for keeping her best friend in the dark, she didn't want to burden her immediately by sharing all the deets of her life in the past two days, which would include sexy Sam, Bulldoze Monster, and her disastrous itchy splotches as well. But she had forgotten that Pia could sniff her mood, even from a distance.

"Hey Nysh! Did I tell you, we enjoyed a full-on strip tease performance at the Club in the Bahamas? One damsel even tried to woo Zain with a lap dance....," Pia stated.

"Ah ha... Yes! That's good," Nysha replied nonchalantly.

"Ok.... there you go. Out with it, sweetheart.... What is it that is bothering you so much?" Pia asked in a serious tone.

"Ah! What?" Nysha was taken aback.

"Exactly! What? You aren't even listening, Nysha," Pia accused.

"Oh, I am so sorry, Pia. I have been dealing with some stuff, and just couldn't concentrate," she clarified.

"Don't be. It's ok, shit happens. Come on, now tell me, you don't have to carry all that weight alone," Pia pushed encouragingly.

"Alright, you got me," Nysha said defeated, partly glad that she didn't have to carry the pile of emotional wreck alone.

As Nysha narrated the incidents of the past two days to Pia, she listened to her best friend with equal sincerity. Once she finished, Pia squeaked excitedly, "Oh my God, Nysha! That's too much happening in your life, sweetie! No wonder you are lost, honey."

"Stranded on a remote island, precisely…!"

"Aww! Poor soul!" Pia exclaimed.

"Now, sweet pea, if you are done feeling sorry for my overtly fucked up life, could you give me some valuable suggestion please, i.e. if you have any, my love," Nysha rebuked.

"Nysha Patel! Let me at least get a hang of things first. We are talking about Dr. Samarjeet Attwal, aren't we?" Pia confirmed.

"Yeah, the same Dr. Attwal…with whom you had almost ended up getting engaged to…when you were playing the game of love, jealousy, and revenge with your now husband, and would be father of your lovely children."

"Child, singular..," Pia corrected.

"With all the coochie-cooing and open display of affection with pathetic restrain, I am sure you guys wouldn't disappoint. There are going to be more," Nysha stated as a matter of fact.

"Such a shameless bitch you are," Pia accused.

"Wait, till I teach your kids the trades of the game..," Nysha threatened.

"Nysha Patel….you wouldn't dare..," Pia shrieked.

"You know me better than that, Pia Shergill," Nysha guffawed.

"Alright…I call for peace…Truce! Now tell me honestly, do you have HOTS for the sexy doctor?" Pia asked.

"Ummm…"

"Cross your heart and tell me the truth..," Pia cajoled.

"I do... In fact, I find him extremely attractive, sensible and good looking. He is a good soul," Nysha replied.

"And he is single..," Pia announced.

"Well, I am not sure about that..," Nysha replied.

"Oh! He must be..," Pia stated confidently.

"Aren't you wild guessing it?" Nysha asked.

"I have a feeling, Nysha... Something is gonna brew soon…," Pia opined.

"I don't know, and truth be told, the last time you predicted something similar, he turned out be not so interested in girls," Nysha teased her friend.

"Come on, sweetie! That was long back," Pia protested. "Seriously though, give yourself a chance, Nysha. Samar is a nice guy. Let go of the past. It's been long anyway," she affirmed softly.

Samar

Meanwhile, Samar's knuckles had turned white with all pressure and might with which he had gripped the poor steering wheel of his car. Facing the wrath of his mental turmoil, while withstanding the physical exertion of his chokehold, it was nothing short of a miracle that the poor inert object had stood its ground, without straightaway snapping into two. His breath now came out in small pants, and in a feeble attempt he tried to clear his unruly thoughts and stop the World from spinning around, but with sparing success.

What the fuck! What the hell had he been thinking, pulling her for a kiss in her own home, he thought.

Had it not been for the phone call, he would have almost ended up taking her savagely on the floor, the living room couch or right against the wall itself! Bloody hell! He most certainly must have come across as a fucking asshole. But then, she hadn't stopped him either. Her soft moans had driven him insane, igniting a bolt of desire deep within. Did she desire the same? He definitely felt that way.... or else, he would have never taken an unwilling girl...... not even in his dreams. Never!

No, this can't happen again. Not between them... But a part of him knew that it was easier said than done. How were they supposed to work together, while ignoring each other at the same time? They were poles apart, and yet he craved her like a druggie craving his next dose of poison injected straight into his bloodstream, or a dying man waiting resolutely to be granted his final wish.

On reaching home, he carefully placed the car keys on the attached key holder on the wall. As he rubbed his throbbing temples to ease the tension, and while running a hand on his forehead and across the back of his head, he could feel a slight headache developing gradually. Understanding that it could progress into an intense migraine, he opened the bedside drawer and immediately swallowed an eletriptan with water. Plonking his ass on the nearby couch, he unlaced his shoes and stacked them neatly on the shoe rack, and without losing any more time, he changed into a sleeveless vest and shorts and headed straight towards the bathroom. He thought he could do with a cold shower, but after finishing one, he realized that a shower could hardly calm his anxiety.

Stepping outside onto his bedroom balcony, he sat on the recliner, listening to the sound of water and watching the rhythmic flow of the waves. Today, however, the usually soothing sound of the sea had failed to provide a sense of calm to his edgy nerves. With each passing wave, the tightness in his chest only intensified. It felt as if the crashing waves mirrored his unrest, and the one thought which encircled his mind was: What was this bizarre connection between them? Was it love…lust…attraction…physical intimacy…chemistry…? Whatever it was, it was wild and driving him crazy. One thing was for sure, what he felt for Nysha Patel; he had never felt anything similar for anyone else. Could it develop into something more concrete and meaningful? Only time could tell…..

Nysha

Readying herself for sleep, Nysha crawled into her bed and switched off the bedside lamp. Her thoughts were still messed up, and a host of jumbled hazy visuals were encircling her mind. She tried shutting them out, but clearly her weary mind was losing all its focus. Twisting and turning in her bed, she remained awake for the longest period of time, until finally sleep managed to sneak in, and she drifted off to an uneasy slumber. Later that night, a re-run of the same dream which she had been visualizing continuously for the past few days upset her sleep. While the handsome hunk was wearing his usual white coat, and had a wide smirk plastered on his face, her heart had started to beat at an accelerated rate. She tried to make an escape, but her arms were held above her head, while his fingers lashed against her wrists and pinned her against the wall with one hand. The other hand wrapped around her hips, keeping her in place. Her legs felt wobbly, and to her horror she realized that they were pinned beneath the weight of his thigh. Even in her state of drowse, a shocked gasp akin to a nervous squeak escaped her lips.

"This is all wrong, and how dare you!" Nysha said, as her voice trembled.

"What do you expect when you fucking keep on testing my limits, Ms. Patel," replied the handsome hunk.

"I don't want this.... not you," she said.

"Too bad... Your eyes tell otherwise. Perhaps you would change your mind once I kiss you senseless," he mocked.

"You wouldn't dare!" she hissed.

He gave her an all knowing cocky grin and slid his hand beneath the length of her hair. Encircling his fingers around the nape of his neck, he pulled her closer until their faces were just a breath apart. A shiver ran down her spine as he bent his head to kiss her lips...

Nysha woke up with a jerk. The AC was set at a chilled to bone Antarctica temperature and yet, her entire body was trembling while droplets of sweat trickled down her forehead.

Holy Hell! She had been dreaming about Samar.... and it had actually felt so damn hot and real!

"Nysha Patel! You are doomed in the pits of hell!" she muttered to herself, as she covered her face with her hands to wipe off her visible embarrassment.

WHAT A MESSY AFFAIR!

While trying to catch some sleep, Samar had spent a difficult night tossing and turning in bed. He got up early next morning, changed into his jogging clothes and headed to the park for a jog. Drenched completely in sweat and panting for breath, he reached home and made his way straight to the exercise room without giving in to the temptation of taking a short break. The room, which was an almost replica of a mini gym, was well stocked and housed all the equipment necessary for a proper workout and to keep in good shape. Grabbing a pair of boxing gloves, he began hitting the punching bag as hard as he could. Sweat trickled down his forehead, and he began to blink rapidly in order to keep it from reaching his eyes. But no matter what he did, there was no escaping the memories of the previous night, which still kept coming back to him at a relentless pace.

Completing a hectic workout regime, he took a quick shower and went downstairs for breakfast. There he saw his parents who were already seated at the table. His mother gave him the most overwhelming smile, while greeting him in her softest and silkiest voice, soothing enough to put even Hindustani Classical singers to shame. But all Samar could feel and hear were warning bells. His mind had conjured the 'danger-ahead' symbol with the deadliest and grisliest 'skull and cross bone' hovering over his head.

"Oh, there you are! Good morning, beta! Come, have breakfast with us," Ms. Attwal said.

She came forward and enveloped him in a big tight bear hug. Samar hugged her back, but his senses by now had got fully activated and he could well perceive the danger lurking around.

"Good morning, Ma. Good morning, Papa," he greeted his parents.

"Good morning, son," replied Mr. Roshan Attwal.

Samar settled down on the chair beside his dad, while his mom lovingly placed a plate in front of him and began serving pohe, his mom's special, and his favorite Maharashtrian breakfast. He was still clueless as to what he had done in order to be subjected to this glorious morning treatment. He eyed his dad with a questioning frown, but Mr. Roshan simply shrugged his shoulders and gave him a silent, 'I don't know, ask your mom look,' and went back to finishing his breakfast. But he didn't have to wait long for his internal query to be addressed. As Samar began pouring fresh kiwi juice into his glass, Mrs. Attwal slowly started to reveal her actual plans for him. Her sweet voice befriended her vocal cords, and she chirped in the sweetest voice ever to grace the human ear, "Samar beta, do you remember I had mentioned about my friend, Anisha Kapoor from Australia."

"Yeah... I guess so. What about her?" he replied nonchalantly.

"Well, the Kapoors are back in India, and I was wondering if we could invite them for dinner sometime."

"Sure, you could... or perhaps you could even zero down a good restaurant and invite them there. That would reduce the pain of slogging the entire day in the kitchen. Besides, you should not exert your flexors, ma. That would only make your tennis elbow worse."

"Aww! That's so thoughtful of you, son. Dekha Roshan ji, a son, would always worry about his mother. Don't you bother beta, I promise not to exert much," Mrs. Attwal replied.

She continued, “And I also wanted to let you know, that the Kapoors would be visiting Akshat Ratna today.”

She spoke as if it were the most natural thing to say.

Samar froze on the spot. Even though he had known all the while, that his mother’s overtly diabetic sweetness was all a facade, and just the cherry topper of a hidden brewing conspiracy theory, he had no idea that this time she had outdone herself, like, totally!

Getting a grip on himself, he asked in a mundane tone, “Why? Are they meeting someone?”

“Meeting?” his mother asked as if he had put forth the most ridiculous query.

“Yeah.... a meeting,” Samar clarified. ‘It is a hospital after all, not a park where they can choose to walk in at any point of time, just for fun,’ he snidely remarked.

“Samarjeet Attwal!” Her voice boomed with a thunderous roar as she called out his name. “You will not use such a disrespectful tone while speaking about family friends. Besides, Prem uncle would be visiting too. He and Ashish Kapoor have been friends for a long time, and uncle wanted to show him around. So, he was just hoping that you would be there to.....”

“To escort him and his guests around..,” Samar completed for her.

She gave him a vicious glare but nonetheless replied in a calm tone, “That’s not how it works, beta. Your uncle just wants the best for you. He thought you could give them company. It’s about time you strengthen your social circle.”

“I am a doctor ma, not some social media influencer who needs a fan following. Uncle is definitely most welcome to the hospital, and he could bring along anyone he wishes to, but I can’t promise I can give them company. I am busy," he said.

"I checked with the receptionist, you don't have any appointments lined up," Mama Attwal stated as a matter of fact.

Sssheesh! He cursed internally. His mother was inexorable. He made a mental note to brief his staff at the earliest regarding a strict 'no schedule revelation' policy to anyone, including his family, and obviously Lalita Pawar topped the list. His mom would have hated the idea of being equated with Lalita Pawar, but he couldn't help much when she was hell bent on playing the 'malevolent matriarch'.

"Well, unforeseen emergencies crop up at odd times," he added, while trying to maintain a straight face.

"We will see to that. But make sure you try and keep your schedule free. After the visit, we are going out for lunch. Prem uncle would be joining in too," Mrs. Attwal subtly ordered.

"We? Lunch? Are you sure you are not missing anything, mother," he said through gritted teeth.

His mother laughed nervously in an offhand manner, as if she had just been caught red-handed. "Ha! Ha! Why would you say that? Can't a mother plan an outing with her son. Even I like showing off my doctor son..," she remarked.

"Show off, pretty much! And to whom would that be?" Samar asked.

"Arrey! Bata kyu nahi dete tussi, Jasmeet ji...?" For the first time now, his father's voice echoed in the dining area. ("Oh! Why don't you just spill the beans, Jasmeet ji...?" For the first time now, his father's voice echoed in the dining area.)

Mr. Attwal continued, "Puttar ji, tenu ma and mama ko lagta hai ki Anisha ki beti, Ishani, teri perfect vohti banegi...Yehi toh khichdi pak rahi hai kabse..." ("Son, your mother and uncle think that Anisha's daughter, Ishani, would make the perfect wife to you. That's the theory which has been brewing for some time now....")

Perfect wife! Samar literally shuddered at the idea of his perfect wife, as envisioned by his mother and uncle.

Mrs. Attwal glared at her husband for ruining her plans, but the old man walked away nonchalantly as if nothing had happened at all, and everything was well under control. Samar doubted if his father was going to return home anytime soon, considering the grave risk he had taken by offending his 'vohti'.

Samar looked at his mother's inscrutable face and then then said in a deadpan voice, "If whatever dad said was right, and that's what you have been planning all along, no way you are going to bait me into this, Lalita Pawar," he snapped.

His mother resorted to her age old blackmail tactics. She let the dam gates open, and there it was... A flood of tears streamed from her eyes, and rolled down her cheeks. And it seemed so damn real! Samar had always wondered where she got her flair for acting from, considering he wasn't aware of any of his ancestors being even remotely associated with 'drama' or 'theatrics'. But then again, there always happened to be a first time for everything, he thought wryly.

"Not again Ma... Nah! That's not working! Not this time," he added unwaveringly.

"Haye! What did I do? I just want you to settle down, and this is how I am being rewarded for the sacrifices I make.... Such ungrateful children!" she sniffed.

"Keep Suhani di out of this. The poor girl is happy and settled," he defended.

"And do you think I am not happy for her, except for the fact that missy decided to marry that professor," she retorted.

His mom made it sound as if her daughter had brought disgrace upon herself and her family by marrying a genius, whilst refusing to marry a Sanitary Hardware Shop owner, or more like the owner of a chain of Sanitary Shops in South Delhi. Rajat Mehta, better known as the hardware prince, was the sole heir to carry forth the legacy of Mehta & Sons Sanitary and Hardware Stores. He was one of those Punjabi men who thought they could get girls based on their financial prowess, but thankfully, his sister had weighed intelligence against the riches. Aditya Mehra was just the perfect man for her. He was intelligent, sensitive, a doting husband, and now a doting father to their five year old daughter, Aadhya.

"For God's sake Ma, he is a Professor of Robotics at Michigan University. Well, of course, most of your friends wouldn't understand that, coz they would be more interested in designer potty seats..."

The words simply slipped off his tongue. He, of course, immediately understood that, without even meaning to, he had crossed a line there. But now that the damage had already been done, his mother shrieked like a mad woman, "Doctor Samarjeet Attwal, you might be a very big doctor, the greatest heart surgeon to be walking this Planet, but I am still your mother, and you will do exactly as told. It has been three years since you liked a girl, and what if it did not work out... She is happy and settled with her star husband, appearing for interviews... and now she even graces the covers of Femina Magazine, disseminating yoga tips for moms in the making...," she concluded.

"Really?" He was interested now.

Saying everything in one shot, she gasped for breath. Then suddenly like magic, she pulled out a magazine from the stack and waved it in front of his face, before pointing out at the cover which featured Pia, donning her yoga attire and doing a 'butterfly pose'. The caption read, 'Sexy and Strong: Pregnancy Yoga for Would-be-Moms.' The girl sure looked radiant in her 'pregnancy avatar.' If only his mom could understand, that everyone deserved their share of happiness. He took the magazine from her hand and blurted out, "Fine! Have it your way, Tragedy Queen," he hissed, before continuing, "I will join you for lunch. But the next time if you plan something which involves me, without informing me, or checking on my schedule, I swear to God, I won't be arm-twisted into toeing the line to suit your whims and fancies," he threatened.

He thought he could see his mother wiping a tear drop from the corner of her eyes with her dupatta, before breaking into an awesome smile. With her antics, she could even put Rakhi Sawant to shame and give her a run for her money.

Holding the rolled magazine in the grip of his hand, he started to walk away. But suddenly on remembering something, he stopped midway and turned around. Pointing at the magazine cover, he hollered at his mom, "And leave this poor girl alone, let her be..."

As he walked out of the house and looked up at the clear blue sky, he muttered to himself, "Mistake! This was all a mistake... What a terrible start to an awesome morning!" he whined.

Occupying the driver's seat, he looked into the mirror and said aloud to himself, "Doctor Samarjeet Attwal, just so that you know, you can always say a No to a forced proposal, without succumbing to parental pressures."

With that slight pep talk to himself, he started the car and drove off.

Breakfast, Parents, Mayhem & ~~Menu~~ Venue!

Nysha looked in the mirror and studied herself. She was wearing a long, floral maxi skirt and a crop top, which displayed a hint of her midriff. The easy-breezy outfit was a perfect choice to beat the scorching summer heat. She had braided her hair after a long time and was happy with the end result. The old-school hairstyle made her look much younger and accentuated her cheekbones. Her rash marks had reduced considerably, leaving behind just a slight tinge of crimson shade. Dabbing some concealer under her eyes, applying her favorite ivory bronzer and a metallic nude lipstick, she grabbed her favorite silver clutch, notebook, and car keys, and headed straight downstairs.

After a long time, she saw Papa Patel seated at the breakfast table, quietly and obediently eating from his bowl of oats. He scooped the spoon into his bowl and put it in his mouth, as if savoring every bite. The reality, however, was far removed from the blissful, picture-perfect moment. She knew how he hated every bite of it but didn't have the guts to invite the wrath of the Goddess. You needed to be either outrageously mad or crazy courageous to do that. Sadly, though, Papa Patel wasn't both. He was a simple, opportunity-seeking Gujju businessman who had displayed a lifetime of courage thirty-five years back when he had wooed her Punjabi mom and convinced her to marry him.

And that was it.

After marriage, the ferocious Punjab Tigress had taken over the reins of the household; Papa Patel's courage had taken a cozy backseat, while his submissive side had shone at the forefront. However, soon after marriage, business prospered, and several milestones were achieved. So, despite all their differences, the one thing that remained constant was the enormous love and respect they harbored for one another while supporting each other in all endeavors. The way they still looked at each other screamed 'couple goals.' Growing up, Nysha had always believed that eventually she too would find her 'dream man,' who unlike the cliché concept of 'perfect,' wouldn't have to fit into the bill for everyone and everything. But it would rather be fair enough if he could simply fit into the shoes of being 'Mr. Perfect' for her. And then she found 'him' and thought that she had probably gotten lucky. However, until then, nobody had warned her that the Universe not only conspired to 'give' or 'bring together,' but sometimes it went behind your back, ruthlessly snatching away your most desired gift or precious possession, thereby jeopardizing your very existence on this 'Celestial Ball.'

Shaking away her gloomy thoughts, she went ahead to greet her parents.

"Good morning, Davesh bhai, healthy morning breakfast actually suits you," she teased with a wink.

Her father at first glared at her but later, giving her a smug smile, whispered playfully, "Why, of course, you should try too...Why don't you ask your mom to serve you some," he shot back.

"Spare me! I have my smoothie savior bowl," she replied.

"So, are you going to the hospital now?" he asked.

"Nope, to Aura Cosmos," she replied. "Haven't been there in a while...I needed to discuss the fundraising strategy with my team and check on the star schedules....If you ask me, there is a shitload of work to be done. I will visit the hospital only in the second half," she continued.

"By the way, aren't you coming?" she asked.

"No, you go ahead," Mr. Patel replied.

"Haven't you been avoiding visiting the hospital after the Pawar incident, fattu Patel?" she accused.

"Did you just call my husband, fattu?" Mamma Patel yelled from inside the kitchen, before coming out with a tray containing three cups of tea, filled to the brim with her special adarak chai.

"Good morning to you, too, matai. And please feel free to ask your h u s h b a n d what he did—or perhaps did not—in order to earn his esteemed title....," she replied.

Sensing that two pairs of eyes were watching him with interest, and in turn expecting a response, Mr. Patel raised his hands in defeat and said, "Between two meddling individuals, do we really need another one? I am not interested in being labeled as the Panga Family, my love," he defended.

"Ah! there he goes....," Nysha said, as she let out an uninterested yawn, and snapped her fingers between her mouth to emphasize on how utterly boring he sounded.

"I am done with your sleepy lectures....You know what, Pawar's son turned out to be more supportive of my plans than you, Daddy dear...," she snapped.

"Pawar's son?" her mother now suddenly seemed interested.

"Oh! So now we are talking...Yes, Dr. Pawar's son..," Nysha replied calmly.

"How is he?" Mrs. Patel bluntly asked.

"More like a grown-up...educated, smart man...," she replied.

"No! No! That's not what I meant....I mean, is he like... call him for dinner types....," Mrs. Patel asked.

Barely had the words escaped her mouth, when Nysha let out a hysterical laugh and said in a hilarious tone, "That's utterly funny, Mamma... But I would ignore your outrageous suggestion anyway. The world does not revolve around me finding my Mr. Perfect and getting settled, only because your friendly neighborhood Panditji had said so....," she scoffed.

"But you said...he is a nice guy...," Mrs. Patel reasoned.

'He definitely is...and I am sure there are many nice guys out there whom I wouldn't marry...He is more like a nice...Good Beast...a Good Giant," she explained.

"The Good Witch," her mother corrected.

"Nope, he is a beast... a good-hearted beast...but not my type..."

Her mother pouted and replied, "Sad! You didn't turn out to be the Beauty to his Beastliness..."

"Urgh!" Nysha shrieked as she got up from her chair. "Stop this madness! And for God's sake, stop watching those firang shows and getting weird ideas into your head...," she reprimanded.

"Even the firangs get married, puttar. Cassie is finally getting married to Dr. Radford...," her mother informed.

"Well, good for her, my best wishes...But sadly enough, some people need to work, cause marriage ain't going to solve any of their problems, as you guys would like to believe...So, excuse me...Ta-ta."

"Ah! Now she is acting like Mayor Tinsdale," Mrs. Patel fussed behind her.

"Spare me!" Nysha yelled.

She picked up her belongings and was about to leave, when her father's voice called out softly from behind. She turned around and asked, "Yes, Papa Patel, now what?"

"Nothing, just that you should know too, we will always support you... no matter what."

She smiled and replied, "Well...have known that for a while now."

"Also, Harsha wouldn't mind you settling down..."

"Yeah, I have always known that too. Thanks, Davesh bhai...," she smiled.

Nysha was in her office, going through the list of celebrities and sorting out the details that Zain's darling secretary, Mehtaji, had sent over. The schedule of the stars and singers, their available dates along with the phone numbers of their secretaries, their current charges, their history of engaging in charity and philanthropic activities, and most importantly, people with whom they got along with...like really along (in the best interest of avoiding cat fights and noisy brawls), it was all there. It also included the voted list of the audience's favorite celebrities, the real-life star Jodis, and favorite onscreen pairs as well. With the whole array of particulars at her close disposal, things had become way easier, and Nysha couldn't have been more thankful to Mehtaji for his ready help. She made a mental note to thank him later with a customized 'gourmet hamper.' Thinking of gourmet food made her stomach let out a low rumble. Oh boy! How she missed her choco-cigar rolls and marzipan bites.

Her prayers were answered when there was a soft knock at the door, and before she could answer, the door went ajar and the beautiful face of Aashita Gogoi peeked in.

"May I come in, ma'am?" she asked playfully.

"Oh my God! Oh my God! Who do we have here?" Nysha squealed as she got up from her chair and began jumping up and down on the laminate floor, while stomping her feet behind her desk, unable to contain her excitement.

Aashita moved forward, and Nysha hurriedly stepped out to give a warm hug to her friend-cum-business-partner.

"Oh, baby! You are back and blushing from your honeymoon," she teased.

"Am I?" Aashita chuckled.

"Of course, Aashita baby...."

"Hey, don't call me that," she giggled as she spoke.

"And this is for you," Aashita said while placing a lovely gift hamper basket on the desk.

"What's this beauty?" Nysha asked, admiring the arresting hamper.

"A goodie basket from Raghav and me, more like a thank-you hamper for friends who are more than family and who have stood by us through thick and thin."

"Oh wow! May I?" Nysha eyed Aashita, as if seeking her permission to open the hamper.

"Of course, go ahead, it's all yours," she affirmed.

Nysha slowly untied the ribbon attached to the top of the hamper and then removed the golden net cloth covering it. It contained an assortment of items, starting from mixed nuts, crackers, jalapenos, nachos and dips, homemade marmalade, gourmet coffee and Assam tea boxes, non-alcoholic beverages, homemade pasta delight, Belgium chocolates, dry fruits, and more. But her breath hitched, and her eyes went fixed on the small green box which screamed out to her to open it up and devour its rich and heavenly taste. Without delay, she unboxed it, and there it was! The crescent-shaped, delicate goodness stared back at her, enticing her to gobble them up, and she did exactly that: she picked up one and popped it in her mouth. Her eyes automatically shut as she savored the richness of its taste and her mind hummed in satisfaction.

"Oh, darling! You are almost having a mental orgasm...," Aashita jeered.

"You bet!" Nysha confirmed.

"Mind if I have one?" Aashita teased.

"Oh, no! No! No! You know what, it's almost a crime to have only one of these marzipan bites. And I might love you a lot—to the moon and back—but no way am I sharing these...," she said as she moved the small box of goodness away from the hamper and tucked it safely in her bag pocket.

"How mean was that!" Aashita exclaimed.

"As mean as it gets....And why the hell are you after my bites? You have Mr. Raghav Baruah to help you experience your share of orgasms," Nysha rebuked.

No sooner had the words escaped her lips than Aashita pressed her palms over Nysha's mouth, silencing her, and muttered, "You are so utterly shameless, aren't you?"

And they both ended up giggling like teenagers at a slumber party.

"I really love this mangalsutra of yours," Nysha said as she eyed the beautiful crescent moon-shaped pendant studded with red and white stones.

Aashita wishfully touched her nuptial chain and replied in a longing tone, "Yeah, I love it too....It's an Assamese traditional design. It's called the Junbiri."

"I would love to have one for myself," Nysha said with an evident yearning in her voice.

"The day you decide to get married, I promise to get you one," Aashita declared.

"Stingy bitch! Which means I am never going to get any...," she charged.

"Oh sure, you will. That's a promise. #Sister Code," Aashita declared.

"Okay, I will hold you to that. By the way, where is Mr. Raghav Baruah?" Nysha asked, shifting the topic.

"As we speak, IPS Mr. Baruah is all set to join as SP, Crime Branch, Nagpur."

"Oh wow! I can't believe you guys are married for real."

"Yeah...it does feel like a dream."

"Dream!' Nysha shrieked before adding, "Aashita Gogoi, let me remind you about the nightmare we all woke up to two years back."

"I know...I know...it was so embarrassing, right? When he actually thought that I was a high-end escort and I thought him to be..."

"A dealer of drugs and girls," Nysha completed for her.

"Yeah, can you believe that?" Aashita exclaimed.

"Not exactly your fault. He was undercover for a covert operation and in the guise of a mob boss with tattooed arms. He looked as sinfully hot and tempting as he looked dangerous."

Aashita threw her friend a wicked glance.

Nysha let out a soft chortle and raised her hands in defeat before saying, "Well, I didn't devour Mr. Choco Brownie; you did."

"Choco Brownie, huh? Actually, more like choco fudge or lava—tough outside but soft and mushy inside."

"Or perhaps sugarplum or hunnie bunch," Nysha teased. "Aashita hunnie, your story is indeed very interesting and might end up as a super-hot romantic flick on 'Netflix' or, better still, on the 'Big Screen.' But believe me, at present there are more pressing matters screaming for your kind attention at Aura. And the first one to top the list is Project Akshat Ratna. So, sweet pea, if you could take your mind off from your sweet and sultry honeymoon memories, I would like to brief you on the current status of the Fundraiser Event."

Aashita rolled her eyes and gave an understanding look before declaring, "Lady, I am all ears. Enlighten me."

For the next few minutes, Aashita listened carefully, and even took notes, while Nysha briefed her regarding the said event. After listening to all that she had to say, Aashita had a grave expression on her face, which in turn made Nysha worried.

"Babes, did I scare you? Your shell-shocked face gives the impression that someone had just narrated the devilish plot of the upcoming Nun III horror flick. Is something wrong with the planning?" Nysha asked, concerned.

Aashita waved her hand in a dismissive fashion and went on to reply, "The planning, your research, the proposed timing of the event—falling on a free, lazy weekend with practically no big events scheduled—everything is just way perfect..."

Nysha furrowed her eyebrows and asked in an exasperated tone, "Then? What's the problem? You are making it sound as if being perfect is a bad thing."

"No, it's not. But not having a venue definitely is," Aashita clarified.

"Of course, we will finalize a venue," Nysha said nonchalantly.

"When?" Aashita asked.

"Soon, of course," Nysha replied.

Aashita shook her head in disbelief. Her aura had now shifted from the girl-next-door avatar to a thorough professional who meant business. She continued, "As much as I hate to terrorize and burst your happy bubble, we are talking about a glam event here. I am sure you have clarity regarding the big shots from the entertainment industry we plan to rope in. Nysha hunnie, we need a top-notch venue. We can't settle for anything less."

Nysha's heart sank a little. Everything which Aashita had just stated made perfect sense. They really had less time to decide and finalize one. God! How could such an important aspect escape her wits? They were dealing with celebs who wouldn't compromise. Agreed, it was a charity event, and whilst a few gentle souls might not charge a penny for performing and gracing the same, their basic wants by no means could be negotiated. Darn! A good venue was definitely a foremost requirement, and if they failed to finalize one, they were sure to be doomed to hell and back!

Nysha's ghastly stupor was broken when Aashita snapped her fingers just inches away from her face.

"You there, sweetheart?"

"Aashita, tell me honestly, are we fking doomed, or do we still stand a chance at making amends?" Nysha asked.

Aashita bit her lower lip, an act she would often engage in unknowingly, only when she was hopelessly confused. This, in turn, made Nysha's insides churn and set her heart racing.

"Great! We really are damned then," Nysha spoke aloud.

Nysha exhaled softly, as if pulling her thoughts together, and just when she was about to speak, Aashita looked straight into her eyes and declared, "Alright, let's do it."

"Wait, do what?" Nysha reconfirmed.

"The event, of course. What else?" Aashita shrugged her shoulders as she spoke.

"But...you aren't even sure about it."

"No, I am not, Nysha...But I do believe that we can make it work... together," she completed.

Nysha let out a weak smile and replied, "Really? So...what's next?"

"Mademoiselle Nysha Patel, I trust you to slog your ass and find us a kickass venue. Can I count on you to not disappoint?" Aashita asked, while a small nervous smile played on her lips.

"Absolutely, Senora, count on me...On it, right away," Nysha assured.

BANTERS, INTROS, MADNESS & MORE...

At around 1 o'clock, Nysha reached the hospital. Quite a lot of things began to play in her mind all at once. But the two concerns which took priority were finalizing the venue and facing Dr. Samar.

Being at Akshat Ratna, of course, did not mean that she by any means was obliged to meet him. But a part of her also knew that, in a way, it was inevitable, since they were expected to work together on a common project and, till the completion of the same, they would be required to meet often, share information, brainstorm and exchange ideas, and most importantly, act and behave civil with each other, without jumping on each other's nerves or throwing themselves into one another's arms. The last two clauses, however, seemed a bit too far-fetched since whenever they happened to meet, they either ended up snarling, glaring, mocking, or almost kissing each other. The fact remained that as much as they repelled each other like similar magnetic poles, at the same time, they were also drawn to each other like a moth to a flame, and both instances could prove outrageously precarious and detrimental to their well-being. Nysha could only hope and pray that her hormones would behave and not end up acting unruly in front of the 'sexy devil' in a white coat or bow down before his 'Highness's testosterones.'

As she pressed the elevator button and stared at the electronic display showcasing the floor numbers via which it passed and halted at times to accommodate people on the different floors, it felt like standing there forever while watching the door in fascination to simply derive the pleasure of seeing it go ajar. But the elevator nevertheless took its own sweet time to arrive. Meanwhile, a throng of people had already gathered in front of the steel door in anticipation of squeezing themselves inside the small tin box. So, Nysha decided to ditch the elevator to save herself the ordeal of squeezing her butt inside the crowded crate, and took the stairs instead, all for, and in the best interest of mankind. A wry smile crossed her lips at her own predicament. Climbing up the stairs slowly as she reached the first floor, she got a call from Harsha Aunty informing her about a sudden OT emergency which would take up some of her time. Nysha halted her steps immediately and tried to reschedule her plans for the day in her mind. She had planned on meeting Harsha Aunty and discussing the key points of her presentation. But now, with Aunty getting busy and her entire routine getting jeopardized, she thought of ways to utilize her free time instead. She began to rack her brain, searching for a plausible solution, when she heard footsteps leisurely descending the stairs while humming 'If it's love' by Sting to himself.

"Wow!" she thought. It happened to be her current favorite track and the one which topped her playlist at the moment.

The footsteps halted right at the end of the stairs, and that's when she saw the familiar face of Dhananjay smiling at her. He had paired a slim-fit black polo t-shirt with a pair of white tailored trousers and was looking really handsome. She noticed that he had a sassy taste in fashion, and though it was quite suited to his personality, at present it felt as if he was a bit overdressed for a typical hospital visit.

"Hey, what are you doing here?" he asked.

"That was supposed to be my line, don't you think so?" she smiled as she replied.

"I came here to meet Dr. Sanghavi," he stated as a matter of fact.

Nysha touched the bridge of her nose and furrowed her eyebrows before replying, "You did? Well, I came here for the exact same reason too."

"But now she is not there...," he said.

"Yeah...she got busy. I did not know she was meeting you today. I thought I was supposed to meet her alone," Nysha stated.

"Perhaps, she wanted to discuss something with both of us," Jay offered.

"Possible...," Nysha agreed.

"Now what?" he asked.

"Ah! We could wait...Aunty's cabin or maybe..."

"Samar is not there," Jay stated plainly, as though reading her mind.

"Oh! He is not...Where is he?" she asked casually, without sounding too curious about Dr. Heartless or his whereabouts.

Jay gave her a mischievous smile and muttered beneath his breath, "Well, the lamb is up for slaughter..."

"Excuse me?" Nysha grumbled, unable to get him.

"A man might have his own secrets, sweetheart," he winked.

"Aren't you getting a bit too dirty-flirty, Mr. Beast," she snapped.

"Beast, me?" He pointed a finger at himself, grinning widely as if she had just cracked the most hilarious joke of the millennium.

"Well, if you remember the ordeal I had to face because of the beast at your home," Nysha reminded him savagely.

"Ah! I had already said sorry about that...And Jahaan is not a beast...," Jay defended.

Nysha smirked and said, "Ah! Of course not. He is your soul brother, the cutest and most adorable fur baby surviving the planet...for all I care. But, you, elder brother, maintain a safe distance from me, got it?"

"Hey, I am clean...I was nowhere near him today, and let me tell you, it takes quite a bit of resolve to do that...," he stated.

"Aww! The poor baby must have been heartbroken," Nysha scoffed.

"Come on, Nysha, why are we even engaging in this shitty verbal duel, that too on a hospital floor," Jay asked, exasperated.

"You started it...," Nysha defended.

"Alright," he raised his hands in defeat and declared, "Let's call a truce. You want to maintain safe distance, I will keep my distance. But let's get out of here. Since it's already lunch time, how about we go and grab a quick lunch somewhere nearby?"

Nysha twisted her mouth into a half smile and considered his proposal. There wasn't any doubt that she was hungry and could definitely do with some good food, before resuming her venue hunting. With a sly smile she replied, "You sure...you came here for a meeting, Mr. Pawar," she teased.

"You sound as though you are accusing me of having an ulterior motive. I said I am clean," he assured.

"Guess you are. So, do I consider this lunch proposal to be some sort of a sorry offering?" she asked.

"Offering sounds so much like a Goddess...," he mocked.

"Oh! I am a Goddess," she said, while pointing a finger at herself in a dramatic fashion.

"Sorry to burst your bubble...but you are more like a chudail...," Jay clarified.

"Chudail! Did you just call me a witch?" she accused.

"I did sweetie, but more like the good one...," he said.

"Ah, another fan of Cassie..."

"Who's she?" he asked, a little bemused.

"She is The Good Witch, Mr. Beast...Come on now, let's go," she exclaimed.

"You quite enjoyed our banter, didn't you?" Jay asked.

"Oh! I simply loved it. Relaxed my stressors, you see," she winked at him.

"Well then, I am happy to help," he winked back.

"But I do have a feeling senior Pawar wouldn't appreciate the idea of us getting cozy at all," she said with a soft chuckle.

"Well, bad for him. But I do like the idea of us...," Jay said playfully, while a small smile played at the corner of his lips.

Nysha gave him a confused look, before uttering, "Us? Eww! Have you lost it, Mr. Beast? You are clearly delusional," she accused.

Jay laughed at her antics, before admitting, "Oh, that was damn hurtful, I was hoping that you would give us a fair chance," he said with a mocking grin.

"Fk off, Pawar junior. Your sinister 'us' recipe has left a bad taste in my mouth. You better make up for it," she threatened.

"Oh, sure, will do, my lady...sure, will do," he repeated in a beguiling manner.

As per his classy taste, Jay took her to a newly opened chic Korean Restaurant. When they entered, the maître d' showed them to a cozy corner table for two. In the backdrop was a large, vintage-themed window overlooking the spectacular view of the hotel's in-house rosarium. Nysha couldn't help but notice the minimalistic furniture and aesthetic decor the place had to offer. The mixes of colors, yellow and green, were used to their best advantage, and it helped to create the ambiance and vibrancy of the 'spring' season.

A waiter served them a complimentary five-flavored berry punch, and as they sipped it leisurely, Nysha took in the lovely decor, making a mental note to take a few pics and sharing the same with Pia, with a view to incorporating a few changes at their own Cafe. The impressive way in which the Korean traditional elements were integrated into the landscape along with the folk art paintings on the wall, gave a mesmerizing and truly authentic 'Korean feel.' The smooth and creamy texture of the drink had already made her hormones happy, and she in turn became excited about tasting the cuisine and indulging in the main course.

As her eyes roved around, they fell on someone, and for a moment she thought that in all probability she was hallucinating. Behind one of the patterned rustic metal frames dividing the sitting area into sections, she could see Dr. Samarjeet Attwal busy in talks with someone, and well, that someone happened to be a pretty damsel. Dressed in a pink salwar suit, she looked every bit of an eloquent princess channeling her inner Barbie traits.

As the sultry minion shared a joke, Samar bent down his head to listen to her, and in the process his arm brushed hers. When she saw Dr. Samarjeet Bloody Attwal's body shaking with laughter, Nysha, in reflex, could feel her insides churn with anger. She had a sudden strong urge to slap his handsome face and wipe away the smirk or better still, throw up on the perfect lapels of his coat.

Holy Hell! What kind of a shameless jerk was Dr. Heartless...and how could he make her heart flutter even from a distance?

His tall frame, broad shoulders, muscular chest, angular jawline, and perfectly fitting sky blue coat gave her a hard time breathing. She remembered how they could have almost ended up kissing in the living room of her home, and her body's response to his touch made her insides twirl in knots.

Yech! Her appetite was ruined now, she thought.

Her mind wandered to her best friend Pia, and the words of wisdom she had spoken to her. When Pia had said that something might end up brewing between her and Samar, Nysha had subconsciously and subtly started to believe that probably 'something' actually stood a chance. Well, what she had forgotten was that the Universe, being a sloth, was totally uninterested in solving her solitary concerns.

She glared daggers at him, and as if sensing her vicious stare, he turned in her direction and caught her gaping at him. His eyebrows shot up and his mouth opened slightly, and she became certain that Dr. Heartless had seen her for sure. When he had caught her eyes, she should have immediately looked away, but her current fked up state of mind didn't allow any of that. In fact, thanks to Dr. Attwal, the little sleeping devil inside her mind had resurrected after a long gap, and it was now dying to unleash its dormant vile potential. In fact, the devil was ready to initiate its first ploy and what's more, the table for six was all set to be served the perfect dessert to mark an end to their scrumptious meal.

Without a word, she got up from her chair with a jerk, taking Jay by surprise, and almost spilling her drink on the embroidered organza tablecloth, while droplets of the same fell on Jay's highly expensive branded t-shirt.

Shocked at her weird behavior, he too got up from his chair with a jolt. As he began to brush off the droplets from his t-shirt, he quipped, "Hey, Wobbly Duckling! What do you think you are doing?"

Nysha gave him a devilish grin and spoke with a mischievous glint in her eyes, "Mr. Jay Pawar, I think we have your family here, and wouldn't it be just nice to go and say a polite hellooooo!" she said in a sing-song voice.

Jay looked at her and then towards the direction she was beckoning with her eyes. His eyes widened in disbelief; obviously, he had no idea that his father and extended family would all be gathered at the same place. Turning towards Nysha, he said in a half-pleading, half-disapproving tone, "Ah! I don't think that's a great idea. I mean, look at them, probably they are in the middle of something important."

She gave him a soft menacing look before replying, "You sure I ain't missing anything here, Mr. Pawar junior?" Nysha said through gritted teeth.

"What? No," he denied.

Not satisfied with his half-hearted response, she continued to glare at him. The poor fellow shrugged his shoulders and finally gave in, "Alright, they are here for a formal meeting..."

"And a formal meeting....would be like...," she probed.

"Like a meeting with prospective in-laws, prospective bride...what do you say, hone wale samdhi–samdhan kind of a thing...," Jay replied in his slightly accented tone.

Nysha quivered internally with anger at his response, but nevertheless maintained a stoic face and replied instead, “Ah! That’s all the more reason to go and say a very polite hello. Besides, I can’t risk my reputation by feigning ignorance about senior Pawar’s presence and come across as being rude and arrogant. You know how it is, we don’t really share a great bond, and he quite doesn’t think very highly of me,” she reasoned.

Jay gave her a level stare before replying, “Sweets, as much as I would like to believe in your innocent words, the murderous glint in your eyes speaks otherwise. And why do I get this feeling that you are up for some mutiny, or rather, a vengeful ploy is at disposal,” he accused.

Jay had quite aptly decoded her current mindset, but since she couldn’t give him the credit for his acute prediction, so she playfully replied instead, “Oh come on Pawar Junior, now you are reading between the lines.”

Before Jay could probe further, Nysha walked up to him and slipped her hand through the crook of his elbow, taking him by surprise. Still smiling at him and leaving no room for denial, she whispered determinedly in his ears, “Now, Mr. Beast, get me introduced to your family, will you?”

Accepting defeat and knowing that there was no room for escape, Jay finally gave in to her demand. As she walked gingerly towards Samar’s table, Nysha could feel his heated gaze on her. His eyes never left hers, and not one to back out easily, she too didn’t break her eye contact with him. The burning intensity of his stare made her steps heavy, and at one point she almost faltered, feeling the weight of her irrational decision to confront him upfront with his family and would-be in-laws. As they neared the table, the people seated around became more prominent. Senior Pawar gave her a nonchalant glare, and though she had wanted to return the favor with equal intensity, she decided to play safe and coy with a polite nod and a soft and mushy hello instead.

Next, her eyes fell on a lady wearing a beautiful henna-colored chikankari suit paired with an elegant rose gold pearl-drop necklace. Even with the subtle signs of aging and wrinkles visible on her face and neck, she still managed to look delicately beautiful. Nysha didn't require any introduction regarding her identity, since she had the same eyes as her son, and even the strikingly similar jawline took her by surprise.

Nysha waited for Jay to make the formal introductions, but to her dismay, the Beast remained silent, almost as if he had gotten his tongue-tied on seeing the nasty and disapproving look on Senior Pawar's face. Sure thing, sulking Pawar Senior could be an actual recipe for 'Bad Omen,' nobody would want to be served on a platter. And though Nysha totally empathized with him and could comprehend his pain, she definitely could not end up looking like some idiot waiting for validation from a group of gaily seated spectators. She tugged hard at Jay's arm to break his state of trance, but before 'His Beastly Highness' could speak, Samar intervened, "Ma, she is Nysha Patel, the consultant who is working with us on the Akshat Ratna project, and Ms. Patel, this is my mom."

"Hello beta...," Mrs. Attwal greeted her with a warm smile.

Nysha's heart thumped loudly in her chest. Suddenly, she felt rather small for acting on her rash instincts and attempting to ruin Samar and his family's lunch outing. She also noticed how he had managed to maintain his cool, despite her crazy endeavor to sabotage his reputation and derive sadistic pleasure out of the same. Nevertheless, focusing her thoughts on the current situation and maintaining a plastered smile on her face, she replied calmly, "Hello, Aunty, nice to meet you."

"Hello beta, it is nice meeting you too. Why don't you and Jay join us?" Mrs. Attwal offered.

"No, Aunty, that's not required at all. We just wanted to say hello, isn't it, Jay?" she replied, while politely declining her request.

This time she tugged even harder at his arm, but the naive idiot still looked clueless. Nysha suppressed a strong urge to whack his arm in turn. However, when she threw him an icy gaze, he took the clue, but muttered a nonchalant, half-hearted and half-muted response, "No, Atya, we didn't mean to disturb. You all continue, please...," Jay responded in a mundane tone.

"We will continue, beta ji, and family does not disturb, isn't it, bhau?" Mrs. Attwal eyed her brother to seek his validation, before continuing, "The Kapoors are family too. Come, sit down, make yourselves comfortable," she coaxed.

Doctor Pawar looked at Mrs. Attwal and then towards her. Nysha's heart did a crazy somersault inside her chest, her nervousness equivalent to that of a kid who had made her very first attempt at cheating on a math paper, only to be caught in the act by the broody and snobbish principal. Her cheeks felt heated, and for a moment it felt as if she had forgotten to breathe altogether.

"Join us, Ms. Patel," Dr. Pawar finally said in a soft, menacing tone.

No sooner had the words escaped his mouth than Samar savagely joined in at the opportunity, "Yes, Jay bhaiya...Ms. Patel, come on now, join us," he said with an unmistakable smirk on his face when his eyes caught hers.

With the tables turned around and almost kicked hard at her, Nysha had zero clue regarding her next move. She turned to look at Jay expecting some help, but he was nowhere to be seen. To her dismay, she found him seated next to his father. She had no idea when the little turncoat had taken the opportunity to abandon her completely at the mercy of Dr. Heartless and his crew. Her mouth opened slightly at his brutal betrayal. She could feel color rising to her cheeks, and even droplets of sweat had started to surface on her forehead, despite the AC running in full capacity. With reluctant steps she moved forward and pulled out a chair. As she sunk her butt into it, she had an almost excruciating vision of herself lying deep in the desert sand, in the midst of the most devastating sandstorm. True, she had seen bad days, even worse, but nothing could beat the insurmountable suffering of slipping into a chair between the 'Beast' and 'Dr. Heartless.'

Finally giving up the idea of damage control, she looked at the floor, half expecting it to explode and rip apart so that she might as well fling herself into the Earth's hollow and get saved from any further embarrassment and horror. Only one thought occupied and screamed aloud in her mind: Oh my God! If only I hadn't been born at all! How on Earth am I gonna face Dr. Heartless and his equally heartless uncle yet again.

A Venue on the Menu

A lunch outing had never been half as awkward and harrowingly as difficult as the present one. Nysha tried to fidget with her phone while maintaining a straight face and a polite smile smeared across her lips. She stared at her phone screen as if her life depended on it, desperately hoping for an SOS call to intervene so that she could declare an emergency and save her butt from any further humiliation. With Samar seated just inches away and her concentration amiss, even the delectable delicacies served on the table failed to fascinate her.

Then suddenly, underneath the table, she felt a slight brush on her leg. Even beneath her long skirt, she could feel a spark ignite and rise to her core. It felt strange how her body reacted to his touch, or how her hormones jumped to and fro in desperation. She thought it to be accidental and slowly tried to move her legs away from his vicinity, ignoring the tingling sensation of his touch. As she tried to shift her focus to the food, she felt his leg brushing against her skirt once again. That's when she realized that Samar's sitting posture was such that it was almost impossible for their legs not to touch.

Bloody creep! Nysha thought to herself and sneered at him. She stared at him with curious eyes, but he was busy stuffing chicken kimbap with spiced soy sauce into his mouth. He seemed to be completely unfazed by their proximity; in contrast, her awareness of his presence was heightened to an extent where she was able to inhale the subtle scent of his citrus aftershave and even feel the unmistakable warmth which his body emitted. His calm and composed demeanor enraged every particle in her body, and it took a hell of a lot of restraint to maintain her cool and not stab him straight in the eye with the chopstick in her hand.

Nysha turned to look at pretty Ishani. Dressed perfectly, with not even a wisp of hair out of place, she looked every bit the designer who had very much been a part of prestigious International Fashion Shows and Beauty Pageants. The way she held her chopsticks between her delicate fingers, while batting her eyelashes and stealing glances at Dr. Heartless, made Nysha's insides seethe with fury. The sultry fashionista at times provided her input regarding the food and purred a 'yes' in agreement with Samar to almost everything that he said. It made her look like a wet kitten with perfectly manicured, but rather blunt claws. Ishani even tried to act jovial with Nysha and Jay, time and again trying to pull them into the conversation, and while Jay merrily joined in, Nysha excused herself with a polite smile. In the current situation, a tête-à-tête was the last thing she had wanted herself to get involved in. Moreover, it wasn't like she and Ishani had a lot of things in common. The way Ms. Pretty Perfect spoke, with her stylish accented tone, and the way she wiped the edges of her thin mouth with smooth gentle strokes using a tissue, was in deep contrast to Nysha, who at all times would be more comfortable wiping her mouth and face with the back of her hand instead.

Finally, when the long and torturous meal almost came to an end—or that's what she thought—Nysha witnessed the most gauche sight of the day. It seemed the pretty princess had smeared some chocolate on her cheek, and Samar, being the perfect gentleman that he was, bent forward and had the honor of wiping it off from her pretty face using a tissue. Jitters ran down her spine, and even the smile that had remained loyally plastered on her face until now went completely missing.

God! She didn't want to witness this! A hard realization dawned upon her, and cold sweat broke out on her face. Behind the camouflaged fancy exterior, this girl was a sneaky snake with venomous fangs who, given the chance, could even bite off a butt. Nysha could bet her only Louis Vuitton pumps that the entire setting of matchmaking was a sloppy external charade, masking the actual agenda of the Kapoors, Dr. Pawar included.

Well, for all she cared, Samar could go ahead and get his butt licked, or better still, get bitten by Ms. Fancy Fangs!

Her weird, sadistic thoughts were enjoying a free rein until a phone call interrupted them. A smile broke on her lips, her joy equivalent to that of a weary, thirsty traveler who had finally managed to locate an oasis to quench his thirst. She excused herself from the group and started walking towards the curved entrance of the restaurant. On reaching the door, she turned around and glanced above her shoulder one last time, only to find the occupants at the table still chatting away merrily.

Should have said a formal goodbye before moving out, she thought. But now was not the time. She opened the door and walked outside, allowing the fresh breeze to kiss her cheeks and ruffle her hair.

By the time she made her way outside, the phone had already stopped ringing since the call had been disconnected from the other end. She could not blame the caller, for it did take her a while to answer. But knowing her friend Pia, Nysha was sure she would be waiting with bated breath for her to return the favor. Without further delay, she called her back, and almost immediately, Pia's restless voice chirped in, "Nysha Patel! Where are you?"

"Hello to you, too, duhling!" Nysha greeted her overenthusiastic friend.

"Oh, drop the formalities! You gotta hear this first...."

"Spill it!" Nysha replied.

"Know what? Mehtaji might have discovered just the perfect venue for your event...," Pia declared.

"Oh my God, Pia! If that's true, I owe him big...," Nysha exclaimed.

"Alright! First listen, and then decide for yourself...You have heard about Celebrity Big Daddy, right?"

"Of course, who hasn't? With cat fights, live smooches, tantrums, bitchiness overload, and the super-sexy Aarav Kapoor hosting it, it's trending, and numero uno on the charts."

"Ah! About that, sweetie! Can we push that discussion for sometime later? I thought we were discussing your venue here," Pia mumbled.

"Aww! Such a jealous Aunty you are, aren't you? Come on now, praising another star would hardly reduce an ounce of your husband's stardom," Nysha teased.

"Don't you dare call me a jealous Aunty...," Pia threatened.

"Then stop behaving like one...," Nysha stated.

"Right! About the venue then, bitchy friend...," she grumbled.

"Hmmm....that's better," Nysha giggled.

"Well, the Big Daddy set is located in Lonavala. The place is absolutely picturesque," Pia explained.

"So? Are you suggesting I parade my troupe of celebrities inside the BD house? Anyway, what harm could a few extra TRP points do, right?"

Nysha could hear Pia snarl at the other end. "Aargh! Can't believe we have been friends for almost 25 years now. You are such a pain in the butt, you know that? Now, If you would let me complete...,"

"Alright! Stop shouting....Please...go on..."

"Have you heard about Noah Jidan?" Pia asked.

"The famous NRI Industrialist?" Nysha replied.

"Yeah, right, him. So, last year, Mr. Jidan had bought an old heritage property in Lonavala, intending to transform it into a 'World Class Art, Culture, and Sports Center.' It's located near Lake Pawna, about 5 kilometers from the BD sets. The entire project is helmed by his daughter, Delizah, and her husband, Bryan. In fact, they are stakeholders in many casinos across India, particularly the ones in Goa and Andaman."

"Are we talking about the famous Del Floating Casinos?" Nysha asked.

"We are," Pia confirmed.

"So, what's in store for us?" Nysha asked.

"Well, Zain happens to have a very good relationship with the couple. In fact, two years back, he had even inaugurated their hotel in Khandala. Plus, Bryan has a half-Iranian sister who desperately wanted to make her Big Bollywood debut. Considering his equation with the Jidans, Zain managed to pull a few strings, and with Director Asif Abassi already on the lookout for a fresh face, Lyanna cleared her look test and auditions effortlessly. She is the next exciting launch from the Abassi camp, and sources say, she might very well be Bollywood's next big find. The Jidans, needless to say, are incredibly grateful to Zain and more than willing to do anything for him. So, this morning, when Mehtaji called Bryan to narrate the entire venue hunt debacle, he was more than happy to let us use the

Sports Complex and the biggie is: they aren't charging a penny."

"You got to be kidding me!" Nysha exclaimed.

"Absolutely not!" Pia assured.

"And how much time until the Center is complete?" Nysha asked.

"The Sports Complex would take another 15-20 days, a month at the max..., which still leaves us with ample time for the preparations."

"It does. And what's in it for them?" Nysha asked curiously.

"For starters, a kick-start celebrity inauguration, and phaadoo publicity at that," Pia trilled.

"I guess, that does make sense," Nysha agreed.

"Totally! I have mailed you a couple of pictures of the property, the indoor stadium, and the landscape. Check them at once."

"I will. In fact, I might as well drive to Lonavala today, and check the facility myself."

"With whom are you planning to go?" Pia questioned immediately.

"Alone, Mrs. Zaidi, does that bother you?" Nysha snapped.

"You can't go alone," Pia stated as a matter of fact.

"And why on Earth would you say that?" Nysha asked in exasperation.

"Because it's already 3:30, and even if you take the Mumbai-Pune Expressway, it will take you at least two hours to reach Lonavala, and driving back home again would be really tiresome, unless, of course, you plan to stay back."

"I have to go, and I don't plan on staying back. Once the venue is finalized, Aashita can take it up from there. Besides, next week is the final presentation. If I don't have a confirmed venue, old goat Pawar is going to breathe fire down my neck. And I can't fking afford it...," Nysha yelled.

"Fine, then take someone along with you," Pia said in her overly adamant tone.

"Look, sweetheart, you can stop worrying about me. I am not your foster child. Your child is on the way; till then get a grip on your momma instincts," Nysha hit back.

"Girl! Stop fussing about everything around, will you?" Pia chastised.

"Seriously! Yeah, right, why am I even wasting my time?"

"Wait! Should I ask Zain to accompany you? His shoot in all probability should be over by now and...," Pia offered.

Pia hadn't even finished, when midway through she heard a loud guffawing sound at the other end. Annoyed with her crazy friend and her equally crazy antics, she retorted, "And what exactly is so funny, you psycho?"

"Funny! No! Your suggestion is absolutely hilarious, my friend. And as much as I love you and adore the cutesy tiny miracle growing in your belly, I would rather give your proposal a miss," Nysha declared.

"Care to explain?" Pia probed.

"Ahem! Pia Shergill, I am already in deep st, and the paparazzi following my butt is the last thing on my bucket list right now. Besides, I definitely don't want to be labeled as the Femme Fatale Husband Snatcher, who takes advantage of her best friend's pregnancy and goes on long drives with her star husband. The media trial would be totally unforgiving, and sweetie, I can't even afford an Ivy League lawyer to support my case."

Having said it all in a single breath, she gasped for air when a voice from behind startled her, almost making her lose her balance. She was about to experience a hard fall when strong hands gripped her upper arm, saving her from a nasty collapse.

"Hey! Are you okay?" he asked.

Nysha was about to mutter a 'sorry,' but one look at her rescuer, and her snooty self was back. Her jaw opened wide and she literally shrieked, "You?"

Samar's eyes widened and he almost immediately left her arm and dropped his hands to his side.

"Yeah...me! Who else were you expecting anyway?"

Sneering at him, she replied, "Not you, of course."

"Oh! That's bad...," he said in a half-mocking tone, further annoying her.

"Pathetic, I would say."

While Nysha's face clearly reflected her evident dislike and frustration, Samar, on the other hand, had a wide grin spread across his lips, while an unreadable expression shadowed his face. This, in turn, managed to infuriate her further. Meanwhile, in the sudden, unexpected face-off between her and Samar, she had completely forgotten that Pia was still on the line and was actively listening to their not-so-jovial banter. Her overtly protective friend was yelling her lungs out at the other end.

"Hello! Hello! Nysha, are you there?"

With a deep sigh she answered, "Hey Pia, I am so sorry...I have to go now."

But Pia being Pia wasn't listening. Instead she had her own jumping queries. "Nysha, who's there with you?"

Nysha eyed Samar and lied through gritted teeth, "No one, it is just the hotel doorman."

"Well, that's quite funny, you know, considering you were engaged in a repartee with the porter," Pia accused.

"Well, why not? Small talk to make the world a better place," Nysha defended.

"Nice try, sweets, but I think I still do recognize Samar's voice," Pia countered.

"It's not him....you obviously got it wrong," Nysha lied.

"Fine...pass on the phone to your doorman then," Pia ordered.

"Are you kidding? What are you going to say to him?" Nysha charged.

"Oh! Just a simple hi, you see...My contribution to making the world a better place," Pia proclaimed.

"Ok, I give up. It is....Samar," Nysha hissed.

"I knew....Why don't you ask him to accompany you?"

Nysha let out a hysterical laugh, and said in a hushed tone, "I would rather let Count Dracula suck my blood than hang out with that weirdo."

"Why are you being such a stubborn shrew?" Pia accused.

"And why are you being such a paranoid elf?" Nysha bit back.

"Don't you follow the news, hunnie? Last week there was a cold-blooded murder on the same highway, and you want me to stay calm. Well, I am not the least bit buying your idea of lone travel down that route. You are having trouble asking him...Fine! Pass me the phone, I will do the honors. If you don't, I will call him up directly or worse, I will inform Aunt Harsha about your crazy exploits," Pia threatened.

"Gosh, Pia! You can't intimidate me. Your pregnancy hormones are acting up, and you are being an annoyingly abusive bully, you know that?" Nysha complained.

"Absolutely! I totally agree. Now, pass him the phone."

"Aargh! You are relentless. Great! Have it your way then. Also, let me warn you in advance, I am going to give you a real hard time, Pia Shergill. You are gonna pay for this...Wait till your kid comes of age. The crazy antics I am gonna teach the cutie pie will be enough to blow your mind away."

"Ha! Ha! Ha! Not worried about that, bestie. Considering I know you so well, I am sure I will figure out a way to deal with those antics of yours. Now if you wouldn't mind passing on the phone, puhlleaze!" Pia added.

Muttering a curse beneath her breath, Nysha passed on the phone to Samar, "Here, Pia wants to talk to you."

Samar shot an eyebrow at her and asked in a surprised tone, "Me!"

"Yeah! Isn't it totally uncalled for? I told her you are a busy doctor. It's okay, I will tell her you are not available," Nysha said in a sarcasm-laced tone.

"Oh! Come on, drama queen...," he said, as he grabbed the phone from her and answered the call, "Hey, Pia, how are you doing?"

"Samar! Hey! After a long time...I am good, how have you been?"

As the long-lost platonic friends shared their life updates on the past three years, Nysha excused herself and stepped away, not wanting to eavesdrop on their not-so-interesting, exchanging-pleasantries kind of conversation. A part of her hoped that Samar would decline Pia's outrageous suggestion, but the other part could take a wild guess that in some time from now, she would have no option left other than to tag along with Dr. Heartless. After all, who could say 'no' to a would-be-momma and, for old times' sake, didn't that always mean something?

"Sure, I got this. You don't worry at all. Take care, bye."

With those final words, he hung up and walked up to Nysha. There was an unmistakable glint of mischief and a subtle hint of triumph in those drowsy eyes. Nysha wanted to dive deep into them. It wasn't a small feat that he could make her stomach flutter and legs wobble simply with his intense gaze. Fearing that her face might give away her actual feelings and make it too obvious that she was drooling, she tried to look away, but Samar was already in her space, standing right in front of her with a raised eyebrow.

"You could have directly asked me out, you see...," he teased.

Nysha furrowed her eyebrows and replied in an indignant tone, "Excuse me!"

"Instead of Pia intervening to explain the situation over the phone, you could have directly discussed it with me. Would have saved us some time," he rephrased his suggestion.

Nysha raised her hand to stop him from speaking further, "Seriously, who says you have to come along? Look, Pia is being unduly paranoid. That doesn't mean you have to listen to everything that she says. And don't worry, I ain't gonna tell her a thing. So, clearly, you wouldn't be harming your clean-slate reputation."

There was complete silence for a few seconds before Samar spoke again, his voice grim. "You know what? I actually don't care what you think. The arrangement is between Pia and me, and I will not lie to her, nor will I allow you to do that. So, if you don't mind, move that pretty butt of yours a bit faster, we don't have all day. My car is parked right at the corner."

Pretty ass! Really! Was that supposed to be a compliment or a badass remark? Nysha mused.

IT'S A CHECKMATE.

Nysha wanted to open her mouth to argue, but one look at Samar's clenched jaws and the heat of his piercing glare, and she dropped the idea altogether. She was clearly being bullied and blackmailed by her best friend and the doctor, but since the task at hand was far more important, she decided to put her independent feminist ego to sleep, all in the better interest of a brighter tomorrow. Samar and Pia were so alike, it was a relief that they didn't end up together. They had the potential to be a real pain in the ass, a tad too over-the-top perfection personified to be handled with grace.

Upon reaching his pretentious SUV parked almost at the end corner of the parking area, Nysha stared at the car door blankly for a few seconds, before turning around to look over her shoulder.

"Damn Nysha! Why the hell don't you get in? And what are you looking at?" he asked.

She gave the most annoying lopsided grin before replying, "Aah! Just wondering, your folks haven't finished yet? Still gorging on the last scoop of dessert, or perhaps finalizing on the roka dates?"

"That wasn't the least funny, you know," he said laconically, and in an exasperated tone.

"Well, it wasn't meant to be...," she hissed under her breath, before dumping her ass on the passenger's seat. Samar looked mad, and made an angry grumbling sound. Not that it really bothered her. In fact, his pissed-off demeanor activated her sadistic pleasure hormones.

The car hit the road, and Nysha settled comfortably in her seat, while Samar shifted his entire attention to the drive ahead. She stole a glance at him and saw him clasping the steering wheel in a white-knuckled grip in total frustration. Considering the display of strength and exertion of force on the poor inert object, it was surprising that it still hadn't snapped into two. Deciding to give him some time to cool off, she turned in her seat and looked out of the window, the blur of fleeting scenery providing temporary relief from the tension within the car. Anyway, a sulking grumpy doctor was hardly a recipe for soulful musings.

Meanwhile, Samar looked at Nysha, who had a certain calm aura spread across her face, or was it calm before the storm, he wasn't sure? Knowing her, he bet more towards the latter, though. She hadn't spoken a word since she had got inside the car. In fact, she had her eyes closed, and her legs were pulled up in a comfortable position, making her look like a soft stuffed pretzel. When she yawned softly, with her lips parting slightly and eyes still closed, it stirred insane feelings inside him. That, coupled with the rhythmic rise and fall of her breasts, made his breath stuck in his chest, and it had taken a strong resolve to keep his emotions in check. He could see that she wasn't happy about being stuck with him, and he echoed her sentiments, unless, of course, she believed otherwise.

Ummm! After nearly 45 minutes of unperturbed beauty sleep, Nysha woke up with a sexy murmur, making his breath hitch in his throat. She stretched her arms and extended her legs to ease the stiffness, before stifling a yawn and cupping her mouth to do the same. Glancing at him whilst still rubbing her eyes in a childlike gesture, she asked him in a soft whisper,

"Are we there yet?"

Samar cast a sideway glance. His eyes bore into her drowsy ones, as he took in the soft, careless beauty of her curls caressing her cheeks. His fingers twitched to tug them behind her ear. Her gaze had an undeniable effect on him, and he hated his body's reaction and the shot of desire and attraction he felt towards her, despite knowing for a fact that it was an insane idea. Samar knew better that they didn't share anything in common, and their coming together was not even remotely possible.

Tearing his gaze away from her, he concentrated on the road ahead before speaking, "You wish, princess! Just so that you realize, we are travelling by a car, and not some private jet which lands its butt straight on your Fort's helipad," he snapped.

She glared at him, her sleepiness slipping straight out of the window, and her mouth curled into an impatient angry snarl.

"You are such a snob, aren't you? Not to mention, a big bore to the core too."

"Call me that again and you will see what I am capable of," he threatened.

She slapped her hands over her mouth, and raised an eyebrow in a challenging manner, before speaking in an overtly animated tone, "Oh my God! Oh my God! I am so… sooooo… scared, you know. What are you planning to do? Push me out of the car, and leave me stranded on a deserted highway. Would you stoop so low, Dr. Heartless?" she said while blinking her eyes quite a few times, making Samar's heart rate increase by several notches. Samar knew that her dramatics were meant to mock him, and yet he found them absolutely adorable. He let out a low growl and took a deep breath in order to control his desires as well as his anger.

"Know what Nysha, go back to sleep. You are better off in an unconscious mode. Consciousness doesn't suit you. Your tiny brain cells get worked up for all wrong reasons," he mocked.

Nysha let out a dry, humourless, and not quite a funny laugh before replying, "Ha! Ha! Ha! Right back at you, take that, Dr. Heartless..."

Before Samar could come up with a befitting reply, Nysha took out her earphones and plugged them in. She had closed her eyes yet again, leaving him seething in fury and desperation.

After almost a two-hour long drive, they finally reached their destination. True to what Pia had said, the Sports Complex was indeed an architectural marvel. Shahzad Qureshi, the Complex Manager welcomed them and showed them around. Since he already had prior information regarding their probable visit, he had made quite a few arrangements. They were served welcome drinks, along with a readymade assortment of savoury items and sweets. Nysha stuffed a few packets of mixed nuts and a few energy bars in her bag. When Samar looked at her quizzically, she replied with a coy smile,

"For the journey back home, you see."

He shook his head in disbelief, but his lips gave away a smile at her crazy escapades. He was finding her behaviour quite amazing and deeply annoying at the same time. But no matter what, Nysha Patel was not someone to be ignored. She was carefree, crazy, and spontaneous from the word 'go'. There wasn't a bone of pretention in her body, and neither did she find it necessary to hide behind the socially acceptable veil of perfection. Nysha was real, and that's what made her attractive. It was a tough bet to spend time with her, and yet not to fall for her. Anyway, Samar's myocardium had already started to pump blood at a faster pace than acceptable under normal circumstances. Clearly, her presence had cast a spell and woven an unfathomable magic around.

Once they were done with the refreshments, Shahzad showed them the rest of the facility, including the stage area in the auditorium, the seating arrangements, the greenrooms, the restrooms, and a Starbucks Cafeteria decorated with an impressive collection of locally sourced artefacts and paintings. The tour left them completely satisfied with their choice of venue. They confirmed their booking and completed the formalities. By the time they were finished, it was already 7:30. Shahzad suggested they could stopover by Lake Pawna, since the lake under the moonlight was a sight to behold. Assuring him that they surely would, they said their share of goodbyes and thanked Shahzad and his team for their awesome hospitality.

On their way back, Nysha insisted on stopping by the lake, and though it was already late, and Samar was sceptical about the idea, he finally gave in to her incessant pestering. He parked his car by the lakeside, and Nysha was about to get down when she heard a taunting warning from behind, "15 minutes, that's all you have. Make it quick."

"Oh! For heaven's sake, can you please let your hair down at times and stop breathing down my neck like old goat Pawar," she chastised.

"Breathing down the neck is so very cringe, do you even realize that? And can you stop using derogatory terms for Dr. Pawar? He is my uncle, goddammit!"

She scoffed dismissively and and made the most annoying face at him before getting down. Samar followed suit.

It was a beautiful night for walking. The moonlight passed through the covering of branches and trees, and bathed the lake in a shaft of silver radiance which shone like a jewel amidst the silver glow. They walked in silence for sometime, engulfed in the cold darkness, breathing in the fresh air as a waft of cool night breeze blew across their faces and ruffled their hair. Right around the corner of the lake, Nysha's eyes fell on a small black iron gate which opened to a children's park. There was a small lock attached to it, but on pushing slightly the gate opened.

"Hey, crazy! What are you doing?" Samar called out from behind.

She turned around and gave a distractingly beautiful smile before adding, "For once, Dr. Heartless, would you follow my lead?"

Before he could reply, Nysha had already made her way into the park. It was dark, and the park was deserted, almost like the road outside, with not even a vehicle passing by. The air around was infused with the smell of wet grass and night flowers. To top it all, the gleam of the moonlight painted a picture perfect canvas. Nysha settled on a swing and tried to push herself. She swung her legs high up in the air and shouted to Samar,

"Will you simply keep staring or be of some help? Come on, push me."

An elegant smile curled up at the corner of his lips. As he approached her, he rolled the sleeves of his shirt up to his elbow and bent down to push her, but before that, he whispered in her ears, "Do you know you are one hell of a crazy woman?"

He pushed her with all his might, and the swing went high up in the sky, and as it came back, Nysha leaned her head back, laughed like a carefree teenager, and hollered to Samar, "And you are a snob, you know that, Doctor… a big one at that…."

The breeze tossed her hair and created a messy riot across her face. Her lips parted of their own accord, and as she let out a carefree laugh, a sweet ache slowly developed in Samar's chest, and he tried to look away from her mesmerizingly beautiful face.

Once the speed of the swing subsided, she got down in an almost breathless state and he asked her, "Done? Let's head back home."

Nysha winked at him mischievously and replied, "Says who? I have just begun… Race you, Dr. Heartless...," she challenged him.

"Where to?" he called after her.

"To the fountain…,' she called out.

They ran like kids. He chased after her, and the sound of her mirth-filled laughter filled the air. Her free, impulsive, and spontaneous movements were sensuous and carefree. She had started this madness, and had pulled Samar along with her. He dived into her merry world and was beginning to enjoy the utterly lunatic symphony of fun and hilarity. By the time they finished, they were huffing, panting, and gasping for breath. Their eyes were watery from excessive laughter, their heartbeats erratic, their legs wobbly and braced for balance, but their hearts were filled with jubilance.

Samar couldn't take his eyes off her. In her quest for madness, a button had loosened at the neckline of her top, exposing the smooth porcelain skin in the valley of her breasts, and as droplets of sweat tricked down the same, she looked like a temptress, hell-bent on inciting lust and passion even in a saint. And damn, he wasn't even half a saint. Down south, Mr. Willy Wong had become deliriously active and was on the lookout for a quick escape route to satiate his sudden insane cravings. Samar was having a hard time keeping its behaviour in check, since it was now beginning to act like a fanatic, going berserk in his pants.

Their eyes interlocked, and his sinfully lustful gaze bore straight into her outright innocent and playful ones. The magnetic pull of her aura had a devastating effect on him. He wanted to look away, but his eyes fell on her lips, which were a delicate canvas of enticement, and the way it had curled into a captivating smile made his heart lose a beat at first, and then several beats altogether in a go. Beneath the trajectory of stars and the glistening blue street lights afar, their rushed heartbeats created a different rhythm altogether. The buzzing electrifying connection between them was too intense to give a miss, and it felt as though time had come to a stand still.

All of a sudden, their stupor was broken when someone flashed a gleam of light towards the park, and in a state of shock, a gasp almost threatened to escape her sassy mouth, when Samar pulled her towards himself. The abrupt forced movement made Nysha's head bang on his chest. He immediately placed a hand over her mouth to muffle her disoriented snivel. Her eyes widened in shock, but nevertheless unlike other times, she didn't protest and let him take charge of the situation instead. They could see a police patrolling car stationed right outside the park. A window pane rolled down, and before someone could get down from the car, Samar instinctively slid behind a tree, pulling Nysha along with him. His hand was curved around her waist, while she tightly clutched on to the lapels of his shirt. Meanwhile, a middle-aged police man got down from the car and flashed a beam of light before shouting,

"Anybody there?"

"Hello! Anyone out there…," he yelled again.

There was silence all around. Apart from the whining of street dogs and an owl hooting at a distance, the only audible sound was that of their rasped breaths. The policeman shouted again, and in reflex to shy away from his line of sight, Nysha snuggled closer to Samar, almost burying her face in the crook of his neck. Her body pressed tight against his, jolted his senses, and every fibre of his being came alive and kicking. Samar let out a low growl, while Mr. Willy Wong's control was barely hanging there by a thin thread. Outside they could hear footsteps pacing up and down the gravel road. It almost felt like eternity since they stood there cuddled in each other's arms and oblivious to the surroundings. After sometime they could hear the engine of the vehicle start, and much to their relief, the patrol car drove off, leaving them behind.

"I think he left," Nysha whispered, as she reluctantly tried to pull herself out of his embrace and proximity. Still in a breathless state, she tried to inhale sharply, when Samar pulled her nearer by grabbing her waist, and murmured in her ears, "Breathe… just breathe in and out...," he ordered.

She passed him a weak smile, and steadying herself, muttered under her breath, "Back to being a snob..."

Barely had the words escaped her mouth, when she felt a tug at her braid as Samar pulled her closer, their faces just inches apart, "Samar!" her voice sounded like a hoarse whisper.

Samar bent down his face and captured her chin with the other hand, "This, Ms. Patel, should be a reminder to not call me a snob ever again."

Before his words could register and make sense, Samar captured her lips in a delicate kiss. Nysha froze; her mind unable to decipher her emotions. The gentle assault of his tongue inside the folds of her mouth played havoc with her senses, and she found herself being consumed by the kiss. Then suddenly, just like it had started, he ended it. They were both out of breath… but between gasps Samar said, "See? Not a snob..."

Nysha frowned at him. Her thoughts were running wild, and her emotions were out of control. She grabbed the collar of his shirt and pulled him towards herself.

"That's for me to decide, Dr. Heartless."

Saying that, she once again latched her lips with his, taking him by surprise. She nibbled slightly at his lower lip, driving him mad. A low guttural growl escaped his mouth and he pulled her closer to himself, his hands firm on her waist. The world around them had disappeared into oblivion. The touch of his fingers had evoked her inner most desires, while her soft moans, as she called out his name in between their passionate rampage, acted like a shot of ecstasy injected directly into his nerves and transporting him to a 'World of Jubilation,' free from the shackles of forced chivalrous behaviour while arousing his wild self, and igniting the fire of need, which coursed through his veins.

Nysha gnawed at his neck and murmured, "Hmmm....You smell so good..."

"And you smell delicious... I am sure you will taste yum too," he teased as he sucked the skin at the nape of her neck, and his teeth grazed against the soft skin above her collarbone sending chills down her spine, and making her giggle in response.

"You little minx...wait till I paint your neck with my mark," he declared passionately.

She pushed hard at his chest, still panting for breath, "We should stop… Samar. We better stop…," Nysha hummed.

"Hell… Why?" Samar protested.

"Seriously! What do you think we are doing, Doctor? Mauling each other in a goddamn children's park," she exclaimed.

Samar raised his head and looked into her eyes, his breath still heavy. Nysha was right. In their smouldering passion, they hadn't even realized that they were behaving like desperate horny teenagers driven purely by lust; who couldn't keep their damn hands off each other.

"Hell! You are right...," he murmured softly, more to himself than to her. His eyes still held a heated intensity, but nevertheless he distanced himself slightly from her. Then cupping her face between his palms, his calloused fingers grazed the soft and sensitive skin of her cheeks, while he ran the rough pad of his thumb above her lips, leaving a trail of heated desire burning deep within her, diving down straight to her soul.

Samar's ministrations to her body made her breath choppy. He observed her face for some time, and then, breaking the palpable connection between them, spoke reluctantly in a baritone voice, "Come, let's go."

He held out his hand to her, and she took it silently. As they headed back to their car, their bodies radiated a different level of tension, and a growing awareness throbbed amidst them, forever altering the variables of the equation between them. For good, bad or for worse, only time could tell.

The drive back home was mostly silent. What had transpired between them was an almost surreal experience, and they were both trying to soak in the flow of events. Finally, they reached Nysha's home and Samar pulled the car into the driveway, and parked it in front of her entrance. She got down from the car and was about to open the gate, when Samar called out her name, "Nysha... wait!"

She stopped in her tracks and turned around to face him.

"Do you wanna say something about tonight? Anything?" he asked.

His query left her stupefied. There were so many things encircling her mind that she was clueless about where to begin. Her feelings for Samar were raw, he was an enigma, almost like the important piece of a jigsaw puzzle which could make her heart complete. She opened her mouth to express her feelings, but words failed her...

"I... Samar... I...," she stuttered.

Samar stepped forward and closed the distance between them. He slid his fingers beneath the nape of her neck and tilted her head forward until their foreheads met. They stayed put for sometime, simply listening to each others heartbeats, while taking in the familiar scent of one another. He then pressed his lips to her forehead and said softly, "Ssshhhh...You need not say anything... But I do want you to know something. You, Ms. Nysha Patel, are special. This evening… tonight, was very special for me, and I meant every word of what I said. Do you understand?" he asked.

Nysha was already overwhelmed with varied emotions. She nodded slightly, but nevertheless refrained from looking directly into his eyes, or commenting a thing.

"Nysha, look at me," he cupped her chin between his palms and tilted her head slightly until their eyes met.

He slowly bent his head and rubbed his nose against hers. Then nibbling softly at the tip of her nose, he moved down and rubbed his nose against the nape of her neck and shoulder blades, while sniffing in her intoxicating scent. He could feel her accelerated heart beat, and a slow, wicked smile crossed his lips.

"Hmm! You look so cute when you are speechless, which I believe is a rare feat," he murmured between his antics.

"Samar… you should leave…," she whispered.

He had a hypnotizing effect on her, and she feared that the intense passion would consume them both.

"Of course, I should," he said playfully, before planting a kiss at the corner of her mouth, leaving her cheeks flushed and eyes wide open with shock.

"Good night, Ms. Patel, and yeah, sweet dreams too," he said with a wink.

As Samar strolled towards his car in a relaxed fashion, Nysha stood there glued to the spot. Before getting inside, he turned around one last time and muttered, "Checkmate."

Finally he drove off, leaving her in a state of daze. As she slowly made her way towards home, a smile curled up at the edge of her lips, the same corner where Samar had kissed her.

She had a hunch, and a sudden, strong emotion engulfed her senses. Despite all her attempts to stay away, her heart was risking it all by falling hook, line, and sinker for the charms of Dr. Heartless...

BREEZY MORNINGS & HEARTY BANTERS

Early next morning, Nysha woke up to the ripples of bright sunrays penetrating her room, doing a happy dance, whilst kissing her face and bestowing upon a radiant glow. The chirping birds outside provided the perfect rhythmic chorus to a breezy and breathtaking morning. Taking a deep breath, she blinked her eyes several times in order to adjust to the morning hues and let the calm energy of dawn seep into her soul.

Letting out a soft yawn, she stretched her arms wide behind her head and looked groggily around her room. Suddenly, she remembered the happenings of the previous night, and her face flushed red and her cheeks heated in embarrassment, as the memories of their wild rampage, the blazing desire, and unabashed craving for each other came back to her. She immediately rose up, and rushed towards the bedside mirror. Positioning herself in front of the mirror, she examined her face from left to right and then again from right to left, and let out a sigh of huge relief. But little did she realize that her respite would only be short-lived. The very next moment her eyes widened, as it fell on a mark on the soft skin of her neck. She leaned nearer to the mirror for a closer inspection, and realized what it was.

It was a hickey! Darn! Sexy Samar had planted an old-fashioned hickey on her neck.

She remembered his words, Wait, till I paint your neck with my mark... and he had!

Holy shit! What was se supposed to do now? And how on Earth would she manage to hide the formidable mark from the treacherous eyes of the moral-policing society.

For the longest time she stared at her image in the mirror, which gawked back at her with equal intensity. Her lips quirked into a small smile, and leaning towards the mirror she whispered softly, “Nysha Patel, you are an absolute nut job, and needless to say, awfully pathetic too.”

Picking up her phone, she began messaging the artist who had created the perfect tattoo master piece on the canvas of her neck.

Nysha: What were you thinking when you had left that horrendous mark on my neck, bloody Dr. Heartless?

Samar: Says who? The witch who uses her nails to scrape the skin and paint my neck?

She blushed hard at his blatant accusation.

Nysha: Oh, stop lying. No way, I am not capable of doing something so LS...

Samar: Ms. Patel, you have an uncanny sense of humour. Otherwise, who in their right mind would call love bites horrendous or low standard…, he replied with a chuckle emoji.

Nysha’s cheeks heated and she could feel the temperature rise up to the tip of her ears at his deliberate teasing. Before she could open her mouth to further accuse him, her WhatsApp notification beeped, and she opened it immediately. Dr. Heartless had sent her a snapshot of her nail imprint on his neck and, Oh My! My! Was she even remotely capable of doing that? His neck displayed light scratches and a dark bruise grazed his skin as a mark of their previous night's wild and uninhibited passionate exploration. She blushed the darkest shade of red, the color of her cheeks bright enough even to put the reddest of cherry tomatoes to shame.

Nysha: Shameless you are, Dr. Heartless, she accused.

Samar: Pretty much, Nysha, hunnie. Guilty as charged, he acknowledged.

Nysha: Aaragh! Get a grip on your wild instincts, Doctor. And dare you try any of your antics at the hospital, she warned.

Samar: Can't exactly guarantee that. It depends actually.

Nysha: Depends, Seriously? You wouldn't dare, she warned.

Samar: You quite don't know my dare yet, Nysha... so let's not even get there. See you at the hospital, he replied coolly.

Nysha: Alright, hospital it is, then.

Accepting his challenge, she closed the chat.

Morning 11 o'clock:

Nysha reached the hospital just in time for the meeting with Harsha Aunty. With her car still parked safely in the hospital parking space, she realized that in a city like Mumbai, taking a cab was an easier and comparatively faster option, since one didn't need to concern oneself with the distressing parking hassles. As she headed towards Dr. Sanghavi's cabin, her heart felt heavy and overly burdened with the weight of the stress and tension of the upcoming presentation due the coming weekend. Though she was thoroughly determined to restore the lost glory of Akshat Ratna, and make the celebrity fundraiser a grand success, deep down, Dr. Pawar and the not-so favourable reactions expected from his team of hardcore loyals had never ceased to bother her. She was only hopeful that eventually the majority of stakeholders would come around to support their noble cause.

She reached Dr. Sanghavi's cabin and was about to enter the same, when she heard voices, and the sound of laughter coming from inside made her halt her steps. As the curious soul inside her tried eavesdropping on their conversation, she overheard things which weren't quite to her liking.

Dr. Harsha: "Nysha is working really hard. I am sure she will find a way out of this crisis..."

Dr. Heartless: "Well, I can see that… She thinks highly of you…."

Ah! That familiar, deep, sexy baritone voice had been messing with her mind lately. It could make her go crazy one moment and, the very next, burn her heart with profound desire. She shook away her steamy, senseless thoughts and was about to knock when she heard Samar speak again, Dr. Heartless: "She just gets a bit overboard at times… I mean, she is too sensitive and naïve about certain issues."

Dr. Harsha: "It's ok to be sensitive at times, Samar…"

Dr. Heartless: "I ain't saying that's a bad thing… It's just that…."

Samar didn't get a chance to complete his statement when there was a loud knock at the door.

"Come in," said Harsha Aunty in a soft voice.

And she barged straight inside the cabin with a scowling face.

[Scowl courtesy: Dr. Heartless (Dare he call her naïve! And what was he; some know-all Saint, bloody Heartless!)]

"Good morning, Nysha. We were waiting for you. Come, take a seat," said Harsha Aunty.

"Good morning Aunty, I hope I didn't disturb the flow of conversation," she said in a sarcasm-laced voice as she eyed Samar in a loathsome manner.

He seemed to have been taken aback by her sudden changed demeanour. Dressed in a formal crisp white linen shirt with sleeves rolled up to his elbows, and paired with smoky grey trousers, he looked sinfully tempting.

God! Who looked this sexy in a tad boring office wear? It was a sin to look this smouldering hot in the office. And darn! He was a cardiologist. With his looks, what was he planning to do? Create some kind of short circuit in her already jammed brain cells, or tug straight at her heartstrings until they snap in two. And why on Earth were her thoughts always this reckless with him around, whereas he seemed to be unscathed by her presence, and in perfect control of his emotions? Damn you! Samar, she thought.

All of a sudden, the medium-sized cabin started to feel like a clogged, pint-sized closet, with less space and even lesser oxygen for intake.

"Nysha… beta, are you ok?" Dr. Harsha's voice broke her stupor.

"Yeah! Absolutely fine, Aunty…," she replied.

"Then sit down, beta…," Dr. Harsha suggested.

"Yes, you should sit down, Nysha… I mean Ms. Patel," Samar added with a soft chuckle.

"I surely will, Dr. Heartle…, I mean, Dr. Attwal," Nysha replied back, matching his tease and tone.

Nysha scanned the room, then, pulling a chair from the corner, she sat near Dr. Harsha, deliberately avoiding sitting near Samar. It earned her a raised eyebrow from Dr. Heartless, but hell, she cared!

She flashed her pearly whites at him and hissed under her breath, "Trust me, air required for breathing, you see…,"

He shook his head at her antics and muttered, "I do. Suit yourself, miss."

Meanwhile, Harsha Aunty suppressed a smile, quite enjoying the hushed banter between two of her favourite young people, and also aware that her small cabin had turned into a battle ground of sorts. However she restrained from commenting, and feigning ignorance asked instead, "Now that you are seated, I believe we could start."

"Of course, we should. We definitely don't have all day," Samar's voice drawled, and Nysha glared daggers at him.

"Right away, doctor…," she whispered.

Once Nysha began explaining the key points of her presentation, both Samar and Dr. Harsha listened to her with complete attention and were quite impressed with her research. She had covered certain aspects that hadn't occurred to them yet, but were nevertheless important for concluding the entire summary. After completing her deliberation, she looked at them for cues to gauge their reactions. While Harsha Aunty smiled warmly, the mischievous grin on Samar's face took her breath away. He was the only person who could make her nerves rattle, turn to mush, and blush all at once. Though she had experienced intense emotions before, none had been as fervent as her current, unadulterated feelings for him. Before she could probe further for feedback, the cabin door flew open, and in walked a beast donned in the season's swankiest outfit. The flashy pastel hues could even put flamboyant actor Ranveer Singh to shame. Nysha had to suppress her strong urge to put on her shades and protect her eyes from the deliberate ordeal inflicted by Pawar junior.

God! What was he thinking when he had picked up this outrageous outfit? she thought.

Before she could gather her thoughts and comment, she saw Samar get up from his chair and walk up to Jay.

"Happy birthday, bhaiya," Samar said as he hugged Jay.

"Thanks, brother," Jay replied.

Nysha's eyes widened and she blurted out, "It's your birthday?"

"Well, that's what I would like to believe," he answered with a raised brow and an amused tone.

"Hey, happy birthday," Nysha said, as she too went ahead to hug him.

"Thank you," Jay replied.

"Happy birthday, Jay. God bless you," Harsha Aunty joined in.

"Thanks, Dr. Harsha," Jay replied with a smile.

"So, what are your plans for the day?" Nysha chimed.

"Nothing much… Join me at the Mahim Retro Buzz tonight at 8."

"Wow! That's an excellent choice. Who else is invited?" Nysha asked.

"You, Samar… a few more friends will join in, that's it," Jay replied.

"Cool… But as much as I would love to, Jay…"

Nysha hadn't even completed the sentence when Jay intervened,

"Don't even get there, Ms. Patel. You are coming. Period," he added straightway, closing the room for further argument.

"It's midweek, Jay. Who gets drunk midweek?" Nysha protested.

"Then don't drink, just come," Jay insisted.

"Mr. Pawar, are you aware of the degree of torture you are putting me through? I mean, who goes to a Retro Club and drinks milk instead," she ranted.

"Make an exception then. Anyway, not drinking midweek is your call."

"That's because I get pretty bad hangovers, my fair-weathered friend, and the next day happens to be a working day."

"Did I just hear fair-weathered friend?" asked Harsha Aunty with a soft chortle.

"Oh you did, Aunty! And please ask Jay to share the deets," Nysha added in her overtly expressive tone.

"She exaggerates, and you know that right, Dr. Harsha?" Jay defended.

"There is no denying that you do exaggerate at times, Ms. Patel," Samar deadpanned.

"Really now! Are you brothers ganging up against me? But seriously, what were you thinking, Mr. Birthday Boy? Wearing these flashy colours to a hospital? Just because your younger bro is a surgeon doesn't mean you can put the life of these poor patients at risk, especially the poor beating heart which pleads to be left alone, and saved from the ordeal of an almost myocardial infarction."

Both men crossed their arms over their chests and looked at her, and then towards Harsha Aunty, in a manner which exclaimed that they had indeed made a point.

"The girl is dramatic, you see," Jay said.

"Quite a handful," Samar readily agreed.

"Great! Now I am not only dramatic, but also a handful! Thankless wizards," Nysha shrieked.

"But you are also a loving witch, my friend," Jay added with a wink.

"Wait! Which precisely translates to pyari chudail in Hindi, right?" Nysha asked.

"Don't always go by the literal meaning, my pyari chudail. Your pitch for the inauguration of a separate Paediatric Heart Surgery Unit was both surprising and electrifying at the same time. In fact, that was the deal-breaker, and mind blowing climax to the entire presentation!" Jay praised.

"You heard? But you weren't even here," Nysha asked, flabbergasted.

"Hey! I was just outside the door. I didn't wanna disturb. So yes, I waited till you concluded."

"And you liked it?" she asked with a hint of doubt.

"Like would be an understatement… I loved it," he confirmed.

"And do you think senior Pawar would like it too?" she asked.

"Well… does he have a reason not to?" Jay replied as a matter of fact.

"I am so glad that you aren't like your father, unlike Dr. Attwal here, who savagely takes after him," she accused.

Jay muffled a quiet chortle, while Samar asked in an impassive voice, his face inscrutable.

"And what makes you say so?"

"You have not uttered even a single word of praise, whereas the entire PHS unit was proposed whilst keeping you in mind," she shrugged.

"I am humbled, Ms. Patel. And it's not that I disapprove of your proposal. It was good, but I'm also aware of the people we're dealing with, and I don't want to say anything that might make you complacent. No doubt you're 90% prepared, but you need to close that 10% gap if we want to win over the Board members, especially Dr. Pawar."

Nysha pursed her lips, gave him a disdainful look, and said, "A dash of optimism sprinkled into your overly pessimistic thoughts isn't going to harm much, is it?"

Samar shook his head at her adamancy and immature shenanigans. Then he said in a soft and sardonic voice, "Good job, Ms. Patel, and all the best for your final presentation. Hope this makes you feel better."

Before Nysha could retort, Samar turned towards Dr. Harsha and said, "I will take my leave, doctor. I have a round to complete. Bye, Ms. Patel."

"Samar, wait! I am coming too," Jay called behind him.

"Dr. Harsha, I will leave too. Bye, Nysha, see you tonight…and no excuses," he said.

As the men walked out of the cabin, Nysha watched their retreating backs until they disappeared completely, once the door closed behind them.

"I should leave too, Aunty," she said, as she collected her laptop bag and got up from her chair.

"Nysha, am I missing something?" Harsha Aunty asked with a frown and a bemused look on her face.

"Excuse me, Aunty. I didn't get you," she replied.

"That's my point, beta. From when did someone's opinion begin to matter so much to you?"

Harsha Aunty eyed her as if she was waiting for her to confess to her crimes, and that in turn made her feel ridiculously small and tongue-tied.

"It doesn't, Aunty," her voice sounded shaky even to her own ears.

"Samar's opinion does mean something to you, doesn't it?" Aunty probed further.

"Is that a bad thing, Aunty?" Nysha asked.

"Of course not, dear. In fact, you are wonderful as a team. Just be careful," Aunty cautioned.

"I will, Aunty. Bye… I will see you on Saturday with the final presentation."

"Of course. All the best, dear."

"Thanks, Aunty."

With the fear of being probed further, Nysha almost scurried out of the cabin. She thought she could hear quiet laughter behind her, reminding her that they were just kids, and well, parents being parents, would always stay ahead one step at a time.

Nysha immediately wanted to get away from the hospital, since she knew that quite a lot of things were pending at 'Aura,' and though Aashita had been managing well, but she could definitely do with some help. However, her immature self and that petty voice in her mind were hell-bent and adamant about not allowing her to walk out of the hospital, not until she had sought an answer for his cold and impassive behaviour. Though he had said that he had a round to complete, she seriously doubted that, coz it seemed more like an excuse to move away, especially from her.

She walked across the corridors, and in no time reached Samar's cabin. Without a word, and ignoring the courtesy to knock, she barged inside and immediately regretted her impulsive move. Samar was busy passing instructions to a nurse when her sudden unsolicited entry took them both by surprise. The nurse almost jumped in her place, while Samar looked at her as in she were some alien who had just decided to crash-land her UFO in his office. His eyes shot electrifying sparks at her, promising a brutal galvanization if possible as a part of her chastisement, which in turn ran shudders down her spine.

Samar cleared his throat, probably buying some time to control his murderous thoughts, before speaking in a perfectly pitched and controlled voice, "Ms. Patel, I wasn't expecting you. Do you have something important?"

Nysha suppressed her inner urge to call him names and laugh out loud at his face, but some remaining shreds of inner decency prevented her from doing so.

Meanwhile, Samar signalled the nurse to leave, and leave she did, but not before throwing Nysha a vicious vamp-like stare. The girl in her mid-twenties, though dressed in her nurse's uniform, was dolled up perfectly, prim and proper, almost like she was there to exercise her seduction skills on her target. And of course, who could be a better target than sexy Sam!

Once she left, Nysha closed the door behind her and walked up to Samar with angry strides. His handsome and equally arrogant face had annoyance written all over it since she had walked in uninvited and disturbed his work, which wasn't the most sensible thing to do in a professional setting. But damn him! He always brought out the worst in her, or perhaps not always, but at most times.

"Well... what are you waiting for? Shoot...," Samar said in an expressionless voice.

"I thought you were intelligent enough to have known without asking," she said, twisting her mouth slightly.

"Ms. Patel, intelligent per se is your forte," he accused.

"Oh, come on now, we are all naive fools here, aren't we? You are the only chosen one, Hawking's incarnation," she retorted.

"Well, you are being presumptuous... But now I know where you are heading to, Nysha. When I said you are naive, I never meant it in a negative sense," he defended.

"Try telling that to your pretty assistant or, better still, the damsel your family has lovingly chosen for you. I am not some bimbo to believe every word that comes out of your mouth."

A faint semblance of a smile tugged at the corner of his lips, and then he said in an annoyingly sexy voice, "Jealous are you, Ms. Patel?" he teased.

"Fuck a duck! Of course, I am not. Who do you think I am? Not your poor little whining girlfriend."

"Why? You do sound like a possessive girlfriend," he added with mirth.

"Possessive, my ass!" she angrily poked a finger at his impossibly hard and perfectly chiselled chest.

"See, that's what I meant by being naive. It's so easy to get a reaction from you," he further nudged.

"Yeah, reaction... right? Coming to that, Mr. Attwal, let me warn you in advance, if at all I make an appearance at Jay's birthday party tonight, dare you step into my personal space, and I sure won't think twice before kicking your balls and fucking the living daylights out of your rude system," she warned.

"I wouldn't dare," he chortled. "But I am still clueless about what exactly are you mad about," he added.

She threw him a murderous glare and hissed under her breath, "Alright, act all naive and dumb as you want to, but if ever again, I am compelled to put on a high-neck formal jumpsuit in this scorching summer heat, just because you decided to let loose your feral instincts akin to that of a Neanderthal, and tie-dye my smooth textured neck, I promise you are not going to live to see the crack of dawn," she cautioned yet again.

"I would love to see you try," Samar jabbed snidely, with a smirk plastered on his face. His voice was barely a whisper, driving her insane and almost daring her to do something foolish. At other times she would have taken the bait, but she couldn't let her hormones act up and let the damn man know about the kind of effect he was starting to have on her.

Without uttering another word, and before he could do or say something which could potentially change her already fucked-up mind, she strode out of his cabin and started walking through the corridor.

Arrogant devil! The words began to play and echo in her mind as she made her way out of Akshat Ratna, away from Dr. Heartless.

Starry Nights and Party Vibes (Chapter I)

"I think you should go," Aashita chimed from behind Nysha.

"Oh, come on! Get off my back now, will you?" Nysha grunted back at her friend.

Ever since her two closest friends had taken their wedding vows, they were hell-bent and adamant about fixing her nonexistent love life. Both had assumed the role of 'Mother Hen,' fiercely protective of her and vouching to safeguard her from predators on the prowl (eligible dating men included). But now both mommies had taken a strong liking for sexy Samar and wanted her to give a shot at a relationship with him.

Relationship! Seriously! They've got to be kidding! Nysha thought.

"Come on! I'm not going anywhere," Nysha said, almost hollering at Aashita, and slicing through her blusters. In turn, she made an annoyingly pouty face and, with puppy eyes and a dramatic flair, replied, "Poor Jay! He would be so very heartbroken, you see..."

"It should suit him fine. Anyway, a superficial heartbreak is only going to make him a stronger beast, what do you say?" she replied with a wink, as she began to neatly organize the printouts and faxes into a folder for the final presentation.

"You sound so much like a she-devil incarnate, akin to Mazikeen, the Archdemon," Aashita quipped while rolling her eyes at Nysha.

"Oh, thanks, friend! Your compliment just did wonders to boost up my dampened spirit," Nysha said with a huff.

Aashita shrugged her shoulders and said, "Fine, don't go. Let Dr. Attwal think that you are so besotted by him that you can't even tolerate the sight of another girl near him."

"Are you crazy and seriously out of your mind? And which girl are we talking about here?"

Aashita winked and let out a low whistle before replying, "We are talking about the sexy siren, Ms. Designer, Ishani Kapoor."

"My love, I really don't care two hoots about Dr. Attwal or his sexy siren for that matter."

"Try saying that to a novice, sweetheart. I know you better," Aashita challenged.

"Fine!" Nysha put the papers aside and gave Aashita a pointed look. Then she said in a serious tone that strictly meant business, "Spill it. What do you want me to do?"

"Nothing much, just that you should accept the invite, go and connect with people, and let your hair down. Why let anyone believe otherwise?"

Nysha shrugged her shoulders and raised her hands in defeat before saying, "Alright, if that's what it takes to get you off my back, you insufferable woman, then so be it."

"Language, lady! And just for once, can you stop being so difficult?"

Nysha made the most annoyingly grimacing face and replied, "Wow! Now I'm becoming difficult as well. Great!"

"Instead of bickering this whole time, why didn't you finalize a gift for Jay instead?"

"Ah, that!" Nysha nonchalantly waved her hand and replied, "I already have the perfect gift in mind for Mr. Beast."

Aashita rolled her eyes and repeated playfully in a slurred voice, "Perfect gift!"

"Of course, La' Dior Perfume for Men! Can you go wrong with that, baby?"

"Excellent choice, Mademoiselle Nysha," Aashita agreed.

"Totally! And we're in love with Mr. Johnny Depp, aren't we?" Nysha exclaimed playfully.

"Aha! Captain Jack Sparrow, an absolute favorite, darling... Not to mention the raw, fresh, and woodsy masculine fragrance of Dior... Aww!" As Aashita began with her description, her eyes closed of their own accord, and it seemed she had an almost orgasm.

"Urgh! You insatiable little minx, spare me the details of your bedroom fantasies with your alpha male," Nysha chastised.

"Nysha Patel, you are incorrigibly shameless. Now go, get the gift and enjoy the party," Aashita stated.

"As you say, Momma..." Nysha sneered.

"And Momma would want the details the next day. No hiding!"

"Crooked Momma!" Nysha scoffed, and both friends laughed out loud, drowning in a whirlwind of carefree laughter.

Mahim Retro Club,

8:10 P.M.

Considering that it was midweek, when Nysha entered the club, she found it unusually crowded. The lively decor of the club, along with the umbrella-shaped shades above and the sparkling golden and red globe lights, provided an aesthetic, retro-themed ambiance. Staying in tune with their vintage theme, a '60s BMW Isetta could be seen perfectly perched atop the bar sitting area. The crowd had already started to move and flock toward the dance floor, and the atmosphere was fully charged and abuzz with activity. The DJ began to play the retro Bollywood hits of the '60s and '70s. As the song, "O' Haseena Zulfonwali," began to play, all Nysha wanted to do was fuck the world, jiggle her booty, and join the folks on the dance floor to "shake a leg." After all, Junglee boy, Shammi Kapoor, was an all-time favorite.

She looked around and tried to locate the birthday boy, but her eyes fell on Samar instead, and, oh boy, he did look gorgeous! In fact, he looked like one of those devilishly tempting models gracing the cover pages of men's lifestyle magazines, who could woo and lead to the "doors of hell," cajole one into eating the forbidden fruit of passion, and thereby lure one into giving in to their inmost secret desires. Dressed in well-fitted black jeans, with a crisp button-down blue ombre-effect shirt, it looked like he was there to play dirty and slay his prey. Nysha tried to look away, but it was too late. He had already caught her gawking at him. The unmistakable twitch of his lips and the slight smirk on his face gave her the apparent hint that she had caught his attention. Their eyes locked, and her heart started to pound violently in her chest. He smiled and walked toward her with suave vibes. As he approached her, his domineering frame became more evident, and it seemed like "Eros" had been way too kind in blessing a mere human with an overdose of "sex appeal." With his "sex on legs" vibes, he could slaughter just anyone tonight. He looked like such a snack that Nysha had to restrain her sleazy thoughts from getting wicked and slipping under the covers.

Damn! The shape-shifter and vampire romances of the paranormal world were surely messing up with her messed-up mind.

Finally, he stood before her; a soft smile played on his lips, while Nysha's eyes fell on his hands. He was holding a glass of what seemed like champagne. The manner in which his fingers curled around the delicate stem of the glass in a firm grasp made her imagine all the naughty things that could be a sheer possibility, with his perfectly crafted hands wrapped around the intimate parts of the human anatomy.

Sheesh! I could do with a breath of fresh air, she thought. The mere thought of all the raunchy stuff made her cheeks flush red and hot with inward embarrassment.

"Hey!" He said with a smile.

Oh my God! Does this man look more attractive up close? It involved an internal brawl not to gawk at him like a lovesick puppy when his six feet of "handsomeness" was standing just inches away. With the top two buttons of his shirt open, the toned muscles of his chest on display, and his sleeves rolled up to his elbows, he looked every bit like the tempting choco-drip cakes topped with strawberries and blackcurrants, too enticing to be resisted when all you wanted was to devour them immediately.

Pulling herself out of her trance, she tried to find her voice and speak with her parched mouth, "Hi," she said.

Her voice sounded more like a subdued squeak, even to her own ears.

She swallowed hard in order to lubricate her voice in an attempt to make it sound normal before speaking again. “Umm! The birthday boy, where is he?” she asked.

“Oh! He just went downstairs. Actually, a few of his American friends are here for his birthday. He went to fetch them,” Samar replied.

“I see.”

“Would you like anything to drink?”

“No, thanks, I’m good. I would rather stick to my no-drinking policy. You aren’t drinking much yourself. Go ahead, finish your drink,” she suggested.

He smiled and replied, “Took a sip. Realized I’m not a fan of this, anyway...” he leaned forward, making her shrug and take a step back instinctively. His proximity fused her brain cells, and though he smelled absolutely gorgeous, he made her feel dizzy and nervous. Keeping his gaze fixed on her face, he lifted his arms and raised his glass. In the process, his hands slightly brushed her collarbone, sending electric sparks up and down her spine. “There you go,” he said, as his aim hit the perfect spot behind her shoulder, and he placed his still half-filled glass on the server’s tray.

As he retreated his steps, Nysha’s heartbeat normalized. But the mischievous and deliberate grin on his lips was hard to miss.

Ah! Those slightly full lower lips, which looked so good on him. And then there was the kiss...The kiss that had burned her soul, the feel of his lips as he had slightly nibbled on her bottom lip, sucking and biting it again. He tasted like her favorite cookies, mocha, and hazelnut...That a kiss could leave her burning with smoldering passion and yearning for more had never once crossed her mind. But now that she had experienced it, could she go back and undo it? Not a possibility. Cause the way Dr. Samarjeet Attwal had kissed her, with the demanding strokes of his tongue, like she were the sole source of water under the scorching desert sun, was an experience and a memory that would remain forever etched in her mind.

She was snapped out of her reverie when Samar called out her name, "Hey... Nysha..."

"Yeah...," she replied.

"What...?" he asked.

"Ah! Nothing...." she was about to respond, when suddenly her eyes went wide, almost bulging out of their sockets. The sight she saw was definitely not a treat for sore eyes. Well, on second thought, perhaps it could be bliss for brutes and pervs who were busy feasting their eyes on the new guest as if she were the last bite of scrumptious chef's special dessert left on the crystal platter. And here she thought that perhaps an enjoyable night awaited her, and anyway, being a bit chummy with Dr. Attwal couldn't be all that harmful. After all, cold and uncaring could be the ways of the world, but not hers. At any given point in time, she would choose to be cordial over being resentful and bitter. But it seemed Mr. Lousy Fate had other plans in store for her. Well, of course, when was the last time that Mr. Fate had shown some real support in favor of her decision? And why on Earth would it belittle itself by changing the habit of a lifetime? So it chose to do what it was best at: cause mayhem and act kaput, heartlessly crushing Cupid's arrows and driving poor Mr. Cupid out into the realms of a parallel universe.

Samar was still eyeing her curiously, clearly expecting an answer. She gave him a rueful smile and then pursed her lips slightly. Taking a deep breath, she tried to answer in an utmost calm manner, which was quite a Herculean feat, considering her insides were seething with fury, akin to molten lava of anger en routing her nerves, and in turn penetrating her bloodstream. She batted her eyelashes in a dramatic flair and spoke in a beguiling manner... "Dr. Attwal, it seems you have company, my friend."

Confused with her response, Samar raised an eyebrow at her, while she beckoned with her eyes toward the club entrance. "Ishani...," her name rolled off his lips in an uneasy drawl.

Nysha walked past him, slightly brushing his arm, and whispering in his ear, "Have a nice time with your vohti, Dr. Attwal."

Samar frowned heavily at her and tried the effect of an icy glare. But she held his gaze in an "I dare you" fashion instead. The unmistakable hint of accusation in her eyes was hard to miss. Sighing deeply, he said, "Look, Nysha, I had no clue that Ishani was invited."

She scoffed and replied, "Of course, Dr. Attwal... Liar! Liar! Pants on fire!"

"Oh, come on, Nysha, if you want to believe... then believe! Or else you can go to hell, for all I care," he replied.

"But isn't that a place reserved for the likes of you, Dr. Heartless?" she gritted through her teeth, while making a pouty face.

"You seriously think I care? You are welcome to think the worst about me. Not that I'm going to die of insomnia."

With electrifying sparks flying haywire, their heated banter had almost transformed the environment into a battleground of sorts. Even with loud music playing in the background, Nysha swore that she could hear gunshots and smell gunpowder amidst cries for help. And just when she was contemplating whether she should use her (un)manicured nails to claw his face, she heard the jovial voice of the birthday boy from behind. "Hey, it seems you guys have already started without me."

Samar took a deep breath and shook his head in a huff as if trying to compose himself, while Nysha flashed her sharp teeth at Jay and spoke in a sugar-laced voice, "Of course not, it's nothing... important."

She went ahead and gave him a hug (more than a friendly one!), which seemed to have unsettled Samar to quite an extent, and that in turn gave a boost to her sadist alter ego.

Jay hugged her back and teased her sheepishly, "Whoa! That was quite a birthday gift, Ms. Patel. I didn't know birthdays did this to you."

Nysha laughed and punched him playfully on his arm before adding, "Quite a talker you are, aren't you, Mr. Beast? But I do have a birthday gift for you."

She handed him the gift bag, and it took him by surprise. He shook his head and said, "Wow! No way could you have known..."

"What?" she asked.

"That... this happens to be a favorite."

"Well, I did. And you simply can't go wrong with Mr. Depp, can you?"

Jay smiled and said, "Of course, you can't," he agreed. "Well, thank you so much," he added.

"You are welcome," she acknowledged.

In their exchange of pleasantries, Nysha had failed to witness that Ms. Kapoor had comfortably settled her ass on one of the cozy club chairs, just opposite to Dr. Heartless. She folded her hands on her lap and crossed her smooth and perfectly hairless legs. It seemed they were put up for display and a little appreciation, too. Looking at her legs, Nysha could only wonder if she was hairless down south, too. Chiding herself, she tried to clear her mind of the obscene thoughts, when her eyes darted toward Samar's face which held a foreboding look, as several defined wrinkles on his forehead marred his handsome features. But her heart skipped a beat, when she noticed that his eyes were fixated on her, as though studying her expressions. He held her gaze for some time, when she saw Ishani's hand reaching out to tap his knee, flaunting her immaculately manicured nails painted in blood-red. His severely creased forehead began to smooth considerably, his body relaxed, and he sank deeper into his chair while his lips curled into a hauntingly beautiful smile, the smile that made her breath hitch in her throat.

That smile...the damn smile should be banned, was the first thought which crossed her mind.

The second being, and especially when it appears like magic on his face at Ms. Kapoor's touch, as if it provided the much-desired soothing effect to his bruised ego. Bloody creep! Nysha thought.

"Nysha... hey! Are you listening?" Her stupor was broken when Jay called out her name.

"Of course... yes, tell me."

"Hmm! You haven't met my friends yet. Come, let me introduce."

"Yeah... sure, I would love to."

Jay reached out to her and gently wrapped an arm over her shoulders as he led her to where his friends were seated, just across from Samar and Ishani. "Nysha, that's Andy, Paula, Edward, and Alice, and here are the famous twins, Shauvik and Shanaya, the potential heir and heiress to the famous International Frozen Dessert Chain, Sugar & Candy Floss," he completed.

Nysha greeted each one of them with a smile. The twin, Shanaya, was an athletic girl who sported wavy shoulder-length hair with streaks of pink and blue. She had some bold tattoo designs done on her upper arm which intrigued Nysha. It made her look like a "Bratva She Boss," but nevertheless she was quite sweet. Nysha was pleasantly surprised that Jay had such amazing friends at his disposal. She easily mingled with them, and the flow of conversation had been so natural that it felt as though she had known them for eons. As the talks continued, Jay suddenly pulled her closer, and before Nysha could react, Shanaya blurted out in an excited voice, "Guys! Are we missing something here? Are you both seeing each other?"

"What? No!" both Jay and Nysha shouted in unison. The intensity of their denial was so strong that it left Shanaya and her friends shocked for a while, with their eyes wide open, but they recovered the very next moment, and all of them were shaking with laughter.

"Whoa! Seriously, guys! That was quite something," Shanaya gasped.

"Phew! Damn, that was hell scary," Nysha muttered.

"Excuse me! And this was quite mean," Jay spluttered out, whilst squinting his eyes at Nysha.

"Really now, mister! What were you even thinking?" she glared at him.

"Come on, stop it, you two!" Shanaya said, raising both her hands and her voice. She then continued, "Though you guys are absolutely hilarious, and we would have loved to witness your annoyingly cute banter, we are actually getting late for the cake-cutting ceremony. Everyone's been waiting."

Turning toward the rest of the gang, she exclaimed, "Aren't we all in agreement, guys?"

Needless to say, there were nods and murmurs of agreement.

As his friends and the rest of the invitees enthusiastically began to surge forward toward the cake display area, Nysha gently nudged at Jay's arm and then lifted an eyebrow at him questioningly, "Mr. Dhananjay Pawar, you owe me answers."

Jay narrowed his eyes at her and smiled mischievously, before replying, "Me? What did I probably do?" he shrugged.

"Mr. Beast, you know pretty well that there is nothing between us, and we aren't involved in a fling, and most definitely aren't a thing, and yet you were trying hard to give the impression that we are an item together... Why?" she asked.

Jay's expression changed, and suddenly it became more solemn. Then, squeezing her hand slightly, he said in the same breath, "Oh! That was just a little PDA at work to annoy my ex."

"Your ex is here!" Nysha blurted out in surprise.

"Hush, woman! You wouldn't want the world to know."

This time, however, Nysha's eyes glinted with mischief, and she said in a hushed tone, while making a feeble attempt at muffling her soft chortles. "Alright! Alright! Who's the lucky girl?"

Jay raised an annoyed eyebrow at her deliberate teasing.

"Aaa! Aah! Pardon, El Senor, slip of the tongue, you see." "Of course, what I meant was, who's the unlucky girl?" Nysha winked.

"Nyra Sharma... she is here with her current boyfriend. They are sitting on the heightened dining platform overlooking the bar area. And don't you dare throw a glance toward them," he warned.

"Are we talking about supermodel Nyra Sharma?" Nysha confirmed.

"Yes, we are. Also, her current boyfriend, Hridaan Roy, is the skipper of the Indian Cricket Team."

Suddenly Nysha's pupils dilated and concern flickered in her eyes. Mr. Beast was actually trying to make his ex jealous. Could he get more adorable? she thought.

Nysha intertwined her fingers with his and gave him a peck on his cheek before whispering in his ear, "Aww, poor baby! Well, let the world imagine that something is actually brewing between us. I'm ready to play along."

Nysha winked at him, whilst Jay smiled at her antics. And they both, together, walked toward the corner where their friends were eagerly waiting to start with the cake-cutting ritual, and also to mark the beginning of a long and crazy night ahead.

Meanwhile, from a distance, Samar had managed to follow Nysha's every move. She was wearing a mauve-colored sequin knee-length dress with an attached floral bow on her left shoulder. With minimal shimmery makeup and kohl-rimmed eyes, she looked gorgeous. But her best feature was her smile; it was genuine and carefree. Her soft chortles and giggles transformed her face from simply beautiful to breathtakingly mesmerizing. Her laughter reverberated in his ears, and it was the sweetest sound he had heard in a while.

"Dhananjay and Nysha seem to be really good friends, isn't that right, Samar?"

His thoughts were interrupted by Ishani's subtle query. Otherwise, from the time she had set foot inside the club, his eyes had hardly drifted away from her. Of course, he hadn't missed her cozy banter and equation with his cousin brother and his friends. And then there was this kiss! Though it had been just a chaste kiss, one perfectly suitable for friends, it had somehow managed to piss him off. He was baffled at how easily Ms. Patel could mess with his mind and tug at his heartstrings, all at the same time. Never had a woman bothered him as much as she did. He ran his fingers through his hair as he tried to shift his attention to the lady sitting right in front of him, clearly expecting an answer. Ishani was wearing a single-strap short red dress (in all probability self-designed) which hugged her curves almost like a second skin and the length of which sparsely covered the twin globes of her butt. With matching red and gold stilettos, big hula-hoop earrings, expertly done makeup, and perfectly painted lips, no doubt she did look stunning, almost like a diva. How she fluttered her eyelashes and the hint of a suggestive blush while talking to him was hard to miss. She definitely tried hard to keep him entertained with customary stories of models, ramp walks, and International Fashion Weeks, but unfortunately he found it boring and hence utterly difficult to follow her continuous jabbering. With his concentration amiss and the line of conversation dragging at a sluggish pace, Samar felt like a detainee who wanted to get rid of the shackles and disappear from the torturous scene, and being unable to do the same made him more and more irate with every passing second.

His mind was preoccupied with the feisty woman, full of spunk and zeal, who never thought twice before speaking her mind. She was like the prohibited fruit, tempting one to taste it, even at the cost of one's health. At the same time, she was also the antidote to cure one's sufferings. Samar had never been in two minds regarding a woman. His contradictory feelings of wanting to come close and yet staying far away from her at the same time were playing havoc with his mind.

"Samar! Hey, are you listening, or getting bored?" Ishani probed again.

This time, however, Ishani's sultry voice broke his reverie and snapped him out of his thoughts. A sheepish smile played on her slightly pouting lips. So, without wasting much time, Samar returned the favor by putting forth his best-practiced fake smile and replied, "Umm! No! Not bored at all. You were asking something."

"Aah! About Dhananjay and Nysha... are they together?" she repeated.

Samar's eyes darted toward Nysha. She was busy sipping her drink and deep in conversation with Jay and his friends. They all seemed to be in a jovial mood, completely enjoying themselves and having a gala time together. Time and again, he could see Nysha punching Jay's arm playfully, or him draping his arm over her shoulders and whispering in her ear, which would lead them both to laugh out loud. But there was nothing sleazy about their movements or body language. They were simply being friends and having fun, and that was the most normal thing to do and expected of a party thrown by a friend for friends. He, too, wished to join them, but instead was stuck up playing pal to the puppy-eyed lady, who expected him to keep her entertained, and now was clearly expecting a response to her query. He shook his head and replied, "Well, I don't think so. They bond well and are good friends."

"They seem to be having a really good time. We should join them too, what do you say?" she purred.

A smile threatened to escape his lips at the very thought of them joining Nysha and her newfound gang of friends. Well, for starters, the fact that she didn't like and approve of Ishani was hardly a secret. Samar could clearly remember the last time when they were all forced around the same table together, and the look of disdain which had crossed her face wasn't quite hard to reckon. Her deciding to give a cold shoulder and act weird with Ishani had confused him. Suddenly a thought crossed his mind. Could it be that she was jealous of Ishani? Damn! Why hadn't he thought about it earlier? Yes... of course, she had been jealous, very jealous indeed. In fact, she had reacted in the same way as expected from a disgruntled girlfriend. And wasn't it similar to what he had felt when he had seen Jay getting a bit too cozy with her. But of course, egoist Ms. Patel would rather choose to keep her feelings under wraps than to be honest and vocal about the same. Then again, he couldn't risk unleashing her firebrand potential by adhering to Ishani's request to join them. Nysha deciding to behave civilly by no means meant that she wasn't capable of turning savage. The chances, though minimal, weren't a risk worth taking. He took a sweeping look at Ishani. Clearly, her Chihuahua avatar wasn't quite a match to Nysha's Bull Terrier. But he couldn't say that to her face, could he? He had to come up with a better excuse, and he did.

"Well, we could. But let me get you a drink first. What would you like?" he asked.

Ishani looked at him as if he had just asked her to make out with him, and then promised a mind-blowing orgasm if she agreed to his request. The flirtatious look that she gave him underneath her lashes made her look like a whimpering kitten, and he couldn't help but wonder if there were special classes for pretend clawing and meowing, too. Anyway, he wasn't interested in an over-the-top seductress act and found it totally overrated. "Aww! How sweet of you! A Moscow Mule for me, please...," yet again she purred.

And could he do anything about it? Of course not... except for replying politely, "Of course, I will get it right away."

Starry Nights and Party Vibes (Chapter II)

Nysha found it really bothersome that Dr. Certified Heartless had nothing better to do other than babysitting a grown-ass Daddy's princess. Time and again as her eyes scurried toward their table, she found them busy talking, and each time Ishani's wide red-painted lips impeccably curved into a happy smile, she couldn't help but wonder if Samar could see through the charade of her celestial nymph act, while using her seductive prowess to the best of her abilities. Anyway, playing naïve and in need of protection was old school and so totally overrated. Though Nysha's heart went out to Samar, who it seemed, was caught up and entrapped in the web of lies and deception spun by the lady in red, there was little she could do to put some sense into his thick head.

Not that Dr. Attwal looked vulnerable or in need of any help. In fact, it appeared as if he was having a gala time and enjoying to the fullest with his "vohti-to-be." When he whispered something in her ears, and Ishani threw her head back to laugh at the 'best joke of the millennium,' Nysha felt something inside snap; her obvious patience and the pretense of acting civil were wearing out. In that single moment, she could have sworn on her forefathers, that given a chance she might have as well considered kicking both their ass cheeks, and sending them flying for an "early moon" to outer space, where they could lick and kiss each other's rears, for all she cared.

"Jackasses!" she thought aloud.

"Can we expect some real action, other than you both eye-fucking each other?" Shanaya scoffed at Nysha.

Taken aback at her raw choice of words, Nysha raised her eyebrows and, feigning innocence, replied coolly, "What are you talking about? And gosh! That was so crude."

"Absolutely! That's because I wanted it that way... Anyway, the point is, why are you wasting your time here, when the sexy siren is busy toying with your property?"

"Dr. Samar isn't anyone's property."

A subtle, coy grin spread across her lips at Shanaya referring to Dr. Heartless as her property. Truth be told, the savage in her loved the idea of owning someone as hot as him. Oh! How she would have loved to squeeze his perfectly shaped ass, one cheek at a time. As though her filthy thoughts had reached him via telepathy, at that very precise moment he decided to turn around. He looked at her with hooded eyes, and Nysha could literally feel color rise up her cheeks and turn flush simply with the impact of his gaze. His eyes traveled the length of her body, making an unhurried perusal of the same, and though she did try to hide her flustered state, she knew for sure that she was doing a pathetic job. With their eyes locked in an intense stare-down, they had both given up on the pretense of a "you don't exist game." The atmosphere felt charged with electrifying tension, when suddenly Shanaya got up from her chair with an abrupt jerk, breaking their palpable connection.

"Alright! Had enough...," she declared.

"Wait! What are you up to?" Nysha asked, bemused.

"Fun time, baby...," she winked.

Before she could prod for further clarification, Shanaya had already made her way to a table occupied by a gang of gorgeous ladies, each sophisticatedly beautiful in their own right. One among them had flaming red hair and was wearing a golden tiara, and a matching sash draped over her shoulder with the words "Bride to be." Surely, they were there to celebrate the bachelorette party in honor of the would-be-bride. Nysha was partly impressed and largely surprised at how easily Shanaya could blend with the girls and befriend them, as if she had known them for ages and had always been an integral part of their inner circle. She watched from a distance, when one girl in the group began to talk excitedly and her eyes shone with great interest. It made her wonder about the bait which Shanaya had thrown their way in order to lure them for a possible challenge and make their fun night all the more interesting.

After what seemed like a satisfactory closure to their discussion, Shanaya returned to her table, sporting a satisfied grin on her face, but it was her eyes which caught Nysha's attention, because they shone bright with evident mischief.

"What did you tell those girls?" Nysha asked.

"Patience, love; I just sprinkled a dash of adventure to make their special night a bit more enthralling. Anyway, the cat would soon reveal itself. Just wait and watch," Shanaya replied.

"Whatever that means!" Nysha shrugged.

After some time, Nysha saw the most excited face of the gang get up and ready herself for the task at hand. She tiptoed her way toward the bar area, swaying her hips in a dramatic flair while placing one foot in front of the other and walking with feather-light steps. Her entire demeanor was flirtatious and screaming for attention, which she got in ample amount. Heads turned as she crossed the tables and several sets of eyes followed her moves, but her eyes were fixated on the object of interest, "Dr. Samar." After all, he happened to be the bait for the night. The pretty lass settled her bottoms on a stool next to Dr. Heartless and tried to strike up a conversation whilst keeping her sultry smile intact. Nysha saw him reply to her queries, but he had a visible frown on his face, clearly annoyed by her moves and overly friendly gesture.

"What the hell is that?" Nysha asked, appalled.

"Hush! It's just a little game of temptation for raising the heat quotient. And don't you worry, no one's gonna seduce your property," Shanaya added with a wink, as if addressing her concern.

"Oh, come on now! For the second time tonight, Samar isn't anyone's property, least of all mine," Nysha quipped.

"Well then, good for you. Clearly, nothing to worry about," Shanaya retorted.

"Now, if you could please throw some light on the nuances of your little game," Nysha asked.

"Aww! Getting impatient, are we?" Shanaya teased.

"Cut the crap, what did you really tell them?" Nysha coaxed.

"I challenged them to a dare where they needed to have a date fixed with the handsome doctor. Simple," Shanaya stated.

"What? Why the hell would you do that? And why on Earth would they agree to something like this?" Nysha yelled.

"For a 100-dollar bill, who wouldn't?" Shanaya replied with supreme confidence.

"Wow! And why would you make such a dicky move?" Nysha asked, astounded.

"A little fun isn't bad, baby... Besides, he isn't even looking at her. I'm sure she's gonna lose."

Shanaya was right. Samar seemed to be in no mood for talks. He was just being gracious enough to acknowledge the pretty damsel's presence.

"Of course, he isn't a prick, who would flirt with other women when his wife-to-be is seated just a few feet away and watching his every move," Nysha defended.

"Really now, wife-to-be! Are you this dimwitted?" Shanaya questioned.

"Why? Did I say something wrong?" Nysha asked.

"Can't you see for yourself, his so-called wife-to-be could hardly hold his attention? Why do you think he has been killing time at the bar?" Shanaya reasoned.

Nysha's eyes scurried toward Ishani, who now had Jay and Paula for company. She looked absolutely gorgeous, and any man would have loved to have her by his side. Then why would Dr. Samarjeet Attwal differ and believe otherwise? Well, truth be told, it shouldn't have been her concern, he could be with anyone he wanted to be, and yet she found a sickening feeling settle in her gut at the thought of his interest lying elsewhere. She racked her mind for a plausible response, when suddenly Shanaya declared, "There, frowning beauty is back. Her scowl and sad pout bares it all. Poor baby, she definitely lost."

Shanaya was right. The pretty lady gave them a sorry stare and showed them a thumbs-down sign as if seconding Shanaya's claim. Her friends tried to cheer her up at her devastating loss. However, Nysha's heart flipped and did a happy dance inside her chest when she saw a seething glare cross Ishani's beautiful face. As hard as she tried to pretend that she wasn't watching, or perturbed at their steamy stunt involving Samar, Nysha had caught her in the act of throwing a disdainful look at sultry Challenger Number 1. Suddenly, Nysha found her bitchy and sadistic hormones becoming fully activated and jumping to and fro, while creating havoc in her system. She wanted to twirl around and dance. But instead, maintaining a stoical expression and her calm, she whispered to herself, "Small triumphs for big kicks! Take them all, Nysha."

Before she could get over her initial victory, she found Challenger No. 2 straightening her back and walking up to him with a vicious zeal to win the dare. Both Shanaya and Nysha followed her moves, and so did Ishani. This one, though, could keep him engaged for some more time in comparison to the first challenger. However, after a few more minutes, she was back in the pavilion without any luck at fixing a date.

One after another, the rest of the women followed suit and came back without any luck whatsoever. Finally, it was time for the bride to try her luck. She put a confident smile on her face and strolled toward Samar. With her red hair swaying and bouncing over her shoulders, she looked irresistible and mysteriously beautiful. The young lady began speaking to him with a small smile intact on her face. At first, Samar seemed to have been taken aback on seeing her. He looked confused and shot up an eyebrow at her. Nysha thought he was probably surprised at looking at her sash. After all, which bride leaves her bachelorette and shows interest in striking up a conversation with a stranger instead? However, after some time, his frown relaxed, and his lips curved into a smile, causing Nysha's heart to sink a little. She tried to spot Ishani to study her expression, but the girl was nowhere to be seen. Meanwhile, Samar and Ms. To-Be-Bride continued with their exchange of pleasantries. It surprised Nysha to see him way comfortable with an unknown girl. Was it because she was younger than the rest of the girls? Or did Dr. Samar prefer his women young and naïve?

Oh, men! How typical! She thought to herself.

As if echoing her thoughts, Shanaya declared in a singsong voice, "Oh! So he prefers younger women."

"Don't tell me you believe in that shit," Nysha gave her a reproachful look.

"Well!" Shanaya shrugged, defending herself.

"Don't you think that's a bit far-fetched a theory for you to believe in?" Nysha reprimanded.

Their arguments came to a halt when the red-haired lady got up from her stool. But Nysha was surprised on seeing Samar also follow suit. They shook hands at first, and then suddenly Ms. Bride-To-Be bear-hugged him tight, taking him by surprise. But slowly, on regaining his composure, he gently patted her back. When she returned to her table all excited, she was greeted with congratulatory thumps on her back, while whistles, hoots, and stomping of feet filled the surroundings at her big win.

Nysha was eyeing their table with disdain, when Shanaya grabbed her arm and pulled her up to her feet.

"Wait! Where to?" Nysha asked.

"Come on, sweet pea, Red Daisy owes us answers."

The very next moment, they reached the super-excited all-girls' table, and without wasting another minute, Shanaya directly came to the point,

"Seems like it's time to part with my dollars. So, you did manage to fix a date, you naughty tease," she winked.

"What? No! Oh my God! He is Samar bhaiya," Red Daisy blurted.

"Bhaiya!" Nysha exclaimed, stupefied, while Shanaya burst out laughing aloud.

Red Daisy looked annoyed and confused at her laughter, but Nysha muttered silently, "Care to explain..."

Red Daisy continued, "Actually, he and my brother are the best of friends. In fact, they went to the same Med School. He used to call me Red Riding Hood, you see."

"Interesting, he is your brother's best friend, and yet you failed to recognize him," Nysha mumbled.

"Oh, that! Actually, my distant sight is weak, and my lenses are causing trouble." She batted her eyelashes quite a few times, as if to substantiate her point.

"Noted, anything else we need to know?" Nysha asked.

Red Daisy winced slightly and replied, "No... Why?"

"That's what we need to know, love," Nysha asserted. "We are good, right? We weren't a part of your cozy stories over there, were we? I would like to believe that you didn't give us away," she stated.

Red Daisy shifted slightly in her chair and looked a bit uncomfortable. When she didn't reply immediately, Nysha's heartbeat began to increase, and her heart began to pump faster with every passing second, rushing blood through her veins. Taking a deep breath, she asked again, "Come on, sweets, we need to know," she pleaded.

Letting out a nervous smile, Red Daisy finally decided to spill the beans, "He took it in the right spirit. There is absolutely no reason to worry," she revealed.

"There-we-go," Shanaya started to laugh hysterically, while Nysha could literally feel tremors beneath her feet.

"I don't think you need to be so upset...," Red Daisy added in a yet feeble attempt to pacify her.

"Well, you know nothing at all," Nysha petted her head, feeling as sorry for the sweet bride as for herself.

"Absolutely nothing!" Shanaya agreed, as she continued with her laughter riot.

"Holy hell! I am a certified nutcase now. Do you even get it?" Nysha announced.

"Calm down, Nysha, you are overreacting," Shanaya tried to convince.

"Overreacting!" she shrieked. "Samar might think that I am a super-obsessed jerk."

"So, what do you propose doing? Now that the damage has already been done," Shanaya asked.

Nysha shook her head, and without wasting another minute, she grabbed her bag and swung it around her shoulder before replying, "Well, I prefer to follow the drill under these circumstances."

"Meaning?"

"Meaning... Exit."

As she darted toward the doorway in haste, all of a sudden, strong hands grabbed her arm and pulled her toward him.

"Fleeing the scene, soldier?" Samar whispered in her ear.

His calm and sexy voice along with his touch seeped warmth through her body.

"Samar! What are you doing? Let me go...," she called out in a hoarse whisper.

He pulled her closer, and she could feel his rock-solid chest and ribcage as her back pressed against his torso. "Let me go, Samar," she wiggled and twisted to get away from his grip, but was unable to do so. His proximity wasn't helping either. It made her weak and lose her mind.

"Easy, soldier! Relax! I mean no harm, but the fact that you pulled that dirty little trick on me, along with your friend out there, I could spank this pretty ass of yours right now, right here," he whispered seductively.

Nysha's cheeks heated and flushed at his upfront accusation.

Good Lord! Did he just use the words, ass and spank, or was it simply a flicker of her imagination? Was Dr. Samarjeet Attwal, the good doctor, capable of using such crude language? He really didn't say that, or did he? She thought.

"Excuse me? I really don't understand what you are talking about, Dr. Attwal. But this boisterous attitude doesn't suit you," she confronted instead.

Samar placed his palm on her waist and in a swift movement turned her around to face him before pulling her closer. "Drop the charade, Nysha, will you? Stuti told me all about your little stunt."

"Stuti!" She asked, confused.

"Aah!" His eyes twinkled and he chuckled with amusement before continuing, "Didn't even bother to find out the name of the bait you and your smart-ass friend there were using against me, did you?" he accused.

"Oh! Stuti...," Nysha nodded, pretending to recall her name.

"Rings a bell? I fondly call her Red Riding Hood. Not sure what you girls call her, though..."

"Samar, you need to believe this... it wasn't my idea, seriously."

His lips twisted in a smile, a bewitching one.

"You are no saint, Nysha. And neither am I. Lies, lies, and all lies, coming from that pretty mouth."

"No... Seriously," she replied indignantly. A rush of annoyance and anger coursed through her. Here, she was being nice to him, and he was calling her a liar, dare he?

Controlling her weary emotions and fighting the strange attraction she felt toward him, she replied with a straight face, "Alright, pull your hands off, doctor. You wouldn't want Ishani to be upset."

"Ishani! Really! Do you see her anywhere?" he asked wryly.

"She left?" Nysha asked, trying hard to control the rush of happy bubbles which floated around her mouth and threatened to escape and spread across her lips into a gleeful smile at her small evident coup.

"Well, thanks to your game. Not that I'm complaining. In fact, I'd be happy to hire your services in the future," he scorned. The next moment, he set her free, with him moving away from her.

Embarrassed, she looked at his handsome features which shone under the neon lights of the Club.

"That was a really stupid thing to do," she said faintly.

"Indeed, it was," he agreed laconically.

"But I will surely make it up to you sometime in the future," she added.

He gave her a hard, pinning glare while crossing his arms over his chest. It made her feel fuzzy and her heart fluttered in her chest like a caged bird. Before she could speak another word in her defense, Jay walked up to them. Standing right in front of them, and defying the pitch of the shrilling and pounding music which the DJ had just begun to play, along with the chiming and jiggling of musical instruments, he spoke in a loud enough voice, "Here you are! I was wondering why my favorite people are missing in action. Come on; join us on the dance floor."

Nysha shrugged her shoulders and spoke close into Jay's ear, "Sorry, Jay, but I will take my leave. I had a wonderful time, really enjoyed myself, enjoyed meeting your friends here... but it's late, you see...," she tried to explain.

"No way, stop being a spoilsport and acting like a nonna. Come on, the fun has just begun. We have the entire night at our disposal," Jay persuaded.

Nysha put her hands on her hips and looked at him with furrowed eyebrows before replying in a defiant tone, "Mr. Pawar, congratulations man... you already seem to be riding high. But you can't really believe that I would be spending the entire night dancing away."

"Stay," a voice commanded from behind.

Both Jay and Nysha turned around at the same time toward the familiar voice. She looked into his somber eyes first, and then toward his face, which held a passive look. The man was good at camouflaging his emotions, unlike her, whose expressions gave away her true feelings. If not a doctor, with his handsome features and acting prowess, he definitely could have become a good actor. When Nysha didn't respond, Samar strolled toward her and stopped just inches away. He bent his head and spoke softly, only for her ears.

"Stay back for a dance with me, Ms. Patel."

His warm breath fanned over her neck and tickled her ear, making her hyper-aware of his woodsy and citrusy scent. She swallowed hard in order to control her rasping breath and then replied indignantly, "Mr. Attwal, I can barely remember giving you the authority to order me around like an arrogant bull."

He tsked in a suave, husky voice which threatened to unnerve her and lose her cool charade. Oh! How she hated being scorned.

"And here I thought you sincerely wanted to make it up to me," he replied in an absolute calm tone, but his demeanor was challenging.

Nysha hated the fact that he could easily ruffle her damn cool feathers and equally calm ocean demeanor. But she couldn't let him know that. She also knew that accepting his challenge would be a stupid move, but her sense of pride wouldn't simply allow her to chicken out and give him the sheer pleasure of having an upper hand over her.

"Fine! A dance it is then. And we are even," she replied nonchalantly, as she spoke through gritted teeth.

"A dance indeed and you sure wouldn't regret it," he said earnestly. The last bit sounded more like a silent promise, but she chose to remain silent.

Nysha somehow knew at that instant that, willingly or unwillingly, she had entered into a labyrinth of emotions where a lot was at stake. That night when they danced to the music, with Samar twirling her around and pulling her back to him, and as she clung to his shirt for support, she realized that in the quest of saving "Akshat Ratna," she could end up losing more than what she had signed up for. She was not only losing the game, but also the battle of protecting her heart from Dr. Heartless himself.

JUDGEMENT DAY (CHAPTER I)

Finally, it was 'D-Day,' and Nysha was having a hard time rummaging and sorting through her clothes, but it was turning out to be a complete waste of time and energy. She couldn't find a proper dress that would look professional, and yet give a classy and ethnic vibe as well. Truth be told, under the current circumstances, dress should have been the least of her concerns, but her instincts hinted otherwise. With most of the Board members proudly belonging to the 'Boomer Gang,' she knew that attire did matter, since it could be her last and only chance to create the right impression and, in turn, convince the members of the absolute need for a 'Fund Raiser Event' involving celebrities.

After careful consideration and thorough speculation, Nysha pulled out and zeroed in on a fuchsia-pink georgette sari, which Akshat had gifted her with his saved pocket money. She had not worn it in years, but somehow, today, it felt like the perfect attire, or rather, the ideal choice for the said occasion. It was her way of paying a silent ode to him, perhaps for one last time, before drawing the final closure.

Nysha could effortlessly drape the six yards of pure magic, thanks to her dadi who would always eloquently vouch for the sari advantage. With a tuck of the sari pleats into the petticoat below the navel, and draping it elegantly over her left shoulder, she took one final look at herself into the mirror and was pleasantly surprised at the reflection staring back at her. With her hair tied in a loose messy bun, kohl-rimmed eyes, soufflé make-up, and shimmery pink lipstick, she not only looked different, but also quite pretty at that. Satisfied, she picked up her crescent moon earrings, matching neckpiece, and completed her traditional look with a matching glittery pink bindi in the middle of her forehead. She took a deep breath and silently whispered to herself, "Nysha Patel, slay it girl!"

It was already 8:15, and since the presentation was due sharp at 10 o'clock, she quickly hurried her way down the stairs. Under no circumstances, could she afford to be late. It would only give Mr. Pawar Senior the sadistic pleasure of jeering at her, and of course she couldn't promise him the satisfaction of the same. Upon reaching the staircase landing, she peeked into the kitchen and saw her mom busy with various chores, aided by Sushi. Nysha enquired about her dad, "Mom, where is dad?"

"He left early in the morning," Mrs. Patel replied. She fumed indignantly and asked, "Don't tell me, he isn't coming for the meeting today?"

Mrs. Patel walked out of the kitchen and looked at her. She took in her sari look, and her eyes held an appreciative gleam. She then replied in a pacifying tone, "Of course, he will. He will be there on time, don't you worry."

"He better be," she replied, still fuming slightly.

"Get some breakfast before heading out," prompted Mrs. Patel.

Nysha shook her head, "Nah, getting late, Mamma. But if you insist..." She quickly grabbed a piece of flat whole-wheat bread placed on the table, rolled it up and gulped it down with water. Then, grabbing the car keys from the punchbowl on the table, headed towards the door. Nysha was about to step out, when her mom called out from behind, "Nysha..."

"Yes Mamma..."

"All the best, bachcha... And you look beautiful in this sari. You sure Harsha wouldn't mind?" she asked tentatively.

"Trust me, Ma, she wouldn't. And thank you."

"Of course, you would know better," replied her Mom with a smile.

Driving through the heated weekday traffic and the swarm of busy, overcrowded pedestrians, Nysha managed to reach the hospital a good 50 minutes before the scheduled time. She directly headed to the Conference Room in order to check the settings, technical aids, and equipment, because she wanted to examine for herself and ensure a smooth presentation flow without any hitch or glitch as such. After conducting a thorough check and being assured about the arrangements, she breathed a sigh of relief. She slumped into a nearby chair and was about to pull out her laptop from its sleeve, when the sudden jarring sound of the door took her by surprise and alerted her mind. She looked up, and her heart skipped a beat when she saw Dr. Samar standing in the doorway.

One look at Nysha, and Samar stood numb and froze on the spot. It took him a moment to register, but when he did, he was unable to take his eyes off her. To say that she looked gorgeous would be an understatement. She looked beautiful—in fact, absolutely regal and stunning. He stood there stunned, taking in her garb. Her dreamy expression lent her a soft, feminine touch, and her honey-colored skin and lush lips made her look mesmerizing. God save him! She was breathtakingly beautiful, and her exotic beauty had forever branded itself in his memory.

Meanwhile, Nysha was hugely aware of his eyes doing a lazy perusal of her being. Sensing his gaze, she looked at him annoyingly, and a small frown on her forehead marred her beautiful features as he still stood in the doorway, completely transfixed and riveted.

"Hey, are you just going to stand and keep staring, Dr. Heartless?" she demanded angrily.

His lips twisted into a small grin at her obvious accusation. "Well, I could keep staring all day, the view from here is lovely," he said mischievously.

"Oh! Come on, will you?" she rebuked.

Samar slowly walked into the hall with brisk steps. He could see that she was apprehensive, and he was eager to join her and help her get over her nervousness. Taking a seat across from her, he asked, "So, you ready?"

"Yeah... well, I really don't know," she replied earnestly.

"Don't worry, you will be just fine," he said with a smile, as he covered one of her hands with his own in an assuring manner, sending a spark down her spine with his subtle touch. For a moment their eyes met, and Nysha wanted him to just hold her in his arms and kiss her "good luck." As usual, his proximity was messing with her sane mind.

Damn! Sexy Sam was a menace, and a handsome one at that, she thought.

Shaking off her stupid thoughts, she quickly got up from her chair and began pacing up and down the room, a usual drill she engaged in to calm her tensed nerves. But today it wasn't helping. Perhaps his company was to blame.

Samar watched her intently as she increased the pace of her strides and began walking back and forth the hall, muttering gibberish to herself and giving out her anxious demeanor. Heaven! The girl was a ball of curled-up mess, and wasn't she messing with his brain cells as well? Unable to take it any longer, he muttered a curse under his breath and rose to his feet. He walked up to her and caught hold of her delicate wrist, taking her by surprise, but nevertheless she didn't pull back; instead, she looked at him with an annoying frown which tempted him to kiss her right away. But he pushed his outlandish thought to the back of his mind.

"Samar, what are you doing?" she asked, bewildered.

"For once, you don't get to question me," he said assertively as he walked toward the door, pulling her along.

"Samar, we can't go anywhere...," she said, as they strolled past the corridor.

"Why?" he stopped for a while and looked at her, challenging her refusal.

"Because... well, we don't have much time."

"We have 30 minutes, half an hour to be precise. Come on, Nysha, you are a nervous wreck right now. In this state, no matter how well you are prepared, you won't be able to deliver. For once, can't you trust me?" he asked sincerely. A small smile escaped her lips at his earnest request, making it hard for him to breathe.

"Did she realize how every small gesture of hers was starting to affect him?" he mused.

She slipped her hand into the crook of his arm and said in a soft slur, "I trust you, Dr. Heartless. Come on, take away my restlessness and soothe my tense nerves."

In five minutes' time they were seated at the hospital cafeteria, with two cups of black coffee (aka muddy puddle water), one empty glass, and a bottle of coke placed in front of them, with Nysha throwing a questioning glance at him.

"Why did you bring me here?" she asked with a raised eyebrow.

"Patience, love," he said, as he took the empty glass and mixed coffee and coke in the proportion of 2:1.

Pushing the glass toward her, he commanded softly, "Drink."

"Seriously, Samar, is this your weird idea of soothing my nerves? And how sure are you that this poison isn't going to kill me?" she charged.

He chuckled softly and replied in an amused tone, "Well, you are right about the poison thing. This is real poison, and it's absolutely wrong on my part to recommend it to you. This could endanger my medical license, love. But sorry to disappoint you, this is non-fatal, and my best solution at present for your edgy nerves. Besides, I wouldn't risk your life for anything in the world."

The last bit spoken made her heart take a flip inside her chest.

"Why wouldn't you risk my life?" she asked curiously.

"Because... I like your..."

"Like my...?" she pushed.

"I like our cute banters, pretty lady," he guffawed.

"Moron!" She said through gritted teeth.

"Now drink, Missy, we don't have all day," he chuckled.

Judgement Day (Chapter II)

With each set of eyes in the room swiveled toward her, Nysha could feel the undercurrent of tension floating in the air. She tried to look all calm and composed, but the reality was way different from her cool exterior. Her insides were literally quivering, and though Samar did teach her a trick or two to do away with the tension and over-thinking, the mounting pressure of performing well, and most importantly, saving 'Akshat Ratna' from falling into the clutches of ruthless, money-minded investors was taking a toll on her mental stability.

She looked around and found the expectant faces of Dr. Harsha, Papa Patel, Jay, and Samar smiling at her encouragingly. While there were others like Senior Pawar along with his friend, Ashish Kapoor (whatever the hell he was doing there!) with their permanently imprinted sneers and demeaning looks, which she gladly chose to ignore.

Taking a deep breath and recalling a small prayer in her mind, she began. After around twenty minutes of continuous speaking, finally when she stopped, there were murmurs and silent whispers among the board members. But contrary to the previous time, this time they were throwing appreciative glances toward her, and from the looks of it, seemed quite impressed with her delivery too. Before she could get a hold of their genuine reactions, there was a round of applause from the corner of the room where her sweetheart cheerleaders were seated. Slowly, the other Board members joined in, and the applause became even louder. But the smug look on the 'Anti-Cheer Squad' retained its place, and though she cared two hoots about the same, somewhere the vibes weren't right. She could sense that something gruesome was definitely on its way, and her instincts proved just right, when Senior Pawar cleared his throat declaring his intention to voice his much-awaited and weighed opinion.

While the entire room was abuzz with activity, and Nysha was looking forward to moving on to the next phase of her plan, Senior Pawar and his bunch of loyalists sported a grim expression akin to attending a funeral sermon. In fact, Senior Pawar's eyes shot angry sparks at her, leaving her to speculate as to what sin had she committed to set his demon soul free and charge at her like a fucking angry bull set loose on the prowl.

"Thank you for your...," Pawar senior paused for a while, as if rummaging through the shafts of his hard-wired brain cells and searching for just the right word from his vocabulary to hurl an insult at her. At other times, it wouldn't have mattered much, but with her loved ones around, it definitely stood a concern, since Nysha could sense his strong contempt for her, and the extent to which he could stoop in order to taint her image was even beyond her imagination.

"Well, that was quite an impeccable presentation, Ms. Patel," he finally declared, with a plastered smile on his lips, which seemed more like poisonous viper fangs, and Nysha had a sudden strong urge to take a step back. But nevertheless, she maintained a straight face, and tried not to flinch, all for the sake of professionalism.

Doctor Pawar continued, "Well, Ms. Patel, I can see that everything about your proposed fundraiser event is hunky-dory. You sure wouldn't mind addressing a few of my concerns, would you?"

"I would be more than happy to rest your concerns, Dr. Pawar," Nysha replied with forced graciousness, when all she wanted was to snarl at him.

He leaned back in his chair and stretched his legs with an air of evident superiority. The likes of Doctor Pawar made her skin crawl with disgust, but then there was nothing she could do to escape the situation, other than wait for him to voice his actual concern.

"Well, Ms. Patel, celebrities coming together for a charity cause to save the grace of a hospital is all very heart-touching. A starry celebrity night with the current crushes and national heartthrobs seems like the promise of a binge affair, which apparently, as we all can see, has managed to impress quite a few in the room," he said with a pause, and then looked toward Jay and his team. His nostrils almost flared as he tried hard to control his irritation as his very own son and nephew had decided to switch sides. For a moment, Nysha's heart went out to him. Can there be a worse betrayal than this? Backstabbers! Jay &... well no Veeru (but sexy Sam!), she pondered. She really felt sorry for him, but regretted the very next moment when he dared to pass an absolute crass comment.

"Well, pardon my words, but just being close to a Bollywood actor can't really be your license to succeed...," he hissed with a contemptuous smile. His words felt like vicious cuts on her skin, as if someone had just stripped her of her dignity in public. The room went completely silent, and her turbulent heartbeat was now audible to her very own ears. She wanted to turn on her heel and make an escape, but her parents had taught her better. No matter what, she couldn't, and wouldn't flee.

Taking a deep breath to lubricate her voice and swallow her simmering anger, she replied, "Dr. Pawar, Zain is family, and if anyone has an issue with that, it's their problem and not mine. Also, I don't remember using him or his stardom as a benchmark for Cosmos's success. I would never speak about something unless I, myself, am not sure of it. Everything represented in the slides was purely based on evidence and research. I, for one, wouldn't engage in a pompous act."

Caught off guard at her assertive retort laced with honey-coated sarcasm, he tried defending himself, but then it was late, because the tigress's manicured claws were already out, and there was no hauling them back without pouncing on a few nasty faces, and scratching them black and blue if required. She held out her hand at him, palm outward, at the very first word which threatened to come out of his uncouth mouth, indicating that he needed to stop, and that she wasn't even close to being done yet.

"Well, on second thoughts, Dr. Pawar, since Zain has been insisting from day one itself that his own charity would be more than willing to actively collaborate on the 'Akshat Ratna Project,' I do think that it's a good opportunity, actually. With his celeb profile and backing, the Event would garner even greater exposure and free media coverage, and that's a recipe for sure-shot success." She paused for a while, and then smiling treacherously, and with a vicious glint in her eyes, she added, "Thanks for the suggestion, Doctor Pawar. As they say, brilliant ideas stem from brilliant minds... and this, Uncle Pawar, is a pure gem. Well, experience does matter after all!" she praised.

Shifting her attention to the rest of the members in the room, she continued, "Well, ladies and gentlemen, the Event just got bigger and better!" (She had wanted to say juicier, but restrained herself). "So what are we waiting for... come on now, put your hands together for a huge round of applause for Dr. Pawar," she concluded savagely.

While the room vibrated with loud cheers and a huge round of applause, it raised the benchmark for a showdown between the adversaries, scaling up the boundaries of their unspoken animosity.

Zain to the Rescue

Angry! Dead angry! Holy Shit... scary angry! Well, 'angry' did seem like an underrated term for what she was feeling at present. She was seething with fury and unadulterated rage. Seated inside Harsha Aunty's cabin, Nysha was burning with frustration in her heart. All she could think of was seeking revenge from monster Pawar for all the unfair things he had accused her of, and belittling her image to that of a bathroom rug.

"Nysha... dear, the presentation went really well. So, what happened? Why simmer your own blood?" Jay dared to ask her, thereby unleashing the fury of the Dragoness.

"What happened? Seriously? The douchebag Pawar happened, Jay... Can't you see how he hates me?"

"That was damn rude!" Samar muttered.

"Oh no! No! No! Dr. Samar, it isn't even half rude, considering what I actually want to do to him."

"And what would that be?" Jay asked curiously.

She squinted her eyes at him and replied, "Trust me, you wouldn't want to know."

"Try us," pestered Samar.

"Alright, you asked for it. I would love to throw him off the cliff, to a bunch of bloodthirsty zombies who would be more than happy to convert him into one of their own kind, or perhaps, feed him to hungry sharks. At least they would thank me for his plump ass."

"Wow! Are you over with your savage ideas, or are there more at your disposal?" Samar asked, part surprised and part amused at her angry disposition and outbreak.

"Well, one more, actually," she replied with a maniacal glint in her eyes.

"Shoot...," said Jay.

"What about locking him up in a room full of vampires so that they can sink their teeth into his neck and suck out his vile blood, all for humanity's sake, of course?"

Harsha Aunty gasped in amazement, while Jay's mouth went agape slightly in rude shock. Nysha threw him a spiteful look and commented with a snobbish flair, "Close your mouth, Pawar junior. All you are attracting are flies."

"You seem to have forgotten that he is my dad, don't you?" muttered Jay.

"And for Heaven's sake, he is a Senior Board member, and my uncle at that," added Samar.

"Alright! That's news! Pawar uncle has admirers, it seems," she guffawed.

"Calm down, baccha, I understand your spite. After all, he has been really mean to you. But currently, there are more pressing matters at hand that you need to be bothered about," Aunt Harsha intervened.

"Well, Aunty, quite a number, actually," she replied softly.

Samar looked at her with slightly furrowed brows, throwing her a questioning gaze. Nysha looked away, pretending to suddenly find the framed pre-pregnancy care poster hanging on the wall more mesmerizing than looking at his accusing eyes.

"Why do I get the feeling that something is really amiss? Care to explain?" Samar asked.

"You simply don't appreciate anything that I do, do you?" she retorted defensively.

"Well, your accusing tone isn't helping much. Penny for your thoughts, Ms. Patel?" Samar inquired resolutely.

"Alright... the bit about Zain's charity being interested was a last-minute add-on," she answered nervously.

"We... all... know... that... and...," Samar said with deliberate and definitive pauses after each syllable. He continued, "But that's the truth, right? Or is there more?"

"I don't know that... yet," she replied with a sorry pout.

"What?" All the three members present in the room exclaimed in unison. A mixture of horrific emotions reflected on their faces, which of course didn't soothe her jumpy nerves. Worse, it made her jumpier.

"For Heaven's sake, you decided to bluff?" Jay started.

"I had to say something in my defense," she declared.

"Ms. Patel, you are not allowed to create feel-good stories with mushy happy endings in a boardroom presentation," Samar asserted.

"I hate to agree with them, but they are right, beta," Harsha Aunty added gently.

"And don't I know it all!" Nysha exclaimed. Taking a deep breath, she continued, "Ok, let me end what I started... Call Zain, and ask what he has to say. Come on; let's hear it directly from the horse's mouth, what do you say?"

The room was still filled with an uneasy silence, but Nysha considered it their silent approval. She went ahead and dialed Zain's number, their final hope and the probable messiah of her current distress.

The call went through, and luckily for her, Zain answered on the third ring itself. "Thank Goodness! You picked up... I thought you wouldn't answer," Nysha cried out in relief.

"Oh, cut the crap, wifey's bestie! You know I wouldn't dare miss your call even if I were off on a Moon mission," Zain replied.

"Well, isn't that a bit preposterous, bestie's hubby? There aren't any mobile towers in space."

"Ok! Perhaps, not a Moon or Mars mission, but I would have answered your call even if I were busy with Oscar-winning director, Kuldeep Ray."

"Are you serious?" she asked.

"Well, actually, no... But I would have answered even if I were to be with any big Bollywood biggie. Like, I am answering now," he stated.

"Now, that's being honest. I thought so. By the way, which Bollywood biggie are you with at present?" Nysha asked calmly.

"Anirudh Ghosh, does it matter? You aren't here to inquire about my upcoming projects, are you? So cut to the chase and spill," he said impetuously.

"Well, I have a problem," Nysha said, coming straight to the point.

"I knew it. Small or big?" Zain inquired.

"Well, it is big. And I need your help, dude," she replied.

"Now, lady... I am listening. Speak...," he coaxed.

"Wait! Zain, could you video call me?" Nysha inquired.

"What? Why should I do that? We are already talking, aren't we?" he asked, annoyed.

"Of course, we are. But I have company, and I would want them to be a part of the bargain too," Nysha pleaded.

"Nysha... honey, I am in the middle of a look test for AG. It's a period drama and fantasy. He would go mad if my look is revealed, and needless to say, throw me out of the project too," Zain replied earnestly.

"Seriously! And who would be interested in doing that? Two senior doctors and an investment banker... Sorry to burst your bubble, Zain, but we don't run a cine gossip magazine, or a cine news tube channel. Besides, don't you trust us?" she said through gritted teeth.

"It isn't a matter of trust. It's about the damn video call," Zain hissed.

"Ultimately, it all comes down to trust... If you do, then please call," she pushed.

"Alright. Have it your way, you mad woman," he sighed exasperatedly.

The very next moment, Zain video-called Nysha. She scouted for a place on the table to position her phone at an angle where the faces of Jay and Samar would be visible, while she sandwiched a chair between them and settled her bottom on it. Then taking a deep cleansing breath, she answered the call, only to find a bare-upper-bodied Zain with protruding muscles staring back at them.

"Holy F*!" the cuss word had almost threatened to escape her mouth, when she bit her lower lip hard and sucked in a swift breath, quickly pushing her panic-stricken tongue inside her mouth, before the words could roll off her lips. Getting a hold of herself, she asked him in an almost calm but shaky voice, "For Heaven's sake, Zain! Why are you dressed...I mean undressed like the Greek God of Desire?"

"Adonis...," he replied.

"What?" she asked.

"Greek God of Beauty and Desire," he stated.

"Seriously! Is that important now?" she shrieked.

"I already told you...I am in the middle of a look test," he justified.

"Where are you now?" Nysha asked.

"In my vanity, why do you ask?"

"Please cover your naked state with something...You are causing visual noise and giving me a migraine."

"And you are overreacting. I'm not someone with a swollen belly from the Bodi clan. I have been working hard on my body. Celeb photographers are dying to lock a date with me for an exclusive photo shoot. You could ask Mehtaji," he further clarified. "And you give me this nasty reaction. That's clearly an insult," he ranted, as he draped a towel around his bare torso.

"I agree...," muttered Jay beneath his breath.

Zain smiled at him, and he introduced himself, thereby making her job easier and sparing her from the added chore of making formal introductions. As far as Samar and Aunt Harsha were concerned, he was already fairly acquainted with them.

"Seriously, guys! To what do I owe the pleasure of calling two very-dumb-headed individuals my close friends?"

"That depends on you," Zain said with a wink.

"When you are in deep waters, you are not really expected to be in a sane state of mind, Mr. Zaidi," Samar joined in.

"Well said, Dr. Attwal...," Zain applauded.

Nysha added with a sly smirk, "Aww! If you guys are done with your super-cute and adorable display of bromance, can we please move on to the actual concern at hand?"

"Sure lady, we are eager and waiting," Zain announced.

The next few minutes were spent on explaining about the proceedings of the boardroom, and also about what had transpired between Dr. Pawar and her. Zain listened to her with undivided attention. Once she was done, he took some time to respond thoughtfully, "Well, that was such a devilishly risky move, darling..."

"I agree. Trust me, I do. But I had no option left."

"I understand... he was being judgmental and unfair... perhaps even nasty... but you can't let that get to you," Zain explained.

"Ok. So, now aren't you getting late for your shoot, or look test, or whatever it is...," she said in a dismissive tone.

"And for once, stop being a loudmouth and a manipulative bully. You need my help, so you've got to ask nicely, like a lady..."

"Like a lady, is it?" she snorted.

"Yes... try it. It isn't so hard," Zain nagged playfully.

"Of course... Puhleazee Zain, would you help your friend in distress?" She rolled her eyes and joined her hands together, and even tried to sound annoyed and fretted. But everyone knew that she clearly loved the harmless harrying by her friend.

"Oh, stop it, miss. You aren't even half convincing... and a terrible actor at that. So save us the torture. Here, I am messaging you Zarin's number. She heads the entire operations at 'Panah-E-Aamna.' Get in touch with her and spare me the horror. She aces the 'Celebrity Game,' and she will help you with the event. In fact, she could even help you arrange for additional funds. You see, some people do have a lot of money. All you need to know are the exact pressure points to extract the same. So, all the very best for your virtuous endeavor, wifey's bestie."

"Thanks a ton, bestie's hubby. You made my day."

"Also remember, Pia and I will always have your back, no matter what," Zain added.

"Yeah, I do...," Nysha replied.

A small frown appeared on his face, before he continued, "Alright, don't take my words too seriously. They were uttered out of sheer courtesy. Don't bother my woman with your calls."

"Really! How very chivalrous! A gentle reminder, moron, your woman was and is my friend first... Your husband's role-playing started quite recently...," Nysha replied savagely.

"Whatever! But I am the leading man... and for God's sake, she is in her last trimester."

"Pia is much stronger than you could ever imagine, Sissy. And that's for us to decide. You don't get to fix the terms of our relationship..."

Nysha was ready to spit some more fire, when Zain waved her off with a dismissive gesture of his hands and said, "Ok, this isn't going to end anytime soon, and I can't afford to lose this much-needed role. So, I will take my leave, gentlemen," he said to both Jay and Samar. Then his eyes searched for Aunt Harsha, and taking the cue, Jay turned the phone toward Doctor Harsha...

"Love you, Harsha Aunty... Any help, just a call away...," Zain gestured with his hand.

Finally, turning to Nysha, he said, "You better rock the show... don't disappoint us."

"I won't... dumb...," Nysha replied with an eye roll.

"And I love you...," he blew her a flying kiss.

"I hate you... moron...," she said with a soft chuckle.

"Suits me... Take care, darling." With that, he finally ended the call.

"Ah! At long last...," Nysha sighed with relief.

After all, superstar Zain did manage to put an end to the cause of all their worries and distress, thereby allowing them to breathe a sigh of temporary relief.

"Alright, guys! Let's set the ball rolling, and kick-start Project Akshat Ratna," Nysha screeched in her trademark over-enthusiastic voice.

LONAVALA CULTURE & SPORTS CENTRE

When Nysha had agreed to a Celebrity Fundraiser, she had no idea regarding the sheer craft, patience, and degree of tactfulness involved in dealing with celebs and their infamous temper tantrums. Not to mention, dealing with their PAs or Talent Managers was a torture in its own right. Because, for one, they considered themselves to be bigger celebrities than the stars they represented, and two, most of them were... well, (pardon the words!) dickheads and nosy oafs with inflated egos.

Nysha was having a hard time overseeing the stage preparations in the scorching summer heat. Though the aesthetically designed, dome-shaped modern-day amphitheater with a responsive artificial intelligence system incorporated into it, and proper vents to mediate airflow and light, was an architectural marvel in itself, but since the carpentry and maintenance crew were still at work, and the installation of air conditioners were yet to be complete, the unendurable heat had left Nysha and her team puffing and sweating like obese WWF wrestlers. Avni, the youngest and the most pampered of their troupe, was drinking water from her personalized copper sipper, while gently dabbing her face with micellar water-infused wet wipes to remove the dirt and sweat from it. Meanwhile, poor Aashita was experiencing one hell of a time trying to schedule the stage rehearsals, while finalizing and supervising the technical aspects of the stage setup. Not the one to take unprofessional behavior lightly, she gritted her teeth while maintaining a forever fake smile on her face when dealing with the stars and their loyalty-galore bunch of sidekicks. Exhausted after an entire day's drill, Aashita settled her ass on the chair next to Nysha and gave her a foreboding look.

"We are in hell! Literally!" she quipped.

"And don't you think I already know that? Don't worry, I will keep you company," Nysha said, as she agreed with Aashita, while rubbing her temples.

Aashita rolled her eyes and scoffed at her in a "dare you" fashion, before speaking again, "Whatever! But what exactly do you propose doing with the goddamn overly friendly designer, Aryan Kundra?"

Nysha shot a questioning eyebrow at her and said, "Seriously, love? I thought we had awfully better tasks at hand. But anyway, what about him?"

"Really, Nysha! Aren't you able to see for yourself... the damn man... is salivating over poor Avni. He is practically a predator on the prowl..."

"Oh, come on, Mother Hen, you are being unreasonable now. You are making it sound like he is a pedophile," Nysha said, as she propped her chin in her palms and her eyes darted toward Aryan, who was wearing a sleeveless gold t-shirt and red-colored dhoti-styled suit pants (whatever it was, the man did justice to it). A smile crossed her lips when she saw him pass a mocktail in a slender, high glass toward Avni. It had a little umbrella attached atop, a curly straw dipped in, along with a slice of lime wedged onto the salt-coated rim (where the hell did he get one!). The young girl sure was enjoying her share of undivided attention.

Nysha hollered at them, "Yo ho! Guys! Over here! Hey

Aryaaaaaannnnnn! Care to pass a few drinks, darling... Come on, we are slogging too... aren't we?" she winked.

Aryan winked back and signaled a thumbs up toward them while a pink blush swept across Avni's cheeks at her suggestive gesture.

"Oh, my God! Is she blushing...?" Aashita asked in an almost accusing tone.

"Shut up, Aashi, don't you dare judge them. I know the poor fellow... he is a harmless flirt... or who knows? Perhaps, he might be serious this time."

"Really?" Aashita slouched back in her chair, while a cute frown and a slight pout adored her beautiful features. "Don't know, but I still find him a bit weird," she affirmed.

Nysha punched her playfully on her arm and whispered in her ear, "Well, too bad... not everyone is lucky enough to lay their hands on one Raghav Baruah."

"Hey! That was so mean... and that's not what I meant...," Aashita was about to offer an explanation, when she saw the mischievous glint in Nysha's eyes, and she stopped. She wasn't letting her friend bait her into snapping back just for fun.

Suddenly, Aashita rolled her eyes in an animated fashion and let out a soft whistle, whilst gesturing toward the entrance. Nysha turned around and found Dr. Heartless, who was walking toward them, and was closely followed by Ishani, the personified queen of animation herself.

Both of them stopped at arm's length, and Nysha could swear, her heart beat had suddenly paced up its rhythm. Ishani had wrapped her hand possessively around the crook of Samar's arm, making her flinch internally.

It took tremendous restraint on her part to camouflage her evident disgust and prevent it from making an appearance on her face. While Samar did manage to gently pull off his arm from her vice-like grip, all Nysha wanted was to channel her inner sorceress potential and make the enticing temptress disappear from the face of the Earth. Nysha was surprised, or rather shocked at her own line of thoughts. She had never come across as a jealous Aunty, and neither did she intend on behaving like one. She had no damn business whatsoever yearning for him, especially when all she ought to be sharing with him was only professional interest, but her treacherous heart, it seemed, was in a mood for rebellion.

Hell! Dr. Heartless always managed to bring out the worst in her. Another reason to maintain safe distance from the potentially dangerous man, she thought.

Schooling her thoughts and issuing herself an internal lecture, she braced herself to face the current not-so-congenial situation. If Samar wanted a prim and proper, sexy siren, possessive, and damn fuckable woman as his arm candy to flaunt out to the world, he could go ahead with it. There was no stopping him. On the contrary, she would wish him all the luck with every torturous minute that would follow him, and which Ms. Pretty Perfect was sure to bring along in her wake. He deserved to rot in hell, and well, Ishani was the perfect choice to keep him company there. In fact, she could potentially dish out a few entertaining recipes for the bored keepers of Hell. In her mental brawl with the taunting, demeaning and overtly critical inner voice, she had almost forgotten about the prying and questioning glances which Aashita was throwing her way. Her generally sweet and patient friend was getting a bit, or rather impatient, now. Taking the cue, Nysha began, “Aashita, he is Dr. Samarjeet Attwal.”

Aashita extended her hand and said, “Finally, Dr. Attwal, pleasure to meet you.”

"Same here," he acknowledged with a smile.

Not the one to be left out, FOMO Queen Ishani extended her perfectly manicured hand with lavender-painted nails toward Aashita and trilled, "Hi, I am Ishani, Aryan's colleague, and partner for his new label, ArIsh."

"Hey, nice to meet you," Aashita offered rather sweetly.

Suddenly, they heard a loud squealing sound which came from the far end of the theater. It sounded more like the harsh shriek of a guinea fowl, and kind of ruined their picture-perfect spell of customary greetings and mushy courtesy exchanges. Upon deciphering the source of the same, they found Aryan waving toward Ishani, who by now was waving back with equal enthusiasm, screaming like a banshee in an attempt at yelling their heads off. Both Nysha and Aashita stared at her with a look of complete disbelief. Just a moment ago, Ishani had presented the picture-perfect version of her calm, composed, most elegant, and collected self. On the other hand, Samar seemed clueless, and he groaned internally when Nysha threw him a cursory icy glance, clearly an accusing one, at his probable choice of women. To make matters worse, Ishani tugged at his arm at the very moment and asked him in a demure tone, as if seeking his permission to go and meet her long-lost friend, "Samar, you wouldn't mind... if I..."

Before Ishani could complete her request, he nodded his head in approval and replied, "Of course, you should. He seems to be getting rather impatient," he added in a brusque tone.

Smiling like a phony bimbette, she scurried her way toward Aryan and Avni. Aashita too excused herself, on the pretext of checking out and scheduling the stage rehearsals with the dance troupes and their assigned choreographers. In reality, however, she had actually wanted to dish out some alone time to her friend and the heart doctor in order to sort things out, as well as to accept the obvious electrifying sparks that existed between them, instead of simply feigning disinterest or opting for absolute denial.

"Umm... So, did you guys come together?" Nysha asked in an accusatory tone.

"What? No! Why would you say that?" he paused and looked at her with furrowed eyebrows before smiling wryly in an amused manner.

"Well, both of you did walk in together, didn't you?" she further added.

"There is a difference, Nysha. And just for the record, we simply happened to reach the same place at the same time. That's hardly a crime...," Samar clarified.

"Hardly...," she scoffed.

Samar took a step forward and held her gaze, as if delving deep into her innermost thoughts. "Tell me, Ms. Patel, what bothers you more? Is it simply my presence, or does that, coupled with Ishani's, make it all the more irksome?"

Undeterred by his proximity and her raging heart, she took a step forward, challenging his superior demeanor, "To bother me, Doctor Attwal, you should mean something to me. I certainly don't remember giving you that privilege. So stop flattering yourself," she said defiantly.

"Ouch! That was savage," he said dramatically, placing a hand over his chest.

"And unlike you, I most certainly don't have time for some cheap antics. So if you could please excuse me, I have work to do," Nysha stated.

"Sure, go ahead, and do whatever you need to do. Who's stopping you?"

"You!" Nysha had wanted to yell out loud, but instead bit her tongue and swallowed her words. She couldn't allow him to walk out with the credit of ruffling her feathers.

"Well, Dr. Attwal, I can't thank you enough for letting me do my job, and you can go back to doing yours," she said with a sneer.

"What do you think I am doing?" he questioned.

"Certainly not your job," Nysha replied.

"Definitely, my job," Samar retorted.

"Wait! You can't be serious about wanting to supervise a bunch of dance rehearsals," Nysha accused.

"Why not? Besides, dance is not the prerogative of only a select few, or is it?" he asked coolly.

"No, suit yourself," she said while stomping her feet, when all she wanted was to push him hard and send him rolling down the stairs.

The air around them thickened with sparks of resentment and tension when Nysha felt a slight tap on her shoulder. It was Aashita. Concerned, she asked, "Hey, is everything ok?"

"Yeah... perfectly fine," Nysha gritted.

"Good, the dance rehearsals are just about to begin. And yes, Avni and Aryan have arranged a crate of chilled beverages and a few snacks," she added with a smile.

"Wow! That was good thinking. She deserves a raise," Nysha praised.

"Ah! Sure she does," Aashita agreed.

Shifting her attention to Samar, Aashita asked, "Dr. Attwal, are you joining us?"

"I was about to..."

Aashita's eyes widened at his response. Clearly, it wasn't something she was expecting. But regaining her composure quickly she said, "Oh! That's really nice."

She threw a fleeting glance at Nysha, who in turn rolled her eyes at her and glared at Dr. Heartless. He smiled smugly at her and said calmly, "All in the best interest of Akshat Ratna..."

"Indeed," Nysha drawled.

THE BATTLE OF YIN-YANG

Moments later, Nysha found herself occupying a seat next to Dr. Heartless, with Aashita sliding in beside her. After some time, Ishani made an appearance. She threw Nysha a swift glance and made a sorry puppy face, as if someone had just threatened to snatch away the cherry topping from her favorite chocolate fudge ice cream. She made a cooing sound and whined with resentment, "Oh, oh, the seats are already occupied."

Aashita looked at Nysha with a stumped expression and whispered, "Is she even for real?"

"Oh, you guessed it right, she very much is...," Nysha replied with conviction.

"Practically, the entire auditorium is empty," Aashita mumbled.

"Yeah, entirely, except for the place near... you know who...," Nysha replied.

"Is she that obsessed?" Aashita asked, befuddled.

"Perhaps, she wants him to behave like Pavlov's dog, salivate at sight, or better still, charm his serpent to do a dirty dance," Nysha replied with a stark, sardonic smile.

However, in her haste to secure a laugh at the expense of Dr. Heartless, she had completely forgotten that all this while he had been sitting right next to her, and now had witnessed and listened to the most unfiltered and vile conversation she had with her friend. And had it not been for Aashita's hilarious eye roll, she would have still continued with her gab.

Holy Mother of God! What was she thinking? And for Fuck's sake, how was she gonna explain taking a sly dig at his dick...? She thought.

She squeezed her eyes shut in sheer embarrassment and tried to plot a quick escape route. She thought she could excuse herself on the pretext of getting a chilled bottle of water. As she tried to leave, her hand was immediately caught in a firm grip. Slowly, she turned around and looked into his eyes which shone with a malicious glint, and a smile curled around the corners of his generous mouth.

"Not yet, miss...," he said in a soft but assertive tone, leaving no room for argument.

Nysha arched an eyebrow at him and replied indignantly, "That obviously... is not for you to decide."

Whatever he had overheard, he should have been mad at her, but instead he smiled and casually leaned back on his seat before replying, "Ms. Patel, are you really gonna pretend that nothing happened?"

"What... do... you... mean...? Anyway, I was just gonna get some water for my parched throat. You have a problem with that?" she babbled.

"I sure don't... But that won't be needed now."

"You can't really stop me...," she charged like a determined, angry bull.

Samar simply tugged at her hand and pulled her back to her seat. He then beckoned with his eyes toward the doorway. Nysha saw Aryan entering the scene, closely followed by servers carrying trays full of bubbling drinks, bottles of chilled packaged water, packets of nachos, chips, popcorn, mixed nuts, gourmet chocolates, and the like. They handed snacks and drinks to everyone present in the room, and needless to say, people were absolutely delighted at the sudden, unexpected indulgence.

Finally, the servers reached the top of the stairs where Nysha, Samar, and Aashita were seated. Before they could grab their share of snacks and drinks, Aryan squeaked and intervened in a sharp voice, "Hey ya guys! Whatcha doing? Look, what I have got for you...," he proudly declared, pointing toward the servers and their well-stuffed trays.

And, well! Well! Did he not have every reason to have his chest swollen with pride, especially when everyone was going gaga over his generosity? At other times, Nysha would have been mightily impressed too, had his timing not been so impeccably and outrightly wrong!

Nevertheless, forced to make peace with her absolutely disheartening fate and drawing an understanding that luck had decided to abandon her in the truest manner possible, Nysha picked up her share of snacks (double the dose meant for an individual), a bottle of chilled water, and stayed put in her own place. In the meantime, Avni too had decided to join them, and before Ishani could throw another feat of tantrum, Aryan had managed to sneak her out of the room, citing a certain wardrobe malfunction of a lead dancer needing her immediate attention. And Nysha couldn't have been more thankful to him, for under the given jinxed circumstances, an air of respite was her much-needed medicament.

Nysha hated the fact that fate always conspired to bring Dr. Heartless and her together under the most unusual circumstances, and she despised it even more when her treacherous heart would switch sides and begin to beat at a faster rate and flutter aloud, threatening to break out from the shackles of her ribcage. Her body's reaction to Samar's proximity was something beyond her understanding and control. She gave him a reproachful look, while he flashed a lopsided grin to address her disgruntled demeanor. His cocky grin was enough to numb her brain cells and peel away the fake layer of sternness, thereby making her heart melt like a puddle of defrosted ice cream.

Shifting her attention from his handsome face, she tried to concentrate on her packet of cheese popcorn instead. As she tried hard to open it by giving it a strong pull, all of a sudden, the packet flew open, sending the entire contents of popped corn kernels flying all over the place, including their seat, clothes, and the floor.

"What the f*... hell do you think you are doing, Nysha?" Samar rebuked.

"What does it seem like, Dr. Heartless?" she retorted.

"Well, can't say for sure, but it seemed you were trying to launch a popcorn missile attack to maim me."

"Aww!! That was so pathetically original...," she guffawed.

"Well... you did elbow me on my ribcage...," he accused.

"You! Forget it!" she stuttered.

She began to collect the scattered popcorn lying on top of their seats. Aashita too started to do the same, but when Samar tried to help them, Nysha glared at him and slapped his hand aside.

"Why don't you just mind your own business," she snapped.

"That is... if you would stop dropping your miniscule bombshells."

She was about to retaliate when the sudden sound of applause interrupted their crazy squabble. Hot star kid Aryamaan Khanna, who was all set to make his acting debut in a scientific action flick, was on stage for practice. Alongside him was his equally cool dance partner-cum-award-winning choreographer, Raisha Anand, and the crowd was unable to keep their calm. There were loud cheers and screams of support and encouragement from the audience. Taking the cue to shut their mouths and reserving their defiant banter for a later date, they settled back on their respective seats.

Slowly, as the rehearsals began to progress, the temperature started to soar too. Nysha wasn't sure if it was the actual mercury levels, or the heat emanating from Mr. Haughtiness, seated right next to her, which was causing her immense discomfort. Whatever it was, she found the entire new situation to be extremely unsettling. After some time, the stage was being prepared for a dance performance by a school of specially-abled children with varied medical conditions, alongside a few noted television personalities. With Avni and Aashita joining in the preps, Nysha was at a loss for what to do next when a sudden, roaring idea struck her. She reached out for Aashita's bag and started to rake through her personal belongings, until she found the real gem which she was searching for, a handheld battery-operated fan with a humidifier and water mist sprayer.

"Ah! My perfect mate," she whispered to herself with a satisfied smile.

This entire period, Samar had been overtly conscious, since the lady seated next to him was practically a ticking time bomb, and it was difficult to guess her next move. Though he knew that he had to watch out for her, and he did manage to keep an eye on her, but never in a lifetime could he have anticipated her next brilliant master maneuver.

He was busy replying to a few urgent emails on his phone when a sudden whirring sound caught his attention. Upon turning sideways, he found Nysha cooling herself off with a battery-operated fan. He could only wish that would have been all, but it definitely wasn't. The very next second, he felt trickles of water wetting his face, for the lady in question had decided to spray water on her face using the misting fan. Though Samar had to admit that the tiny droplets felt refreshing on his skin too, there was no way he was going to confess that to her and let her derive pleasure from her crazy antics.

"Really now! You've got to be kidding me!" he charged instead.

In return, she simply stuck out her tongue at him before turning the fan toward him. She then pressed the mist button, thereby spraying water all over his face and taking him by complete surprise.

Damn! The girl was more childish than he had anticipated! He thought. And though her naive gesture should have pissed him off, instead it had ended up delivering a different sort of kick to his libido. He could only imagine different ways to put that tongue to better use rather than mindless sticking out. Getting a grip on his lustful thoughts, much to the fervent protests of his treacherous dick, he bellowed, "Oh, come on! Switch off that thing, will you?"

She gave him a nonchalant look and continued to spray water mirthfully. Finally, having had enough of her silly stunts, he snatched the fan away from her hand and switched it off. Without further ado, he shoved it inside his pant pocket. She glared at his audacity and was about to make an attempt to reach out for it when the sudden announcement regarding the commencement of the children's performance made her halt. She, of course, couldn't jeopardize it for her own selfish motive. Hence, she refrained from creating a scene, and for the time being, pushed behind the idea of getting back her possession.

The rest of the rehearsals went by smoothly, concluding with a breathtaking finale performance by a Choir Band from the northeastern state of Meghalaya. Also, with the AC installation work finally complete, the cool breeze fanning their faces made for a perfect ending to a long, ever-tiring day.

Slowly, as everyone began to exit the auditorium, Nysha found Aashita already waiting for her down the stairs. Quickly, she grabbed her friend's hand and led her out into the parking area.

"Hey, what's all the rush about? At least, wait for Avni...," Aashita exclaimed.

"No rush... just that it's late. I have texted Avni, she should be waiting in the parking lot," Nysha replied.

"Did something happen up there? It seems you didn't have a good time with Dr. Heartless," Aashita asked.

"Horrible is the word," Nysha grumbled.

"Aww! My poor baby!" Aashita said with a mocking, self-satisfied sneer.

Nysha was about to snap back, when the sound of footsteps behind them made her turn around. "Really! Are you following us?" she snapped.

Instead of replying, Samar let out a low snort and addressed Aashita instead, "Your friend here is really delusional, isn't she? The last time I checked, this was still the parking area."

"Oh! It is... and sorry about that...," she replied, blabbering as she tugged hard at Nysha's arm and rolled her eyes in a suggestive manner.

Nysha scrunched her face but, taking the hint from her friend, chose to remain quiet. She opened the door of her car and gestured for both Aashita and Avni, who were waiting behind it, to take their respective seats. Once they were both settled, she slid into the driver's seat and slammed the door shut. Without saying another word, she reversed and pulled the car out of the driveway, driving off into the dark, empty streets of the Mumbai-Pune Expressway.

Samar shook his head and muttered under his breath, as he headed toward his car. He unlocked the door and got in, but just when he was about to sit, a bulge in his pocket reminded him of Nysha's fan still neatly tucked away. He pulled it out and switched it on; a faint semblance of a smile crossed his lips as the mist sprayer wet his face.

"Quite an immaculate gadget!" He thought, holding it in his hands for a moment before opening the glove compartment and placing it inside.

"Not giving it back," he reflected as he started the car and headed home. But the defiant, faint smile remained intact on his lips, permanently etching itself and refusing to fade anytime soon.

FAIR CHANCE AND FRIENDLY RANTS

On their way back home, they were all quiet for some time, until Aashita decided to break the tense silence between them. "Babes, are we going to keep up with the silent game? Come on, we did put up a fabulous show out there, and deserve to be happy about it, not pout and sulk...."

"Yeah, we did," Nysha agreed. "Sorry, I had been a bit distracted," she added.

"Sure, you have been... and don't mind me asking, but aren't you giving Dr. Samar more leverage than necessary?" Aashita accused.

"That's not true," Nysha outrightly denied, but avoided looking at her friend's face.

"Ah! Try telling that to someone else. He sure gets under your skin," Aashita charged.

Nysha took a deep breath, and letting out a loud sigh, moaned inwardly before replying, "Yeah, you are right, he does... And I hate to admit that I can't seem to do a thing about it."

"Oh sweetheart, he is just trying to get a reaction out of you, or perhaps it is his way of expressing interest. Have you ever considered that?" Aashita asked.

Nysha looked at her with wide eyes and laughed a dry, humorless laugh before responding, "Well, that's a first. But as much as I appreciate your little theory, my love, there is nothing romantic between me and Dr. Haughtiness. He hates me as much as I dislike him."

Aashita let out a low whistle before screeching out loudly, "Or is it His Hotness instead? Honestly, leave aside hate, which definitely is a more intense emotion, I failed to find even a trace of dislike in his eyes. All he wanted was to nudge you a bit, which he did and he was quite successful at that."

Before Nysha could reply, they heard a muffled laughter coming from behind them. In their playful banter, Avni's presence had completely escaped their minds. Both Nysha and Aashita turned around, only to find the young intern smiling nervously at them. Nysha shook her head and said in a bossy tone, "If a word of this conversation makes its way to the office grapevine... at least I know whom to find."

"My lips are sealed, ma'am...," Avni replied earnestly.

"Well, we would prefer the deaf and dumb act more...," Aashita intervened.

"Then deaf it is, ma'am...," Avni murmured in agreement.

"Ah! That's our smart little girl. Now, plug your earphones in place, and go back to listening to your favorite K-Pop number," Aashita commented.

After some time, they reached Avni's home, and dropped her off. Next, it was Aashita's turn.

"Ah, finally we are back. Home sweet home, here I come," Aashita squeaked melodramatically.

"Get down, O' drama queen," Nysha said with a smile.

"Of course... of course, but aren't you coming in?" Aashita asked.

"No, my love, I would rather take a rain check. I don't wanna ace the kill-joy act, dragging my ass between two lovebirds."

"But you won't... Raghav is in Pune," Aashita whined.

"Oh! My poor baby... As much as my heart pains for you, I guess you could use this time to get some good night's sleep," Nysha suggested.

"Guess... I could," Aashita agreed with a fake yawn.

"Alright, I should leave. I could do with my beauty sleep too," Nysha added.

"Ok, love, and do think what I said about Dr. Samar. He sure has the hots for you," Aashita continued.

"Like hell, he does... Don't put ideas in my mind," Nysha rebuked.

"Nysha, I am being serious. You should think about it, give him a chance," Aashita coaxed again.

Nysha looked at her friend with disbelief and rolled her eyes hilariously before replying, "Really? You think so?"

"I really mean it, my friend. He deserves a chance. Think about it," Aashita urged.

Nysha shook her head and replied, "Ugh...! I can't promise... but I will try."

"That's more like my girl," Aashita approved with a satisfied smile.

Two days had passed since the rehearsals and dramatic episode at the Center, and both Nysha and Samar had been too busy discharging their worldly duties, and hadn't found the time to see or hear from each other.

However, on the third morning, Samar reached the hospital at 8 o'clock sharp, since he had an early surgery scheduled. After reviewing his schedule for the day and leaving instructions for his assistant Trisha at the reception, he hurried to the surgery room.

After almost three hours, when Samar came out of the OT, he was starving. Just then, Trisha informed him that Harsha Aunty had called to inquire about his whereabouts. He realized he was running late for the meeting. Although the operation had taken a bit longer than expected and had thrown his schedule off, he wasn't complaining, since the joy of conducting a successful surgery at any point outweighed his falling behind schedule. Checking his watch, he decided against grabbing a quick lunch. Instead, he hurriedly changed out of his hospital garb and headed straight to Dr. Harsha's cabin, postponing his lunch plans until after the meeting, despite fervent protests from his rumbling stomach.

Upon reaching Dr. Harsha's cabin, he found the door to be slightly ajar. Just as he was about to enter, he heard a soft, soothing voice, busy in conversation. It didn't take him long to realize that Nysha was already inside.

"Oh! Such a good boy you are! Which girl wouldn't want you? Of course, I love you... And thanks for the lovely flowers... Not really! You made my day... Such a perfect gentleman... unlike a few others...," she continued, oblivious to his presence.

Darn! Did everything coming out of her sassy mouth have to sound sexy as hell? He thought. Now along with his rumbling stomach, he had managed to get Mr. Willy Wong so excited that it had begun to twitch. He couldn't help but wonder the intoxicating effect those words would have had on him, had she chosen to whisper them straight into his ears. With her full lips and her sultry breath wafting and caressing the soft and sensitive skin beneath his earlobes, for sure he would have dived straight to Heaven. So much for being labeled as a good boy! He sighed deeply and tried to rework his energies to focus on mundane activities, like Mrs. Sarma's BP count, or better still, negotiating ideas for his office supplies. Getting a grip on his feelings, he finally pushed the door, sending it wide open.

His sudden intrusion took her by surprise. Her eyes went wide initially, but quickly she regained her composure and continued her conversation over the phone, shifting her response to monosyllables and riddles instead of a full-bodied tête-à-tête. Clearly, she wasn't expecting him, and most certainly was not very keen to see him. Meanwhile, Samar's attention shifted to a bouquet of mesmerizing pink carnations and Asiatic lilies neatly placed on the table. As much as the sender's flamboyant choice in flowers had managed to impress him, he was also intrigued to discern his identity. But the sudden pang of unwarranted and illogical jealousy threatening to engulf his chest managed to amaze him as well.

Finally, Nysha ended the call and looked at him with a raised eyebrow. "You...?" she said.

"Yes, were you expecting someone else?" he asked curtly.

"No, of course not..."

"I see...," his voice drawled.

He strode toward her with slow, calculated steps, but his eyes were locked on her. Her pulse began to quicken, matching the sudden uneven escalation of her breath. Damn! Even her unscrupulous nipples had chosen the very moment to play the sneak-peek game of arousal. She was afraid; he could see her hardened nipples brushing against the soft fabric of her top. His heightened awareness made her uncomfortable and she crossed her arms over her chest in an attempt to cover herself, and calm her jumpy nerves.

He came too close to her, clearly defying every idea of personal space and comfort. His sudden presence in front of her seemed rather overwhelming, and her heartbeat quickened as the strong, musky, male scent engulfed her senses. He swept past her, brushing his arm against her, sending a jolt of desire and tremors down her body. Nysha's breath hitched in her throat and her belly twisted in knots. She had to take a step back to break her trance, while Samar gave her an all-knowing, curled-up smirk. He slowly bent down and reached out for her bouquet of flowers. On overturning the small card attached to it, as the name of the sender became evident, a furrowed look of dislike and annoyance crossed his otherwise handsome features.

Next, he let an almost frustrated growl escape his smug mouth before blurting out in a rather blunt tone than he had intended. "Why the hell is Jay sending you flowers at the workplace?"

It took Nysha a moment to make sense of the exact meaning of his words, and upon realizing the same, she couldn't believe that he had just poked his bossy nose into something which by no means should have been his business. That, topped with his equally domineering tone, threw her completely off, and an inflated surge of anger erupted in her chest. She frowned and threw him a menacing look.

"How dare you, Samar?" she hissed softly. "Besides, that's none of your bloody business," she added.

"Oh, it definitely is, especially since this is a hospital, and not some fancy club for playing lovey-dovey games," he shot back.

And that was the last straw. With him uttering the pair of rhyming words at the end of his muttered statement, her barely-there thin string of patience snapped into two. She glared at him, her eyes blazing as she gritted through her teeth, "I most certainly don't need to learn the ABCs of workplace ethics and professionalism from you. Now before I lose my cool, get out of my sight," she growled.

But instead of following her order, he inched closer to her, giving her all the more reason to hate him with equal fervor. "This, Ms. Patel, is Dr. Harsha's cabin, and who stays and who leaves, it is only for her to decide, not otherwise," he challenged.

Nysha and Samar were standing so awfully close to one another that with their faces just inches apart, they could even feel each other's breaths tickling their faces. With a smug and grim look plastered on both their faces, they engaged in a severe stare-down battle, with none ready to back out whatsoever.

Finally, Nysha broke the silence, "Fine, I will leave. I forgot that the world is full of misogynistic morons, you just happen to follow the lead," she belittled him.

"Watch what you say," he gritted out.

"Oh really! I repeat, 'You. Are. One. Big. Misogynistic Moron'," she spat each word on his face with disdain.

"Try saying that again...," he dared, his eyes fixed on her lips.

"I said...," she began... Before she could finish, he pulled her closer by her waist, sending shock waves down her spine. "Watch out for what you say, you wouldn't want to regret," he hissed in her face.

"Bossy, are we?" she accused.

"Mule-headed, aren't you?" he retorted.

"Tell me, Dr. Heartless, what is it? Don't tell me you have been keeping tabs on me?" she pressed.

"Hardly!" he spat.

"Then, are you one of those entitled phony jerks for whom the general standards don't apply?" she asked.

He furrowed his eyebrows at her and threw her a questioning gaze, before asking in a hoarse voice, "Where are we heading, Nysha? What's been bothering you all this time? Come on, tell me."

She looked into his eyes and saw genuine concern and empathy. It felt as if his eyes could infiltrate right into her soul. His closeness had caused her skin to erupt into goosebumps, and with her heartbeat already racing, she feared her heart would melt into a puddle of creamy fondue, giving him access to her vulnerable self. She hated the fact that he could do that to her, always...

For a moment, the urge to melt into the embrace of his muscular arms was so overwhelming that she had to fight hard in order to shake it off. Then she remembered that he was bad for her system. She definitely couldn't trust him with her heart, surely not when in all probability he didn't see her in the same light as she did. Her insides twisted with rage when she remembered Ishani accompanying him to the rehearsals the other day. Of course, the cozy family dinner pictures, along with the mirror selfie of the power couple in the making, all of which were posted on Ishani's Insta account and garnered likes and mushy comments at lightning speed, only made matters worse. It made the inner wild pig crawling inside her chest go 'oink-oink' in a full-on beastly mode. Not that she had any business getting jealous, i.e., only if she could control her disruptive emotions.

Realizing that Samar was still awaiting her response, she looked at him with her jaws taut in rage, and replied whilst giving a slight push against his chest, "It's nothing... nothing has been bothering me... nothing that should be your lookout. Now, leave me," she lied as she squirmed in his arms.

Samar shook his head in disbelief, but didn't flinch an inch at her push, instead his grip around her waist tightened, and he pulled her even closer, "Shhh!! Relax...," he said. "Now, until you speak the truth and only the truth... you aren't going anywhere," he declared.

Her eyes widened at his audacity and her lips parted in shock of their own accord. To Samar, it sure as hell felt like an invitation to a different sort of "Heaven," stirring a strong temptation in his chest that he had to fight hard in order to resist.

"Is that a threat?" she confronted.

"More like a promise...," he replied with a side smirk, while grazing her lips with his long fingers in an attempt to close her parted mouth. His simple gestures made her shiver, turning her into a puddle of lust in an instant. Heat traveled down her body, and she knew she had to stop the torture by answering him. Even if it meant accepting defeat, then so be it.

"Fine!" she shrieked. Then looking into his eyes she said, "Leave me, and I will tell you what you need to know."

He took a sweeping look at her face before releasing her from his grip. "Out with the truth!" he ordered.

"Don't push me..., Dr. Heartless," she glowered.

"Do I need to?" he scorned.

"Know what, you are one of the most infuriating men I have seen!" Saying that, she paused for a while before throwing her hands up in the air and continuing, "Ah, correction! Actually, you are the most infuriating man I have ever come across in my entire life... You are a kind of mean, annoying, bossy jerk and... and...," she panted and gasped for breath, while he casually crossed his arms across his chest, unperturbed by her accusatory calls. This further annoyed her to bits, and she glared at him. Samar, on the other hand, was enjoying her theatrics. It was finally comforting to know that he wasn't the only one suffering because of this maddening woman. She was equally affected by his presence, and wasn't immune to him either.

"Hey! Short of words already?" he asked with a taunt. "Perhaps you could use some help; how about interesting, intriguing, challenging, or irresistible, and daring...," he concluded in good humor.

"You are pathetic, Dr. Heartless... one cold-blooded pretentious jerk who goes all turncoat the very next moment that he gets a chance to."

Samar shrugged his shoulders in an offhand manner. With all her baseless and rather mindless accusations, he was getting a bit impatient now. "Well... well, turncoat is a very strong term indeed, and rather demeaning at that. I am sure most people find me chivalrous and loyal, and if you think otherwise, you clearly need to explain," he taunted.

She rolled her eyes at him and replied, "What if I don't want to? Anyway, we already have had enough for the day. I am sure your plate is full, and so is mine. Leave it, Samar, this isn't going anywhere," she protested.

Her last words were uttered in dejection, and Samar hated to see her that way. He could handle a feisty Nysha, but a gloomy one wasn't his best bet. Nevertheless, he wasn't letting it go. Their conversation needed closure. Their mindless banters weren't without any significance. She was definitely not going anywhere, and if it were for him to decide, he wouldn't let her go... not now, not ever... He, himself, was shocked at his intense thoughts, which made him sound like a possessive jerk. He was relieved that he had not said them aloud, as doing so would have given her another reason to either loathe him or lecture him on 'feminism,' 'equality,' 'women empowerment,' and what not. Probably his hunger pangs were messing with his mind, or so he thought. Currently, he couldn't think of a better excuse to defend himself internally. He realized that he still hadn't responded to her, when he saw her staring at his face, almost like studying the play of various emotions dancing across it.

"No...," he replied curtly.

"No!" she repeated. "What do you mean?" she asked.

"I mean, finish what you started, Nysha," he insisted. "Why do you think I am a turncoat, or mean, or for that matter, even infuriating...? I surely must have done something really admirable to be bestowed with these enviable titles," he scoffed.

For the briefest moment she looked at him wishfully, and her eyes conveyed an emotion which Samar had been longing to see for some time now. But before he could be sure, it was gone and replaced with a nonchalant expression.

"Alright, Dr. Heartless!" she said with a huff... With her legs slightly apart and with her hands on her hips she proclaimed, "Danger tides ahead, don't complain that you weren't warned prior in time. Once I start, there is no stopping, and unfortunately there isn't anything which you could do or say, to make me stop. So, are we doing this right now, in Harsha Aunty's cabin?" she reaffirmed.

"Well, darling, don't you think it's already a tad late for that?" he asked. He had uttered, "darling" simply to tease her, and as expected, it had the desired effect. She blushed, and her skin turned a brilliant shade of crimson. With a satisfied grin on his face, he added, "And as far as I am concerned, don't worry; I am tougher than you think I am... So shoot!"

"Why are you doing this, Samar?" she asked again.

"Doing what exactly, Ms. Patel?" he countered.

"Playing games, dammit! One day you make me feel special, and the very next day I find your ass plonked comfortably beside your oh-so-soulmate...," she accused.

"What are you saying? This is all rubbish... delusional, aren't you?" he denied her accusation.

"Right, Mr. Heartless, I am the one who is lying now, aren't I? Well, let's see, what about the couple-goal selfies, and groufies posted as 'badge of honor' in your partner's Insta account. Let me guess, those were lies too... such a shame, isn't it? To waste that billion-dollar smile of yours on something so immaterial and insignificant," she scorned.

"And how do you know about that?" he asked calmly.

"Know about what?" she replied, befuddled.

"The dinner selfie," he clarified before continuing, "Unless, of course, you have been stalking me... and Ah! The 'billion-dollar smile' comment, I take that as a compliment," he said, his voice drawling.

Her knees went all wibble-o'-wobble with nervousness at his observation. No wonder she came across as a dangerous stalker, digging into the personal lives of almost strangers, whilst burrowing deeper into their social media profiles.

Damn her! For not being careful before ranting in frustration, she thought. "I am not stalking you, why would I?" she made a pathetic attempt at blurting out a lie.

He scanned her face for a long time, her face revealing nothing. But clearly, he did not believe her. He had no reason to, and obviously he could see through her evident lie.

"Why do you care?" he asked softly.

"I don't," she lied.

"Liar!" He called out.

She opened her mouth to defy him, but unable to curate the exact choice of words, ended up biting her lower lip instead. As the center of her teeth tugged softly at the flesh of her lower lip, it did unimaginable things to his body, things he wanted to avoid thinking about in a hospital setting. He pulled her closer once again, and as her lips parted in shock, it seemed to him like an enticing invitation, and he thought he would be damned to pass up such a close call. He leaned down and brushed his lips softly against hers. As his breath caressed her skin, jitters ran down her spine.

"You can't kiss me...," she muttered in a shaky voice.

"I just did... and you liked it," a hint of amusement flashed in his eyes, and his lips adorned a smile.

"You are such a cocky and manipulative jerk. Forget liking, your touch makes me nauseous."

He eyed her for a second, before sliding his fingers into her hair and gently tugging her head backward. He looked into her eyes, before caressing her ears with his lips and speaking in an almost whisper, "You can lie all you want, Ms. Patel, but your body betrays you... its reaction to my touch can hardly be dismissed as dislike or disgust, and if you say so, then you are in absolute denial."

"Damn you, Ms. Patel...!" He groaned.

And the very next moment his mouth came crashing on hers. This time there was no prior warning. He did it as if it was the most natural thing to do. A guttural sound escaped his mouth, one which he himself wasn't able to identify with. It sounded like a mix of victorious growl, combined with a desperate, searing need of passion. He kissed her as if his life depended on it, and when she responded to the same by cupping his head in her delicate palms, his heartbeat perked up insanely. He deepened his kiss, sucking at her lips and absorbing away all her cynical thoughts. Time seemed to stop around them, and only their mouths meddled, and tongues danced in a soft, entwined rhythm, while their hands explored each other, shedding inhibitions which had stopped them for long. His touch ignited fire within her and made the erogenous zones of her body come alive, zones which she never knew existed. As she moaned softly into his mouth, Samar was lost in her sweet, and yet potentially intoxicating and dangerous taste which threatened to consume him completely.

Finally when his mouth left hers, they were both breathless, and the consequence of the kiss was not lost on them either, nor could it ever be. For they had both crossed the line of sanity and had knowingly or unknowingly stepped across the threshold of the very formidable "zone of affection," by falling hard and head over heels in love with each other.

HEARTFELT CONFESSIONS

"I hate you," Nysha said, while running a finger over her well-kissed lips.

In return, Samar simply shot her a twisted smile and replied with all sincerity, "I know... but believe me, I will make it up to you," he winked.

"You are despicable...," she whispered.

"Well, that's bad... since you love this despicable man, don't you?" he replied with spunk.

"Ever heard of overconfidence ruining the show? You are insufferable... and yet somehow I can't stop thinking about you," she groaned.

"Ah! Now that's some serious confession in the making...," he said with a playful taunt before continuing, "and while you aren't exactly the distressed damsel or dream princess type...You, Nysha Patel, are the cause of my tachycardia. My cardiovascular system has never ever been so worked up... behaving irrationally, acting weird, and making my cardiac muscles pump blood through the vascular system at the pace of a bullet train. You keep my thoughts occupied, and every time that I think of you, my heart never fails to skip a beat. You are an annoying brat who has managed to turn my life upside down ever since the day you decided to set foot on it." He took a meaningful pause, before letting out a soft sigh whilst shaking his head in disbelief.

"Oh, and I hate to admit it... but you have also made my life really beautiful, meaningful, and need I say... complete, Ms. Patel," he concluded.

For a brief moment, Nysha looked at him with a bemused expression, as if she was finding it difficult to make sense and accept his heartfelt confession. Finally, she decided to break the silence with a soft giggle, "Whoa! Now, that was some declaration...," she said with a mischievous grin.

"You are incorrigible, aren't you? Does all of this seem like a joke to you?" he asked, annoyed, while she batted those ridiculously long and beautiful eyelashes at him.

Nysha raised her hands up in the air as a sign of defeat in response to his infuriating glare, before inching closer to him and throwing her arms around his neck. Still smiling at him, she replied, "Oh, no! No! No! Don't get me wrong, Dr. Samar Heartless Attwal, but you better mean every word you just said with that sexy mouth of yours, because I am a greedy bird, and once you commit, I want everything — all of it — starting with love, lust, friendship, dedication, sex, marriage, kids, and the list goes on. For starters, I need a lifelong commitment, and no, you aren't allowed to back out. Do I have a deal, Dr. Attwal?" she asked.

"You have my word, Ms. Patel... A man's promise," he assured.

Saying that, he slid his fingers through her hair, beneath the nape of her neck, and with a slight tug on her scalp pulled her closer for a quick kiss, before whispering playfully into her ear, "You have no damn idea what I wanna do to you..."

Her heart began to pound hard against her chest simply at the anticipation of his words. A whiff of desire shot through her. Dr. Heartless was definitely a magician with his hands. Prior to this, she had no idea that a simple tug at her hair, or simply words, could be so stimulating. As if reading her thoughts, his lips curled into a wicked grin, "Can you please get a grip on your horny thoughts, you naughty girl...," he teased.

"Don't blame me, you started it...," she replied, trying hard to hide a blush at his apparent teasing.

"Don't worry, I wouldn't disappoint you...," he stated.

"I know... not the least of my concerns...," she replied.

"And I am not into biting... unless of course, you are into such stuff...," he said with a chuckle.

"Stop it, will you?" she smacked him hard on his arm.

Suddenly, the cabin door flew open, making both Samar and Nysha jump slightly in their respective places. While a smiling and absolutely unsuspecting Dr. Harsha entered the scene, it definitely left the newly dubbed 'OG Lovers' in town feeling a bit unsettled.

"Oh, I am so very sorry! The allotment of clinical postings took longer than I had anticipated...," she uttered her sincere apology, completely unaware of the recent developments, cupid attacks, and changed equations that had occurred behind her back, right within the confines of her very cabin.

"It's ok, Harsha Aunty, not a problem... seriously...," Nysha muttered softly, throwing a nervous glance at Samar.

"Yeah..., that's right, Dr. Harsha. In fact, we were discussing about the upcoming event," Samar confirmed.

Argh! Seriously! How believably original! Nysha groaned internally. The person was a real stick-in-the-mud. How would he explain standing and discussing such an important event? And for the record, what were they even discussing anyway, aside from their mind-blowing kiss, of course, she thought.

"Oh! Really?" Dr. Harsha furrowed her eyebrows and gave them both a skeptical, "don't attempt kidding me" look. Well, it made sense, since she was kind and gentle, not stupid and naive. Her gaze flickered back and forth between Samar and Nysha, and her scrutiny left them both flustered. As if satisfied with what she saw, she let out a soft chuckle, and a small smile teased the corner of her lips, "Alright, children, actually I am famished. Perhaps, you could enlighten me with your perspective over lunch. We definitely have a lot to discuss, and I am so looking forward to it." Then shifting her attention toward Nysha she said, "Nysha beta, perhaps you could order some Chinese."

Nysha coughed hard at her request and glared at Samar as if he were the cause of her embarrassment. In response, he glared back. Meanwhile, an amused expression flickered across Dr. Harsha's face, and Nysha could tell from the look of it, that good old Harsha Aunty was in a mood for some playful repartee. She had definitely caught the whiff of something brewing behind her back, and wasn't letting it go until she uncovered the truth.

Well, where were the demons and vampires from Dracula's squad, when you really needed them to gulp you down? She thought to herself as she fished her phone out of her pants pocket and scrolled through the food delivery app. After all, she had Chinese to order, didn't she?

Seated across the table with a spread of Chinese delicacies sprawled out before them, Dr. Harsha gave them a look, which was a dubious mix of suspicion thrown in with a dash of amusement. Samar was trying hard to twirl around the long strands of noodles around the prongs of his fork when he caught Nysha's furrowed eyebrows and her absolute disapproving glare.

"Does that taste right to you, Dr. Attwal?" she enquired brusquely through gritted teeth.

Caught off guard at her query, he replied bluntly, "It's fine... just a bit bland perhaps... Would you mind passing me the sauce, please?"

"Sure, why not?" Nysha muttered through clenched teeth. She grabbed a sachet of ketchup and slammed it right beside him, literally banging on the table, and making the water inside their respective bottles ripple in effect. Quickly picking up the sachet, Samar ripped off its corner and squeezed the sauce in a zig-zag fashion over the contents of his plate, thereby making a sorry attempt at displaying his pathetic artistic skills.

Meanwhile, Nysha pierced a slice of cucumber and cherry tomato with her fork, and scooped a piece of feta cheese, before putting the mixture into her mouth. The way she clenched tightly at her fork, it seemed she would rather pierce a hole straight into Samar's heart, or better still, stab him right in the eye, than sit through the dreaded ordeal. She drew in a deep breath to control her murderous thoughts, while reading her mind and accessing her lethal ideas, a muffled gasp escaped Samar's mouth. Dr. Harsha gave them both a meaningful look, and while all three of them made an attempt to eat their food in silence, with the only occasional audible sound of cutlery hitting their plates thrown in, the air around them, especially the blanket surrounding Samar and Nysha, was anything but cordial.

After what seemed like a lifetime of chewing, munching, nibbling and gnawing at their food, finally Dr. Harsha decided to call it quits and end the torturous game of silence. Well, she had made up her mind... arm-twisting them into making a confession wasn't going to help, but perhaps the age-old game of jealousy could just do the trick. Dr. Harsha comfortably leaned back in her chair, and crossed one arm over the other before starting, "Alright, Dr. Samar, tell me how's it going with Ishani? Well, she's a nice girl, and your mom seems quite eager to welcome her into the family."

Nysha furrowed her brows together at her weird query, while Samar shrugged and looked clearly embarrassed at her sudden intrusion into his personal space. What else could justify her changed demeanor, if it weren't for traces of unwarranted substances? Samar cast an uneasy glance toward Nysha, and she glowered back at him.

"Well... nothing much to say... We haven't quite decided yet, not that there is anything to decide. You know how it is...," he blabbered.

"Oh! Is it?" Dr. Harsha replied.

Nysha noticed that Harsha Aunty looked quite disappointed at his response... God! Could someone tell what was wrong with her? Since when did she become a nosy poke... or was it a first? she thought.

"Umm! Maybe we should get back to business, Harsha Aunty... All these tinder thunder can wait. I believe we have more pressing matters at hand, don't we?" Nysha eyed Samar, savage intentions clearly written all across her face. As if taking the hint from her harrowing glare, he nodded in agreement and replied, "Ah! Well, Nysha is right, Aunty... We sure need to discuss about the upcoming event."

"Oh, but we will," she said with a dismissive flick of her hand before continuing, "I just thought we could have a personal one-on-one first," the enthusiastic gleam in her eyes was hard to miss.

Urgh!! What has gotten into her? Nysha wondered. Wasn't she letting go of her matchmaking session? Another mention of the #Samar-Ishani saga... and she would definitely end up throwing up, she thought. But surely her internal thoughts couldn't telepathically make their way to

Harsha Aunty's mind. At the very next moment, she dropped a bomb which rendered both Samar and Nysha dumbstruck. They had not seen it coming. Nope, not even in their wildest dreams.

"Samar, your mother happened to mention about the roka ceremony too!" she squealed, her excitement matching that of a 5-year-old upon spotting her favorite candy in a giant pile of Easter goodies.

"Roka ceremony! Really!" Nysha exclaimed aloud.

"Yes! Roka ceremony, baccha, where a prayer ceremony takes place, along with the exchange of rings and gifts... and..."

"I do know what a roka ceremony is, Aunty. My mom is a Punjabi, and so is my best friend," she said sharply, her eyes fixed on Samar, a glint of accusation shining bright in their depths. As if reading her thoughts, Samar shook his head and replied with his eyes.

Trust me, I had no fucking idea.

"Congratulations, Dr. Samar. Guess, you weren't planning on informing us anytime soon, were you?" she gritted out.

But her sarcasm wasn't lost on Dr. Harsha, who was quick to chastise, "Oh ho, baccha! What has bitten you today? I know you are raised better than that," Dr. Harsha intervened.

Great! Now she does the policing job too, anything but doctor duties, Nysha thought wryly.

"By the way, Jay called up...," Dr. Harsha stated as a matter of fact.

"He did? Why?"

"You weren't answering his call, and he got worried. He was inquiring about you," Dr. Harsha replied calmly.

"Really?" This time Samar probed in, scrutinizing her face with his accusing eyes.

"Oh, that! I was probably driving... But we talked...," Nysha responded.

"Oh, you did! Good then...," Satisfied with her response, Harsha Aunty smiled at her before continuing, "I think he genuinely likes you. Have you ever thought about it? Or considered giving him a chance? Maybe you could go out on a date," she suggested.

Nysha could almost feel the heated gaze of Samar's stare, potent enough to burn her. Her own breath clogged in her chest, and she struggled to find her voice, since her brain had chosen that very moment to fog out, and go on a sleepover vacay mode. Upon receiving zero words and an absolute blank expression as her only response, Dr. Harsha shifted her attention to Samar instead...

"What do you think, Dr. Samar? Jay is your cousin, right? Nysha and Jay... they would make a lovely couple, don't you think?" she squealed animatedly.

Samar turned red and looked all uncomfortable at her query. He didn't know what to say. He ran a shaky hand through his hair and mumbled, "I guess that's for Nysha to decide. However, if you were to ask my opinion, I wouldn't recommend him, even though he is my cousin. He tends to be more of a player."

"And you most definitely are a saint!" Nysha snapped back... her vicious mode on point...

"Come on, Nysha, we are not doing this again, are we?" Samar bit back.

She rolled her eyes at him and continued, "Oh yes, we are! My life's decision should be the least of your concerns, when you have already decided to move ahead with your roka ceremony, Dr. Heartless," she spat.

"Oh please, must we play these silly games? I thought we were beyond this. Learn to act a bit mature, Nysha...," he suggested.

"Oh yes, like you have been acting mature...," she scoffed.

"Probably not by your standards... But getting close to Jay just to get a reaction from me can hardly be considered as being mature..."

"You make me sick, Dr. Attwal. I would prefer Mr. Dracula sucking my blood rather than be with you...," Nysha retorted.

"As if... Vile Dracula needed Her Highness's permission," he guffawed.

"Quiet! Both of you! Now...," the shrill commanding voice of Harsha Aunty got their attention... Both of them paused, and for a second the room went completely silent.

"But, Aunty...," Nysha started.

Dr. Harsha raised her hand to stop her from speaking further. "When I said quiet, I meant it, baccha," she stated coolly.

Nysha stopped; she couldn't bring herself to argue with Harsha Aunty. She struggled to suppress the smile which almost threatened to escape her lips at their wild escapades and the sulks they were throwing at each other. Nysha still wore a formidable mutinous expression on her face, while Samar let out a non-committal snort. Nevertheless, both knew better not to indulge in a squabble with her, since for one, their Indian values discouraged such behavior, and second, they were conditioned to adhere to the authoritative voice of their elders without questioning. Dr. Harsha clasped her hands in front of her and began the drill, "Well, children, now that I have your attention."

Children! Really! Nysha thought.

While a spontaneous giggle escaped her mouth, it made Samar's skin prickle at the tingling sound of her laughter, which sounded very much like an opera overture. Till now he had no idea that a stifled giggle could sound sexy as hell! He wanted to kiss that sultry mouth of hers, and render her both breathless and speechless. Samar couldn't help but marvel at his outrageously pitiable luck, on being stuck with two women who were poles apart, and yet could somehow make him feel like a juvenile adolescent, all at once. The very thought made him squirm in his chair.

"You guys left me with no choice... Just a while ago, both of you were practically at each other's throats, beating around the bush... hiding behind the facade of despise and jealousy, while missing out on the most important declaration."

"And what would that be... Dr. Harsha...," Samar mumbled.

"Oh, stop pretending, Samar... both of you love each other, don't you? Is that really so hard to confess?" she asked.

"But he did... just confess... or maybe we both did... confess...," Nysha muttered softly, looking into Dr. Harsha's eyes.

"You did?" Dr. Harsha asked Samar with a raised eyebrow.

"Yeah, we did...," Samar reaffirmed.

"And then?"

"We messed... fought like children," Nysha confessed, unabashed.

"Yeah... literally and figuratively...," Samar added, rubbing his slightly throbbing temples now.

"Love is hardly about who's got a bigger dick vs. a pert ass...," Dr. Harsha spoke as a matter of fact.

"Aunty!" Nysha exclaimed. Her eyes widened as she slapped her palm over her mouth.

"It's ok... Been there, done that...," Dr. Harsha continued.

"Yes, and we are doctors. Dick or ass, it just happens to be a part of the human anatomy...," Samar added, while a mischievous glint shone in his eyes.

"Really? Noted, Dr. Heartless, I will hold you to that," Nysha spoke softly, while the corners of her mouth twitched wickedly.

"Ahem!" Dr. Harsha cleared her throat. "Shall we move to the important bit...," she said, as her gaze rested on Nysha.

"I... Ah! Am I supposed to say something?" Nysha blushed.

"Great! Now she acts feather-brained...," Dr. Harsha mumbled with an annoying snort.

Before more words could be exchanged, Samar blurted out, "Be mine, Nysha Patel... today, tomorrow... forever..."

"Samar!" She sighed and spelled his name softly. It almost sounded like a faint whisper escaping her lips.

"It might sound cliché, and insanely cheesy, but I mean it, every word of it... Ms. Patel...," he added.

His words made her heart beat increase. Her heart pounded hard in her chest, almost threatening to break free from the shackles of her rib cage. Samar pulled her chair closer to him and wrapped his arms around her, bringing his head down to rest on hers. Needless to say, her heart momentarily stopped beating altogether. A soft sigh escaped her lips as she allowed herself to get lost and mellow down in his warm embrace, whilst soaking in the comforting heat of his body. Getting a grip on her galloping heart, she lifted her head and looked into his eyes. Then she caught hold of his shirt's collar and tugged it hard before speaking her heart out, "I love you, Dr. Heartless, more than you could ever imagine, I do. And forget the roka ceremony, if ever again, I happen to spot you and Ishani in a close vicinity, I swear to God... I am going to kill you... or better still, chop off your balls with a blunt razor...," she cited maliciously.

"Hey, that's so mean... I can't really take the guarantee of Ishani or her antics," he laughed a carefree laugh, full of love and life.

"But you could surely take the guarantee of your balls," Nysha spoke with mock anger.

"Yeah sure... I do take the threat to my balls seriously," he chuckled softly.

"Good, you should. And don't ever think of lying or keeping a secret from me," she warned.

"Never...," he muttered beneath his breath, and pressed a kiss on the corner of her mouth. That was the only way to shut her up, and it worked. She tucked her head into the crook of his neck and whispered softly, "So, we really are a thing, then?"

"Yes, we are. But more than that, we are a team... forever...," he whispered back.

"Forever," Nysha agreed.

THE FINAL REHEARSAL AND MELODRAMA

"You better have a real good reason for having that stupid smile plastered on your face, since our asses here have been practically on fire," Aashita said in a deadpan voice, her face devoid of even a thin semblance of a smile. It made her look like the beautiful and fearless Black Canary, ready to unleash her sonic "Canary Cry."

"Duh! I am so sorry. Did I miss something, my love?" Nysha asked, giggling at her friend's comment.

"Nah! Nothing much! Just that your freak of a designer friend, Aryan Kundra, and his equally psycho co-designer, Ishani Kapoor, aren't answering my calls," she said in a sharp and absolute no-nonsense tone, which could put even a boor or a snob to shame.

"Ok, look, I understand we have a problem here. But I would appreciate it if you could please throw some light on its origin," Nysha grimaced.

"Alright! For starters, freaky Kundra called up this morning, citing that he had made certain design changes to the outfits of our anchor couple." Aashita took a deep breath and paused.

"And...?" Nysha asked with a scrunched nose and furrowed eyebrows.

She knew better than anyone else that a minor dress change definitely couldn't be the only reason to get Aashita's panties in a knot. To ruffle her perfect feathers, both the crime and the criminal had to level up.

"Ok, I am not worried about Rijvi Hasaan throwing a moody tantrum. That guy is a rare gem. But sheesh! Do you have any idea how fussy Malini Khanna can get if things don't work out her way? As it is, the last time, she had agreed only after several inputs and crazy alterations. Her PA mother personally cross-checks every small detail. How do you think we are gonna manage this crisis?" Aashita whined.

Nysha let out an exhausted puff of breath before speaking again, "So, that's it... right? The dress and the designer are our problem then."

"Of course not, there is more," Aashita hollered.

"And more would be...?" Nysha asked.

"Mehtaji wants certain last-minute adaptations to Zain's performance," Aashita clarified.

"Mehtaji! Really? What changes could he possibly expect now?" Nysha asked curiously.

"He wants Zain's performance to be a stunt-based one," Aashita answered in a breath.

"Stunt-based? Wow! And just when did his hyperactive brain-ware conjure up this brand new upgrade and revamped idea? Clearly, the old-age bug has stung his ass. Next time, do remind me to inform Pia and Zain to get him treated of his hysteria before it manages to get even worse," Nysha replied savagely.

"Ok, just so that you know, he was being serious."

Already expecting a sharp retort from her friend, Aashita replied in a straight voice, bursting Nysha's complacency and know-it-all bubble.

"He can't be... Was he?" Nysha asked again, her voice slightly shaky now.

Without another word, Aashita pulled open the top drawer of her side cabinet and took out a sheaf of papers, placing them neatly on the table. Then she beckoned toward Nysha with her eyes, urging her to check and judge for herself the truth behind the steadfast claim.

"These were personally faxed by Mehtaji. Please turn to page 3, Exhibit 3.1, which clearly mentions that Aerial Loop and Fire Twirling are to be mandatory parts of Zain's performance. So, the stage needs to be readied accordingly. Seemingly, Mr. Superstar's next release is a Hollywood-inspired action flick backed by a hotshot Richie Rich producer from the industry, and this guy's craving for the limelight and extravagance is practically insatiable. His back itches to hog the limelight, and we gotta scratch it for him by coming up with a kamar tod, stage fadu performance," Aashita concluded.

"Really...? You've got to be kidding me. For his tod-fod performance fetish, he expects me to risk the bones of my best friend's husband. As it is, Pia hates him doing those hazardous stunts. And for God's sake! She is in the last trimester of her pregnancy. I don't think even Zain would agree to do something that would freak the hell out of his wife at this point," Nysha countered.

"Well, I think he already knows. Cause if he were not to approve, these papers wouldn't have reached us," Aashita stated.

Nysha pondered over Aashita's claim. Well, she did have a point. Drumming her fingers against the wooden chestnut table, she asked her friend, "What do you suggest? Should I call Zain and ask him?"

"That wouldn't be such a good idea. Agreed, he is a friend and a well-wisher, but he has already done so much. Calling him for every trivial matter would not only make Aura look unprofessional, but also inefficient," Aashita replied earnestly.

"But this isn't something trivial," Nysha protested. "I wouldn't have worried a dime if this was just about any dance performance. Even with his eyes closed, Zain could get his steps correct... But to perfect a stunt, you need practice... and our reckless superstar doesn't have any time for that. For Pete's sake, Aashita, we are left with only 8 days for the finale."

"And that's exactly why I have placed my bet on the industry's best. Vardhaan Kapadia is our man of the hour," Aashita replied.

"Aashita Gogoi, are you out of your freaking mind?" Nysha yelled. "Vardhaan Fucking Kapadia is your idea of a best bet? That guy is craziness personified, and I am ignoring the fact that he is a malevolent narcissist, a shameless skirt-chaser, and his ego is bigger than his venomous mouth."

"Aren't you back to being dramatic and pushy, Ms. Patel? Listen to me; he is a national award winner in Stunt Choreography. Well, you have a better idea; I am all ears," Aashita added cynically.

Nysha wrinkled her brows in confusion and looked wishfully at her friend. Then letting out an exasperated sigh, she murmured under her breath, "God, Aashita! Why? Do you even realize this is going to be one hellhole?"

"Trust me, Nysha, this happens to be our only getaway plan. There isn't a plan B," Aashita said wryly.

"I trust you, my friend. I swear I do," Nysha concluded in a flat and dejected tone.

When life hands over rotten lemons and takes an equally rotten turn, agreed, it could be hard to squeeze it into lemonade. But who says it couldn't find its way straight into a jerk's eye? And with a platoon of jerks to tackle, Nysha was ready with not just one or two, but a basket of rotten lemons at her disposal—one lemon at a time for one bloody jerk. Life for sure couldn't have gotten more interesting than it already was, or so she thought. That was until "he" decided to walk in.

Well, if the Devil were to walk the Earth, and if he were to have a face, for sure he would resemble Vardhaan Kapadia. With his sharp, sculptured jaw hard enough to cut glass, chiseled abs, protruding muscles, a sharp, defined nose, jet-black eyes, golden-olive skin, wavy shoulder-length locks... and lastly, those kiss-worthy, tempting lips, which, if they happened to curl into his trademark, sheepish, cocky grin, could weaken the resolve of even the most gallant hearts (gender, an absolute no bar). In short, he looked like the modern-day version of Adonis (raised on steroids).

When Vardhaan walked in through the door of the Auditorium of the Sports Complex, wearing a paper-thin off-white t-shirt with a deep V-neck, he not only put up his chest on a full frontal display but also ended up revealing a generous amount of golden curls covering his torso. That, coupled with his extremely brash idea of matching it with a pair of navy-blue dance shorts with a side slit at that, clearly exhibited his muscular, toned legs and left little to the imagination of the onlookers. Not that it bothered him. In fact, deranged Kapadia enjoyed every bit of the attention he was garnering with the spectacular performance that he had put up. Nysha scanned the room and its occupants. The stats clearly indicated that the number of females between the age group of 25 to 35 years outnumbered the males of all age groups, which kind of explained the shrill cry akin to that of banshees at his sudden apparent arrival. Both Nysha and Aashita looked at each other, gravely aware of the folly committed. Of course! It was their damn mistake that the outright importance of attaching a strict set of rules for "acceptable attire" along with the contract documents had skipped their feather brains. And since every mistake had its consequences, they were now going to pay the penalty for the same. The girls ogled at the rippled muscles of his chest as if he were a loaf of freshly baked bread, straight out of the oven. Now that the women were practically drowned with lust or rather paralyzed with the same, Nysha couldn't help but wonder about the tough times they were going to face ahead in getting some real job done.

"Oh my word, Bou! When you had asked me to join you for today's rehearsals, I had no idea that it was going to be so much fun," an amused voice called from behind, and both the women turned around and glowered at the source of the gleeful giggling voice. A young girl with a riot of expressions dancing on her face, ranging from delight, to excitement, to a hint of gambol stared at them. But what stood out was the unmistakable glint of mischief in those beautiful eyes. She smiled and looked at them, as if she was having the time of her life at their expense.

Investigative Journalist, Aarhi Baruah, a fresh journalism graduate from a leading Ivy League Institute in the UK with a specialization in Crime and Criminology, and presently, assistant to current Media Magnate and former God of crime reporting, Suhas Dasgupta, was clearly enjoying the unabashed show of brawniness galore.

"Don't even think about it," Aashita uttered a strict warning to her sister-in-law, followed by a pointed look.

"But I haven't said a thing...," Aarhi defended herself whilst giving an adorable puppy look.

"I know that look. I've seen it before, and I do know what it means," Aashita affirmed.

"Oh, bou, you are simply too much. In fact, you are beginning to sound so much like dada. One Hitler is just fine, we don't need another," the young girl laughed, while tipping her head back and flipping her wavy curls over her shoulders.

"Trust me; I am the gentle one," Aashita winked.

"Oh! And don't I know that already? I was just thinking of having some fun," Aarhi stated.

"Hard luck, love," Aashita said with an eye roll. "Instead, why don't you try doing the job you are here for? Filling in for Jacob Sebastian, your friendly neighborhood reporter," she taunted.

"Tabloid reporter," Aarhi asserted with an annoying side smirk.

"Whatever!" Aashita countered.

"Well, the good news is, I have the perfect headline in mind for Mr. Smart Pants."

Aashita noticed the playful flicker in Aarhi's eyes. She could have sworn that the girl was up to something naughty. As if in a reflex, she uttered, "No..."

"What now? I didn't say a thing...," Aarhi asked, flustered.

"I think I have a glimpse of your thoughts... They don't seem too friendly," Aashita rebuked.

"Oh, come on, bou, marrying Hitler has dulled your sense of adventure. After all, it's not every day that a loaded choco-chunk cookie on legs approaches you at their own behest. It's a sin not to indulge."

Aashita was about to retaliate, but before she could frame her precise response, the cookie in question had already stepped into the trio's zone of personal space. It was offensive, but hell yeah, Mr. Dick Kapadia had never really learned and bothered about the ABCs of the proximity game. In fact, he considered himself to be the "Demigod of Passion" and the "torch-bearer of lust."

"Oh, my God! Are my eyes playing tricks on me, or is the hottest duo of Professor Maverick's class standing in plain sight, right in front of me?" said an annoyingly handsome man with the cockiest grin ever plastered on his face.

"Oh hell yes...Dick Head Kapadia. It's been how many, like 6 years," Aashita said with a wink.

"Ah! Precisely...It seems like you missed me too, Cookie," he jeered.

"You still think so very highly about yourself, don't you, Prince of Morons?" Nysha said with a smug smile.

Aashita let out a soft chuckle, while Aarhi didn't even bother to muffle her loud snort, followed by an amused laughter.

Vardhaan paused for a second, while his eyes rested on Aarhi's face. Her skin was an enticing caramel color, bearing a resemblance to his favorite biscoff pudding. She was wearing a short jumpsuit with a boat neck and multi-colored polka dots, and it reminded him of school-going kids who sported two perfectly done plaits or ponytails, while pretending to act all big. She had tied her hair in a high ponytail, but the loose strands still managed to kiss her face. For a split second, his hand itched to test the softness of her skin and feel the riot of curls beneath his palm. A crazy desire to set her hair free from the elastic clutches of the hair scrunchie and see it splayed across in all directions rose in his chest, which he had a hard time crushing and looking away. But the very next moment, his eyes fell on her slim and delicate collarbone, and he cursed himself internally. True, he had a reputation of a debauch, but surely he didn't have to live up to it or do insane stuff just to protect it. Before his thoughts could get more haywire and wild, Aarhi snapped a finger right in front of his eyes, bringing his attention to her face, "Hey, right up here... Mr. Kapadia," she said whilst flashing an amazingly adorable smile which stirred his insides.

Extending her hand forward for a handshake, she proudly announced, "Aarhi Baruah, Investigative Journalist, The Hurricane." He took her hand and wrapped his fingers around her slender ones, appreciating the feel of her soft skin against his.

"Hey, sweet pea, aren't you a bit too young to play Enola Holmes?" he scoffed. "Love, you should be going back to playing tea party with your friends instead?" he added with a wink.

Aarhi's gaze hovered on his face for some time, before dropping to the wide expanse of his chest. His transparent t-shirt, of course, did very little to cover up for his part nudity, or his toxic masculinity. In fact, the flimsy material could hardly camouflage the hard planes or solid pecs which lay beneath. The person was very comfortable with his body, as if being ogled or drooled at were a part of his daily ritual. For a crazy second, she wanted to trace the outline of his muscular chest and see if his muscles would warm and quiver underneath her fingers.

Hell! Focus, Aarhi! And stop behaving like Lady Lech! She schooled her thoughts.

"14 years...," she huffed and almost spat out those words on his face. Her voice came out louder than she had expected.

"Pardon... love?" Vardhaan inquiringly raised an eyebrow.

"Enola Holmes was only 14 when she started... I am way older," she replied haughtily.

"Right so... But a day or two doesn't count, Cookie," he countered.

"And stop calling me cookie, or love, or sweet pea, or any such fancy syllables with which you are used to addressing and objectifying women. I would appreciate something more formal. For starters, a bit more professionalism," she replied coolly.

"Sorry, sweetie, I don't remember agreeing to any code of professionalism with you," he hit back.

"Ah! My bad, I never got a chance to actually mention this before. I want you to do an interview for 'The Hurricane'," she stated.

"An interview? Interesting...," he sounded as though he was taken aback. Then slowly, with his long legs, he strode toward her, and in just a few steps he was close to her, practically looming over her. It didn't take her second-guessing that in some deranged way, he enjoyed looking down upon her 5'6" frame with his over 6'1" frame. As she craned her neck to look at him, she saw his caramel-brown eyes filled with mirth.

"What? Do you want to intimidate me with your Hulky frame?" she charged indignantly.

"Do you ever get intimidated?" he asked, brimming with amusement.

"Nope... never!" She drew herself up and replied in a no-nonsense tone, expecting it to compensate for her average height.

"Well, I thought so, Sweetie," he replied with a satisfied grin.

"Aarhi," she asserted.

"Alright... Aarhi sweetie, look at me, love," he said, pointing toward his broad muscular chest. "I don't do interviews. In fact, I don't need to... when practically every other day, Page 3 tabloids, local rags, celeb columns, entertainment websites, gossip queens, or entertainment influencers are brimming with articles or cramming with information about me. You see, people are utterly obsessed with me. Not that I am complaining. I know I quite have that effect on them," he stated arrogantly.

Aarhi watched him for some time, wide-eyed in shock, before bursting into a whirlwind of loud and unapologetic laughter, as if it was the funniest jab she had heard in years. It was a loud, rumbling laughter that practically brought tears to her eyes.

"God! You are the most obtrusively self-obsessed and annoyingly arrogant person I have ever come across," she said, still laughing and wiping away the tears of mirth from the corner of her eyes. "But having said that, when I said interview, I meant some real stuff, and not just Page 3 Hush Hush Scandalous Whispers or Overrated Purple Prose, which talks more about your harem of girls and less about your achievements, wherein the actual equation should have been vice versa."

She put her hand into her jumpsuit pocket and fished out a card, handing it to him. "Nevertheless, if you ever have a change of heart, and want to tell the world your true inspirational story, you know whom to reach," she said, exhibiting an air of supreme confidence.

"Well, I will certainly remember that, my love," he said, his eyes twinkling.

"Muy Bien, Mr. Kapadia. I hope your good sense prevails," Aarhi added.

She started to leave, took a few steps, and then suddenly stopped in her tracks. It seemed as if she had forgotten something important. Then turning around she gave him the most amazing smile possible. It lit up her face and made her look magnificently gorgeous.

Fuck! She was beautiful, Vardhaan admitted internally.

"Adios, Mr. Kapadia... Hope you make up your mind soon," Aarhi stated.

She walked off, leaving a hint of a smile tugged at the corner of his lips, along with the Herculean task of normalizing and calming down his hitched-up breath.

"Hot chocolate... mint and paprika infused," he muttered softly.

"Someone seems to have finally met his match!" The known voices of Aashita and Nysha echoed in his ears.

He turned around, only to find them flashing a knowing smile.

Creepy ladies! He thought.

"I thought the organizers had work to do," Vardhaan gritted out.

"Sure, they do. That doesn't mean we aren't entitled to our share of fun," Nysha added.

"Plus, my sis-in-law is way out of your league, Kapadia. So don't even go there," Aashita added.

"And you two must be her self-appointed mother hens," he said with a playful taunt.

"Ok, enough of the jibe-exchange marathon," Nysha declared with an all-new, serious tone. "The stage is free, Kapadia, have it orchestrated your way for the practice; Zain is just about to reach. And trust me, we can't afford to disappoint our biggest star performer and highest contributor."

She looked at Aashita, who nodded and replied, "Noted."

"Don't worry, I have got you covered, cookie," Vardhaan said, slowly tracing his steps toward the stage.

"And shove that cookie into your fucking ass...," Nysha yelled behind his retreating back. Of course, it didn't bother him. Nothing did. He could bring out the worst in others, but his own restraint was stronger than a Himalayan hermit.

"Asshole!" Nysha grumbled.

And the Melodrama Continues...

After an affable banter with Dick Kapadia and assuring Pia over the phone that her husband was in safe hands, Nysha settled herself on the soft cushion of the front-row VIP seat and ran a hand along the intricately carved and delicately embossed wooden arm of the chair. Their uptight schedule and the mess thrown in had left them with practically no time to appreciate the beauty and artistic grandiosity of the auditorium. Designed by renowned Belgian architect, Victor Lambert, the dome-shaped structure was an architectural marvel and a modern wonder in its own right. Letting out a sigh of relief, she looked up at the stage and was totally mesmerized by what she saw. Truly, it was a sight to behold. It was amazing that they had managed to bring two of the industry's most gorgeous men together for a dance performance.

The Aerial Loop managed to combine the beauty of dance and soft silk, making the audience delve deep into the artistry and remarkable choreography of their performance, while transporting them into a high pedestal of awe, and the Fire Act transported the spectators into an unmatched Parallel Universe of 'Flame and Fun.' The powerful impact of skillful choreography, coupled with the fine show of muscle dexterity and energetic stage performance, culminated into an indescribable feeling of joy and complete exhilaration. Nysha had a real hard time controlling her surge of high emotional hormones, when all she wanted was to stick two fingers into her mouth and blow out a loud, long wolf whistle, sharp enough to deflate eardrums, join the background dancers and break into a 'kamar tod' gleeful dance, or simply jump up on the stage, fling her arms around Zain's neck, and thank him for being their life-saver, and an absolute darling. It took her a Herculean effort to restrain herself, act mature, and pretend unperturbed, all for the sake of being taken seriously and behaving like a grown-up, and not some deranged and fucked up Aunty.

Once the show was over, Aashita whispered softly, "Spectacular, aren't they?"

"I couldn't agree more," Nysha nodded, letting out an almost regretful sigh, as the bout of magnificent spell came to an end.

"I guess your doubts rest in peace now, Madam Organizer," Aashita enquired.

"Hmm...," Nysha let out a soft, blissful moan before replying, "Well, it most definitely was a mind-blowing start."

"Touche, my friend! Touche!" Aashita agreed.

But their happiness was rather short-lived; it died an eerie death the moment Malini Khanna walked in through the door, closely followed by her helicopter mother, whose rotor blades were overtly protective and frustratingly manipulative. Fashion influencer-cum-Travel Blogger-cum-Reality Show Winner-cum-Current in-Demand Host-cum-...Well, her list of achievements was practically endless. Making it to the 4th place in the list of "Asia's Most Sexiest Women," declared by the UK New Times, happened to be the latest addition to her crown of pride, which was kind of great, except for the fact that the brilliance of her feats wasn't lost on her either. Of late, she had earned widespread odium owing to her ill repute for a wide array of reasons. She was labeled unprofessional for her late arrival on the sets, catfights with fellow female actors, temper tantrums with crew members, and her nosy mom, who followed her almost everywhere like a shadow in tow. However, in the quest of protecting her naive daughter from the big bad wolves of the glamour world, Mrs. Khanna had contrarily ended up being a dreaded influence upon her, while casting a gloomy shadow upon her career, even before it could take a decent flag off.

"Think about the devil, and the devil surfaces," Nysha mumbled.

"She Devil, to be precise," Aashita rectified. Besides, "Hell hath no fury as a newbie celeb scorned."

Nysha scowled at her friend, "What's with murdering the proverb? And she has no reason to scorn."

"Really? If you say so. Anyway, good luck with convincing Aunty. Last she called, she clearly believed that there were enemies on the prowl, hell-bent on sabotaging her daughter's reputation by staging a wardrobe malfunction," Aashita added with malice.

Nysha shrugged her shoulders and raised a questioning eyebrow, "God! You are clearly into exaggeration, aren't you? I could surely do with some empathy at the moment," she stated.

"I could give you a proverbial dose of pseudo-sympathy or an honest opinion, I simply chose the latter. And if you don't mind me asking a favor, could you please deal with Malini and her entourage? I can't stand that woman and her whimsical antics, and she reciprocates with equal fervor," Aashita stated as a matter of fact.

Nysha nodded, her face masking her annoyance behind the charade of understanding. "Alright... I am in. Anyway, I am sure it will be a cakewalk," she grimaced.

However, when Nysha had agreed to convince Malini and her mom about how great the design changes were, or how elegant she would look in the new ensemble, she had no clue what she had signed up for. Both mother and daughter were epitomes of egocentrism. Their rejection of the design was not so much for their dislike of it, but for their non-inclusion in the proposed alteration. Nysha was having a hard time breathing, since the mother-daughter duo had decided to put her patience to a good test by fiddling with her strings of endurance and checking on its elasticity and snap time. She would have almost exhausted her daily quota of sanity, had it not been for Aryan's influx and his thoughtful and much-desired intervention. Not only did he manage to contain the diva's reluctance to try the new outfit, but he also promised her mom a new exclusively designed dress, especially for the gala event. The next thing Nysha knew was that they had decided to bury the hatchet and call it a truce as if no hard feelings had ever existed. Wow! And all in the name of a designer and his designed dress. While it had taken Aryan a while to coax them, but finally when he did, he had done a fantabulous job of wrapping the pair around his little finger like a flexible band, and Nysha was pretty sure he could have as well used his allure and charm to make the ladies eat out of his hand.

Nysha could feel exhaustion slowly seeping into her system and making its way at a leopard's pace down to every bone in her body. She stifled a yawn and rubbed the back of her neck, aware of the tension and stiffening that had settled there. Clearly, she had pulled a muscle or two. Ignoring the slight ache, she looked around the auditorium, in awe at the plethora of activities surrounding it. Starting with Vardhaan and Zain, who were now perfecting the last couple of steps and trying to ace their performance with their final recipe for finesse, the anchor couple, Malini and Rijvi, who were busy rehearsing their lines, with Malini stealing occasional shy glances at him, and poor Rijvi being adorably clueless about her affinity toward him. Also, there were the crew members who had their hands full and were scurrying around from pillar to post, juggling various tasks, as well as meeting the expectations of the performers and their attendants. Aryan on the other hand, was trying to engage Avni and flatter her with his swoon-worthy sugary talks, and while she did pretend her best to be unfazed by his romantic advances, her eyes betrayed her true emotions. The devil's seductive charms were not lost on her either. She was as besotted by him as he was with her. Poor girl! Nysha thought...If she couldn't restrain her heart, the devil might as well succeed in possessing her innocent soul. Then her eyes darted toward the tail end of the room, where both Aashita and Ishani were slouched on a black, old leather sofa, apparently a makeshift seating arrangement, engrossed in what seemed like an important discussion. While Ishani spoke in her usual animated fashion, with her hands and eyes being equal participants in her exchange of words and wisdom, Aashita's stoic expressions provided the perfect masquerade for keeping her true inner feelings under wraps. However, knowing her friend well, Nysha could bet that her non-committal look suggested that she was bored to tears with her present companion's ridiculous show of emotions.

Nysha shook her head and let out a quick huff of breath. She decided she needed a breather, and a walk in the orchid garden could provide her with the same. Excusing herself from the troupe, she strode across the grounds. As she walked, she whipped out her phone from her pocket to check the string of missed calls and messages. Ignoring the cacophony of beeping and flash notifications, she scrolled right to that one message, which could lift her spirits and make her lips twist into a smile.

"Hey, I know you are gonna be insanely busy this week. But I wanted to let you know that, no matter what, I have got your back. Also, you are going to slay it, my queen..."

A crazy, wide, unabashed smile crossed her lips, and she was thankful to be alone, within the confines of the Victorian-style Gazebo, which provided her the liberty of soaking in the warmth of Samar's words, away from the prying eyes of her friends and colleagues. "Queen!" he had called her his queen. A shot of ecstasy traveled through her entire system, making every fiber of her body come alive. She was filled with a sudden fanatic urge to call him and hear his voice. The need to experience comfort in the warmth of his embrace, and the urgency to taste his tongue and let him devour her lips whilst he filled her senses with his scent, was intense. Without letting another torturous minute pass, she dialed his number. The call went through, but there wasn't any answer. She tried a second time, this time again, the phone rang for a long time but no one picked up. But just when she was about to hang up, convinced of the fact that Dr. Heartless was in all probability busy fixing hearts and saving lives, he finally answered, "Hey, missing me already?" he asked in a tantalizing tone, making her heart skip a beat and skin erupt into goosebumps. Of course, she missed him... She loved him, and she missed him bad. But she wasn't going to admit it and come across as desperate for His Highness's kind attention.

"High hopes, Dr. Heartless. No, I'm not missing you. Frankly, where is the time for that? My hands are full, and yeah, I am surrounded by too many lovely people to be missing you," she lied.

"Ah! Interesting!" He said in a deep, husky voice. "Where are you now?" he asked.

"The usual... auditorium," she replied.

"Liar!" he called out softly.

"And what makes you say so?" she challenged.

"Because... there is no noise or any commotion in the background... If you were to be surrounded by your so-to-say lovely people, I am sure the clamor would have been hard to miss. Nothing rocket science, my love," he replied calmly.

"Impressive, Sammy... Doctor Heartless goes Sherlock, not bad...," she teased.

"Now tell me, where exactly are you?" he asked.

"Garden...," she replied.

The damn place has at least five gardens. "Which is your chosen one?" he asked impatiently. His words made her laugh like a hormonally imbalanced, giddy teenager. The fact that she could annoy him and rattle his perfect demeanor, made her smile internally. Slowly, she was getting to know him better. In fact, it was a fine revelation that even the slightest of things could manage to irritate him. Without pushing any further, she replied, "Gazebo @Orchid Maze Garden," but why do you ask? "It is not as if you are planning to materialize out of thin air like Kal-El," she stated.

"Now, who the hell is he?" he gave a disgruntled response.

"Your IQ is really small, sweetheart, clearly disappointing. Kal-El is the other name of Superman. He is the greatest superhero of all time. Hopefully, your other physical organs are not as tiny as your brain," she sniggered.

"Watch your words, lady. Now you are hitting below the belt. You might not like the consequences," he threatened.

"That kind of depends on what you have in mind," she said suggestively.

"Well, you are going to find out soon. What about spanking for starters, honey?" His deep, rhythmic baritone voice suddenly breathing down her neck left her startled. She turned around in a jiffy, and the sudden movement made her tipsy, throwing her off balance. Samar caught her hand in a firm grip, pulling her closer to himself, making her face land smack dab on his chest, with her nose crushed beneath the hard planes of his torso. His proximity and the whiff of his manly smell sent a jolt straight to her gut. She tried to pull herself away from him but instead found his hold tightening around her waist. His gaze bore into hers, and his lips lifted in a smirk at her shocked expression. Taking advantage of her befuddled state, he grazed the back of his fingers against her lips, making her moan softly in return. The sweet, sultry sound went straight to his groin, making Mr. Willy Wong highly active and buzzing in anticipation. He slightly squeezed her perky rear, making her call out his name.

"Samar, stop," she whispered softly.

"Hush... love, you have no idea what I want to do to you?"

"You really aren't contemplating spanking, I believe?" she asked in a hushed tone. Her witty remark earned a croaky laughter from him. She looked up at him, feigning annoyance, but was lost in his eyes instead. His deep hazel eyes reflected various emotions, from mirth to passion and a dash of lust. He was wearing a simple V-neck T-shirt, which revealed a hint of his hard chest, and a pair of faded denim that clung to his taut butt like a second skin. And God! She was doomed, for he looked just like a hot, freshly baked crème brûlée to be devoured straight out of the oven. Damn him! For managing to look gorgeous even in the plainest, most boring, and most predictable clothes of all time.

A slight tap on her cheeks pulled her out of her reverie. There was no denying that she was full-on mush and yearning for this man. "Spanking isn't even close to what I would actually fancy," he whispered in her ear. His warm breath tickled her sensitive earlobes.

"What would you fancy then?" she asked, suddenly emboldened and looking straight into his eyes.

"I would love you splayed across on the OT Table like my personal gourmet spread and ravish you to the core. I fantasize about hearing my name from your sexy mouth again and again. By the time I am done, you won't remember your name. And I wouldn't settle for one. I would claim a repeat performance with the same vigor. But for the time being, we could settle for a kiss... a mind-blowing, toe-curling, air-sucking kiss," he completed.

His words left her flustered, but his demeanor remained unchanged, calm, and composed like he was discussing a corporate case or the next performance in a row. If his words could unnerve her to such an extent, she imagined the kind of mayhem his promised kiss could cause. Slowly pulling herself out of his proximity, she tried steadying her rattled nerves, before speaking again in a groggy voice, though it failed to sound half as convincing even to her very own ears.

"This isn't fair, Samar," she pleaded.

"Excuse me... What isn't fair?" he asked, bemused.

"You coming here and playing games with my mind. Talking dirty and wreaking havoc in my already tired brain cells... not fair, you don't get to do that," she pouted.

"Oh! Poor baby, you don't like me coming over to cheer you up?" he asked.

"Don't baby me, Samar. I am serious," she claimed.

"Alright... Perhaps, this would help to change your mind, my stubborn princess," he stated confidently.

Before she could get the inkling of his next move, he bridged the distance between them, dug his fingers into her hair, and pulled her mouth into a scorching-hot and all-consuming kiss, drowning them both in a bubble of lust. They were completely lost inside their cozy bubble, oblivious to their surroundings, until Aashita suddenly manifested out of thin air and they got... Well, they were, "busted!"

Confessions, Mayhem & the Final Wrap

"Holy Mother of God!" "What the fuck, guys!" The shrill voice of Aashita called out from behind, taking them both by surprise. Nysha stilled, unsure of how to face her partly annoyed, partly irate, and at present, utterly mad friend. However, acknowledging the inevitable, she slowly turned around to face Aashita, who had a pissed-off look marking her features, and an end number of questions oscillated on her beautiful face. Questions she expected answers to, and answers without which she wasn't going anywhere.

Nysha attempted a feeble smile, but the smile seemed to have lost its path and bounced off track upon witnessing Aashita's unceremonious glare. She stood there with her hands crossed while giving them a stare-down of a lifetime, making them feel like two horny kids who were caught experimenting, while making out in their neighbor's backyard.

"Look, I can explain," Nysha offered.

"Seriously, can you?" Aashita countered.

"Listen... you aren't making this easy," Nysha said.

"You aren't either... But anyway, I am listening," Aashita replied.

“I wanted to tell you...,” Nysha stated.

“When?” Aashita asked.

“Today... Even yesterday... but you were busy cribbing. Not that I blame you,” Nysha clarified.

“Ah! That’s really sweet...,” Aashita gritted. “So, you guys are serious?” she asked, her eyes darting between Samar and Nysha.

“Yes, we are. I love her... damn very much,” Samar declared, even before Nysha had a chance at putting forth her side of the story. Aww! And did the mushy declaration melt her heart? Oh, surely, it did. Her chest swelled with inflated pride, like that of a baboon, and her heart began to beat at top-notch speed, putting Schumacher’s Formula 1 to shame. She wanted to pull him for a mind-numbing kiss, but quickly dropped the idea upon seeing Aashita’s lip, which was drawn into a thin line and her brows pulled together into a visible frown. She looked far from being cheerful. In fact, she looked like a murderous and cheated girlfriend who had just stumbled upon her lover making out with her best friend.

“Yikes!” Nysha’s wild thoughts sent her into a full-on frenzy mode. A barely-there smile crossed her lips, but it failed to escape her beau’s attention. He raised a questioning eyebrow at her, making her flash her pearly whites at him while batting her eyelashes in a dramatic flair.

“Can you stop drooling over the doctor?” Aashita hissed.

“I... don’t... drool...,” Nysha defended.

“You clearly were, just a few seconds back,” Aashita accused. “Which reminds me... who knows about this new development?” she added.

“No one,” Nysha replied.

“Pia?” Aashita asked.

“No,” Nysha responded.

“Aunty? I mean, your mom,” she enquired.

“You’ve got to be crazy,” Nysha retorted.

“You sure?” Aashita questioned.

“Yes,” Nysha asserted.

“He?” Aashita confirmed.

“Double that,” Nysha nodded.

“Hmm... Alright,” Aashita concluded with a satisfied grin.

Samar had a hard time following the monosyllabic exchanges between the two friends. Sure thing, they had mastered the art of minimalistic communication, but it was driving him crazy now. After what seemed like ages, finally, Aashita hugged her friend tight and said, “Oh dear, I am so very happy for you.”

Then turning toward Samar she added, “Congratulations, Dr. Samar. Welcome to the family.”

“What she means is, madness...,” Nysha quipped.

“Why am I not surprised?” he replied with a raised eyebrow.

“Ok. Now, can we all go inside, please...I came looking for you before thunder struck. Aryan wanted to have a word with you. In fact, I won’t be surprised if he is pulling his hair by now, unable to deal with Miss Malini,” Aashita clarified.

“Don’t tell me, what now? Anyway, I have full faith in him. He will manage with his charm," Nysha claimed.

"Oh, I am not so sure. Even charms have a shelf life, but Malini and her antics are incessant," Aashita replied.

Slowly, Samar strode down to where Nysha and Aashita were standing. He leaned toward Nysha to give her a slight peck on the cheek, but Aashita stepped in between, giving them both a slight push against their chest to shove them apart, while at the same time wrapping her arms around them, and drawing them closer, almost squishing them into a warm bear hug before whispering, "Guys! Lovers or not, there are smartphones all around. The last thing we can afford right now is a viral news flash with the paparazzi going crazy over a smouldering kiss o' passion. We have worked very hard for this event to let a kiss decide its fate. Not that I don't trust my friends... but..."

"But...," Nysha pressed.

Aashita paused for a few torturous seconds before speaking, "But I don't trust brand new lovers to keep their hands off each other."

Her words were like a bucket of cold water dousing their red flame.

"Thanks for your concern, friend, but we don't need your chastisement. We are grown-ass adults," Nysha replied, her voice triple-barreled with sarcasm.

"Aww! But it's not every day that I get to pull your leg, Nysha sweetie. I wouldn't miss this opportunity for the world," Aashita winked.

"Wicked Maleficent," Nysha muttered.

Aashita laughed aloud and then turning toward Samar added, "You will have your time with her, Doctor, but until then, I play the chaperone. She comes with me. Even if it means ducking out a few silent, half-muttered, and covert curses hurled across. I think I will survive."

"You are crazy," Nysha sniggered.

"I sure am," Aashita admitted, before dragging her friend toward the hall, leaving Samar to trail behind the two guffawing teens. But it wasn't before hurling certain inaudible profanities and accusations inside his head, meant for the girls, but confined strictly within his mind. After all, he was a model of restraint, and couldn't allow his cool and composed demeanor to slip off. Not that easily at least...

As she stepped inside the auditorium for the second time that day, Nysha could sense an absolute madness encasing the entire setting. But she wasn't complaining, for the scene that unfolded in front of them, was not only the kind of creative frenzy she had been expecting all through, but it seemed that finally, they had succeeded in attaining the unattainable. It took her a moment to ensure that whatever she saw was not some dream, but indeed a reality.

The stage was cleared of all the equipment, and rugs, carpets, and mats were spread out at the base. In a thoughtful gesture, a few chairs had been arranged for the older staff and crew members who had difficulty sitting on the floor, so they didn't feel left out or missed out on the fun. Inside the circle, Zain, Aryan, Vardhaan, Avni, and Aarhi had plonked themselves on the ground. Zain had a guitar placed on his lap, and his agile fingers were strumming expertly and roaming over the strings in a magical fashion. As he played the tune of, "Gazab Ka Hai Din," an '80s all-time romantic favorite; his close-knit spectators went crazy with happy screams and loud cheers. The magnificent roar was madness personified. Not that she could blame them. A superstar showing off his guitar-playing skills was not an everyday affair, and his fans and supporters couldn't get enough of clicking photos and capturing videos.

Nysha was getting impatient now. As much as she wanted to join in and have fun, she also wanted to know how they had achieved the impossible. The way these guys had bonded, they looked like a close-knit, happy family with a common goal, and "Mission Akshat Ratna" already seemed to be a cohesive, successful affair and not some distant reality anymore. As though sensing her thoughts, Avni spotted them and made her way to them, a big, broad smile still splayed across her lips. She halted right in front, and without wasting a minute, Nysha directly came to the point.

"How?" she asked.

"Pia ma'am," Avni replied instantly. Nysha's eyes widened and her mouth fell open in surprise at her response.

"Don't tell me Pia is here, and I missed her," her eyes scurried back to the stage while attempting to spot her missing friend.

"Not Pia ma'am, but lunch boxes from Sinful, with personalized gourmet hampers arrived. Each hamper has an attached personal note and an exclusive Sinful membership card, meant only for high-end patrons. Needless to say, our pack here is overwhelmed with the gesture. And ma'am, the food was simply...," she paused, while searching for the right word.

"Orgasmic," Nysha completed.

"Seriously?" Samar raised an eyebrow and threw her an amused look.

"Of course, we are talking about Pia and her amazing cooking skills here. No wonder, these guys have already attained Nirvana."

"They have managed to scrape even the last bit off their plates," Avni added.

"What is inside the box? I am getting curious now," Samar asked.

"Creamy butter chicken lasagne," Nysha exclaimed.

"Prawn Tempura," Aashita added.

"And Sinful's signature rainbow cupcakes and black rice pudding," both, Pia and Nysha screeched together in a practiced chorus.

"God! Are they right?" Samar asked, turning toward Avni.

"Absolutely... every word," Avni confirmed.

"Would you like to know the contents of the veg box too, Samar sir?" Nysha asked, and her lips twitched slightly as she set herself up for the challenge.

"No, my love. I would appreciate it if I could get my box instead. I am starving," Samar replied.

At their open display of affection, Avni stifled a giggle, while Aashita issued them a warning glower.

"I will get your boxes right away," Avni stated, still smiling.

As she excused herself, Aashita warned, "Guys, can't your very public display of affection wait... or be postponed until the show's end? Word spreads fast, especially the grapevine... we don't want that."

"She started it," said Samar.

"You challenged," Nysha countered.

"As if...," Samar huffed.

"For Fuck's sake, stop it guys... Stop behaving like teenagers," Aashita hollered.

"Who's behaving like teenagers?" a deep, rumbling voice spoke from behind.

In their crazy banter, they had failed to notice that Zain had already finished playing and had strode up to them.

"Hey!" Nysha said, as she gave him a quick hug.

"You didn't answer... Is everything ok?" he repeated.

"Don't mind, it's nothing," she gave a nonchalant shrug. "By the way, when did you uproot yourself from the center of gravity, and what's with those mean guitar-playing skills, Mr. Superstar? Don't tell me, you want to hog all the limelight for yourself...," she taunted playfully.

"Yes please... of course... you got me!" he replied with a dramatic smile on his face, making Nysha and her friends laugh aloud at his crazy shenanigans.

"Jokes apart, Zaidi, but thanks for the lovely surprise. It was amazing," Nysha affirmed.

"Don't thank me. It was all Pia...," he replied.

"I know, but you did a fabulous job of putting that friendly musical jam together, and considering the complex crowd at your disposal, it sure wasn't an easy task."

"Hell yeah, but you tend to forget about my charms, Patel...," he added with an arrogant smirk, suddenly wrapping his arms around her shoulders and tugging her closer to himself impishly, while she wriggled in a futile attempt to free herself from his grip.

"God! You are an incorrigible jerk," she said, while slapping her palms on his chest and managing to free herself. "I still wonder what Pia saw in you... My friend is a gem... you on the other hand..."

"Stop right there... don't even think of grumbling something offensive," he threatened.

"Yeah right... I better call and thank Pia," Nysha stated.

"You should...," Zain affirmed.

"Though I fail to understand why she had to take all the trouble, especially in the last phase of her pregnancy...," before Nysha could complete, Zain intervened, "Well, I am glad she did. You know what food means to Pia..."

"Certainly not something to simply fill empty tummies," Nysha replied.

"Nah! It is an emotion and a lifelong memorable experience. Considering her current mental state, with her hormones wreaking havoc, I can't tell you how happy she was to curate these customized boxes and hampers. Like she was having a therapeutic experience, and compensating for not being able to do much."

"Hmm... That's Pia, always thinking about others. I hope you are being good to my friend. It's a hard time for girls, balancing their fetus, their career, and what not..."

Before she could complete it, Zain cast an irked look.

"What?" Nysha asked.

"Can you please show some respect for my offspring, and call it baby instead of fetus," he pleaded.

"Oh! So sweet! Already being a touchy parent, aren't you?" Nysha said in a sing-song voice.

He was about to retort, but a sudden loud ring on Nysha's phone broke their exchange of unpleasantries. "Yes, Avni...," Nysha answered. As she listened to the voice at the other end, her face lit up, and she muttered an earnest thank you before hanging up. While a smile still played on her lips, she saw curious expectant faces eyeing her with interest, clearly anticipating an answer.

"What?" she asked.

"We get to ask that, Patel," Zain replied.

"Curious much," Nysha asked.

"Very," Zain said.

"Well, lunch has been arranged," Nysha replied.

"Kaha, madame?" Samar asked.

"Ah! At last, the doctor speaks... I thought you had gone on mute mode," Zain joked.

"Trust me, that's not a bad option," Samar winked.

"Now, if you are done with your bullish tête-à-tête, move your asses. Delizah and Bryan are waiting to have lunch with us," Nysha growled.

"Delizah and Bryan! They are here? Why didn't they call me?" Zain whined.

"Oh, sure they did, Mr. Superstar, but it seems the objectionable instrument is nowhere in your close vicinity. Probably it's beneath your Highness's dignity to answer the calls of your mediocre subjects," Nysha shot back.

"Can you stop your cringe fest? With your flair for coming up with the most obnoxious response, you can surely give the C-grade dialogue writers a run for their money," Zain scoffed.

"I will surely contemplate," Nysha huffed.

"Shut up! Shut up! Shut the fuck up!" Aashita screeched. "You guys are making me nauseous with your stupid squabble. One more word, and I swear I'm gonna puke right on your shoes."

"Yuck! Please!" Nysha muttered with disgust.

"Hey, chill! What's wrong with you?" Zain asked as he took a step forward.

"Patience snapped, period. Don't try your luck too hard, Mr. Superstar. It's not like your shoes aren't an option. I won't back off from throwing up on your shoes either. In fact, the bigger the brand, the better it is," she said with a devilish grin.

Zain looked at her as if she had just threatened to upload the pirated version of his unreleased movie on an illegal streaming website. "Seriously, are you out of your mind, lady? These are a pair of Tod's Limited Edition Moccasins. You wouldn't dare," he threatened.

"I am sure you don't want to find out," Aashita added viciously.

"Alright, guys! Let's call it a truce... a ceasefire... before Ares decides to walk the Earth," Nysha proclaimed.

"Who's Ares now?" Samar growled.

"Oh my dear doctor... Trust me, ignorance is bliss... and now, please follow me...," Nysha replied.

"Dear... doctor?" Zain muttered under his breath, with calculated skepticism, as if something utterly distasteful had hit his tongue and made him gag. He eyed Aashita with a questioning look, and she glowered back. But her subtle warning did little to curb his curiosity. He whispered softly into her ear, "Something's fishy, isn't it?"

His query was met with a severe frown.

"You don't give up, do you? Aren't you turning into that infamous director, always digging for Celebrity Gossip and releasing them on his chat show... hell-bent on compromising consent for the sake of TRPs. What was his name?" Aashita asked.

"Hush, woman! You don't want to be the death of me," Zain gritted. "Talks are underway for a three-film contract with his production banner. I wouldn't jeopardize it for some shady tittle-tattle, my friend," he schooled.

"You are such a snob in the making," she guffawed.

"God! Your hunger pangs are getting the worst out of you. Come on, let's get you something to eat before you turn ballistic," Zain scoffed.

"I hate you and your antics," Aashita muttered.

"Oh! Trust me, I have seen worse... You have to try harder, my friend," he sharply retorted.

"Ass...," she muttered.

"Harder," he challenged.

"Shameless," she chuckled, and her mouth tugged up in a wide grin.

Friendly Lunch, Unfriendly Jibes & Past Revelations

Lunch had been arranged in a room adjacent to Bryan's cabin. By the time Nysha and her gang reached, the rest of the members were already seated around the table, waiting for them. As they walked inside, Delizah looked up at them and came forward to greet them, while a broad smile graced her lips.

"I am so glad that you could stay and we could meet," she said while giving Zain a quick hug.

"Of course, sweetheart, I am glad too," he said earnestly, hugging her back.

Bryan closely followed behind his wife and added, "We have been married for like five years now, and yet I can't help but get insecure upon seeing my wife's greater affinity toward you," he said playfully.

"Well... well! There's no cure to jealousy it seems... and let me remind you, I have known your wife long before you, mister. Our friendship dates way back, and the bond that we share is special," Zain replied.

"Very special...," Delizah affirmed while throwing Bryan a mischievous look.

“Teaser,” he said, his eyes filled with mirth at his wife’s antics.

Zain cleared his throat and declared, “Now, if you are done with using me as a prop, and channelizing your internal flirtatious self, can we please begin? I am famished.”

“Aww! So sweet! Just to remind you, that the food has been prepared by your dear wifey,” Delizah remarked.

“Precisely, greater the reason for my impatience.... for my wife happens to be the best.”

“You guys are couple goals! Matching Gala outfits, public display of affection, always holding hands, having eyes only for each other... Oh My God! Pia truly is one lucky girl,” Delizah responded.

“Everything you just said is quite true... except that I am the lucky one to have Pia in my life. She is my calm amidst chaos, sunshine amidst the gloom, and my smile and hope in times of despair,” Zain affirmed.

“Aww! Wow, so romantic!” Aarhi shrieked aloud, and all eyes turned toward her. Realizing that every eye in the room was fixated on her, she gave a sly smile and said, “Sorry, guys; I got a bit carried away... But Zaidi sir, your declaration of love was super cute, sexy, cool, and so damn utterly romantic that you can’t totally blame me for going berserk.”

Zain gave an understanding smile and said, “Don’t worry, dear. I am used to getting that reaction, and it always feels great.”

“Sir, on a serious note, your love story can shame even the YRF Love Sagas,” Aarhi continued.

“Flattered....Now, coming straight to the point, little one. What do you want?” Zain asked.

"I would love to do a story on you and Pia ma'am," she blurted.

"Oh! Girl, that was fast," Zain remarked.

"Oh, trust me; you don't know her at all. She can be a super-fast shifter. Moments ago, I topped her to-do list of Celebrity Interviews," Vardhaan scoffed.

"The offer still stands, Mr. Kapadia. Let me know if you make up your mind," Aarhi gritted.

"Alright, let's cut to the chase and spare the drag of an episodic daily soap. If you have something worthy to catch my attention, I might as well give it a thought," Zain assured.

"You aren't kidding? Are you?" She asked him wide-eyed and mouth agape, still regarding his proposition.

Zain shook his head to suggest that he wasn't kidding. "No, I am rather serious. But though I am a nice guy, I am not exactly known for my patience. So if you really wish to catch my attention, you better be quick," he added.

"On it... and I won't disappoint," Aarhi promised.

"Issue settled then...," Zain concluded.

"Absolutely, and thank you for trusting me," Aarhi exclaimed.

Once the pleasantries and greetings were exchanged, everyone took their respective seats around the table.

"Aryan and Avni, do they join us?" Nysha asked.

Aashita shrugged, "No, I asked them to... even Delizah did, said they were more than welcome to join us. But they preferred not to, politely declined."

"Come on, Aashi, sometimes people prefer to be left alone. It's ok to want some privacy... or some us time," Nysha clarified.

"Of course, I do understand the need for us time," Aashita nodded, while an eloquent smile tugged at the corner of her lips.

"Well, I can't wait any longer to gorge on the food," Nysha confessed.

"Go ahead, who is stopping?" Aashita remarked.

As Nysha excitedly opened her box, the smell of three-cheese infused, fresh-baked lasagne wafted through the air.

"Hmm! it smells delicious! Heaven!" she uttered.

"I am sure it would taste even better," Samar mentioned.

Nysha took her spoon and dug out a large scoop, but just when she was about to put it inside her mouth, Bryan got up from his seat and declared, "Ah, there you are. I thought you are not going to make it."

Everyone turned around to acknowledge the novel presence. However, Aashita and Nysha's eyes widened upon seeing the late attendees. But before they could react, their shocked expression caught Delizah's eyes and she enquired, "Girls, is everything alright?"

"Ah! Well, we thought, lunch was meant to be an intimate affair," Aashita said, beckoning toward the newly arrived father-daughter duo. While Mr. Kapoor took a seat near Bryan, Nysha realized with a near sinking feeling that the only empty seat available was near Samar, and Ishani heartily settled her ass into the plush cushion. As usual, she looked immaculate with her perfectly done hair which fell like a cascade of waves over her shoulders. Her impeccable makeup screamed of a little touch up done right. Overall, Ishani's flawless demeanour was a sharp contrast to her own muddled self.

"It is. But Mr. Kapoor is Bryan's new business partner, so the invite. Is there a problem?" Delizah asked in a hushed tone.

"Well, he probably was interested in buying Akshat Ratna. But since that is clearly not happening now, so yup, all good," Nysha assured, conveniently leaving Ishani out of the picture. She had no intention of letting the world know about her not-so-friendly equation or her near-perfect animosity with the Billionaire heiress. Though a strange sense of unease had settled in her gut, she tried her best to act normal while sporting a weak smile. But that was until her eyes wandered to Samar and Ishani, and the sight she witnessed sent her wheezing. With her head bent down, Ishani tried to whisper something into Samar's ears. In her lousy attempt, her lips almost brushed his earlobe, which made Nysha's insides twist in reflex. A sense of raw anger crept into her body, while a surge of indescribable jealousy seeped through her veins. Her massive appetite for food was now lost. Instead, suddenly, she missed Spooky, the demonic Chihuahua of her neighbor, Gupta Uncle, terribly. He was one and the only one, who in all capability could relieve her of all miseries by biting off a part of Ishani's perky rear, so that each time she would try sitting on her sore and sorry ass, it would serve as a reminder to stay away from her man. The very thought of her uneven ass brought a smile to Nysha's face. As if sensing her wild inner thoughts, Ishani turned her head toward her and faked a big smile, before greeting her in an equally fake and honey-laced tone, "Oh! Hi Nysha, I didn't know you were here, sweetie."

Ishani's outward sweet and sultry voice did little to hide her inner despicable tone, and though it did get on Nysha's nerves, there was no fucking way she was letting her the gratification of knowing that she could make her lose control.

"Well, here I am. But clearly, you were expecting someone else," Nysha replied begrudgingly, but a fake smile still adored her lips.

"Oh, no! That's not what I meant. Did that sound rude?" Ishani asked, peeking through her perfect eyelashes, while faking a mock concern.

All previous thoughts of being in control and playing it cool were threatening to abandon Nysha's mind. All she could think of was fisting her fingers into Ishani's hair and banging her head straight against a concrete wall, everything with the hardcore intention of deriving pleasure from her shocked expression. Later, of course, an apology would follow, for her not so meaning to be rude behavior, and deemed to be unfit action. She took a deep breath and was about to retort, when Aashita cut in, "Of course, she should be here. In case you haven't noticed, she is in charge and leading the entire event," she added defiantly.

Nysha was filled with a sense of pride and deep-rooted admiration for her friend. She knew that somehow she had managed to stir Aashita's protective instincts, and sadly for Ishani, the mother hen was in no mood to kiss and spare.

Also, their cold exchange of words and the not so subtle meaning behind them had now garnered the attention of those around them. Caught off guard by Aashita's accusing tone, Ishani shifted uncomfortably in her chair, "Look! I was misunderstood and I apologize... I meant no harm, and demeaning Nysha was never the idea...," she clarified.

Sensing things might get a bit overboard, Nysha intervened, "It's ok, Ishani, no need to apologize. Everyone is just doing their job, so no hard feelings," she said. "And Aashi, it's ok, chill!" she added with a wink to lighten the mood.

Ishani reached across the table and gave Nysha's hand a slight squeeze before saying, "Oh, sweetie, thank you so much for understanding. I just thought perhaps you would be more interested in attending Akshat's anniversary prayer service than this impromptu lunch meet-up, but clearly,

I was wrong. Anyway, I am so glad that you have decided to move on. After all, we all deserve a second chance," she gave her hand another firm squeeze. Finally, with a vixen-like smile spread on her lips, she meted out the ultimate blow, "Ah! And one more thing, please call Dr. Harsha once you are free. She was worried sick about you, said you aren't answering her calls, and it is so unlikely for you to forget dates. I told her it must have slipped your mind, and that I will surely try and inform you. I believe my job here is done. I just remembered I need to make an urgent call. So everyone, kindly excuse me, I will take my leave. Enjoy your meal. See you later. Ciao!" She pushed back her chair with a sharp scrap against the floor, and left without uttering another word, pretty confident that the resultant damage from her well-played move would most certainly be to her absolute sadistic liking.

Nysha's face turned red, and it seemed like Death Eaters had managed to suck out all the air from the room, and also from her lungs, leaving her drained off completely. A flood of crazy old memories came rushing back in a flash, in bits and pieces, making it insanely difficult for her to draw a breath. And suddenly it all came back...Him going down on his knees, her giggling, calling him crazy, the ring, the heart platinum band, the cake... the cake... the choco-mint ice cream cake... the accident... and him gone, gone forever...

Her breath came in small puffs, and her restlessness began to increase. She tried to push away the dreaded memories behind, but they refused to leave. She tried hard to figure out what was wrong but couldn't do so. The only thing she remembered was, that something terrible had happened in the past... and probably it was all her fault... all of it.... As she tried to get up, her steps faltered, and she tightly gripped the end of the table for balance. A strong arm encircled her waist, keeping her in place. Her cheeks were plastered against his chest, and his familiar scent hit her nostrils, making her feel comfortable, relaxed, and hopelessly miserable, all at once.

From the corner of her eye, she saw Samar's blurry outline. The unmistakable hint of concern and helplessness was evident in his eyes. She tried to say something, but her voice slurred and her words refused to come out, whilst his soothing voice echoed in her ears, "It's ok... Nysha, I have got you, love... Breathe... please breathe......," he kept on repeating. She grabbed a handful of his shirt before whispering, almost pleading, "Samar, I can't breathe. I can't... please help me."

As her vision began to blur... she heard Samar's panicky voice calling out, "Nysha! Stay!...Stay!...Please... Somebody get help fast.... we are losing her." Then everything went murky... faded in front of her eyes.... until there was a complete blackout.... And only darkness prevailed....

Several hours later, when she finally woke up to the worried faces of her friends and well-wishers surrounding her, it took her mind on an unwarranted guilt ride. The pain and fear which still lingered on their faces and in their eyes, was all her doing. Unable to look into their anxious eyes, she turned her face around and tried to take a few deep breaths. Aashita slowly sat beside her, and in a comforting manner wrapped an arm around her shoulders, and when she didn't pull away, she quickly encircled her with the other one as well. Nysha heaved a sigh and was glad to return her friend's embrace, while soaking up her warmth and comfort. Aashita softly patted her friend's back and whispered, "It's ok... I am here. We are all here for you....," she asserted.

As tears of remorse slid down her cheeks, Nysha asked in a rueful tone, "How did I forget, Aashi? How could I? Does that make me a terrible person?"

"What? Are you mad? You are one of the most amazing people I have ever come across, and I consider myself lucky to have you in my life,"

Aashi assured.

"But....," Nysha began, when Zain intervened, "Besides, you don't need validation regarding your awesomeness from anyone... not me, not Pia, not Aashi... no one, fucking no one can make you feel awful," Zain said, as he held her hand between his own.

"What he means is.... definitely not some snarky bitch...," Aashita added.

"Holy Lord, Woman!" I never said that. You sure have no filters in your mouth, and you are a menace... In fact, you are formidable for my PR," he exaggerated.

His sudden outburst had the desired effect, and though Nysha tried her best to stifle her giggle, she lost control; and ended up laughing frenziedly until tears streamed down her cheeks. They carried an array of emotions, from grief to an overwhelming sense of relief, and laughter, and most importantly, they made her feel alive and kicking again.

"Ishani is going to kill us," she said in between her soft chortles.

"Kill us? Are you serious?" Aashita shrieked. "Given a chance, I am gonna skin her alive, or better, bury her in the desert sand."

"There goes the demoness!" Zain exclaimed. "Tell me, who has activated this violent streak of yours? My bet is on Mr. Baruah."

"Of course not. Raghav is a thorough gentleman...," Aashi defended her husband.

"I agree. This isn't Raghav's doing. Both my friends are practising their motherly instincts on me," Nysha explained. "Speaking of which, did you mention anything to Pia or Harsha Aunty? Not to my parents, I believe," she looked meaningfully from Zain to Aashita.

"Not your parents... of course, since they aren't here. But Pia, and Harsha Aunty, we had to," Aashita stated as a matter of fact.

"Oh, No! Why? You shouldn't have...," she sulked.

"We didn't have a choice. They would have found out anyway," Zain defended.

"He is right. Not left with a choice really," Aashita supported Zain's statement.

"Pia.... What was her reaction?" Nysha asked tentatively.

"She was freaking worried... but calmed down after speaking to Samar. By the way, since we got you here, your man has been working relentlessly, only to get you better. His external calmness is quite a contrast to his inner chaos. He is a gem, Nysh, a real gem. Don't let him slip away," Aashita coaxed.

"I am not sure.... not anymore...," Nysha said ruefully.

Aashita fumed at Nysha and gave her a menacing glare. She could almost feel the heat emanating from it. Her glare, in all probability, could thaw a polar ice cap or even melt the 'man of steel.' Locking eyes with Nysha and containing her irritation, Aashita spoke with an audible sigh... "Well, at least give your relationship a fair chance. He deserves it... In fact, you both do."

Sensing the tension in the air, Zain intervened, "Alright... we will have the time for this. Now, if you are feeling ok, let's get you home."

"Yes please.... I would love that," Nysha agreed.

"Very well then, let me talk to your man," he winked.

"Moron!" Nysha breathed out.

Zain walked up to the door, but before he could open it, the door flung open, and Samar walked in. A grim expression marked his features. "We have a situation, guys.... A problem!" he stated.

"What now?" Aashita pouted.

"The paparazzi have surrounded the entire hospital building like vultures. There is media frenzy all around," he said in a deadpan voice.

"Holy Fuck! How did they get to know?" Nysha questioned.

"Someone must have tipped them off," Zain answered casually. The perks and pitfalls of being a numero uno superstar weren't lost on him.

"Do you think it could be someone from the hospital?" Aashita enquired.

"Can't say, it could be just anyone... They have their sources...," Zain said softly.

"Now what?" Samar asked.

"Give me a minute, I will ask Veer to check," Zain excused himself. After talking to his bodyguard for around five minutes, Zain disconnected the call and looked at his friends, before speaking in a sombre voice, "The problem is real, guys. Few of the notorious and pushy ones are in close vicinity. Some sneaky oaf had spread the word that Pia had gone into labour. But there is nothing to worry about since Veer has managed to clear the air for now. However, exiting through the main entrance is not recommended. The blinding flashbulbs and the snap-snap from the barrel of camera shutters could be disturbing."

He then turned toward Samar and said, "I believe we have a backend entrance."

"We do...," Samar replied.

"I trust you to take the girls and make a safe exit. Meanwhile, count on me to divert the media and use it to our advantage. I will try to provide them with all the updates regarding our upcoming event," Zain added.

"Master Manipulator, aren't you?" Aashita guffawed.

"Trades of the game, sweetie," he replied.

Before leaving, Zain walked up to Nysha and hugged her tightly. He kissed her head and whispered assuringly against her hair... "I trust the doctor to keep you safe. And you are my brave girl, stay strong."

"Thank you... I will," she replied softly while hugging him back.

A Long Ride Home

Samar led the ladies to the backend exit, where the security personnel had already parked his car.

“If you don’t mind, I would like to take the back seat,” Nysha said.

“What happened? Are you ok?” he asked, concerned, instinctively reaching out to touch her forehead and neck with the back of his hand.

She blushed and smiled faintly under his touch, “Don’t worry, Dr. Heartless, I’m slightly under the weather, a bit nauseous. All I want is some good sleep,” she whined playfully.

He smiled back, partly relieved that she was back to being her usual self. Pulling her closer to himself, he brought his head down to touch hers before whispering softly, “Ms. Patel, you scared the shit out of me today. Don’t you dare repeat this performance, ever again,” he warned.

“Trust me, this isn’t a performance I am very proud of,” she replied.

Aashita cleared her throat and hollered, “And trust me, I am not very keen and proud to be the third wheel and interrupting your, ‘the moment.’ But lovebirds, can we make it quick, please? We don’t want to risk ourselves running into some scheming paparazzo, who, by the way, would be insanely happy to capture you both making out in the wild.”

"Eww! You sound insufferably gross," Nysha shrieked.

"I agree, you do," Samar stifled a smile, and muttered under his breath.

"Not even half as gross as those slimy, sneaky bastards, though," Aashita defended.

"Slimy, who?" Nysha questioned.

"Oh, my word! Don't you know the latest goss?" Aashita asked.

"I don't... but I trust you to enlighten me," she said, sporting an amused smile, while slipping into the backseat of the car, thankful for its dark, tinted windows.

"I suppose you have no idea what the paps did to Ayesha Kapur?" Aashita asked.

"Ayesha Kapur? Rings a bell," Nysha replied.

"Of course, it does. Former Beauty Queen, Vogue India's current cover star, and the reigning queen of fashion and style who took the internet by storm with her free-spirited, boho-chic photo shoot, and instantly went on to be declared as the national crush."

"Ah ha! Now, I remember... She is also UNICEF's Goodwill Ambassador for children, along with Zain and other celebs, and in a week, she is getting married to real estate magnate, Abhiram Khanna."

"Oh yes... about that...there seems to be a change of plan...," Aashita clarified.

"Really? Correct me if I am wrong, but last week they threw the grandest pre-wedding bash and an insanely chic cocktail reception at the Rustic Palm Resort in Alibaug. It was attended by the likes of pop divas, like Anastasia Andreev. So, what changed?" Nysha asked.

"Well! A lot, actually...," Aashita replied.

"Fill me in, gossip girl. I am wide awake," Nysha squealed.

"Of course, you are...," Aashita winked.

Samar muttered a silent thank you to Aashita, grateful for her quick thinking and ability to get Nysha's mind off negative thoughts. He looked into the rear-view mirror and saw a happy gleam in her eyes. Despite the evident tired circles, she seemed all geared up and excited to contribute her two cents to the spicy conversation. Girls and their love for goss! he thought.

During the next half an hour, Samar had acquired quite a substantial amount of information regarding the love tangles of Ayesha and Abhiram, fairly enough to appear and clear a bite-sized, multiple-choice objective test on them. Right from their chance encounter at an LA Fashion Week, which happened to be Abhiram's sister, supermodel Shreya Khanna's first International Runway Debut, to meeting again at an after-party, their instant rapport and click, with sparks flying and Cupid striking. They dated for three years, deflected the media, and avoided bad press, until finally deciding to proudly declare their "In relationship" status, engraved boldly on their social media handles. There had been no respite after that. With the paparazzi following their tail like mad hounds on the prowl, the camera flashes and clicks descending from all angles—top, down, and middle. The media going berserk at their every damn appearance, buzzing around like a swarm of agitated cicadas, and the scandalous whispers becoming more and more prominent with each passing day, the lovebirds had aced the "flaming the paparazzi" game. Every time they stepped out hand in hand and posed confidently under the harsh scrutiny of the cameras, it sent the media into a full-on frenzy mode. Soon, they became the "most talked about" and "media favored" couple, with their stories and PDA plastered across Page 3 tabloids, magazine covers, and entertainment websites. Everything was going on fine for the power brand couple, until the day, when their perfectly balanced castle came crumbling down. On the day of their pre-wedding party, a shutterbug loitering in the dark had captured Ayesha kissing a masked man in a secluded corner of the hallway. The next day, a generous glimpse of their moment of vulnerability flashed across the tabloids and social media pages. With the picture going viral in record time, and with netizens eager to share their valuable opinion on the designated act, the comments section on the said piece flooded with unsolicited gyan, slut-shaming, and of course, moral policing on the outright immoral act. The desi aunties' "Kitty and Satsang Gang" weren't left behind either. The subtle, nonchalant remarks by Abhiram's mother, Mrs. Sunita Khanna, and her best friend, Gaurika Sachdev, added fuel to the already sparked controversy, making their dislike for the would-be-bride rather evident to the world. Ex-supermodel, Gaurika Sachdev, rechristened as Gauri Ma at present, was a Satsang expert and spiritual consultant. A self-proclaimed celebrity healer and natural coach, she was quick to shift the blame on Ayesha and her negative aura for her reprehensible deed. A dosha in her kundali wasn't left behind either, terming her as an "unsuitable bride" for the most "suitable bachelor."

"And that sure would make for an awesome movie plot. But girls, we are home. We could have taken a detour, in case you wanted to continue your rejuvenating conversation," Samar teased.

"Oh, come on, Dr. Heartless, don't be so mean. A girl's reputation is at stake, yet Abhiram has chosen to remain silent. This surprises me more," Nysha clarified.

"Don't be so quick to judge. If he truly loves her, then he might be planning something to clear the air. She has got to trust him," he assured while opening her side of the car door and helping her out.

"But some people are simply vile, Dr. Samar...You need to drop your gentleman's hat and act fast. Perhaps give them a taste of their own medicine," Aashita said. "He might be planning something for the upcoming press conference. Not sure though," she added.

"They have a press meet planned...Wow! And where do you get all the updates?" Nysha asked.

"Stay tuned for saucy news updates...courtesy Journalist Aarhi Baruah. Like, Share, Subscribe...," Aashita mimicked.

"Of course... How can I forget? You have a journalist sister-in-law. By the way, the man whom Ayesha kissed, why was he wearing a mask?" Nysha asked.

"Duh! Because it was a masquerade party...," Aashita pointed.

"Le!! It could have been Abhiram then...Big deal for nothing...," Nysha exclaimed.

"Don't jump to conclusions, sister... If it was him, why would he keep mum for so long?" Aashita asked.

"Don't know, maybe they were testing the waters, checking the loyalty quotient of their people. Categorizing friend and foe...," Nysha said.

"You don't really believe that, do you? Putting so much at stake to test waters," Aashita asked with a hint of skepticism. "But perhaps, I could give you the benefit of the doubt here. Vade Log Toh Vadi Vadi Baatein. Everything is possible in love, un-love, k-drama, and jung," she sighed.

"Alright, enough of the Ayesha-Abhiram saga," he said. "Now that we are home, you need to rest," Samar affirmed while ringing the doorbell.

The door swung open almost immediately, and a lean girl with a worried expression written all over her face stood at the doorway.

"Kitni der kar di, didi. Padesan ho gayi main. Aap thik ho?" Sushanti asked.

("It took you so long, sister. I got worried. Are you ok?" Sushanti asked.)

"Ab tu shuru maat ho jana, Sushi. Main thik hoon," Nysha assured her firmly, and stepped inside the house with a practiced smile plastered on her lips.

("Now you don't start, Sushi. I am ok," Nysha assured her firmly, and stepped inside the house with a practiced smile plastered on her lips.)

Sushi, of course, wasn't very convinced; but knew better than to pester further. With furrowed eyebrows she said, "Main oats strawberry smoothie banayi hoon, aur aapki favourite kimchi, and fried rice bhi... Aap fresh ho jao. Main garam karke lati hoon."

("I have prepared oats strawberry smoothie, your favorite kimchi, and fried rice too. You go and freshen up, while I will go and heat some food for you.")

"Wow, Sushi! Kimchi, ha? Kaun sikhaya?" Aashita asked.

("Wow, Sushi! Kimchi? Who taught you?" Aashita asked.)

"Pia didi sikhayi na... yeh bhi... aur bahut sari foreign recipes, aur wo kya kehete hai... ma--ca--rooo..."

("Sister Pia taught, this, and many more foreign recipes, and also... what do they say... ma--ca--rooo...")

She tried hard to pronounce it correctly, dragging the letters a tad too far, when Aashita completed it for her, "Macaroon bhi! Barhiya hain! Sushi, tu toh next season ka Master Chef join kar hi le, aur Chef Vikas Khanna bhi toh hai na, tere favorite...," she teased.

("Macaroon too! Very nice! Sushi, now you can join the next season of Master Chef. Also, Chef Vikas Khanna is there too, your favorite," she teased.)

"Kya didi! aap bhi...," Sushi blushed hard, as much as she beamed with pride.

("What, sister!" Sushi blushed hard, as much as she beamed with pride.)

"Alright, everyone, get back to business. Aashita, you should head home," Nysha intervened.

"Are you out of your mind, girl? I am not going anywhere, no fucking way," Aashita opposed resolutely.

"I am alright now. This is home, and nothing here would trigger an attack again," Nysha tried to sound convincing.

"I know that, but why can't I just stay? Look, I don't want a share in your gourmet meal. I will order online if that's what you are worried about," Aashi argued like a pesky kid.

"What? Are you mad? I am worried about Raghav, you idiot. I already know that I ruined your dinner plans. But at least you could spend time with him before he leaves for Delhi tomorrow. I don't want to be the reason for kalesh (marital discord) between newlyweds," Nysha clarified.

"Hmm...," Aashita contemplated for some time before speaking, "Well, even though you are partially correct, it's already late, darling. Nothing much to do, go home and sleep like the dead," Aashita explained, sticking out her tongue to justify her stance.

"Or maybe, make love," Nysha lip-synched and muttered the words in a barely audible whisper. But her measured diligence got lost and wasted when Aashita responded to her romantic suggestion in an over-enthusiastic flair.

"What? Really! Are you and Samar planning to break the ice and make love tonight? That's why he can stay, while I have no business staying," she quipped. Her eyes widened at her sudden intelligent discovery and deduction, while a mischievous, self-satisfactory smile played on her lips. As if her skewed and half-baked analysis wasn't enough to cause a major stir-up and embarrassment, she continued with her self-crafted sorry saga. "Of course, what business do I have playing the third wheel," she muttered. Her self-sympathetic charade was on a full-on active mode, and nowhere close to reaching an end.

What was meant to be a hush conversation between two close friends was now out in the open. While Nysha cursed her considerateness and foolhardiness for making the impromptu suggestion, Samar on the other hand, pretended to have not heard a thing, and she couldn't agree more with his current tactic. When one had potty-mouthed friends like Aashita, playing deaf and dumb could be the only way of dealing with unwanted and unwarranted shitty shit.

"You are shamelessly impossible," Nysha gritted through her teeth and gave her friend a disapproving glare.

"Aww! Is my poor baby embarrassed?" Aashita teased, feigning innocence.

"Yes, I am. Precisely the reason why you will be leaving right now," Nysha declared, while giving her friend a slight, friendly push.

"Alright! Alright! Are you sure you will be ok?" Aashita reconfirmed.

"I will be fine, drama queen. Now, take my car keys and leave before I call Raghav and lodge a formal defamation complaint for slander," Nysha threatened.

"Oh! Damn, girl, I am leaving. So much for your newfound mate," Aashita whined, as she stepped out of the house with the keys.

"Bye, Aashi, see you tomorrow," Nysha said while rolling her eyes.

"Bye, Nysha, bye Samar and Sushi," Aashita bellowed. "And darlings... restrain yourselves, I trust you kiddos to behave and not break any moral code of conduct," she added with a chuckle.

While Nysha gave her friend an incredulous stare, she thought Samar's face had lost some color out of sheer mortification, and while she did want to kiss away his fret, she had to hold herself back due to Sushi's presence. She couldn't afford to make the girl uncomfortable with her "dil maange more" act. But she could at least try and pacify her doctor. So once Sushi retreated to the kitchen, she said, "I am sorry... Unlike Pia, Aashi can get a bit blown up. But she didn't mean any of it."

"She didn't?" he asked bemused.

"Of course she didn't," Nysha clarified.

"Oh!! I see," he said with a smug smile plastered on his lips.

"You aren't weaving any ideas, are you?" she questioned.

"Well, a man can always hope, Ms. Patel," he said. He lifted her chin using his thumb and index finger, while a teasing smile played on his lips. Nysha's heartbeat increased pace in raw anticipation at his nearness.

"Samar...," she murmured softly... "I need to go... freshen up," she mumbled.

"Of course... I was planning to do the same... If we do it together, maybe... we could save some time," he whispered in her ear. His warm breath fanned her earlobes and goosebumps skittered throughout her body. Her breath hitched in her throat at his wild suggestion, and his slow, husky, and inviting words were like a wicked torture to her being. As if sensing her dilemma, an unhurried, lazy smile grazed his lips.

"What's so funny?" she frowned.

"Your thoughts... they are ludicrous...," he chuckled.

"You don't know them... you can't...," she challenged.

In a quick move, he pulled her closer by the waist, and tucking a strand of hair behind her ear, whispered softly and seductively, "I know more than you think I do, Ms. Patel. Trust me, your dreams... your feelings, each one of them... however insane they might seem, will all get fulfilled someday... it's just not today. Do you trust me with your dreams, Nysha?"

Her name on his lips sounded like a warm caress against her skin... a silent, affectionate promise, and a murmur of togetherness... As she nodded in agreement, a grin spread across his lips, making him look as sexy as sin, and Nysha could only imagine the latent potential the man possessed to grace the cover of Maxim India. A heart doctor with drop-dead gorgeous looks could be a game-changer for the sponsors. Her thoughts were interrupted when Samar placed a chaste kiss on her forehead and said in an authoritative but well-meaning tone.

"Go, freshen up. Meanwhile, I will use the guest bedroom downstairs. Sushanti has asked me not to leave. In fact, she has also started calling me, bhaiya. I think she already likes me," he said, beaming with pride.

"Of course, she likes you. She is a smart girl, Dr. Heartless," Nysha said with a wink and a little giggle.

"What's so funny, you brat?" he asked with a glimmer in his eyes.

"I think what she likes more is the fact that you are a doctor. You see, Sushanti is a big sissy, and overtly protective of me. And now that she was informed about my attack, she would rather let a stranger of a doctor stay at home than bear the burden of my well-being alone. And undoubtedly, my girl gang has trained her well. So don't get deceived by your brotherly instincts. There's more depth to the waters than you can actually perceive," she concluded.

"Vicious ladies!" He said with a twist of his tongue as a quick, wicked grin graced his lips.

"Trust me... you have no idea," she said while running a hand over the sexy contours of his jaw, and feeling his day-old stubble beneath her palm. He caught her wrist and placed a kiss on her palm and also the back of her hand, before confessing with all sincerity, "Just that you know... I love you, Ms. Patel."

"Ah! Well, about that," she said with an elfin wink. "Maybe I love you... maybe I don't," saying that, she giggled, and without giving him a chance to respond, hurriedly made her way up the stairs.

"Liar!" he smiled and called out behind her retreating back.

Addressing the Past, Present, and the Uncertain Future

Part 1

On the way to the guest bedroom, Samar's eyes fell on the array of tastefully selected photographs that adorned a section of the living room wall. Though he had already seen them before, this time he did an unhurried perusal of the same, staring at them for a long time. That's when one particular photograph caught his attention. It was an old picture of Nysha, alongside a boy her age. They were at the stadium, wearing Team India jerseys and floppy hats, flaunting the victory sign while smiling at the camera. They looked adorably cute and happy together. Though Samar never had a chance to meet Akshat personally, and neither had he seen his pictures before, somewhere in his heart he knew instantly that the boy in the photograph was him. Earlier, when he hadn't known about the entire Akshat episode, he had thought of him as just another friend of Nysha, or maybe a cousin. His heart sank a little at the thought that Akshat was no more. The man had died young, leaving behind a grieving mother, loving friends, family, well-wishers, and a lover. Samar couldn't even imagine the unfathomable heartache Nysha had to suffer at such a young age and the terrible loss she had to endure at the sudden demise of a loved one.

If previously Samar had been proud of her and her achievements, now he was simply in awe of her endurance and everything that she stood for. He considered himself lucky that she had healed enough to let him into her life. His thoughts shifted to her panic episode earlier that day. Though he had a fairly good idea about what, or who in particular, could have triggered it off, there was much more to her condition which he still didn't know, but intended to know soon. In addition to dealing with the ordeal of losing someone dear, was the idea of imprisoning oneself with their memories for the fear of forgetting and eventually replacing them with someone else over a length of time. The worst happened today when she was forced to take a guilt trip down memory lane while remembering things that seemed to have been pushed behind her realms of consciousness for a long period.

He inhaled sharply and heaved a long sigh before retiring to his room. He had just closed the door behind him when the phone in his pocket rang. While pulling out the same and seeing the caller's name on display, a smile crossed his lips before he answered, "Hello Samar, right time or not, we need to talk," said the authoritative voice at the other end.

"Hey, Pia! Trust me, I have been meaning to talk to you all day," he replied earnestly.

A sigh of relief heaved at the other end of the line. "Very well, Dr. Samar, let's begin by throwing some light on the real Akshat Sanghavi and why Project Akshat Ratna is so important to Nysha and us," she said softly.

"Go on, Pia; I am listening," he said.

Part 2

Nysha woke up with a start. Beads of sweat trickled down the length of her face, and her heart thudded loudly in her chest. She looked sideways and found the sleeping form of Sushi, with a smile tugged at her lips. Not wanting to disturb the young girl's sleep, she slowly got up and sat on the edge of the bed for some time. Upon pressing her hands against her throbbing temples, she realized that a dull headache had slowly begun to creep in. As she reached out for the water jug placed neatly on the bedside table and tried pouring some water into a glass to satiate her parched throat, she realized that her hands were quivering.

The awful visions were coming back again. She tried to bolt those dreadful memories, push them away, but instead, they kept haunting her, repeating the same traumatic cycle. Her palms felt sweaty and sticky, and her eyes failed to see smooth movements. Everything seemed cloudy and jumpy, and her vision was blurred. She clutched tightly to the edge of the bed, blowing air through her mouth and taking deep breaths, trying hard to stabilize herself and regain her composure. She couldn't let it happen again, and cause distress to her loved ones.

"Get it together," she murmured.

"Nope, not going down without a fight," she promised herself. Repeating the mantra inside her head with conviction, she slipped out of the bed and tiptoed her way out of the room. Taking the stairs down the hall, she made her way toward the guest bedroom. The room was still dimly lit, and she contemplated whether to knock. What if he was asleep? Was it ok to disturb him at this hour of the night? She thought. She fought the urge to retreat to her room for fear of allowing him to see her in her most vulnerable state. Suddenly the door went open and he stood at the doorway. His eyes widened for a moment in surprise, but it was soon replaced by concern.

"Hey! Not sleepy yet?" he asked.

"I-I...," she tried to explain but realized that her words wouldn't come out.

"I am unable to sleep," she blurted out.

There was momentary silence between them, and she realized that apart from his sleeves rolled up to his elbows, he was still completely dressed, his hair was neatly brushed back; in fact, everything about him was so immaculate that he almost seemed ready to step out for a photo shoot. A stark contrast to his perfection personified was her messed-up self. Her hair was pulled up in a messy bun, with loosened ends kissing her cheeks, and she was wearing her favorite Hello Kitty pajama shirt and shorts. In fact, in comparison to him, she felt miserably underdressed.

"Oh Shit!" she whispered,

"What happened?" he exclaimed, his mouth agape.

"No-nothing, you should go back to sleep. Sorry, I-I wasn't thinking," she fumbled.

"Come on in," he said.

Before she could protest, his warm hands wrapped around her wrist and pulled her inside his room, closing the door behind them. "But I am in my pajamas," she protested, finally finding her voice.

"You look cute," he assured.

"But you are overdressed, it's not fair," she grumbled.

"That's because, I wasn't given an option, you see," he complained.

"Oh! I am so sorry about that, it slipped my mind completely. I will get you my dad's clothes."

"Shhh! Relax Nysha, I am good, and so are you... Trust me," he said in a soothing voice.

He sat on the couch and pulled her along, encircling his arms protectively around her fragile form. Her body relaxed, and she snuggled closer to him, absorbing the warmth of his body and feeling safe—truly safe.

For the first few minutes, they sat in complete silence. Her head rested against the hard ridge of his shoulder. Samar gently dug his fingers into her hair, and with a slight tug untied her bun. As her hair tumbled down, cascading around her shoulders like waves, he slowly began to run his fingers up and down her hair in smooth strokes, akin to a soothing massage.

"Nysha," he began.

"Hmmm!"

"We can sit in silence or talk, it's totally up to you... I am ok with both," he assured.

There was an elongated pause before she broke the silence, "I remember him... Akshat... He was the wittiest, kindest, and most affable human being I have ever come across. And I say this not because I loved him, but because it's true. It was probably easiest to love him, or perhaps it was most difficult to know him and yet not to fall in love with him."

She lifted her head and looked into his eyes. He nodded and held her tightly, before placing a soft kiss on top of her head. She continued, "Our families had been friends for generations. Growing up, there had been several opportunities for us to meet – from common parties, festive celebrations, family get-togethers, social events, and so on and so forth. We had experienced several of our firsts together – first pub, first karaoke, first gin, first kiss." She let out an audible exhale before continuing, "Every moment with him was fun. My friends simply loved him. It was so easy to love him. My fondest memories are of the times spent with him and my friends. His family adored me, and so did mine. It was an unspoken accord between us and our families that someday in the future, our names would be clubbed together. My friends believed that we were destined to be together."

"Together!" she repeated, laughing a mirthless laugh, and a lone tear escaped from the corner of her eye and trailed down her cheek. Samar caught it with his thumb, and whispered, "I love you," he said. He took her hand in his and squeezed it slightly. Kissing her cheek, he repeated, "I love you. We don't have to do this, Nysha. You don't need to relive the pain again," he persuaded.

"But I want to. It's been long, Samar. It's time to let go," she insisted.

He nodded understandingly, allowing her to complete. "It was a double celebration that day, Christmas Eve and a commemoration party for Akshat. He had gotten admitted into his dream culinary school, Culinary Art Academy, Italy for the spring semester. He had always wanted to become a chef, and opening his Indo-Italian restaurant in the suburbs of Mumbai had been his lifelong dream. He wanted to master the art of food and cook for the connoisseurs of exemplary food. That day, we were all enjoying ourselves, when suddenly out of the blue, Akshat took out the ring. It was a beautiful ring, a platinum heart band. To this day, I fail to understand the whim behind his sudden action, yet it was the most joyous moment of my life. Little did I realize then that it would soon turn into one of the worst nightmares, the one that would haunt me for life."

She gasped for breath while trying to restrain the flood of tears threatening to cascade down her face. Her voice quivered, yet she spoke more to herself than to him. "Back then, we were all young... immature, living in our make-believe cocoon of happiness, hesitant to come out of it, probably too naive to even believe that something could go wrong with us..." She paused...before continuing, "And yet it did go wrong...Everything went horribly...wrong...I-I-don't-know, what had gotten into me that day...I insisted on celebrating with my favorite choco-mint ice cream cake. It was past 12, and though I knew it was a fucking crazy request, I wouldn't budge. Not many parlors were open, and though Akshat tried placing an online order, as luck would have it, while a few parlors had already closed, the ones open had run out of stock. He promised to get it the next day... double the size... double the celebration... but I was adamant... Finally, he gave in... And we rode pillion, gliding through the flooded Christmas streets, lanes lined with food and gift stalls, under the vibrant hues of the sky and the canopy of amber lights. The chill in the air and the contagious Christmas energy didn't bother to spare us. We screeched at the top of our lungs, wishing passersby a Merry Christmas and a Happy New Year until we found our own sacred destination, 'The Messy Gelato & Honeycomb Bar.' The place was practically thronged with patrons. Young and old, everyone wanted a share of their scoop of happiness with extra sprinklers, and we were no different. We were parked on the other side of the road, about to cross it together, when a sudden influx of an energetic bunch of teenagers with an assortment of musical instruments, starting from a saxophone to a tambourine, a guitar to a violin, and a harmonica to sleigh bells, caught our attention, especially mine. As they began dancing to their music and singing the all-time favorite carols, a few spectators joined in, and taking the cue, I too tried a small twirl and gave in to the temptation. Though Akshat was too shy to join in, looking at my enthusiastic demeanor, he didn't have the heart to stop me either. So, he whispered into my ear, loud enough to be heard over the sound of pulsating music, 'Stay,' he said, as he kissed my forehead. 'I will get the cake.'...Those were his last words... and the kiss, the last one... both his and mine."

Part 3

"My subsequent memories hereafter are all a haze...," she whispered. One moment he was waving at me, winking and flaunting the large cake box in his hand, and the very next moment, a speeding delivery van knocked him off, dragging him along with it, before throwing him a few feet away from the actual place of the hit. I don't exactly remember how I reached Akshat Ratna. The doctor informed that he had sustained several injuries, including to the cervical spine, and was declared dead on arrival. By the time our families, friends, and well-wishers arrived, I was still in a trance, refusing to shed even a drop of a tear, refusing to accept the unacceptable. For two complete days, I behaved like the living dead, neither eating nor drinking, nor talking or crying. But on the third day, Pia did the unthinkable, or probably the inevitable, she placed the Asthi Kalash with his mortal remains on my lap, urging me to accept the bitter truth of our lives, that Akshat was no more, he was gone. He wasn't even a body now, and what remained of him were ashes or simply asthiya which needed to be immersed into the river for the soul to be liberated and to attain absolute salvation."

"That day I cried. I broke down completely and howled my lungs out... until my throat went parched and my vision went blank."

For the next couple of minutes, they sat in absolute silence, with none attempting to speak after the heartfelt and heavy disclosure. However, after some time, when his shoulder drooped and the weight on it got heavier, he realized that Nysha had fallen asleep. The load of her profound confession had most certainly taken a toll on her. Carefully, he carried her to the bed and tucked her beneath the covers while placing a pillow under her head. He looked at her sleeping form. Her hair, a tangled mess cascaded around the pillow, a small frown marred her beautiful features, and with nothing to hide, she appeared tired and vulnerable, but a goddess nevertheless... his goddess... his to love, worship, and protect. Samar was surprised by the sudden spur of protectiveness he felt for her. He had never felt likewise for anyone else...

God! He loved her... And he would be damned if he let anyone or anything hurt her... ever again, he thought.

With that silent promise to himself, he slid into the bed next to her, encircling his arms around her in a warm embrace. Burying his head into the crook of her neck, he slipped into a peaceful slumber.

Part 4

Nysha awoke the next morning and blinked her eyes quite a few times to adjust to the new surroundings. The first thing she realized was that she wasn't in her room...but before panic could sink in, a surge of relief coursed through her upon comprehending that she was in her own house and that she had slept in her guest bedroom. As she tried getting up, a muscled arm around her waist pulled her back, cuddling her and anchoring her in place. A smile crossed her lips, "Possessive much, Dr. Heartless!" she whispered softly, before placing a kiss on his nose.

"I really don't like this name. This needs to change...," Samar protested with a wink.

"You weren't asleep. Cheater!" she accused.

"Well, I was, until you decided to barge into my dreams," he defended with a sly smile, while he lay on his stomach, with his head propelled up on one of his elbows.

"Liar, Dr. Dimwit," she said, as she got up from the bed.

"Come on, this is low even by your standards, Nysha. I trust you to do better than that," he teased.

"Challenge accepted! What about Dr. Doofus or... better, Dr. Dickhead?"

"Brat!" he chuckled, as he caught her wrist and pulled her to himself. Tugging a strand of hair behind her ear, and caressing her cheeks with his thumb, he asked in a tender voice, "Are you ok?"

She paused for a while before replying, "Well... I think... I am... I genuinely feel alleviated. Thanks for being so patient, Samar. Thanks for not judging... and allowing me to be... just me."

Samar placed a chaste kiss on her forehead and said, "Thanks for trusting me. Can I ask you something?"

"Of course."

"After everything you went through, did you seek any professional help?"

"You mean... like a therapist?"

"Yes! Sort of..."

"No. Do I need to?" she asked.

"Well... we could. A little help wouldn't hurt," he suggested.

"Perhaps, you are right," she said.

"That's more like it...," he praised.

"Samar, do you think I am damaged?" she asked.

"Of course not... But to think of it, we are all a bit damaged, aren't we? I guess that makes us all... very human," he said.

With a faint smile, she replied, "You make it sound good and simple."

"That's because I love you," he professed.

"Ah! About that, Mr. Sweet Talker, we still need to get certain things straight, I am not sure if I love..." Barely had the words escaped her lips when Samar pulled her closer and brushed his lips against hers. With their bodies pressed together, a reverberating sensation traveled through her body. Pulling herself away, Nysha asked, "Wow! What was that?"

"My part of the deal... I said, I love you," he said with a goofy grin.

"And I said I am not sure," she said, sounding like a pouting child.

"We will see to that, Ms. Patel," he said as he pressed his lips against hers for a second time, and this time, with a silent promise to himself.

"She was his, and he was never letting her go..."

THE FINAL DRILL, CURTAIN CALL & A LOT MORE

The backstage had transformed itself into a war zone of sorts. It was hugely crowded, and the air was thick and filled with tension to the brim. Aashita looked like a meddling mediator, making her way amidst the crowd, pushing herself between people while muttering a barrage of profanities under her breath. Dressed in a pre-draped turquoise sari pantsuit with matching designer zardosi sneakers, she looked as breathtakingly beautiful as she looked alluringly professional. Holding her clipboard close to her heart as if her life depended on it, she waved at Nysha while barking instructions to the crew members into her Bluetooth earpiece. Famous for losing her temper and her OCD need for perfection, she looked like a war lady ranting her infamous battle cry and ready to behead those found guilty at the slightest slip.

"Props! Costumes!"

"Sound check!"

"Focus lights! Yes... Tweak the angle to the middle... Right there, toward the main spot!"

"Sound check! Remember to run a quick check on the mic ASAP."

"Suck it up fast. We don't have the whole day...," she yelled.

Sensing the urgency and palpable tension in the air, Nysha walked up straight to her friend and squeezed her shoulders empathetically before handing her the iced hazelnut coffee tumbler.

"Thanks for the caffeine shot," Aashita said. "Might as well have one before someone gets murdered tonight," she added.

"Tham ja veere, there is no reason to panic. You are doing great, my friend. We are in a good space," Nysha assured while giving her friend a warm hug.

"You wish! Makeup Dada is hell-bent on giving me a minor attack. The man hasn't arrived yet whereas bitchy Malini has, and her mother was threatening me with a legal suit."

"You got to be kidding me," Nysha guffawed.

"No, I am not... She did," Aashita gritted.

"Well, you should have given her the go-ahead then," Nysha suggested.

"Frankly, I was at a loss for words... That fuck-face, prat of a woman threw me off guard with her chipmunk-sized brain," Aashita grimaced with spite.

"She is Mother Godzilla, isn't she? By the way, what was she suing you with?" Nysha asked.

Aashita rolled her eyes, "Oh, trust me, you wouldn't want to know."

"On the contrary, I do," Nysha insisted.

"Alright then, brace yourself. She said she could sue us for wasting her and her daughter's precious time."

"Her time! Really? Now that's something. What is she, some crème de la crème?" Nysha asked.

"Hush! You wouldn't want Aunty to hear and take offense. Also, she mentioned something about neeet-worthh," Aashita mimicked. "Nysha, hunnie, do you have any idea what that is?" she asked.

Nysha bit back a smile, "Oh wow! No! No idea... Guilty!" she said with her hands raised in the air.

"Thought so."

"Did she mention the project which has been keeping her daughter busy, apart from hosting our paltry event, of course?" Nysha asked.

"Oh yeah... she did. It's horror maestro Devang Kohli's latest horror flick, where our lady is supposed to play the female lead."

"Wow! Good choice. Firstly, she is born bitchy, so playing chudail would come naturally to her. Secondly, these movies aren't even horror; on the contrary, they are a satirical take on horror. Besides, they are jinxed... they bomb at the box office, thereby dragging down the actors' careers along with them. The poor fellas either end up judging reality shows and faking cringe tears, or in the worst-case scenario, get featured in soft porn packaged as pseudo mystery or fantasy drama. So I would say it's pretty much a match made in heaven. She should go ahead. My best wishes."

"Oh, my word! That sure was a vile comeback, my friend," Aashita added while hugging her friend. "And did I tell you that you look like hot brownie fudge in this ivory lehenga dress paired with the tiniest choli ever possible? And as much as I love your bomb avatar, it gets me worried about the sanity of my male crew. How are they supposed to keep calm and think straight, when every inch of that gorgeous and spotless back is up for display? By the way, has Doctor Handsomeness seen you yet? Boy,

I would have loved to see his reaction."

"Damn, girl! That was crude! But knowing you, I would take that as a compliment. And no, Dr. Heartless hasn't arrived yet. I am not even sure if he can make it or not."

"Don't say that? Why?" Aashita asked worriedly.

"Well, duty calling! It's an emergency. The CM's father, 78 years old, suffered a massive embolic stroke this morning. It was an urgent medical condition requiring immediate surgery. And since Samar happens to be the best, he got tied up. I spoke to him before the surgery, and though he assured that he wouldn't miss the Fundraiser for the world, my hopes aren't very high."

"Aww! Poor baby! I am sure he will make it," Aashita pacified.

"I hope so. But that's alright. He is busy saving a life, and I am proud of him," Nysha confessed.

"Of course... you are. We all are," Aashita added.

"Don't worry, Nysha di, he is going to be here."

The sudden voice from behind startled both friends. They glanced over their shoulders and found Aarhi walking up to them, munching a pita sandwich and sipping her latte.

"Look, who do we have here?" Nysha squealed. "And how do you know Samar is going to make it?" she asked.

"Well, I am a journalist and have my own strict can't-reveal sources."

"Oh come on!" Aashita intervened. "We don't have a reason to believe tabloid journalists, Ms. Baruah," she said with a smirk.

"That was pretty rude and insensitive, bou. Inside sources at the hospital have confirmed that the surgery was a success and that the CM's father is stable now."

"Is it?" Aashita winked playfully. "Well, I am happy for my friend. By the way, where did you grab those sandwiches and drink?" she asked.

"Vardhaan gave them to me," Aarhi said.

"What? Seriously! Take my advice, stay away from that man."

"Just a plain sandwich, bou...No reason to get hysterical," Aarhi said defiantly.

"Yeah... right? Isn't your tabloid stint getting far too stretched?" Aashita hissed.

"You don't seem to be very happy? Don't worry, this happens to be my very last entertainment assignment," Aarhi assured.

"It better be," Aashita cautioned.

"You are turning devilish, bou. Raghav Baruah has managed to create another monster," Aarhi jeered.

Before their episode of banter ran out of control, Nysha intervened. "Ladies, my heart is choked with gestures of your overwhelming and heart-warming sisterly love and relentless cheering for each other. However, before a cloud of unwavering emotions envelops my being and I succumb to tears of endearment, would you be kind enough to step out with me, please?" she mocked, her tone laced with sarcasm.

"Whoa! What was that? Are we playing some Victorian vocabulary game here?" Aarhi teased.

"You guys are demented! Seriously! Follow me now," Nysha huffed.

Without another word, the crazy duo followed her to the main stage area, but their silent giggles continued, which she happily chose to ignore. Well, Nysha knew that when you have friends who are certified lunatics, there is hardly much left to do other than ignore, of course.

The stage outside looked like a piece of art and was mesmerizingly beautiful. The arc above with its orange hues appeared like a picturesque sunset, while the crystal and glass backdrop complimented and blended with the earthy white, brown, and green elements. The warmly lit chandeliers along with the golden and red drapes looked as captivating as they looked surreal. Also, the floor decor with its high-gloss metallic finish and colored LED lights with dynamic effects ensured a cohesive look and provided an aesthetic appeal. The rows of chairs covered with the best quality of Egyptian cotton in neon ombre hues, combined with Japanese cherry blossoms and carnations enveloping the grand pillars, accentuated the entire setting, transforming it into a visual spectacle of sorts.

“Wow! This is aweeeesomeee...,” Aarhi stretched the word for effect.

“It sure is! Days of hard work and a shit load of effort. And here we are!” Nysha reminisced. “And we are going to rock it, Aashi, aren’t we?” she asked, seeking validation.

“Well, my friend, we sure will. There is no reason to believe otherwise. We are going to triumph.”

As Aashita went forward to cuddle her friend, Nysha slipped into her warm embrace, while Aarhi looked at them longingly and purred, “Aww! Can I join in?”

“Well, you could always squeeze in, Ms. Tabloid,” Aashita sniggered.

“That shouldn’t be a problem, until you promise to give us an awesome coverage,” Nysha agreed.

"Hold on, ladies, I am having a major FOMO now...," the deep voice of Jay boomed from behind.

"Oh My God, Jay! What a lovely surprise!" Nysha exclaimed. "Where have you been?" she asked.

"Well, I had been busy settling some pending business chores... But here I am now. And..."

"Oh, just shut up! And squeeze in!" Nysha yelled.

"Alright! Alright!" he appeased.

As the four friends snuggled in a warm huddle, an unexplainable sense of relief and contentment washed over Nysha. Here she was, with friends and well-wishers, and life, of course, couldn't have gotten any better.

After two hours of witnessing a line-up of spectacular performances in a row, the moment for which everyone had been waiting with bated breath finally arrived. It was time for Zain to take the stage and set it ablaze. Nysha had no doubts that he would do the same, literally and figuratively. Defying the laws of gravity, the superstar suspended himself in the air and performed a blindfolded acrobatic aerial stunt with a bonus fire-twirling feat, sending the audience into a full-on frenzy mode. That, combined with Vardhaan's sensational dramatic descent on stage alongside Zain while holding the Indian tricolor in his hand, as he joined him for the finale act, made the packed auditorium explode in elation. With a mixed bag of patriotic songs reverberating throughout the auditorium, the spectators were caught in nationalistic fervor, and the duo's performance had enhanced the bar of live concerts several notches higher, thereby earning them a standing ovation from their fans and extended fandom alike. Their joyous disposition knew no bounds when a foreign news correspondent informed them about securing a position in the "Guinness Book of World Records," for waving the maximum number of tricolors simultaneously on a live performance stage. The Gala Night and mind-boggling spectacle finally concluded with an extraordinary and gripping rendition of the "Vande Mataram" by Music Maestro and International Globe awardee, Nazim Saeed. With the celebs and performers joining him on stage, the audiences were enchanted to witness a phenomenal performance that sent silent tremors down their spine. The hall froze for several moments, the spectators trying to absorb the artistic spell, and awakened again to a thunderous applause, screams, screeches, cheers, and whistles. The roaring applause resounded throughout the auditorium. It died down slowly, only once the curtain fell and hid from sight, one of the most magnificent feats they had ever witnessed, the one they would cherish for years to come, and the memories and experience of which would last them a lifetime.

THE AFTER PARTY: MAYHEM & MADNESS

The After Party

The poolside after-party by the Jidans was an absolutely enticing affair. Known for throwing lavish parties and playing the perfect host, the grandeur of their parties always left everyone spellbound. The venue had transformed itself into a dazzling and vibrant Moulin Rouge backdrop. A variety of scrumptious snacks and drinks were served by waiters dressed in opulent costumes complete with feathers, rhinestones, and sequins, doing justice to the French Cabaret theme. One such server approached Nysha and held out a tray in front of her.

"Rainbow prawn crackers, ma'am. House special," the young waiter added with a smile.

"Of course," she smiled back.

As she picked one martini glass off the tray and tasted it, she was enthralled by the array of flavours that exploded in her mouth: Worcestershire sauce, egg mayonnaise, horseradish, cayenne pepper, and pickled ginger. The combination was perfect, and so was the balance.

"Wow! This tastes awesome," she said while picking up a second glass.

"Sure it does, ma'am. I meant it when I said it's a house special," he beamed.

"Rightly so. Give my compliments to the chef," Nysha added.

"Thank you, I will."

As the server left, Nysha saw Aashita making her way through the throng of people and approaching her. She plonked herself on the sofa next to her and gave her a meaningful look.

"Is this supposed to be your hideout throughout the party?" she accused.

"Says who? I'm still trying to recover from my bout of hyperventilation," Nysha defended with an eye roll.

"Funny indeed, but I wasn't born yesterday. Now stop sulking and join in."

"Join in, as in drink and get wasted? No, please, thank you. I would rather give it a pass."

"Look around, everyone has a drink in hand. You really don't believe that each one out there is wasted, do you?" Aashita questioned.

"Well, I am speaking for myself. Can't comment on others," Nysha defended.

"Is it about Samar?" Aashita asked.

"Of course not... Why would you say so?" Nysha denied.

"Are you sure?" Aashita pressed, placing a hand over Nysha's.

"Okay, fine... Maybe, it is," she raised her hands in surrender and confessed, "I miss him, I really do. I wish he could be here... with me... with us to celebrate."

“Of course, you do. To think of it, he might have wanted the same. But, love, he’s got a job to do. He is busy saving a life or perhaps lives. You ought to give him that benefit,” Aashita stated.

“Whose side are you on? You sound like Team Samar,” Nysha said, scrunching her eyes.

“Well then... maybe, I am,” Aashita winked.

“But Aarhi said the operation was a success. So what got him tied up for so long, Aashi? He missed the entire event,” Nysha sighed.

“You believe tabloid journalists? Really? They lie all the time...”Aashita clarified.

Before Nysha could protest, her cell phone rang, and the name of the very person whose whereabouts were bothering her relentlessly flashed on the screen.

“Hello, Dr. Heartless, you missed out on all the fun... All of it...” she spoke with marked excitement.

“Nysha...” the voice at the other end sounded grim.

“Samar? What is it? Is everything okay?” she asked, concerned.

“No, I’m afraid not. We have a situation here,” he stated.

“Tell me about it,” she said, her heart thudding violently.

“Alright! Listen! There’s no reason to panic...” Samar began.

“Samar, you’re scaring me now... Spill...” she gritted out.

“Okay... Here’s the thing: Pia’s early labour has begun. They are getting her here... now.”

Mayhem

"Now? Fuck! Shit! Who told you? How do you know? Oh my God! The baby wasn't due until two weeks from now. Why did it decide to arrive early?" she ranted in panic.

"Nysha! Nysha! Listen! You're freaking out! Calm down. These things happen... Relax!" Samar placated.

"Are you mad? This isn't an everyday occurrence, Dr. Heartless. Why would you want me to be calm...And my God, who is with her? I'm here. Zain is here..." Nysha continued.

"She's not alone. Shergill Aunty is here... In fact, she's the one who called Dr. Harsha," Samar cut her off.

"Yes... Of course, she's there. Even uncle is there," she heaved a sigh of relief.

"Yeah... and mom would be here too," he said.

"Wait! Your mom?" she asked, bewildered.

"No, dumb! It's your mom we are talking about," Samar clarified.

"Oh!" she blurted.

A sudden gush of inexplicable emotions swelled inside her chest. Her heart expanded of its own accord, with pride and happiness. He had addressed her mom as 'mom.' It was a small gesture, a spontaneous minuscule act, which probably meant nothing, and yet her foolish heart couldn't stop gushing and melting into a puddle of mush.

"Nysha...you there?" Samar asked.

Samar's voice brought her out of her ridiculous reverie.

"Yeah... Sorry, it's just that you called my mom your mom, so..."

"So? I guess eventually I have to call her that..." he stated as a matter of fact.

"Oh! So that's it. Very practical indeed," she hissed. It felt like someone had just splashed ice-cold water on her wishful thinking.

"What's wrong with you, Nysha? Is this important now?" he asked, irritated.

"Of course not!" she snapped. "Only you could have ruined a perfect moment like this, Dr. Heartless," she huffed.

"Wait! We were having a moment, and I wasn't even aware of it?" he asked, confused.

"Oh! Just forget it!" she surrendered.

"Nysha, I hate to say this, but it seems as if your ability to think straight has vaporized into thin air. Clearly, you are unable to handle the pressure and are acting delusional. Do you have anyone near you, preferably with a perfectly sane mindset, and someone capable of taking in a few simple instructions...," he spoke softly, each word rolled out with the precision and the calm of a practiced shrink.

"Fine! Aashita is here. I'm putting it on speaker mode... Rattle it out," she growled.

After the discussion, both Aashita and Nysha had one question in mind, a rather simple but important one.

"Right now, we are in Lonavala. It will take us at least two hours to reach Mumbai, sans the traffic, and preposterously assuming that we are super lucky. How do you suggest we beat that?" they asked.

To which Samar replied in his trademark composed demeanor, "Come on, ladies, talk to Zain. The guy has a gazillion fans spread across the world, fans capable of pulling off unimaginable stunts to impress him or simply to gain even a sliver of his attention. Now is the time to use his charm and reap the benefits of his staunch fandom. Tell him to pull a few strings, or several at once, and do whatever it takes to get back as soon as possible. Remember, it is his wife we are talking about here, the one he made a promise to... a promise to be by her side...Well, a good man always keeps his promise, and a superstar at that definitely does," he concluded.

"Duly noted, Sir," Nysha replied, a small smile curled up her lips and brightened up her face.

Madness

It took them less than an hour to reach Akshat Ratna. Zain, his bodyguard Veer, Nysha, and Aashita were joined by Jay, Vardhaan, and Aarhi. Upon learning about the sudden contingency, the Jidans did not waste a moment in making the requisite arrangements. Their private chopper dropped them off at the helipad positioned atop their luxurious hotel's roof, The Monarch's Lair. A grand seaside paradise, the hotel was off-limits for most people, and only the crème de la crème, the richest of the rich, and the most affluent of the affluent could probably afford a stay there. As they disembarked from their chopper, wind from the heavy helicopter blades tousled their hair, and a man who looked like security personnel walked up to them. He greeted Zain, while acknowledging the rest of them with a polite nod.

"Mr. Zaidi, welcome to The Monarch's Lair. It's an honor to have you and your friends with us. I am Steve Polanski, the Security Head," he introduced himself.

"Hello, Steve... nice meeting you, too," Zain replied with a sincere smile.

"Sir, would you and your friends stay back for refreshments, or would you prefer to start immediately?" Steve asked politely.

"Thanks, Steve. We will take a rain check today. You know the circumstances, but we will surely come back some other time," Zain replied affably.

"As you wish, Sir," Steve confirmed.

As Nysha watched the courteous exchange, she was truly filled with admiration for her friend. Despite experiencing an undercurrent of tension, Zain still was able to hold himself up, never once letting the mask of tranquility slip off his face. He was considered a superstar for a reason.

Steve led them off the helipad and into an elevator that took them down to the parking area. A luxury sedan was already parked there. As they got inside, a gourmet welcome hamper from the hotel was neatly placed on their seats. Needless to say, each of them was amazed by the grand welcome and exceptional hospitality. However, only Vardhaan voiced his extreme delight while savoring a packet of stuffed caramel churros. Not bothering to control the annoying sound he made while speaking through a mouthful, he said,

"Wow! This is awesomeness galore... Just yummylicious!"

"Can you not speak while eating? You are acting like a grunting pig," Aarhi schooled him.

"Did you just call me a pig?" Vardhaan asked with furrowed eyebrows.

"Of course not. I would never insult a pig...or any animal for that matter," she replied, faking a coy demeanor while batting her eyelashes with a dramatic flair.

Vardhaan was about to give a befitting retort, but Aashita's booming voice cut him off,

"Shut the fuck up...both of you. Not a word till we reach the hospital... Period."

Nysha's eyes darted toward Zain. She placed a hand over his and whispered,

"Don't worry, she is in good hands. She will be fine. She is a fighter."

"I know...," he replied with a small smile.

"We are almost there...10 more minutes," Aashita confirmed.

Zain nodded understandingly.

Nysha reflected on the events of the past few hours. It had been one hell of a crazy rollercoaster ride. She recalled what Samar had said about Zain. This man was clearly something. It didn't matter that he was one of the highest-paid superstars in the country; there had been many in the past, and there would be many in the future too. But what mattered was that he had a heart of pure gold—rock solid. He was totally cool about his stardom, never letting an ounce get to his head. In fact, on several occasions, he allowed his friends to have a good laugh at the cost of his movies without taking a shred of offense, sometimes even joining in the fun. His movies, though worldwide box office hits, for some stupid reason seemed to defy the laws of science and lack simple logic, and they, being morons, never missed an opportunity to point out the same. However, what Nysha figured out today was that Zain's rabid fan following wasn't just confined to the teeny teenage girls or Gen Z youngsters, but his charm wasn't lost on the country's Richie Richest too. He was, in fact, worshipped, and she was pretty sure that if needed, people wouldn't hesitate to line up his path with flower petals, merely to ensure that their superstar was comfortable.

The simple fact that he breathed and was alive meant everything for the 'Zaidians.'

"Zain," Nysha called.

"Hmm..."

"You know what, you will be a fab father..." she said sincerely.

"Thanks," he replied with a wide smile, and his entire face lit up like a 1000-watt LED bulb.

AKSHAT RATNA REVISITED

Upon arriving at the hospital, Zain and his team were immediately escorted through the rear entrance via a platoon of serious-looking security personnel. At other times, Zain would have greatly disapproved of making a fuss about his visit to a place, especially a hospital. But the circumstances were entirely different today, and he was convinced by his trusted aides, Veer and Mehtaji, that this happened to be a necessary evil, just in case things flared up. The security had been instated, not only for him and his family but also for the hospital staff, patients, his loyal fans eagerly waiting outside for a glimpse of their superstar, as well as the crazy paparazzi who were now hovering around the entire building like a swarm of wasps, with highly activated stingers.

They reached the third floor, and on seeing them coming, Samar immediately went forward to greet them.

"Thank God you guys are here! I was starting to get worried," he spoke to Zain, but his eyes darted toward Nysha. While he did a slow perusal of her form, an unhurried smile crossed his lips. Warmth flooded through her because she could interpret that look well. It was a look that held genuine appreciation, akin to being worshipped by one's lover.

Nysha tried not to blush and turn crimson when his eyes shifted to trace a path from her neck down to the hollow of her cleavage. Realization dawned on her upon recalling the kind of dress she was wearing. The revealing choli and the half-width dupatta did little to cover the expanse of her chest. This wasn't the dress you were expected to wear in a hospital. Moreover, this wasn't even her taste. Damn! The designers and their outfits..., she thought.

As she made a futile attempt to cover herself with her barely-there dupatta, Samar tried hard to shift his gaze, straining his eyes to look above her head. However, the chart showcasing the cycle of obesity and its various health hazards, which hung loosely on the wall just behind her back, was a sorry replacement, barely able to compensate for skipping the magnificent glory in his line of sight.

"Where is Pia?" Zain asked, interrupting the silent yet smouldering exchange between the two.

"In labour...," Samar replied. "I think you should go too...," he suggested.

Zain raised an eyebrow and gave an incredulous look as if he had just mentioned an impossible feat.

"What? Are you out of your mind? What will I do there?" he bombarded Samar with an array of questions. Unable to get a grip on his emotions, he continued his tirade, "And where is ma-in-law? Why isn't she here?" he asked.

"Oh, come on, Zain, you can do better than this... Stop spluttering your testosterones hither thither," Nysha intervened.

"I guess she is right; you need to calm down... Relax!" Samar said. "And don't worry; Pia and Nysha's mom are in Doctor Harsha's cabin. Having them walk the corridors would do no good," he spoke as a matter of fact. "But you, my friend, need to be with your wife. If I were you, I wouldn't miss it for the world," he said suggestively.

Zain looked from Samar to Nysha and back to Samar again before speaking.

"Well, I am pretty sure about that. And can you stop being a hero at my expense, please? You are a doctor. When your time comes, of course, you will go inside without any qualms. But I have a thing for blood; I hate the sight of it...," he defended himself.

"No way!" Aashita exclaimed. "How do you go about doing the action sequences flawlessly then? With blood spattering all around... especially the recent gore one, where you play a savage Alpha brute," she asked.

Zain bit back with an eye roll, "Pardon my words, Mrs. Baruah, but for a decorated police officer's wife, you really are a sorry excuse. That thing in movies is anything but blood. It's a mixture of different ingredients... from corn syrup to food coloring, to paint, and whatnot...But that's hardly the point. And about the Alpha Brute jibe... the critics loved my work, and the movie might just be considered for the National Award. So take back your words... Chop Chop!"

"That's definitely not important now," Samar impatiently cut them off. "Zain, do you suffer from hemophobia?" he straightaway asked instead.

Zain shrugged his shoulders and replied, "Nah! Not that extreme, I believe... But yes, I do fear blood, and Pia knows about it."

"All the more reason that you should go; she would be so proud of you...," Samar asserted.

"Zain, do you want to be with your wife?" Nysha asked.

"Yes...," he said, without batting an eyelash.

"Decided then... Let's get you in, Mr. Superstar," Samar confirmed.

"Aww! How adorably sweet!" Aarhi spoke for the first time since they arrived. "If it were up to me, your love story would have made it to the front page," she cooed.

"Oh! I am so glad it's not up to you then,' Aashita said. 'Private lives aren't up for display, not even for celebs," she snapped.

"But love stories sure are, bou," Aarhi countered.

Aashita made an annoying 'pfft' sound and was about to retort. However, before the spat between the sisters-in-law could escalate, Vardhaan wrapped his arms around Aarhi's petite form and said with a sly smile, "Hush love! You are parched. Let's get you something to drink."

Aarhi glowered at him, but he, in return, pulled her closer, whispering something in her ears, the plastered smile remaining in place. Slowly, she pulled herself out of his embrace and gave a reluctant nod before muttering a half-hearted yes.

"Alright, let's go. By the way, what's the treat?" she asked.

"Chilled beer and Korean pulled chicken bao," he replied with a wicked grin.

"Well, that sounds like a real deal," Aarhi replied, controlling her frantic heartbeat at the sight of his engaging grin which had lit up his face, making him look breathtakingly handsome.

"It is," he agreed.

Aashita shook her head and tsked in disbelief when she saw them walking down the corridor.

"Come on, she is an adult," Nysha whispered.

"But he is a pervert...," Aashita replied.

"You know what, drop your diapers and pull your adult pants up, cry baby," Nysha snapped.

"She is right, you are overreacting...," Jay said, while Samar agreed with a silent nod.

"Whatever!" Aashita sighed in resignation.

THE LABOUR ROOM ~~DEBACLE~~/OOPS!! MIRACLE/MIRACLE(S)

"Pia! Pia! Pia! Hold on for some more time, love. The baby is almost here!" Zain was part whimpering and part pacifying his pregnant wife, who was experiencing severe contractions now.

"No. It's not, Mr. Zaidi. Not even close," a mean voice echoed from the other end of the room, dismissing his claim completely. 55-year-old Gynac, Dr. Venuka Hattangadi, who until now was immersed in a pile of files, completely unfazed by the guttural and painful cries of her patient, removed her specs and slowly walked up to them. She checked Pia's drips, monitored her blood pressure, and then pulled on a pair of gloves over her calloused hands and conducted a vaginal examination to check dilation and determine the position of the baby's head. Once finished, she removed her gloves, sanitized her hands, and rattled off a few instructions to the assisting junior, Dr. Afreen Faizi.

"How much longer, doctor? She is in extreme pain," Zain asked impatiently.

His query was met with a severe frown. Nevertheless, she answered, "Of course, Mr. Zaidi. This is a labour room. What were you expecting?" Sarcasm dripped from her tone.

Zain wanted to give the old lady a piece of his mind but thought better of it. Flashing his billion-buck alluring smile, he asked with great restraint, "Pardon my unsettlement, doctor, but it pains me to see my wife like this. I was wondering if we could, you know, do something to reduce her discomfort. Well, that's about it," he said while cupping Pia's hand with his in a comforting manner.

"The pain is what gets the baby moving, young man. Don't worry, your wife is stronger than you think she is...," she reassured.

"I know she is, but even if she were lethal, it's been almost seven hours now," he reminded.

"Oh, Mr. Zaidi, you are living in your filmy world, aren't you? But I am afraid the real world tends to operate differently... It takes what it takes... A bunch of idiots cannot pull off a pregnancy stunt with a vacuum and an inverter. Well, you live in a superficial daze...," she called out sympathetically.

The environment inside the cabin became tense. While Dr. Faizi passed him a nervous and apologetic smile, Zain had somehow managed to decipher the behavioral hegemony of the lady in white. He had encountered several in his lifetime who had disparaged his line of work, thinking that it only required feather-brained nitwits to shine in the entertainment industry, while intellectual supremos like her were responsible for saving the world at large. Myths! Myths! And only Myths! The truth of the matter was that every craft required hard work and dedication. But self-obsessed, high horses, thought otherwise... and since it was hardly the time to chastise, he asked politely instead, "So what now, doctor?"

"Your wife is lucky, Mr. Zaidi. First-time labor can last way longer than this, but since Pia's somatic contractions have already started, we expect an early delivery. The baby should be out in the next 30 to 40 minutes. I will be back after my round. Dr. Faizi is here; she will administer an epidural and inform us when the baby descends. Until then, hold your horses, and everything is going to be just fine," she assured.

"Thank you, I will...," he smiled while squashing his internal grimace against the old woman.

Dr. Venuka had hardly stepped out of the room when Zain bent down and whispered in Pia's ears, "That woman is evil, a demoness incarnate."

"Shut up, Zain," Pia smacked his arm.

"Ouch! For a delivering mom, aren't you a bit too strong?" he asked, kissing her forehead affectionately.

"Why did we agree to a normal delivery? And why the hell didn't you stop me?" she accused him between screams of distress.

"I thought you loved the idea; your doctor convinced it to be the best procedure," Zain offered.

"You should have outrightly rejected the idea...," she continued.

"Love, I have always respected your decision. But I will remember the next time...," he assured.

"What? Are you kidding me? There is no next time. There is never going to be one...This is the one and only time...," she shrieked in protest.

"What if in a few years, you forget all about the pain and insist on planning a second issue?" he questioned skeptically.

"Come near...," she said, gasping between breaths.

Zain closed the distance between them and bent his head. Pia tugged at his shirt and pulled him closer, her lips almost grazing his ears. "If I insist on something this stupid the next time...," she let out a breath and paused... before adding, "Shoot me! And if not, then I will shoot you."

She loosened her grip on his shirt and smoothed the creases with her palm before letting him go.

Zain gave Dr. Faizi a vulnerable smile and asked her while caressing his wife's belly, "Do you think it's time to check the baby's descent? If not, his or her Abba might not quite survive to see the noor of his eyes."

The kind doctor gave him an empathetic smile and assured him, "I will check right away, Mr. Zaidi."

Meanwhile, Zain bent down and kissed the swollen belly button of the woman he loved—the one who would soon become the mother of his child. Whispering atop her stomach he said, "Remember, kiddo, your Abba might be soft, but your mom is lethal. I would rather you be like her..."

He stepped aside to let Dr. Faizi check the baby's descent into the pelvis. Excited about her sighting, she called out, "Congratulations, Mr. and Mrs. Zaidi, the wait is over. I will call Dr. Venuka right away."

Fifteen minutes later:

"Push! You can do this, Mamma," the doctor said encouragingly.

Zain held her hands, while an opaque screen in the middle separated Pia's upper and lower body.

"Why does it feel like I need to go to the washroom?" she yelled.

"That's a good thing. It means the baby is going to be out in minutes...," Dr. Faizi assured.

"No minutes! No! I want it out now...," she howled.

"Hold on, love! You are my strong girl...I am so proud of you...," Zain comforted.

Another wave of contraction hit when the baby's head came and rested on Dr. Venuka's hands.

"Ah! Here it is...," she proclaimed.

"Where? Is everything okay?" Pia gasped.

"Almost," Zain said. He had switched sides and was now standing at the opposite end.

"What's that supposed to mean?" she asked, petrified.

"Don't panic, love, but the baby isn't completely out. It's only the head now, and though smeared in blood, it's still miraculous...," Zain answered.

"What is it, a boy or a girl?" she asked.

"Can't say... Like I said, it's only the head now."

"Oh! I want to see it... hold it."

"For that, Mrs. Zaidi, you need to finish pushing first," Dr. Venuka added.

"I think it's here, doctor," Pia said, as she felt another wave of contraction. Grinding her teeth together and letting out a feral cry, she pushed the rest of the baby out.

This time, the whole baby landed on Dr. Venuka's hands.

"Congratulations, Mr. and Mrs. Zaidi, it's a baby boy," she announced with a smile.

"I want to hold it...," Pia cried out in excitement.

"Patience, new Mamma, we need to clean up your prince first," the doctor explained.

"Can I at least have a look?" she urged.

The doctor nodded and passed the baby to the assisting nurse, who, in turn, held it closer for her to admire. The newborn opened his eyes as if taking a moment to greet his mom. Pia's heart swelled with pride at the tiny miracle they had managed to create; their very own little bundle of joy.

"Welcome aboard, Piyansh Zaidi...," Pia beamed.

"Piyansh! A part of Pia... Fair enough...," Zain agreed with a smile.

"How are you feeling, Mrs. Zaidi?" Dr. Venuka asked.

"I am not sure, doctor. There is a strange feeling in the gut. It feels like I am in for a second phase of contraction," she stated, confused.

"Oh no! That's not possible. You might just be experiencing an after-effect of your labor cramps," Dr. Venuka explained, as she went closer to examine.

"No! No! No! This is as real as it can get, doctor. This is definitely a contraction, and not my imagination," she spoke between gasps, as beads of sweat trickled down her forehead and traced a path down her face, despite the freezing OT temperature.

"It's pounding again, doctor...This is unmistakably a contraction," Pia winced and wailed aloud... "Please do something...," she pleaded for help.

"Wait! Wait! I am here, right here...," Dr. Venuka pacified. She went ahead to examine closely and exclaimed in disbelief, "Oh my God! It's a miracle... Mr. and Mrs. Zaidi, you have another baby in waiting..."

“Twin babies,” both Zain and Pia bellowed together.

“A twin?” Dr. Faizi asked, her eyes widening with surprise. “How is it even possible that it went undetected?”

“Very rare, but not unheard of...It’s the hidden twin, strategically hiding behind the other and sharing the same sac...,” Dr. Venuka explained.

“Strategist? What is it, the Elon Musk of Babywood?” Zain exclaimed.

“Stop spewing nonsense, and get it out...,” Pia burst out, her patience depleting with every passing second.

“Alright, Mamma... you know the drill. Push again, a strong, hard push, and let’s be done with this.”

“Yes, baby.... Push! One last time,” Zain encouraged.

“I hate you for making me go through this,” she yelled at Zain, while swearing a few authentic Punjabi cuss words.

“I will make it up to you, love...,” he assured, before adding, “But look at the bright side, there will be no next time... just how you wanted it... In a way, God answered your prayers,” he mollified.

“You are a dead man, Zaidi...,” Pia threatened. But before she could fling a few more abusive swears, the pain heightened, and in one final push the whole baby was out. It let out an ear-piercing cry, declaring its arrival, and obvious displeasure at being uprooted from its cosy and comfortable resting place.

Dr. Venuka smiled and declared, “Well! Well! Congratulations! It’s a baby boy again.”

‘Twin boys!’ Pia muttered, looking pale and ready to faint at the news of bringing up two boys.

Dr. Venuka continued, "This tiny one is definitely the naughtier one. The way he took us oldies for a ride and tricked us all along...I must say, he is your own Little Prankster!"

The newborn stopped crying as if taking a moment to absorb the worthy praise bestowed upon him by the doctor.

"Welcome aboard, Zeeshan Zaidi," the proud new father declared.

Epilogue

The news about the arrival of the celebrity twin baby boys spread fast and wild across the corridors of Akshat Ratna, and a paramount emotion of celebration began mounting in the hushed corridors of the hospital. After a long time, the dark gloom of uncertainty was cast off, and the staff at the hospital was able to breathe a sigh of relief. The long-impending issue regarding the lack of funds was finally taken care of. They also knew they were safe and that their jobs were now secure.

The security at the hospital had been beefed up by Veer, and strict no-outsider visits and no-photography policies were set in place. Even visits by relatives and acceptance of congratulatory gifts were stalled for the time being. Meanwhile, the PR team under the aegis of Zarin posted a message on various social media handles of Zain, informing his fans and well-wishers regarding the arrival of their twin bundle of joy.

The message read:

'With hearts filled with double the happiness and twice the love, we are thrilled to announce the arrival of our twins, our blessed baby boys. We thank everyone for bestowing upon us all your love, prayers, and good wishes. Pia and the boys are healthy and fine, and we are beyond excited to start our journey as a family of four. We request and hope that you can respect our privacy at this juncture.

Love and Hugs,
Zain'

Soon after the message was posted, congratulatory messages began pouring in from both filmi as well as the non-filmi quarters alike. The paparazzi outside the hospital were going berserk and conceptualizing strategies to capture a moment of the mother-sons trio. One such crazy reporter had almost managed to sneak inside the hospital while posing as a doctor, only to be caught by the security personnel right on time. He was dragged out of the hospital, kicking and screaming throughout the corridors.

After the said incident, security was tightened round the clock, which, in turn, had dampened the spirits and squashed the hopes of a section of the paparazzi. Their dream of capturing the pictures of the newborns and garnering laurels and recognition for the same was now a lost cause. But at the same time, there were a relentless few who didn't mind spoiling the broth if they couldn't get a spoonful of it. Hence, with the power of deepfake and AI, and channeling inner creativity at its best, a number of morphed images of the mother and her newborn sons began doing the rounds on the internet, a few even going viral in no time. The PR team was now having a hard time rolling out clarifications about the insane number of fake images, a few of which were meticulously edited, leaving little or almost no room for doubt about their authenticity.

Amidst all the chaos and utter confusion, a different kind of celebration was underway in one of the silent upper corridors of the hospital, near the abandoned nurse station of the old building. The new masi of the twins was unable to keep her calm. She clapped her hands loudly and leaped high, doing a mid-air twirl, before landing perfectly in her beau's arms. Samar looked lovingly into her eyes and said, "Excited much, sassy masi?"

She wrapped her hands around his neck and pressed her lips softly on his, before replying in a sultry tone, "Of course, sexy masa ji."

Samar let out a low, throaty groan. Her soft body pasted against his hard ones made him lose control. The wild sensation traveled straight to his groins. Pulling her closer by her waist, he hissed, "If you don't drop the act and continue with your teasing, I might just end up taking you against the wall," he threatened. "As it is, you have been testing my patience throughout the evening with your enticing backless dress," he confessed.

Nysha smiled; a soft, flirtatious giggle escaped her lips, which made his skin tingle. In response, he made a low grunting sound and said, "Damn, woman! What's wrong with you?"

"Nothing, it's just that this feels like my dream."

"Dream?" he asked with a raised eyebrow.

"Yes, my dream...," she continued, "where a hot, handsome doctor kisses me in the hospital corridors. I have been having a re-run of the same flick for months now."

"Oh, I see. In that case, I would love to make your dream a reality. Will you allow me, Ms. Patel?" he asked playfully, lifting her chin with his fingers.

"I wouldn't mind that... Ah! But actually, there is a slight problem though...," she said, tapping her fingers against her chin and throwing him an assessing gaze, her eyes roving up and down the length of his body.

"What now?" Samar hissed.

"The doctor in my dreams...He was donning his white coat, and oh my God! Did he look handsome? Well, your coat is missing, Dr. Heartless," she stated as a matter of fact.

"Really, my coat? Are we discussing that now?"

"Oh, we are not?" she asked, pouting.

"Tease, aren't you? Turning the moment into a damp squib...," he accused.

"Impatient, are we?" she purred. Tilting her head up, she looked into his eyes. Their lips were now barely apart. Her warm breath fanned across his face, and a restrained gasp escaped his lips. Satisfied with his response, a seductive smile curled up her lips as she whispered in his ear, "Also, the doctor in my dreams kisses like a sin. Do you think you can match up to him, Dr. Heartless?" she asked.

"Well, we can always find out," he replied earnestly.

He sank his fingers into her hair, dislodging her high bun and scattering the tiny pins that had held it in place. Tilting her head back, he claimed her lips. This time, she let out a shocked gasp. For a moment, her mind went blank. The kiss wasn't frivolous; it was feral, and a play of pure dominance. With every suck at her lips, the duel of their tongues intensified. Nysha held on to his shoulder for support, as Samar's fingers dug deeper into her hair, keeping her in place while his tongue explored the depths of her mouth. Scorching desire hummed through the length of her body, and she moaned into his mouth. As she cried out his name in ecstasy, the doctor of her dreams became a distant haze, while her senses were filled with a new reality.

By the time his mouth left hers, they were both panting for breath. Samar's kiss was both demanding and all-consuming, leaving no room for doubt as to whom her heart belonged. He had marked her. She knew that she was his, and only his. No other person could kiss her and make her feel wanted and worshipped like he did.

"I love you, Dr. Heartless," she confessed, as tears of contentment flowed down her cheeks.

"I love you more, sweetheart... today and forever," he declared, kissing her forehead.

"Forever?" Nysha asked.

"Yes, forever," Samar promised.

Somewhere, a 15-minute drive from the hospital

"Oh my God! What is this place?" Aarhi asked, matching the excitement of a 10-year-old.

"A haven for privacy lovers," Vardhaan offered.

"That's funny!" She chimed.

"And what's so funny, princess?" he asked with a shrug.

"Nothing... Just that, you don't seem to be someone who values privacy," she quipped.

"Judgmental, are we?" he scrunched his eyes.

Before she could counter, a girl in her early twenties, wearing an almost see-through neon net dress, walked up to them. A familiar stupefied gleam shone in her eyes.

"Excuse me, you are the famous choreographer Vardhaan Kapadia," she stated.

He raised his hands in the air in an animated fashion and answered with a wide smile plastered on his face, "Guilty as charged, honey!" He replied with sass.

Aarhi couldn't help but notice his magnificent dimpled smile. It managed to transform his face completely. He was sexy; there was no doubt about it. Her fingers itched to touch the slight stubble on his jawline and trace the contours of the dimple on his cheek. Fuck! Think straight, Aarhi..., she schooled her thoughts. He could get his smile insured and avail a lifetime of benefits from it. Shit! Her treacherous thoughts were in no mood for control.

Meanwhile, the tête-à-tête between Vardhaan and his besotted fan continued. “I loved your dance number at IIFA this year,” she purred.

“Really! Thanks,” he acknowledged.

“Can I take a selfie?” she asked.

“Sure, why not?”

As he posed for a selfie like a pro max, Aarhi couldn’t help but admire his chiseled torso, which was cut to perfection for display. As it is, his barely-there transparent body-hugging shirt left little to one’s imagination. Aarhi feared that at any moment if he stretched his arms, the buttons would go flying haywire, scandalously revealing his delectable pectoral muscles.

“Hey! If you don’t mind, could you please click a picture of us from my phone?” the young girl asked Aarhi, breaking her chain of thoughts.

“Of course, why one, I will click many,” Aarhi agreed with a wide smile.

Vardhaan gave her a knowing glare. After the third click, and before Ms. Skimpy Dress could pose a new request, or Aarhi could think of a new tease, he intervened. “That should be it. I am sure you have clicked well,” he turned to Aarhi.

“Yes... Of course, here you go,” Aarhi said while handing back the phone to Ms. Skimpy Dress.

“Thank you so much. It was a pleasure meeting you,” the young girl acknowledged.

Vardhaan and Aarhi gave her a goodbye wave before Vardhaan shifted his attention back to Aarhi.

"You are so dead!" He said, while jokingly symbolizing choking her with his hands.

She snorted and replied, "Oh, come on! Who said, 'privacy lovers'?" she rebuked.

"It's not my fault that I have fans all around...," he bragged.

"God! You are incorrigibly self-obsessed," she stated.

"While I would like to differ and put forth a few points in my support... but forget it. Let's talk about you instead. Do you like this place?" he asked.

"Of course! What's not to like? I love it... It gives a spooky shack vibe. It rekindles childhood memories; it's like being on the set of an intriguing spy thriller or a Count Dracula movie of the '90s... a casual seating arrangement... beanbags...cane swings...macramé hammocks...I am loving it... Who owns it? How come I haven't heard of it? And how come you know about it?"... She continued with her relentless rampage.

"Whoa, lady! Take a pause... Give your journo instinct a break and simply enjoy the moment," he suggested.

"Well... for once perhaps, you are right!" Aarhi agreed while flashing him a cheeky grin. "And they serve mind-blowing, orgasmic dessert too...," she added, scooping a spoonful of tiramisu into her mouth...

"Mmm, this is something," she closed her eyes and licked the spoon.

Her soft moan traveled straight down south, and now he was having a hard time breathing. It seemed like she was actually having an orgasm and would be coming apart right there.

Fuck! This woman made him lose it. With every lick of her lips on the spoon, he was losing his mind, imagining all the better uses for that sexy tongue and mouth.

She opened her eyes and asked, "I simply love desserts...," she said, running her moist tongue over her lips. "Would you like some?" she asked.

Only if you feed me with your sexy mouth, Vardhaan thought... But he wasn't voicing it... Still...

"Oh! Really! It's hard to guess," he deadpanned instead. "Thanks for the offer though, but I would rather pass. I am not a fan of sweets, and unlike you, I value my hard work at the gym, you see," he taunted.

She squinted her eyes and replied, "Hey! You are being too mean and judgmental now...," she charged... "Besides, who doesn't like desserts? And to deny something this heavenly...is an offense...an utmost sin to say," she concluded.

"Of course, princess...You are damn right. I am a sinner. But allow me to order a second helping for you," he offered.

"Now you are faking chivalry," she accused.

Before he could reply, her phone buzzed... Aarhi looked at the caller's name and sighed, "Boss lady calling, I will need to take this," she said.

"Yes, bou...," she answered.

Something was spoken at the other end, which made her excitement level soar several notches higher. Vardhaan looked at her face, mesmerized by her spark and the play of various emotions on her face. He noticed a tiny chocolate smear on the corner of her lips. Her face was now almost devoid of any makeup, with loose strands of hair all over her face. She was messy and a far cry from perfection. But God! Messy suited her. She looked untamed, wild, free-spirited, uncaring, and beautiful! She was genuine...He had forgotten the last time he had seen a girl giving in to her indulgence, unabashed and unapologetic about it. He was tired of people faking around all the time, people who picked up a lettuce leaf, or a bowl of quinoa salad, or a low-carb zucchini, chickpea, feta salad, and posted hashtags on the gram. #healthyeating, #cleaneating, #nutritiousfood...

#fakers, he concluded.

"Why... of course, bou... Really! You are the best." Her eyes then darted toward Vardhaan, as she kept on responding in a low-pitched voice... "Come on... Oh yes, he has been good... Place? I don't know... Yes, I am sure... No, there is nothing to worry about at all. Please! I am hanging up now... Yes! Yes! I love you... love you... Byeee..."

"That was quite a convincing act... Hope Aashita bought it," he said.

"Not really," she rolled her eyes before continuing, "You guys must have quite a history together... She was paranoid when I told her I didn't know what place this was. I am confused. Care to explain?" she asked.

"Not today, love. Maybe sometime in the future, not sure though," he raised his hands uncertainly before continuing, "For now, all I can say is, your sister-in-law and her friend do not have a very high opinion of me. They have their reasons, which I will neither refute nor accept completely," he sighed.

"Alright... forget it! You guys are overthinkers," she said, changing the topic. "Well. I have news," she added, rubbing her palms together...

"Shoot."

"Pia just delivered twins... unexpected... totallyyyyyy..." she stretched the word for effect.

"Wow! Twin babies! That's wonderful news...," he stated.

"It is...Twin boys. And guess what, I get to do an exclusive interview with the new parents...The first to know their reaction...An unfiltered, dil-se conversation. Isn't it great?" she asked with gleaming eyes.

"Of course, it is," he agreed, while his gaze drifted down her face.

She caught him staring and asked immediately, "What are you looking at? Is something wrong?"

"There is a chocolate smear at the corner of your lips," he said.

"Where?" she asked while darting out her tongue to wipe it off, nonetheless missing the actual spot.

Raw desire pulsated through the length of his body...He tried looking away, but the naive girl wouldn't let him.

"Here?" she asked again.

"No."

Once again, she pushed her tongue out, and he had to suck his breath in. That was it; he was done.

"Why don't you use your mobile camera, or I would be happy to kiss it off," he suggested. His voice sounded gruffer than he had expected.

She looked at him with wide eyes. Her mouth went agape with the blunt audacity of his words. She tried to say something, but couldn't find her voice. Without another word, she took out her phone, switched on her camera, and wiped her lips with the back of her hand.

"There, it's gone. Happy now?" she said, burning with rage. "And don't you dare talk to me like that, ever again. Got it?"

"Noted... Nevertheless, I got you."

"You! You didn't mean what you said?" she asked, confused.

"I don't kiss without consent, honey... Contrary to others' opinions about me, I am not a dick and hardly a satyriac. So chill!"

"Satriii...A...What?" she asked with furrowed brows.

"Satyriac, someone with the satyriasis syndrome, i.e., the sexual urge to bed every female with an excessive hotness quotient," he explained.

"This is a word?" she asked, while a soft blush swept up her face.

"It is...You can run a search," he replied confidently.

"Mr. Vardhaan Kapadia, what are you?" she asked. "You are the most infuriating man I have come across, and at the same time, you are also the most interesting person to cross my path. You intrigue me like no other. I would like to know more about you."

"Be careful what you wish for, honey," he replied with a wicked grin.

Smiling, she stretched out her hand to him and said, "You know what, Mr. Kapadia; it was a pleasure spending time with you. I thoroughly enjoyed it. You are not that bad after all."

He took her hand in his, warmth spreading through his body. Her small, soft hands were a stark contrast to his large, rough ones. Nevertheless, it fit perfectly. She seemed like a ray of light in his sea of darkness. Sucking in a deep breath, he replied, "You aren't that bad yourself, sweetie. It was indeed a pleasure...," he winked.

And then she giggled—a soft giggle that sounded like the tinkling music of wind chimes. It managed to prickle his skin into tiny goosebumps. She laughed again, a carefree sound, and lust spread through his body.

Fuck O' fuck! He was so doomed!

Superstar wife gives birth to twin babies via normal delivery, squashing the stereotypical belief, 'too posh to push.'

Aarhi Baruah

Entertainment Desk, The Hurricane

Sept 16, 2024; 11:45 IST

Superstar Zain Zaidi and Pia S. Zaidi became proud parents to twin baby boys on Monday after the star's wife delivered at the renowned Akshat Ratna Hospital in suburban Mumbai. Addressing the press, superstar Zaidi said that his wife, Mrs. Pia S. Zaidi, gave birth to twin boys via normal delivery. Choosing a normal delivery over a C-section, Mrs. Pia S. Zaidi conveyed a powerful message while putting to rest the commonly used phrase, 'too posh to push,' concerning star wives and celebrities.

Award-winning gourmet chef Pia S. Zaidi, who is a noted celebrity in her own right and head chef and partner at Cafe Sinful, the first of its kind in Mumbai to serve authentic Italian cuisine and desserts along with pan-Asian flavors with a twist, was determined to go for a normal delivery from the very beginning. Mrs. Zaidi's efforts were lauded by several city doctors.

Noted gynecologist and research expert, Dr. Venuka Hattangadi of Akshat Ratna Hospital, stated, 'Mrs. Zaidi should be considered a role model for all would-be-moms. Women have always been strong, but thanks to her, now women can choose what is best for them.'

Earlier today, following the announcement of the twins' arrival on superstar Zaidi's official gram account, congratulatory messages began pouring in from all quarters, including from the Chief Minister of Maharashtra, Shri Ajith Deshpande.

The management and staff @The Hurricane extend their heartfelt congratulations to the new parents on the arrival of their twin bundle of joy and wish them a wonderful parenting journey ahead.

www.ingramcontent.com/pod-product-compliance
Lightning Source LLC
Chambersburg PA
CBHW050521240926
51846CB00003B/639
* 9 7 8 9 3 9 5 6 9 7 4 8 4 *